LAKES HOCKEY FOUR

STAND AND DEFEND

SLOANE ST. JAMES

Line Editing by Dee Houpt | www.DeesNotesEditingServices.com
Developmental Editing by Rachel Jeter | DevEditingWithBri@gmail.com
Formatting by The Nutty Formatter | TheNuttyFormatter@gmail.com

1st Edition 2024

CONTENTS

One-handed reader shortcut

STAND AND DEFEND PLAYLIST

BY CHAPTER

Lakes 4: Stand and Defend

1 - Labour - Paris Paloma
2 - Modest - NEFFEX
3 - Love Ain't - Eli Young Band
4 - Drinks - Cyn
5 - Treat You Better - Shawn Mendes
6 - Minefield - Nic D
7 - You Don't Own Me - SAYGRACE (feat G-Eazy)
8 - Never With You Again - Chri$tian Gate$
9 - American Jesus - Nessa Barrett
10 - Statement - NEFFEX
11 - Can I Kiss You? - Dahl
12 - Carousel - Melannie Martinez
13 - Man's World - MARINA
14 - How Villains Are Made - Madalen Duke
15 - Destiny - NEFFEX
16 - Can I Get An Amen - RuPaul (feat. Martha Wash)
17 - Twist Again (La La La) - Chris Webby
18 - Oxytocin - Chandler Leighton
19 - Falling Slowly - Vwillz
20 - Fictional - Khloe Rose
21 - Down to the River - Mitchel Dae
22 - American Money - BORNS
23 - Good for Her - MOTHICA
24 - Powerful - Major Lazer, Ellie Goulding
25 - About Love - MARINA
26 - Here With Me - Marshmello, CHVRCHES
27 - Tie Me Down (Slowed) - Gryffin, Elley Duhe
28 - Thing For Ya - Chri$tian Gate$
29 - Please - Omido, Ex Habit

30 - Charades - Beautiful Beats
31 - Beautiful People - Ed Sheeran, Khalid
32 - Portrait - Unprocessed
33 - Aphrodite - Ethan Gander
34 - Grave - Nessa Barrett
35 - New Bad Habit - Adam Jensen
36 - Rare - NEFFEX
37 - Without Me - Halsey
38 - Love the Way It Hurts - Cloudy June
39 - Trapped in a Dream - RudyWade
40 - Lego Blocks - NERIAH
41 - Dangerous State of Mind - Chri$tian Gate$
42 - Say Don't Go (Taylor's Version) - Taylor Swift
43 - Merry Little Christmas - Phoebe Bridgers
44 - Better With You - Virginia To Vegas
45 - Tattoo - Layto
46 - King of my Heart - Taylor Swift
47 - Butterfly 2021 - Ekoh, CrazyTown
48 - Flirt - NEFFEX
49 - x2 - Anne-Marie
50 - Beggin For Thread - BANKS
51 - Love into a Weapon - Madalen Duke
52 - Dangerous Hands - Austin Giorgio
53 - I Did Something Bad - Taylor Swift
54 - Supernova - Nic D, Loveless
55 - Lover - Taylor Swift
56 - I Need You - Chri$tian Gate$
57 - The Show Goes On - Lupe Fiasco
58 - Us - Clara Mae
59 - Playlist - James TW

MINNESOTA LAKES

TEAM ROSTER

Left Wingers
#16 Jake "Jonesy" Jones
#89 Matthew Laasko
#77 Teddy Leighton
#65 Oleg Pushkarev

Centers:
#46 Camden "Banksy" Teller (C)
#71 Shepherd Wilder
#28 Joey Broderick
#65 Colby Imlach

Right Wingers
#33 Barrett Conway (A)
#18 Ryan Bishop
#48 Brit O'Callahan
#21 Reggie Daniels

Left Defensemen
#5 Rhys Kucera
#39 Dean Burmeister
#20 Doug Elsworth

Right Defensemen
#14 Lonan Burke
#52 Burt Paek
#3 Cory Dopson

Goaltenders
#29 Sergey Kapucik
#40 Tyler Strassburg

TROPES

Hockey romance, ex's best friend, friends with benefits, who hurt you?, playboy hockey captain, situationship, protector, runaway bride, forced proximity, all the banter, villain era FMC, melt your kindle, strong FMC, cocky MMC, happily ever after.

TRIGGER CONTENT WARNING

This book features an abusive, controlling relationship between the FMC and a previous partner. It contains gaslighting, fatphobia, stalking, verbal abuse, emotional abuse, financial abuse, and graphic descriptions of physical domestic violence. In addition, there is cheating (none by main characters), recreational drug use (cannabis) by main characters, a police traffic stop (no police brutality takes place), spitting (including mouth), and needles (body piercings).
If you are triggered by these situations, please skip this one.

In addition, if you know someone being abused, or if you're experiencing abuse yourself, please seek assistance and know there is nothing you have done or are doing to cause it. It is always the choice of the abuser to continue. Help exists, even in impossible circumstances.

For anonymous, confidential help, 24/7, please call the National Domestic Violence Hotline at 1-800-799-7233 (SAFE) or 1-800-787-3224 (TTY). If you are in immediate danger, call 9-1-1.

To my readers—

May you find your inner villain,
and a partner worth taming it for.

ONE

Jordana

"Get in the car, Jordana."

I close my eyes and exhale. I hate when he calls me by my full name but stopped correcting him when it was clear after the first few weeks of dating that I was wasting my breath. *"I'm not going to call you a boy's name."*

"I'm in, I'm in—Wait, I forgot my water bottle!"

"You should have thought of that earlier. You're always making us fucking late."

"It's two o'clock. You said to be ready at three."

He climbs into the driver seat, and we pull out of the underground garage of the condo. Bryan slams his hand on the steering wheel. "Why would I say three o'clock? That doesn't even make sense . . . All I ask is for you to be on time."

I swear, he told me three o'clock, I know he did.

I hadn't finished packing before he was tossing my bag in the trunk at two o'clock. I'm parched, and my lips are dry, but it's not worth the fight. Not when we're on the way to our "*party for the wedding party*," where we're expected to show up head over heels for each other.

I can't believe we're going to another one of these events. It's overkill. We've already had two engagement soirees; how many does one couple need? With each party, my future grows darker, like this marriage is looming over me like a raincloud.

Most women light up when they speak about their weddings and can't wait to marry the love of their life, then there are women like me. Not thrilled but willing. It's not uncommon for industry tycoons and finance moguls to orchestrate marriages for their offspring. Technically, Bryan and I met in college, but our parents know each other and served on the same board of directors back in the day.

Much of our lives are decided before we're even born. From the subject we major in to who we walk down the aisle to—in my case, Bryan Davenport. It's a "smart move." He's fine. Neutral. Predictable. Sometimes he has a temper, and our sex life isn't over-the-moon spectacular, but that's nothing unusual. Our relationship is normal. Our parents set us up, and this is the natural progression of the plan. While I don't always agree or like their choices, I love my family and know they have my best interest at heart. Most people marry for love—and most divorces happen within five years. Love is overrated. Life is meant to be filled with hobbies, like traveling, Netflix, and reading. When it comes to love, the book is always better.

"How was your day at work?" he asks, checking his emails while driving.

"It was good. Jennifer and I went out to lunch today."

"Where did you go?"

"Waterhaus." It's one of the nicer restaurants in the area. I wanted to take my coworker out to celebrate her two-year anniversary with the company we work for, H&H Holdings. Bryan Davenport Sr., a.k.a. my future father-in-law, is the CEO.

"Hm," he tuts. *Now what?* "My parents aren't paying for that lunch." I resist rolling my eyes, not wanting to give him the satisfaction. Every time he refers to H&H as *his parents*, I internally cringe. God forbid a multimillion-dollar-parent company foot the bill on a couple salmon Caesar salads with dressing on the side.

My response is already on my tongue, but I'm careful not to cut him off. "I didn't charge it to the company card, I paid for it out of pocket."

"Well, do you think that's the best use of our money?"

Is he fucking serious? Combined, we have more money than we could ever possibly spend in a lifetime. He's all about living the lavish lifestyle until I'm the one swiping the credit card. I've regretted allowing him access to my accounts since the day *he* made me do it. At the time, it didn't seem like a big deal, however, I didn't realize he'd be scrutinizing every measly purchase.

"Who else went to lunch?"

"Just Jennifer and me."

He mumbles, "Yeah, right . . ."

He's in a bad mood. Ugh, it's going to be a long weekend at the cabin—if you can call a sprawling hunting lodge on eighty acres a "cabin."

My phone dings, I flip it over to see a text from Carl, a colleague on my team. Tapping the screen, I respond with our project update and let him know I won't have great cell reception for the rest of the weekend and to contact Jennifer if he has other questions.

"Who are you texting?"

"Carl from work," I mutter as my fingers tap out a message regarding the contract status for the Redding Group, a new H&H acquisition.

"Why's he texting you?"

"He wanted to know where we left off with the Redding financials. Why? Are you worried about Carl?" It's a slight jab, but Carlton is a colleague twenty years my senior who's happily married, not that it matters.

"Hell no, I'm not worried about him! Why would you even say that? He could never give you what I can, and he knows it too." He smirks. *Gross.* "What did you tell him?"

I hold back a sarcastic response about sending nudes.

"I forwarded him the last update I had and told him we were heading up north for the weekend."

"Great!" He scoffs, hitting the steering wheel again and glares at me, taking his eyes off the road. "So now he knows not to text you all weekend since your fiancé will be around. Do you think you're being sneaky? Why would you say it like that?"

"What are you even talking about?!" Even for him, this is paranoid. Does he *want* me to have an affair with Carl just so he can be right?

"*This,* Jordana. *This*! You don't know how to talk to people! You don't *think*!" He stabs his finger into his temple. "You're so lucky I put up with you. I don't know any other man who would tolerate your behavior. Why do I put myself through this? God, if people only knew—"

"There's nothing going on between us, I'm sorry!"

"How would I know if you're always telling men when it's safe to text and when it isn't? Maybe someday you'll learn how to show me the same amount of respect I show you. I mean, are you the stupid one or am I?"

I stare straight ahead at the road.

"Who's stupid, Jordana. You or me?"

Does he really expect me to answer?

This time he raises his voice louder. "Am I stupid for putting up with you?"

"No," I whisper, hunching in my seat.

"So, you admit you're the idiot. Glad you got that figured out. Start using your brain." He shakes his head and sighs. "I'm sorry. I'm just trying to help you. If we're going to get married, we need to learn how to communicate."

Don't react, it only makes these conversations last longer. My head is spinning. I want to stop fighting and move past this.

For the rest of the car ride, we remain silent. The less we say, the better, and the less he'll have to criticize. But I can't help but wonder if he's right. Was it weird to text Carl I was going away for the weekend with my fiancé? Is that some rule I don't know about? Did I give the wrong impression? *Fuck.*

I lay my head back, and the endless pines that line the long two-way highway blur as we whiz by. Closing my eyes, I enjoy the warm strobe of shadows and sunlight on my eyelids. There aren't many weeks of sunshine left.

When we arrive, he retrieves our bags from the trunk, slams it, and turns to me.

"Give me your phone."

"Why?"

He grits his teeth. "*Because I said so.*"

I hand it over; he already knows the password. He swipes

and scrolls through my text messages, then wrinkles his nose when he doesn't find anything.

I don't know what makes me say it . . . "Let me see *your* phone."

Bryan scoffs and shakes his head. "No."

"You get to look at my phone, why can't I look at yours?"

"Because I'm not the one doing shady shit. You are."

I roll my eyes, and he drops my phone in the gravel drive, picks up our suitcases, and carries them toward the house.

Holding my breath, I retrieve my phone from the ground and breathe a sigh of relief when the screen isn't cracked. That should be the least of my problems, but it's the little things.

Bursting in the front door, Bryan weaves his fingers with mine and dons a big fake smile. "We're here!"

The massive family cabin has been transformed into an upscale party. White panels of fabric are draped between the exposed log beams above. Strands of Edison bulbs span the room. They're trying to make it look more rustic despite this being an eight-thousand square-foot luxury lodge.

An open bar with two attendants has been set up on one end, and cocktail tables are evenly placed, each featuring a centerpiece made of greenery and fresh flowers. The large stone fireplace that reaches the ceiling at the other end of the room has had the logs replaced with about fifty tall white pillar candles in various sizes. The mantle is adorned with greenery that matches the centerpieces.

I recognize a few of the staff from the hospitality service they use for the quarterly H&H stockholder meetings. I would put money on some of his father's business partners being here too. It's supposed to be a wedding-party-only event, but leave it to the Davenports to find an excuse to do a little dealmaking on the side.

Our families cheer at our arrival, and I do my best to match my fiancé's artificial joy. At the bar, a cork pops from a bottle of champagne, and they pour the bubbly. He raises our joined hands like I'm some trophy. Why shouldn't he? After all, we're the happy bride and groom-to-be.

"Can you believe I get to marry this girl? Look at her, isn't she gorgeous?" he announces to the room before planting a kiss on my cheek.

I force a grin and make sure the corners of my eyes crinkle for good measure.

"Luckiest man in the world!" Some guests sigh and *aww*. He leans in and whispers, "This weekend is about us, let's just enjoy ourselves." At least he's not angry anymore.

The speedy click-clack of high heels grows louder, and when I look in the direction, a real smile takes over my face when I see Veronica, my best friend and maid of honor, running toward us. Well, as fast as she can while teetering in sky-high heels. *Thank God she's here.*

"My turn! I'm stealing her!" She wraps me up in a hug and tugs me toward the open bar, shoving a flute of champagne in my hand. "You look phenomenal in this dress. Holy shit."

I laugh and bump her hip. "Same to you. Purple is your color."

She twirls and does a little shimmy. "To us being irresistible."

"Cheers." Our crystal flutes clink.

"I'm starving," I say, looking around. "How's the catering? Will they be passing the hors d'oeuvres soon?"

"Yes, but none for you. Only eight weeks left until the wedding, and we can't risk you losing your measurements. But don't worry, I made you a salad with a delicious lemon vinaigrette."

I love Veronica, but her lemon vinaigrette tastes like lemon-scented Pledge. It's a secret I'll take to the grave. She's my closest confidant, well, my *only* confidant. When you come from wealth, true friends are scarce. People only want to get close so they can get something out of you, which leads to never letting anyone in.

I groan. This stupid fucking wedding diet is gonna kill me. I'm always hungry. How am I gonna last eight more weeks of starvation? Why can't they make the dress fit me as I am now? Why do I have to drop into single-digit sizes? It's ridiculous and archaic.

She takes a sip and smiles. "So . . . how are things going?"

I sigh. "We kinda got into another fight."

She rolls her eyes. "Now what?"

"Same shit, different shovel. His trust issues are out of control. Telling me I'm flirting when—I swear, Roni—I'm just talking to people!"

"Are you sure? You know I have your back, but sometimes you can come off a little flirty . . ."

What? "How?!"

"Don't get defensive! It's a tone thing. *I* know you don't mean anything by it, but maybe the men you speak to don't. I dunno, forget it. I'm probably wrong."

Well, shit, now that's gonna be sitting on the backburner of my brain for the rest of my life. I'll never be able to have a normal conversation with another person as long as I live because I will constantly second-guess my speech. *Was my hello friendly or more than friendly?* Goddamn it.

"I guess it's something I'll pay more attention to. But I really don't think that's happening."

"You're probably right. You know Bry? He loves to overreact."

Bry? I swallow my thoughts and take a sip of my champagne instead.

She waves her hand, as if to erase the conversation. "Let's have fun tonight. We're celebrating, right?"

I raise my glass again and nod.

TWO

Banksy

If this asshole doesn't stop texting me, I'm gonna skip the trip altogether. It's bad enough he's getting married on a game day, but thankfully, the game starts four hours after the ceremony. I'll be able to make it work, but it's still a lot of added stress. Might have to live stream my best man speech from the locker room.

I missed the engagement party due to an away game, but I was warned the wedding-party weekend was mandatory —*according to Bryan, Jordana is quite the bridezilla.* Doesn't matter, I'm only staying for one night. I have to return to the Twin Cities tomorrow for practice, so I'll be outta here before breakfast.

The pleasant AI voice breaks through the car's speakers. *"New text from Bryan."*

"Read text," I command.

"Where the fuck are you?"

Normally, I'd take the Ducati, but it's in the shop. If I were on the bike, I'd probably be able to make up time since I'm a speed demon. I'm running behind, but practice went late and I had game footage to review.

"Reply to text . . . Twenty minutes out."

Bryan's always had a thing about being on time. He puts up with a lot of my shit though, considering my calendar is nuts and we don't get to see each other nearly as often as we used to. We've gone our separate ways since high school. I was drafted early on, and he went to an ivy league school on the East Coast. We have our different lives, him with Jordana and me with a revolving door of beautiful pussy. We've always been understanding of each other's lifestyles and busy schedules. Especially now that I'm the new team captain.

Still can't believe they gave me Sully's spot. I'd never admit it, but it's fucking terrifying. It's a lot of pressure to keep the boys in line and make sure we all are getting along and doing what we're supposed to. Sully was quiet but strong —and one hell of a fucking leader. His best friend, Barrett Conway, is retiring at the end of the season and staying on as an alternate cap. I appreciate that he gives advice without being a dick about it.

It's given me some perspective; I can see why I pissed off all my previous captains. Stirring up shit on the ice is my specialty. But now that I'm the one wearing a C on my sweater, I'm the one who speaks with the stripes, so I can't get into fights, or I'll lose all credibility and respect from the officials . . . which results in penalties, fines, and coaches up my ass.

I'm done starting fights. From now on, I only finish them. Gotta say, I kinda miss the chaos, but having the added responsibility gives me more control over my contracts, boosts my sponsorships, and my favorite of all: *women love fucking the captain.*

It's dark when I pull up to the hunting lodge. I haven't been here since I was a teenager, but even in the low light, it's clear the Davenports have been keeping the place in mint condition, or at least the landscapers have, as per usual of their properties. Back in the day, Bryan and I used to ride quad-runners here and get into all kinds of mayhem. A couple of privileged rich kids escaping the rules and letting loose in the country. Unsupervised, nobody could tell us what to do or how to act. No itchy neckties and stiff shoes. Some of the most fun I had in my childhood happened here.

Although Bryan and I have grown apart over the years, our friendship is resilient, even though we don't talk much. Now he's getting married—fucking wild. He's head over heels for Jordana; she's hot as fuck, but it sounds like she has him on a short leash. I've reached out a few times, and he's always going on about having to "check with the boss." I can't relate. Asking permission has never been a good color on me. Rebellion brings out the hazel in my eyes.

I enter through the huge oak door. Inside, Bryan strides toward me. "Finally!" He claps my back. "Good to see you, man."

"You too. Sorry I'm late, Friday rush hour."

"No worries. Come on, I gotta introduce you to everybody."

Shrugging off my leather jacket, I abandon my bag at the door.

Beyond the luxurious foyer of the vacation home, we enter the great room that's been transformed into a formal event space. High-top tables, an open bar, caterers, and a few ice sculptures replace the aged leather furniture that normally can be found here. A pianist in a tuxedo plays in the corner. Bryan and I took piano as kids, and memories of us playing Metallica on that Steinway make me chuckle. His mom hated that shit.

"Place looks great," I say.

His fiancée appears at his side, and he wraps his arm around her lower back. "There you are," he says.

Jordana looks . . . *tempting*, it's a struggle to maintain eye contact. She's like a curvier Blake Lively. Everyone expects me to look, this time though, she's my best friends fucking fiancée—I'll keep my eyes up. Her dress is white, short, and somehow, the long sleeves and high neckline make it even sexier. Her light-blonde waves are styled in this half-up, half-down fashion that show off how naturally beautiful she is. The kind you see in Miss America pageants—I'd know, I've fucked a few *states* in my time.

"Jordana. Congratulations again," I say.

"Same to you. I hear you were offered the position of captain this season. You must be thrilled." Her answers are clipped, and she's grinning, but it doesn't reach her eyes. I get the sense she'd rather be anywhere else. Or perhaps she simply dislikes me.

"Thank you. Hopefully I'll be able to rise to the challenge. I have some big shoes to fill."

Another tight smile. "I'm sure you'll do well. You had a very accomplished season last year. How many points did you score? Eighty-one?" For whatever reason, it bothers me that I'm having difficulty reading her.

I grin. "Eighty-two."

"Didn't know you were such a hockey enthusiast, babe," Bryan comments, furrowing his brow and waving over my wedding counterpart from across the room.

"I've always been a Lakes fan," she defends before quickly following up with "But I'm just regurgitating what the sportscasters say."

Bryan rolls his eyes and mutters, "Lovely word choice, Jordana."

A pretty brunette stalks closer. "Veronica, have you met

Camden yet? Veronica is Jordana's best friend and maid of honor. Veronica, this is my best man, Camden Teller." He leans in and whispers, "Don't fuck her."

I recognize her from social media. The three of them are often going to brunches and other Davenport social hours.

"I don't believe so!" She holds out her perfectly manicured hand for me to shake and doesn't let go until I pull back. Veronica leers at me over her champagne flute, telling me *she's down if I am*.

I'd rather fuck the same girl twice than stir up drama with the bride's best friend. Hard pass. In my experience, bridesmaids are fucking nuts. We'd fuck, she'd want to do it again, and I'd have to turn her down. I don't do repeats unless they bring a friend. One ticket per customer, no mulligans. Blame it on my strong moral values.

"Hey, babe, grab us a couple of beers, would ya?" Bryan says, pulling away.

Jordana grabs Veronica's arm, then they walk toward the open bar on the far east wall. With Veronica trailing behind Jordana, Bryan has his eyes fixed on the maid of honor's ass.

"Whoa. Down, boy," I comment.

He doesn't pry his eyes up, even while he answers. "She knows I look. Jordana doesn't care where I get my appetite as long as I eat my meals at home."

I cross my arms. "And do you?"

He winks. "What do you think?"

That wink brings more questions than answers. It's none of my business.

I consider whether I could ever settle down with one person . . . I can't picture it. In Bryan's case, his fiancée is drop-dead gorgeous and, other than the resting bitch face, she seems like a decent person, if you've got a Stepford wife kink.

His dad interrupts and thrusts his hand in front of me. "Congrats, Captain."

Grasping his palm, I look him in the eye. "Thank you, sir."

Even though I've been around this family a thousand times, Mr. Davenport has always remained a stranger. He's quiet and has a temperamental disposition. I've never seen him smile. Bryan used to be terrified of him, and I'd put money down he still is. His dad always ran the house with an iron fist.

After acknowledging me, he moves on to the other guests at the party, which appear to be mostly investors, based on how people are dressed and the bits of conversation I've picked up on. The Davenports are one of the wealthiest families in the area, not as rich as Jordana's family but still fully loaded. They work hard to keep it that way. Image is everything to them. The family business has its fingers in nearly every industry, including politics.

Veronica returns with two beer bottles, and Bryan's jaw tics. "Where is Jordana?"

He's kinda weird tonight. I take a drink. Damn, Citra makes great beer.

"She went upstairs for a minute, said she'd be right back. It's fine," Veronica answers.

"Excuse me," he murmurs, turning away.

I hold my arms out. "Come on, I just got here. She said she'd be right back." I don't want to get stuck talking with Veronica one-on-one.

He ignores me and strides toward the stairs, taking a long swig from the bottle and setting it on a high-top table as he passes.

The brunette angles herself in front of me, and when I glance behind, Bryan has disappeared. He's probably going up there to fuck. Not surprising with how good his girl looks tonight—I sure as hell noticed. When he had his eyes on the maid of honor, I had mine on his fiancée. I'd never make a move, but if he's not going to appreciate the way her ass looks in that dress, I will.

"So how long have you been playing hockey?" Veronica asks.

"Going into my ninth season."

Her eyes grow large. "Wow, how old were you when you started?"

"Eighteen." I'm already bored with this conversation. I've had it a thousand times. "So, do you and Jordana go as far back as Bryan and me?"

I avoid asking people questions about their careers. It's something that's always irritated me. As if your job is indicative of the type of person you are. I'm sure sometimes that's true, but "*And what do you do*?" always gave me the same vibes as "*Which one of us makes more money*?"

"No, only since college. We were in a sorority together and did a lot of mixers with Bryan's frat."

"Oh, so the three of you have been friends for a while."

"You could say that. What about you? You guys grew up together, right?"

"Mm-hm," I say, nodding and taking a drink. "Our parents used to dabble in the same business ventures. We grew up attending the same galas and banquets. Bryan and I used to sneak off and get into trouble."

"I can appreciate a troublemaker."

I tip my beer to her. "Me too." *But not tonight.* "Hey, my bag is still sitting at the front door. I'm gonna bring it up to one of the bedrooms. I'll be back in a bit." I cringe, realizing how that sounded like an invite. It's like I can't turn it off.

"I can help you find an empty one," she offers. If I wasn't

seeing her again, I might fuck her in the bathroom. Instead, I'll probably hook up with a cute catering waitress before the end of the night, that's always a sure thing.

"Nah, I'm good." I hold up my hand. "Thanks, though."

As I climb the stairs, the gentle piano keys fade and are replaced by Bryan's muffled voice. He's annoyed with something, and I chuckle. *Bet he got busted for checking out Veronica's ass.* I don't know Jordana, but I doubt any woman would be cool with her fiancé ogling her best friend. He'll have to keep it in check when we go to Vegas in a couple weeks.

The first four bedrooms are occupied with coats and bags from other wedding-party members staying the night. The closer I get, the more I hear. The dim hallway reveals a light shining under the crack of a closed door, and I enter the room next to it, relieved to see an empty king size bed with no suitcases. My ears prick when I hear my name. I gingerly place my duffel on the floor and press my ear to the shared wall.

Jordana sounds like she's trying to pacify him.

"All I said was he had a good season."

"It wasn't what you said, it was the way you said it."

Wait, what? Is he accusing her of flirting with me? I'm very attuned to when a woman is coming onto me, and that's not at all what I was getting from her. The way she said it couldn't have been more stiff.

"I was being friendly, Bryan. Can we please go back downstairs and enjoy the party? Remember, this is for us."

"You may think you're being friendly, but that's not the way it sounds to everyone else. You sound like a whore. I would never, ever talk to another woman the way you talk to my friends. You send out signals to every man you speak to. This is what I was talking about earlier, you don't know how to speak to people! I don't know if I can trust you anymore."

The hair on the back of my neck stands up, as I heard his words in my biological father's voice. It's so similar to the way he spoke to my mom when I was young.

"You can't trust me? Fine, what about the black bobby pins on the floor of the BMW? I'm blonde! What about how late you've been working? The hotel receipts?"

"Jesus, the fuckin' bobby pins again? You're losing your fucking mind. You really are. You have black bobby pins. You can go home right now and check the bathroom drawer, you'll find a whole pile of them! This argument is ridiculous. Stop deflecting. You aren't going to escape the consequences for acting like a fucking cocktease right in front of me. Are you trying to humiliate me? There are important people down there! This isn't a game, Jordana. You're engaged now. Engaged to me."

What the actual fuck?

I lose the rest of the conversation when I exit the room to pound on their closed door.

"In a minute," Bryan barks.

I turn the handle and push the door open.

"I said we'd be out in a minute!"

My eyes drop to his grip on her arm. He turns his head to look at me, and his eyebrows relax. He releases her, and I can't tell how hard he was grasping her because of her long sleeves, but the fact he let go so quickly tells me it was probably firm enough to turn her skin white. I know Bryan, he would never hurt a woman. We've talked about this shit before, he knows about my childhood. He makes an annual donation to my charity for survivors of domestic violence, for Christ's sake. There must be something I'm missing.

"Everything okay in here?" I mostly keep my eyes on Jordana to examine her body language. It's an unconscious habit after all my DV training at the center. She rolls her eyes, looking more annoyed than fearful.

"Mind your business, Teller. We'll be out in a second," he says firmly.

She moves toward me, and I step aside, giving her space to slip out of the room. As she passes, the smell of her perfume wafts in the air. I don't know what she's wearing, but it's nice. No matter what kind of disagreement they were having, I don't like what I heard. My mom stayed in her marriage far too long—it wasn't until he raised a hand to her that she packed up my sisters and me and left.

The way Bryan leers at her gives me those same sinister vibes. I've never seen or heard him like this. It's unlike him.

"How much have you had to drink, man?"

He clears his throat and points his finger at me.

"Don't give me that shit. You're taking this out of context." Like a switch is flipped in his brain, the taut expression is erased from his features. He chuckles. "We had an argument earlier, and she likes to push my buttons. You know how it is."

I don't—and this interaction doesn't sit well with me. Even though my childhood is long in the past, the unease in this room fills me with anxiety. It left an impact on me and my older sisters—they remember more than I do, but the memories I have are enough. It's why I've dedicated so much of my time and money to creating resources for people like my mom. It's hard for me to picture Bryan being one of those guys. We grew up together. I know him, we were practically brothers. Hell, he was my best friend and the guy I talked to when I was scared of my biological father.

"Well, go easy on her, you don't want a runaway bride before the wedding even begins."

I turn to leave but hear him mumble, "She's not going anywhere."

"What was that?" I spin around and narrow my eyes at him.

"Jesus, not like that! I meant we're perfect together, why would she leave? I give her everything she wants. Cars, designer clothes, purses, shoes—I gave her a top spot with H&H. She's just one of those girls who's never going to be happy. It's never enough! I do everything for her, and she doesn't appreciate any of it."

This is all new information, but it's not like Jordana can't buy her own things. Her family is richer than the Davenports and Tellers combined. "Are you sure you want to go through with this? I mean, are *you* happy?"

He thinks on it and exhales through his nose.

"I will be."

THREE

Banksy

Fuck, I love Vegas. Pretty women everywhere. Unfortunately, they've combined the bachelor party with the bachelorette. It was made apparent early on there would be no strippers this weekend. Isn't that the point of having your bachelor party in Vegas?

Bryan insisted on planning it this way, so I let him. Normally, I'd call bullshit—assuming Jordana wouldn't let him have a stag bash, but he seems pretty obsessed with her. He's been texting me about how great she is since the weekend up north a couple weeks ago. Personally, I understand none of it. Love makes people fucking stupid. It's why we're at an XS nightclub tonight and not a strip club. I'm not complaining, the women here are as gorgeous as the ones on the poles.

At least we've got separate hotel suites from the girls. Maybe I can take someone back tonight. If I'm in Sin City, I'm getting laid. I've been putting in so many hours at the arena, and three weeks is way too long to be celibate. Especially if I gotta look at Jordana, Veronica, and the rest of their group in these tight-as-fuck dresses for half the weekend.

Sexy curves are everywhere. It's hell being around this many attractive women and not fucking any of them.

"Shots!" Veronica yells, gathering the glasses from the bottle service cart next to our table. She pours the liquor, then grabs the decanter of fresh-squeezed pomegranate juice to top them off. I shoot the alcohol, and window-shop the women standing outside the VIP area in our vicinity. *Time to make some friends.*

I make eye contact with one of them, and she has a nice smile and an even better backside. *Perfect.*

I nudge Bryan and tip my head in her direction. "You mind?"

"Nope. Have fun."

I leave our couch and step outside the roped-off area to introduce myself. Her name is Kandii, "with one K and two i's." She asks what I do for a living, but I brush it off.

"So, what's it like being in the NHL?"

"It's the dream. I get to play the greatest sport in the world and meet gorgeous women like you. Pretty nice."

She grins. "I'm definitely a perk." *And perky.*

Jordana bumps into me as she and the other girls head out to the dance floor. She's wearing the same perfume as she was last time. Like a total asshat, I can't help but follow the bride-to-be with my eyes as she dances. Christ, what is it about her? It's gotta be some forbidden fruit thing that's happening. *Wait, what were we talking about again?* My job. I refocus on the person in front of me.

"It's more work than people realize. I don't often get to travel for fun. I pretty much live at the arena or training center, there's injuries and bruises, and traveling nonstop can be brutal—"

"Oh my God, totally! I know *exactly* what you mean. I went to *Ibitha* last month and we were so jetlagged. It was crazy! I didn't go to any of the clubs for like the whole first day."

My eyes glaze over while she goes on and on about the parties in Ibiza. I know Ibitha is the proper Spanish pronunciation, but she's name-dropped the island so many times, it's sounding vain.

I gotta learn to say "Hockey is great" and move on. Besides, there's nothing for me to complain about, playing for the Lakes is fucking awesome. Sure, in situations like this, it draws fake friendships and superficial connections, but when the women are this gorgeous, do you need anything else?

"Yup. It's just like that," I say with a smile. She can't tell I'm being facetious, and that's okay.

"Except for the bruises . . . or are you giving me those tonight too?"

Off to the races.

"Depends on if you're a good girl or not."

Our table is now empty. Bryan and the other guys must be out dancing with the group. Might be a good time to bring Kandii to our suite. It's on the same property as the club, so I could probably be back in less than an hour.

We chat a little longer, and the more I try to stretch this conversation, the more she hints at sex. I usually get to know the woman I'm with for a little while before I take her back to my place. It's been about fifteen minutes, but in Vegas, that's the equivalent of an hour anywhere else, right?

"What hotel are you staying at?" she asks.

"Encore . . . want to see it?"

Her smile grows twice as big. "I'd love to."

Our table is still empty, and I could text him to let him know where I'll be, but he probably won't even notice I'm gone. Even if he does, he knows I'm a hoe.

She hooks her elbow in mine, and we head toward the

exit. A small hand grabs my bicep, and I spin around to see Jordana. My date drops my arm, probably because she thinks this is my girlfriend.

"Are you going back to Encore?" she asks.

"Uh, yeah." I link my arm with Kandii to put her at ease.

"Can you see if Bryan is there?"

I furrow my brow. "I thought he was with you?"

"He was, but I turned around and he was gone. I can't find him anywhere. He mentioned having a work call—it just seems like it's been a while."

I peer behind her, and there's a swarm of people dancing. I've got pretty solid eyesight and still can't see for shit in this nightclub. "Where's Veronica and everybody else?"

"I lost them in the crowd. I'm gonna head back to the table. We said if we got separated we would meet there."

"Do you want to come with us and check the hotel to see if he's there?"

"No, I don't want Veronica to think I've abandoned her. I'm going to wait here for them. Besides, if Bryan caught me leaving the club next to you, he'd have a fucking conniption." She laughs it off, but it rubs me the wrong way. "I don't want to deal with his temper tonight."

"Is that a common occurrence?" On the plane, he went on and on about how solid he and Jordana are. Yet, walking out with me would make him lose his shit? The more I'm exposed to their relationship, the rockier it appears. I hate to put such strong accusations on my best friend, but something about this feels off. Could I be naive about the way he treats her? I mean, maybe? But this is Bryan we're talking about.

"We're fine."

Not the right answer. She didn't deny it, and simply brushed off his behavior like it's nothing.

"Well, I'm not going to leave you here by yourself."

"No, I'm good, really. You enjoy . . ." She looks at my date.

"*Kandii.*" Kandii introduces herself.

"Kandii—nice to meet you." She smiles and shifts her gaze back to me. "I'm going to wait at the table. See you later."

Scanning the crowd, I see none of the other groomsmen or bridesmaids. Fuck. "'Kay. Stay behind the ropes. If I find him, I'll send him down. But if he's not there, I'm coming back to make sure he shows up."

"Thanks, Cam. I'm sure it's not necessary."

Cam. Jesus, why does her shortening my name like that make my dick twitch? I need to get laid worse than I thought. Now I *really* want that motherfucker to be up there. I need to get him back to Jordana so I can take care of this hellish dry spell. I track her as she walks away and don't turn around until she's behind the bouncer manning the VIP area. Kandii takes my hand, and we head toward the exit.

On the elevator up to our suite, she kisses my neck, and I'm already getting hard. *See, this is all I needed.* After this, it will all return to normal. When the elevator dings and we step out, I fish my phone from my pocket and open the hotel app to unlock the door.

As soon as the light flashes green, I push the door open and freeze.

"Shit."

"Fuck!" Bryan shouts.

He's got Veronica against the wall, her legs are wrapped around his waist, and he's balls deep. If it weren't happening in front of me, I wouldn't believe it. It makes my fucking heart sink. I've played with guys who cheat on their spouses before, but none of their affairs have ever put a knot in my throat like this one does. I've known this guy his whole life. How could he do that to her?

"Goddamn it, Teller! What the fuck?! I've got the room, get out!"

I stumble back into the hall but only close the door enough to block my view of them. I caught him, and his response is to *finish*?

"That's fucked up, man. Her best friend?"

God, she will be devastated.

He swings the door open, his pants pulled up but not buttoned.

"If you say one fucking thing to her, you're out of the wedding and our friendship is over!"

Promise? What a piece of shit.

"Hey, it's none of my business." I avert my gaze. If I look him in the eyes, I'll punch him. "But Jordana's alone down there, so I'm going back to sit with her until you two get your shit together. Don't leave at the same time."

Kandii's eyes are wide, and her jaw is on the floor.

"We gotta go."

Thankfully, she nods, understanding that tonight isn't happening.

I can't believe he's fucking her best friend. *Her best friend.* Veronica's helping Jordana with all this wedding shit while fucking her fiancé at the bachelorette party she probably helped plan. Is this why he wanted to combine parties?

Jordana's likely still sitting at the VIP table—because she didn't want to abandon Veronica. *Ugh.*

The Bryan I knew would never do something so abhorrent to a woman he loves. The worst part is, I could tell it isn't the first time. This isn't some drunken accident. They seemed way too familiar with each other. How long has the affair been going on?

The whole way down the elevator, my head is spinning. You could hear a pin drop until she breaks the silence.

"You're gonna tell her, right?"

It'll cost me my friendship, but if he's threatening to "unfriend" me over his fuck-up, then our friendship wasn't strong to begin with. How could he toss aside a woman like Jordana—who looks like a total fucking smokeshow, by the way—and fuck her best friend? How the hell could he not appreciate how good he has it?

"Yeah . . . I think I have to."

Kandii nods. "She seemed sweet, and that guy's a dick. He doesn't deserve her." When the elevator doors open, she steps out and throws her thumb over her shoulder. "So, I'm gonna go back and find my friends."

"Sorry about tonight."

"No worries. Good luck with everything." She cringes. Yeah, I wouldn't want to be in my position either. Shit, this sucks.

"Thanks."

When I return to the club and our table comes into view, Jordana is sitting with some of the other bridesmaids. They're all *his* cousins. I didn't notice it earlier, but how doesn't she have any other friends in that group? It's weird.

The bouncer nods to me and unlatches the rope for me to pass.

Jordana stands up. "He's not there?"

I motion for her to step to the side with me, out of earshot from the other women. She swallows hard and absently rubs her forearm. I'm suddenly paranoid about the rest of the wedding party. Did they know? Does *she*?

"He was in the hotel suite."

Her eyes are so big and dark, they're haunting. I suck in a breath. I don't want to hurt her. Fuck Bryan for making me do this. My mouth opens to speak but no words come out.

"Okay . . . So, is he coming down?"

I exhale and stare into those dark pools that seem to have me hypnotized. *Tell her.*

"He wasn't alone, Jordana."

She crosses her arms. "What do you mean?"

"I think you know what I mean."

She shakes her head, and her eyes shine with tears. It's killing me. "Where's Veronica?"

I wince. Fuck, she has nobody.

She swipes at her eyes and scans the dance floor. "Camden. Where's Veronica?"

"Does it matter?" The last thing I want to do is hurt her more. Why twist the knife? She doesn't need two heartbreaks in one night.

"Where's Veronica?" Her gaze snaps back to mine, and this time her eyes are cold and shut off.

It's as if she already knows but needs someone else to say it. "She's with him."

With a bitter smile, she shakes her head.

"I'm so sorry, Jordana."

"It's Jordan. I hate being called Jordana." She turns to grab her purse off the table, snags her phone, and taps away on a rideshare app. Saying goodbye to the rest of the wedding party, she tells them she's not feeling well and is heading back to the hotel.

"Where are you really going?"

"Home."

She strides past me, and I catch up to her. "Are you good?" *Wow, that's a stupid fucking question!* I hang my head.

"I'm fine, I just want to get out of here."

"Don't you need to get your things?" I nod toward our hotel.

"Veronica can have my things. She's taken everything else, right?"

I will not let her wait alone on the Vegas strip.

"When's the next flight?"

"When I arrive. I think Bryan can pay for a charter, don't you?"

I smirk. *Atta girl.*

Ubers are about as common as herpes in Vegas, so her car is waiting by the time we make it out the front doors.

I open the rear passenger door, and she slips in the back-seat. She pauses before closing it.

"Thanks for not covering his ass. You're not as big of a dick as everyone says you are."

"Oh, yes I am."

She doesn't respond, simply yanks the door shut, then a second later, the car pulls away from the curb. I'm left standing there, wishing I were beside her so I could go home too. The last thing I want to do is face the drama that's about to explode inside.

I'm too tired to deal with airports and shit, but I'm definitely getting a new hotel for the night. I'll fly out in the morning. On my way back, I run into Bryan—sans Veronica.

"Did you say anything?"

I can't believe that's his first question. "Dude, you know my dad used to have affairs, you saw how that shit played out. And her best friend? That's so fucked up."

"It was a mistake! It won't happen again. I'm drunk, she was getting handsy, it just happened."

Bullshit. I made that same trek with Kandii—he had plenty of time to reconsider, but he went for it anyway.

"Whatever, I'm going to bed."

"Where is she?"

"No idea. I assume she's still at the club with the girls." *I'll cover for her instead.*

He claps me on the back. "It's just bachelor party shit. It won't happen again."

Unbelievable. I head toward the hotel.

An hour later, as I'm watching ESPN highlights in my new hotel room—five blocks away, my phone buzzes.

BRYAN DAVENPORT

You're a fucking dead man!

Huh. He seems irritated.

BRYAN DAVENPORT

Wanna tell me why her last location is the fucking airport? This is all your fault!

He tracks her location? Of—fucking—course he does, because *she's* the one who can't be trusted. I roll my eyes.

Let's get one thing straight, this is YOUR fuck-up. Not mine. And what makes you think I told her? Maybe you should check with Veronica before you start throwing out accusations.

BRYAN DAVENPORT

Veronica isn't going to tell her.

Sure about that? Because when I got back to the club, the girls said Jordana wasn't feeling well and left. I haven't even seen her since I left XS to go to the hotel.

If she found out, it's because you weren't careful about covering your tracks. Don't come blaming me.

BRYAN DAVENPORT

Was it that girl you were with?

Dude, I have no idea. Look, I'm going to sleep. I've got an early flight home tomorrow. This is too much drama, even for me.

BRYAN DAVENPORT

K.

FOUR

Jordana

The flight home is exhausting. All I want to do is pass out and pretend tonight never happened. My mind won't stop replaying the expression on Camden's face when he told me. His eyes were so full of pity. That man is basically a stranger and was the only one with the decency not to lie to me. I saw the way the other girls looked at me when I got the news. It's like they already knew. How humiliating.

Normally, I eat when I'm stressed. This time, I've lost my appetite altogether. Funny how I've been starving myself for weeks for that stupid fucking dress. *Shit, Bryan, you shoulda told me you were fucking my best friend back then, this diet would have been a breeze!* I'm done with that. No more skipping my iced mochas, no more salads, and sayonara to those revolting protein shakes that taste like chocolate Pepto Bismol.

The seatbelt light dings, and I slide open the window shade. The Twin Cities come into view, and it feels good to be back. *But where do I go*? I want to talk to my best friend about it. I want to cry to her and scream about him.

They did this. They did this together.

The signs were there—the random bobby pins in his car, the work trips—but to sleep with my best friend? The woman who was supposed to be my maid of honor at *our* goddamn wedding? Gotta say, he caught me off guard with that one.

I should've known his jealousy stemmed from a guilty conscience. And how could *she*? And for how long? Has it been happening all along right under my nose? It really is lonely at the top. If I can't trust my best friend or fiancé, who's left?

I'm such a fucking idiot.

The plane lands with a gentle bounce, and I turn on my phone to twenty-some missed calls from Bryan. Ten from Veronica. I call my mom to pick me up from the airport. She's not happy about the 4:00 a.m. phone call, but thankfully, she asks no questions. I don't know how to tell her my fiancé, the one she and Dad love so much, betrayed me and I fell for it.

I stand outside near the charter jet hangar, still in my white bachelorette dress. *The one Veronica helped me pick out.* The nightclub feels like it was days ago, not hours. The Vegas strip is a lot warmer at night than the forty-degrees in Minneapolis. I could wait inside, but I welcome the numbing temperatures; I'd rather not feel.

As soon as Mom's car arrives, I climb into the passenger seat.

"Where's Bryan? Where's your stuff?"

"It's just me, Mom."

"I don't understand." She gawks at me.

"Bryan . . . Bryan was caught with Veronica. In our hotel room."

She pinches the bridge of her nose and sighs. "Oh, honey. I'm so sorry."

As soon as I hear the softness in her voice, I break into tears. "I hate them. I hate them both so much! How could they?"

"I'll have your father take care of this."

She pulls me into her arms, and I tremble, letting out all the feelings.

When I'm empty, I detach from our hug and wipe the remaining tears from my face. "There was so much time and money put into this wedding. I'm sorry, Mom." She nods solemnly and puts the Rolls in gear to head toward the private airport's exit.

We sit in silence as she merges onto the highway.

"I don't think we should do anything rash."

My head snaps to face her.

"He slept with *my best friend*," I say slowly. *Not do anything rash? Like canceling our engagement?*

Mom exhales, and I feel like there's some devil's advocate bullshit about to spew from her lips. Please, not now. Read the room—or car, whatever.

"You know, sometimes accidents like this happen. It's not fair, it hurts, but men are idiots and occasionally forget to think. You and Bryan have been together for so long, do you really think it's worth throwing away your relationship?"

I stare at her in horror. "What?!"

The orange streetlights along the highway maintain a steady strobe of light inside the car, and I wish I could see her face clearer.

"Jordana, there are relationship counselors that deal with this kind of thing every day."

"Mom! You can't be serious!"

"Look, you're not even married yet. He's probably trying to get it out of his system before the vows."

My eyebrows shoot up. "I can't believe you're taking his side," I whisper.

"I am *not* taking his side! What he did was wrong! I'm simply trying to help make sense of it. That's all."

My hands are shaking. "What they did is unforgivable."

"We'll stop by your place, and you can pack a bag. All I'm saying is that you should take some time to think it over, after you get some sleep. You can stay with us for now, but we're heading to Monaco in a few days. Your father will talk to the Davenports and get this all straightened out. It's gonna be okay."

There's nothing to straighten out. I come from a reserved family, and a broken engagement will stir rumors. Is that what she's worried about? Who cares! On top of that, she doesn't even seem surprised, she's more concerned with how to get the train back on the rails. It's like I'm stuck in a nightmare and unable to wake up.

If I screamed, would anyone even hear me?

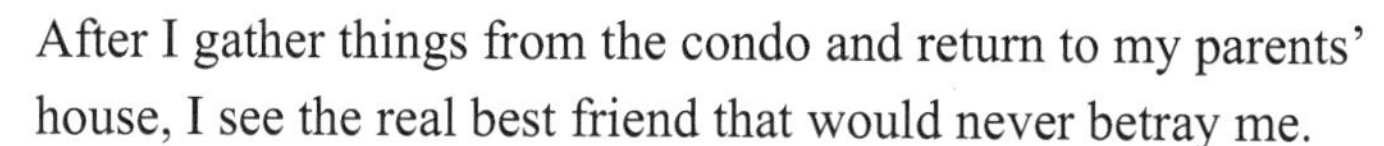

After I gather things from the condo and return to my parents' house, I see the real best friend that would never betray me.

"Chicken Salad!" My big fluffy Alaskan Shepherd mix gallops into my arms and knocks me down. She whines and hops about, trampling me, and I wrap my arms around her big furry neck. I missed my dog so much. We sit up, and she trots in place before rolling onto her back so I can rub her belly.

"Someone's happy to see you." My mom chuckles. Bryan is allergic to dogs, so I couldn't take Chicken Salad with us when we moved in together, and it broke my heart. I still come back to visit her often, but it's not enough.

"Come on, pup. Let's go to bed." I stand, pick up my

things, and head up to one of the guest bedrooms. I take off the couture dress and pull my soft oversized college hoodie over my head—my emotional support sweatshirt.

My cheeks itch with dry tears. After I wash them and the makeup away, I'm ready to sleep. Hopefully, for days. The sun is peeking over the horizon when I draw the blackout blinds to the room. After wiggling under the covers, I realize how tired my body and mind are. I slap the top of the mattress, and Chicken Salad bounds up on the bed beside me.

She circles a few times, then drops down so she's wedged against my side and lets out a deep exhale. We are reunited again, and all is right in her world. Mine is falling apart. I drape an arm over her warm back and haul her closer as a lump forms in my throat, aching like it does right before I cry.

FIVE

Banksy

It's been four days since I've returned from Vegas. A lot of that time has been spent at the arena and weight room, but it's recovery day, so I get to relax. It's been a weird few days. Bryan is pissed. I don't have to worry about any more wedding festivities interrupting my schedule. At least, I assume the wedding is off, based on the way she left Vegas without even getting her stuff from the hotel. That was some heavy shit that went down.

I can't imagine what Jordana—*Jordan*—is feeling. I've received more accusatory texts from Bryan, trying to blame me for how his dick found its way into Veronica. Sometimes they're threatening, but Bryan's all talk. And I haven't admitted to anything. He deserves to be in the hot seat for a while. I'm no saint, but that was a fucked-up thing to do. I don't regret telling Jordan. Ever since the night at the lodge, I've been suspicious.

I take another sip of my large black coffee at my favorite hole-in-the-wall coffee shop, Uncommon Grounds, and the simple act of bringing the mug to my lips makes my overworked muscles ache. I should have stretched this morning, but I had to get here early so I could get my hands on two jumbo pumpkin muffins before they were gone.

This place makes killer fucking muffins, and I wait all goddamn year for the pumpkin ones. Call me a basic white boy, I don't give a fuck. You'd do the same if you knew how good they tasted. The owners already had them set aside; they know me well. This place is mostly frequented by an artsier crowd. I've learned over the years the majority of them aren't concerned with NHL standings or anything hockey-related, so I get to live in anonymity and enjoy my coffee like everybody else. This place is my best kept secret.

A woman reads the newspaper at the table next to mine, and I lean over and clear my throat. "Mind if I steal the sports section?" She smiles and separates the pages for me, handing them over.

"Thanks."

She nods, and we both go about our reading. *God, I love it here.*

A few more customers trickle in, and the ambient noise of steaming milk and cups clinking have blurred into the background. The article I'm reading criticizes the Lakes for choosing such a young captain to take over Lee Sullivan's spot. As I'm peeling the second muffin from the paper liner, the barista calls out a name that cuts through the haze.

"Jordan. Small iced mocha with heavy cream."

My gaze instantly snaps up to the counter, and there she is.

No fucking way. It's creepy seeing someone right after thinking about them. And here, of all places. What are the odds? I would have taken her for a Starbucks girl. She drops a few dollars in the tip jar and smiles at the man behind the counter before finding a table on the other side of the café. I dip my eyes back to the article, but it's impossible to focus on the words. Peeking up again, I give her a once-over. Not a stitch of makeup, her hair likely hasn't seen a hairbrush today and is piled on top of her head in a messy bun. She looks so different, but no doubt, it's Jordan Landry.

I never noticed the freckles over the bridge of her nose. She must cover them up, because there's no way I'd forget those. I have a thing for freckles. Her tight leggings show off her figure, but the rest of her is swimming in an old college sweatshirt with a stain on the sleeve.

It's fascinating to see this version of her, knowing how much money she comes from. The Landrys run in some of the same circles as my family. The top one percent are very aware of each other and their business dealings. In my family, appearance is important. Prestige is everything.

I suppose that's the difference between old money and new money. Old money knows they're rich, they don't need to show it off. New money has something to prove. Jordan is definitely the former. She doesn't show off labels or flaunt designer purses, she's always dressed conservatively . . . but never slouchy. Which is why her current ensemble captures my interest.

Am I supposed to say something? Shit. Give her my condolences? I don't want to be some shoulder for her to cry on. The only body part I want on my shoulders are legs. Besides, she's better off this way. But damn, she's been betrayed in the worst way possible—ugh. Fuck. Before I realize it, I'm already picking up my things.

She catches me striding across the room and cocks her head to the side.

"Hey." Her eyes are tired, but she greets me with a lopsided smile. "What are you doing here?"

I smile back. "This is my place."

"Your place? I've been coming here for years. They know me by name," she chirps.

"Do you think that makes you special or something? They know me by name too."

She holds up a white paper bag. *Why is she still wearing her engagement ring?* "They had my bakery order ready. I'm *very* special. So, suck it." Her bright, clean perfume wafts toward me when she sets the bag down.

I present my matching bag as I pull out the chair across from her and sit down. "Checkmate," I counter.

"Oh, would you like to join me?" she asks, rolling her eyes.

I smirk at her. She takes a sip of her coffee and leans back in her chair, regarding me in silence. I don't like how exposed I feel. The air between us wanes. "So . . . how are things?" I ask, equally sarcastic.

"Can't smile wide enough." We're on the same wavelength. Glad she's not going into more depth, I'm not in the mood to listen to a sob story. I sip my coffee and open the sports section again.

"I'm sorry, but . . ." She looks around. "Why are you here?"

"Pumpkin muffins. Why are *you* here?"

"I mean, why are you sitting at my table?"

My lips curve into a half smile. She really doesn't give a shit. It's intriguing. "Answer my question first." I fold the newspaper and set it down.

She taps her chin and narrows her eyes. "Well, let's see. My ex-fiancé hasn't stopped calling or texting since a few days ago when my mother picked me up from the airport after I left my own bachelorette party because he slept with the maid of honor of our wedding. Before we even got to my condo to pick up some clothes, my mother informed me that sometimes 'accidents happen'"—she uses air quotes—"and he's probably trying to sow his wild oats before the wedding. So I've spent the last however-many days being told I'm overreacting. Like, fuck me for expecting my fiancé to not sleep with my best friend, right?" She throws an arm out. "Oh, and I really like the apple-cinnamon scones, so I've been stuffing my face to pass the time."

She takes a deep inhale and presses her palms into her eye sockets, mumbling something about how she can't believe she's talking to me about her problems. When she drops her hands and locks her eyes on mine, I almost choke on my bite. She's got some of the richest chestnut-brown eyes I've ever seen. Jordan doesn't look at you, she looks *into* you. It's something I've picked up on before, but this is the most attention I've ever received from her, and it's coming at full force.

I nod, giving her a minute to get everything off her chest while she blows off steam.

"My pumpkin muffin is better than your scone."

She laughs. "That's all you're going to say? After everything I just told you?"

I shrug. "It sounded like you needed a little normalcy. And what am I gonna say? Sorry about your shitty life?"

"Hm." She crosses her arms.

"Let me try a bite of your scone."

She studies me. If she thinks I'm about to get in the middle of their situation, she's wrong. I'm not gonna say shit about their relationship or tell her what to do. I don't care.

"I'll let you try my muffin . . ." I coax.

"Bet you say that to all the girls."

At least she's got a sense of humor. She slides the scone sitting on top of the bakery bag across the table, and I hand her my last pumpkin muffin. She doesn't even realize the sacrifice I'm making.

I break off a piece of hers and pop it in my mouth. Meh. Not bad, but it's no pumpkin muffin.

"I shouldn't eat this, scones are my ride or die. Feels like I'm cheating on them." She turns the dark orange piece of muffin in her hand, and her eyes grow large. "God, this must have been how Bryan felt. How tragic."

I stare at her with a single raised eyebrow, my hand frozen, half reaching for the pastry.

Her lips curve into a half smile. "Too soon?"

I grin back, surprised by her unexpected dark humor. She's never been this candid with me before. We share the same defense mechanism.

She chuckles, tears off a small piece of the pumpkin muffin, and savors it. "Mm, tastes like infidelity."

Shaking my head, I take a sip of my coffee. My gaze drops, and I stare at the massive diamond on her finger. "So, are you wearing the ring because it matches your outfit, or is it stuck on your finger?"

"It's stuck on my finger."

I laugh, but her face is sober. "Really?"

She nods. "I'm an emotional eater. Now that I'm off Bryan's wedding diet, I've been hitting the baked goods —*hard*."

I love challenges. "Let me take off his ring."

She holds her hand out. "Good luck. It was tight when he gave it to me."

"Why didn't he get it resized?" I suck her finger into my mouth down to the knuckle, and somehow, her already dark eyes get even deeper. She tastes like apple cinnamon. I swipe my tongue around the taut metal band.

"I thought you were going to use butter or something, you fucking psycho." She stares for a moment then clears her throat. "He said it was motivation to help with the wedding weight loss. It was supposed to fit once I hit my goal."

Well, if that's not the most fucked-up thing I've heard all year.

I pull her finger from my mouth. "You're joking."

She shrugs. "Wish I was."

I can get it to turn, but it's not budging. She wasn't lying, it's stuck. "Fuck, this thing is stubborn," I murmur, working on it.

"I know, I've got an appointment with the jeweler this afternoon." She withdraws her hand and gazes out the window while trying to twist it off. She winces, tugging at it like it's burning her flesh.

"One sec."

I walk up to the counter and grab a thin wooden stir stick from the jar. "Hey, Carol. Do you have any string back there I could have?"

"We have baker's twine. How much do you need?"

"Twelve inches or so?" She cuts me off a piece, and I head back to the table.

"Okay, new tactic."

Using the stir stick, I push the end of the string under the ring and leave a short tail sticking out a couple inches. With the long end, I wind it around her finger tightly and tie it off around her manicured nail. Taking the short end, I unwind the string in the opposite direction, and her eyes light up when the ring moves.

"Oh my God! It's working!"

Her eyes are glassy and full of anticipation. As soon as we get to the knuckle, I pause and stare at her. "Ready?" She bobs her head up and down, and I unwrap the string two more times and slide it off her finger.

Her other hand rubs the red indent around the base.

"Holy shit. Thank you!"

I inspect the ring. It's gaudy and pretentious. Not something I would pick—not that I'd ever buy an engagement ring.

"Your ring is ugly."

"Dick."

"Be honest, would you have picked this?" I hold it up.

She purses her lips but doesn't deny it. She knows I'm right. The corner of her mouth tips up slightly. "You think that's bad? Check out the engraving."

I spin it until my eyes catch the words inscribed into the silver band. I read it aloud and instantly cringe.

"I love you this much."

I stare at her with my head lolled to the side. "And you *still* said yes? Talk about low standards."

I'm not romantic by any stretch of the imagination, but even I know that's bad. Bryan's worst quality is assigning the things in his life with monetary value. Even people. Who's well-connected, who has money, which important public figures would be valuable to have in his corner. But to put *that* on an engagement ring? *Damn.*

"I tried to look at it through his eyes. Like, maybe that was his way of saying he loved me a lot? It sounds stupid when I say it aloud. The diamond was expensive, but his words cheapened it. I'd rather be proposed to with a Ring Pop than have a dollar sign in front of my worth."

She's hurting.

Trying to make light of the situation, I chuckle. "I mean, better than a Ring Pop that says *I love you this much*, right?"

She stares off into space for a moment, and I don't fill the air. Truthfully, I don't feel the need to. The silence doesn't sit heavy between us. She's lost in her thoughts, but when she returns, she gives a tight smile and eats another piece of muffin.

"You're right, these are pretty good—" She chews while tilting her head. "But the scones are better."

She reaches across the table and pulls it back to her side.

"You're so full of shit," I say, beaming. The scones are good, but these particular muffins are leagues above.

She shrugs and takes another bite, then wipes her hands clean of crumbs and holds out her hand. I drop the engagement ring in her palm, and she leans over to tuck it into her messenger bag slung on the back of her chair. When I first sat down, I assumed the conversation would be forced and awkward, but she's easy to talk to. I'm actually enjoying myself.

Zipping the bag closed, she sighs. She's dressed like a bum. No prim manners or empty boring complacencies like everyone else who comes from rich families like ours. She doesn't carry herself with any entitlement—so different from Bryan. She's unapologetically herself in her stained baggy sweatshirt and leggings. Her legs are tucked under her, almost like a child. It's a little unnerving, if I'm being honest. At first, I thought it was because she was depressed and neglecting her appearance, but she has a sparkle in her eye she didn't have before. It's authenticity. Maybe this is the version of her she hides.

Or maybe I'm looking into it too much.

"Can I ask you a question?"

"You just did," she says in a dopey voice, then sticks out her tongue. *Smartass.* I haven't heard that response since grade school. It's stupid and nostalgic enough to make me smile. "What do you wanna know?" she asks, picking at her scone.

"We've only ever spoken when Bryan was around, but

you seem like a completely different person away from him. You're very . . . informal. So, why were you even dating? Was it like an opposites-attract thing?"

Her shoulders rise as she takes a deep breath and then blows it out slowly. "It's something our parents set up. I mean, to a degree. We're the ones who kept dating and going along with it. They thought our *union* would be beneficial for both parties. There's always been an understanding we would get married. Our relationship was not a fairytale by any means, but whose is? Fairytales aren't real, ya know? We got along, we had similar goals, we knew what we wanted in life, my parents loved him."

This kind of thing isn't uncom-mon, it's definitely something Bryan's parents would support, though.

"What about you?"

"Did I love him?" She sighs and ponders the question. "I don't know."

One of my rules in life is if it's not an enthusiastic *yes*, then it's a *no*. "*I don't know*" is what you say when you can't decide what to eat for dinner. It's not the answer you give when asked if you love your fiancé. And refer to it in past tense. I'm not surprised. Until the other night, every time I've seen her with Bryan, their interactions were stiff, like they're following a script. Though, I never would have guessed their relationship was this *transactional.*

"So, what's the plan?"

She shrugs. "We haven't sat down to talk about it. There's a lot wrapped up in this. It's not like I can just walk away and never speak to him again. We live together, there are wedding plans, and there's all the family involvement. My parents left for Monaco this morning. When I waved goodbye, I saw

Bryan's car near the gate. I need to deal with it, but I don't want to."

"You don't have to play nice, you know."

"What do you mean?"

"I mean he cheated on you—with your best friend—and yet you seem so pragmatic. Why don't you teach him a lesson or something?" Bryan's a friend, but he fucked up. "Every time he does something stupid, he gets a pass. Don't give him one." His actions are constantly excused. Even as kids when we did something we weren't supposed to, I'd be punished and he'd get a slap on the wrist. I kinda wanna see her give him hell over it.

"What's done is done. I'm hurt, but I'd rather not rock the boat and make this more tumultuous than it needs to be."

Rock the boat? He had an affair with her best friend. I'd say she's entitled to a little rocking. I pause for a moment, not quite sure how to ask my next question, but it's an important one.

"Are you safe with him? Before Vegas happened, I mean?"

She narrows her eyes. "What do you mean?"

I rub my jaw as I formulate my words. "Remember that night at the lodge, when I walked in on you two talking?"

"Yeah . . ." She takes a sip of her iced mocha.

"I'd been eavesdropping and heard the way he spoke to you. Does he do that a lot?"

"He's jealous and paranoid." She waves a hand. "The irony, huh?"

"That can be a dangerous combination." Bryan and I were best friends, but since that night, it's like I'm seeing this darker side to him. The anger, the cheating, even his attitude is different. "It's your life, you know your relationship best, but just . . . be careful. There are people and resources I can hook you up with if you feel like you can't cut things off."

She averts her eyes and nods. I can tell she knows what I'm getting at. Which makes me think the thought has crossed her mind before.

"I'll be fine. I can figure things out on my own."

Talking about him makes her tense. She's back to staring out the window, which normally would look casual, but her shoulders are hunched, and I wonder if she's thinking of other times he spoke to her with that tone.

"So, can I get your number?"

She flicks her gaze to mine. "Seriously? Are you really trying to—"

"Glad to see his cheating hasn't changed how highly you think of yourself. I meant, exchange numbers for platonic purposes. If you ever need help *with him* or whatever. It sounds like you're going through a lot, so if you need something, I want you to call me."

I can't believe I'm even offering to do this for her, I shouldn't be getting involved, this is stupid.

"Shit." She winces, letting out a nervous giggle. I find her embarrassment kind of adorable. She pushes her unlocked phone across the table toward me. "Yeah, we can exchange info."

After saving my number in her phone, I smirk and raise my eyebrows. "I mean, if you *really* wanna get back at him, I'd be willing to . . ." I'm only teasing, but my brain gets stuck on the image of being her revenge sex. My eyes drop to her chest. *She's got nice tits, it's a shame she's hiding them in that oversized sweatshirt.*

She rolls her eyes at me. "Please, I've read the tabloids. I know all about you, Teller."

She proceeds to nibble on her scone, and my shoulders drop.

"You read about me, huh? Well, don't keep me in suspense . . ."

After she swallows her bite, she smiles and dusts her hands clean of crumbs, preparing to give me the rundown. "You play hard, you party hard, and you—"

"Fuck hard?"

"*And you're a womanizer.* Just because I was in a committed relationship, doesn't mean I can't spot a fuckboy. You're not coming near my vagina."

"I could come on your back if that works better?" I wink, and she actually blushes. She's cute. Most of the beautiful women I talk to are trying to sleep with me. It's easy to accidentally fall into the flirty version of myself.

She scoffs. "Okay. I'm not a bunny, so this"—she waves her arms around—"*thing* you're doing, I'm immune to it."

That kind of pisses me off. I don't like being judged as if sex is a bad thing. "And what would work on you? Being a narcissistic egomaniac? Is that more your type, Sunshine?"

"No, you're not my type at all."

I laugh. "Well, that's good, because I only take home good girls who ask nicely."

She tries to act flippant, but I saw her pupils dilate. *Somebody's got a praise kink . . .* She studies me with narrowed eyes, almost as if she's considering it. I already know what my answer would be.

I realize I've made a grave miscalculation when she starts laughing. It's a laughing *at*, not *with* situation.

"Oh my God, is that what you say to women—*that's* your line? And this works for you?"

She plucks the last bite of *my muffin* off *my plate* and pops it between her lush lips.

Goddamn it, I was going to eat that.

"Yep. Scones are definitely better."

Standing from her chair, she gathers her coffee and messenger bag and swallows the bite. *My* last bite. With my tongue tucked inside my cheek, I shake my head.

"See you around, Teller," she says, pushing in her chair and starting toward the door. Her smile is forced and doesn't wrinkle the corner of her eyes.

I call after her, "I meant what I said earlier. Reach out if things get tough."

She's already stepping out the door but holds her hand up to let me know she heard me.

I shake my head and smirk. "Jordan—fuckin'—Landry."

I'm glad she's not marrying that prick; motherfucker didn't even know what he had.

SIX

Banksy

"Good game, boys! Good game!"

Coming off the ice after a win feels great, feels even better when you're undefeated. We've hit our mark against Florida. I'm not ashamed to admit I love sending teams home on the plane with an L. My goal didn't hurt. It's hard to be humble when you're the best. I wait until every guy is off before I follow them into the tunnel. Captain's the last to leave the ship—and last to leave the ice.

In the locker room, the guys cheer while I check the whiteboard. Normally, I'd be the first one to suggest we hit up the bars, but these days, I take care of some housekeeping before I party. Work hard, party hard, like Jordan said. Wish I could stop thinking about her. I gotta make sure we are ready for our next away game.

"I'm skipping bikes tonight, I'll burn it off with Bridg," Lonan Burke says. He's obsessed with his wife.

"Don't you have to wait to have sex after having a baby?" O'Callahan asks. Lonan and Bridget had their son, Ethan, not long ago.

"Hit our six weeks on Sunday. God . . . her fuckin' tits right now . . ."

"Listen up! Before you fuckers get too riled—flush ride or cold tub!" I instruct, then turn to Lonan, pointing a finger at him. "Mandatory ice bath. Nobody wants to bike next to your boner."

"Fuck you, too, Cap." I'm still not used to them calling me captain, I've always been Banksy. A stupid nickname, originating from Bank Teller, based on the number of commas in my family's bank account. Bank Teller morphed into Banks, and eventually Banksy.

I chuckle as I untie my skates. After dragging my sweater over my head, I remove my padding, taking the time to listen to the team to get a read on where everyone's head is. I'm also doing cold therapy; my muscles need it. I grab a Gatorade and go into the therapy room in my boxer briefs. Lonan is getting into his therapy tub when I enter.

"Fuck, I hate these." Lonan groans, sinking into the cold water.

"Try doing it with seven bars in your cock," I growl, submerging. "Acts like a fuckin' heatsink."

"Hard pass. How do you jack off with that shit? Your dick looks like Inspector Gadget."

"Very happily." I love my ladder, and so do all the women that climb it.

"Seriously?"

"Yeah, it's way more sensitive. Feels awesome. You should get one, I bet Bridget would like it . . ."

"How about you don't mention my wife while talking about your dick?"

"Fair. How's dad life?" I say, changing the subject.

"So far, it's great. Having a kid is a trip."

"I'm happy for you, man."

"Thanks." He pauses. "I understand why Conway's retiring. Traveling is a lot worse when you have a kid. I just want to be home with them."

I shake my head. "You better not fucking retire. I can't have two guys leaving at the end of the season."

He half smiles. "Nah, I'm not done yet." Looking forlorn, he picks up his phone, texting his wife, I'm sure. I can't imagine what his life is like. I don't want to. It's better to be a lone wolf with a job like this. I see the benefit in having the stability of a relationship, but missing out on all the different pussy? Fuck that. I love variety.

Speaking of, I'm annoyed by how long it's been. We had a rare one o'clock game, but Top Shelf will still be packed with people celebrating our win, so I can find a bunny.

Two beers, three-quarters of a pizza, and one Erica—the hot-as-hell puck bunny next to me—and I'm still not in the mood. She's the kind of girl I usually go for, but it's not doing it for me. With one arm around her, squished together in a booth with the team, my palm drops to Erica's thigh. I grip it. *Nothing.* No excitement, no anticipation. Maybe I need to see a doctor. *Fuck, is this erectile dysfunction?!*

Can't be, I still jack off normally. Although, I'm ashamed that before the game, I saw Jordan's face when I came. How fucked up is that? My phone has been burning a hole in my pocket ever since I got her number. She's off-limits. Which makes her more desirable. I can't figure out this weird attraction I have to her. I mean, yeah, she's gorgeous, but it's something else.

Pity? No, that's not it. Maybe because my brain gets off on breaking pretty things. The thought of corrupting daddy's ivy-league princess gets me hard. All that money spent on finishing school only to be finishing on my cock with a big smile on her face. *I'm sick.*

I shake off the visual of Jordan bouncing on my dick. I should see if this bunny wants to get out of here, this has to be one of those things where if you don't use it, you lose it. Maybe I've forgotten how good it feels to have my cock sucked or something.

"You having one?" Wilder holds a shot glass in front of me. *I wonder what she's doing right now.*

Fuck it. I shake my head and pull my phone out, letting my fingers do the thinking.

Hey.

Three marquee dots blink, and I smile. Why do those dots give me the jolt of anticipation I'm looking for? Jordan's response to "Hey" shouldn't be more exciting than the prospect of taking home the bunny next to me. I'm hanging out with too many married dudes. It's messing with my head.

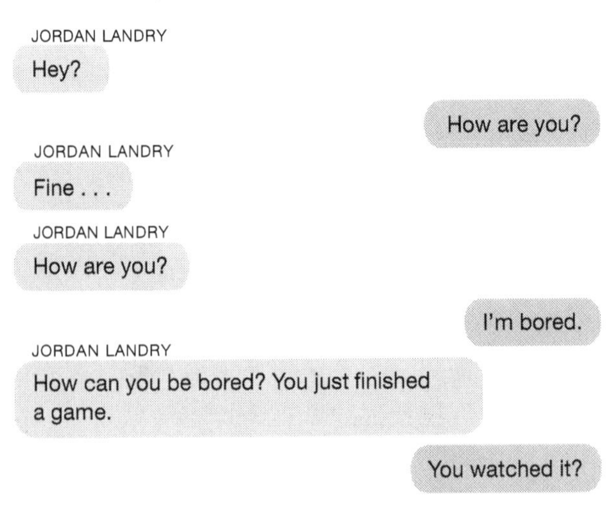

JORDAN LANDRY

I caught the last half. Kapucik did great on that power play.

And . . .

If she saw the last half, then she saw the two goals I made.

JORDAN LANDRY

. . .

What about me?

JORDAN LANDRY

What about you?

Okay. I see how it is.

Erica snuggles closer. “It’s really crowded here,” she says. It’s not that crowded. I retract my arm from behind her and lean forward so I can text easier.

JORDAN LANDRY

Sorry. Kinda having a bad day.

Bryan?

JORDAN LANDRY

Everything.

I crane my head forward to glance outside. Clear skies. Temps are nice . . .

Want something to take your mind off it?

JORDAN LANDRY

You’re not my type.

I got my bike back from the shop and am going for a ride. Wanna join?

And btw I’m everybody’s type.

JORDAN LANDRY

Bike like bicycle or motorcycle?

It's a Ducati

(motorcycle)

JORDAN LANDRY

I know what a Ducati is.

So you wanna go for a ride, smartass?

I bet Jordan would make a good backpack. Maybe she rides, pretty sure her dad has bikes. My foot taps while I wait for her response, but this time there are no dancing dots at the bottom of the screen.

I wait.

And wait.

After a couple minutes of radio silence, I assume she's not interested. *Oh well.* I'm about to stuff my phone in my pocket when it vibrates again.

JORDAN LANDRY

Are you a safe rider?

The safest.

Well, I am when I ride two-up. My last beer was washed down with half a pizza.

JORDAN LANDRY

I highly doubt that.

I'd be safe with you.

JORDAN LANDRY

K. I'm staying at my parents'. Here's the address.

She sends me a pin with her location. I've got my spare helmet with me, and it won't take too long to get there.

Be there in 20. Wear something warm. Gloves if you have them.

JORDAN LANDRY

I'll wait outside. If I'm not there, go to the cemetery at the end of the road.

The corner of my mouth curls up. Finally, something more interesting than sitting here. I've been wanting to get in a couple rides before it gets too, cold anyway, and there's only a handful of nice evenings left. The cemetery thing is a little weird, though.

"I think I'm gonna head out," I tell Erica.

"Where are we going?"

"I don't know where you're going. I'm meeting a friend."

She furrows her eyebrows and serves me a fuck-you glance.

"See ya at practice tomorrow, boys."

We tap knuckles, and they give me a small wave, returning to their conversation about some of the new hockey gear the org wants us to switch to. I wasn't paying close attention. When I get out to my bike, I chuckle at the second helmet strapped to the side. I figured somebody like Erica would wear it on the way back to my house to get my dick sucked. Instead, I'm taking my best friend's girl out for a platonic early evening ride. Although, we're no longer best friends—*and she's not his girl anymore.*

Exactly twenty minutes later, I turn onto the road that leads to the huge Landry estate. The Landrys—and a few others—are considered the ultra-wealthy in this area. Someday, my sisters, stepbrother, and I will inherit the Teller fortune, but for now, my wealth comes from the NHL. All the money I have, I've earned. My house is nice, but the Landrys' house is more similar to my parents'. Fucking massive.

Jordan and I grew up surrounded by people who use the

word summer as a verb and shop on James Edition instead of Amazon. But where my family's wealth stops at material things, her family's doesn't. They buy power, influence, and time—yes, time. The world waits for them, not the other way around.

Her parents have a net worth of over a billion, yet she's sitting on her ass on the dirty curb, waiting for me at the end of the long private drive. She stands as I pull up, wearing only a sweatshirt and leggings, but at least she's wearing a pair of gloves.

"You gonna be warm enough in a hoodie?" I ask, syncing up the intercoms on the spare helmet.

She crosses her arms over her chest. "Yeah."

I adjust the straps and hand it to her. She shoves it over her head and works the clip under her chin, making sure it's tight. She looks kinda cute. I test the intercom function.

"Can you hear me?"

"Ha! Is this like a walkie talkie?"

"Bluetooth, grandma. Ready to get on?"

"Yeah, how do I do it?"

I cock my head to the side. *The fuck?*

"Doesn't your dad have a bunch of motorcycles?"

"Yeah, he collects them. He doesn't ride them."

Typical.

"So, you've never been on a bike before?"

Her head shakes back and forth. Thankfully, she can't see my big-ass smile through the reflective visor on my helmet. *This will be fun.* I relax my jaw before flipping up our visors.

"Do you trust me?"

Her gaze bounces between my eyes, and after a second, she nods.

"Okay, come over on this side." I tap behind me. "Make sure to keep your leg away from the exhaust." I show her where to step, and she swings her leg over, straddling the seat behind me. She's left a gap between us, sitting right on the edge, like she's trying to not get too close. "Where are you?"

"Here."

I can't see where *here* is. Reaching behind me, I hook under her knees and yank her forward, wrapping her arms around my stomach.

"You're supposed to be *here*."

She clears her throat.

"Ready?"

"Wait, wait! Is there anything I need to do?"

I turn my head to the side. "Hold on around my waist. In turns, look over my inside shoulder and lean with me. Keep your feet on the foot pegs, even when we're stopped. And don't wiggle your ass around. I'm sure that last one is gonna be really hard for you to follow but try your best."

"Okay. Waist. Inside shoulder. Lean. But what if I forget something?"

"I'm not going to be taking any fast corners on your first ride. Just focus on holding on and keeping your feet on the pegs. Cool?"

She blows out a breath. "Uh-huh. Okay, I'm ready."

"It'll be fun, I promise."

"Just don't kill me."

I chuckle as I hit the kickstand with my heel to put it up, engage the clutch, shift the bike into first gear, and take off slowly. We head to the end of the road, and as soon as we pick up speed, she squeezes me. *Solid grip.* I check in at the last stop sign before we hit the main road.

"Still good?"

"Still good."

"Okay, let's go."

I take the back highways—heading to the quieter smooth

roads where I ride when I need to think. We'll be going slow until we get out of the evening traffic around the cities. As the sun sets, the chatter of teeth come through the bike intercom.

"Sure you're warm enough?"

"I'm fine. Keep going." She shivers again. I should have made her grab a jacket.

I huff. "No, you're not." If she's cold now, she'll be freezing once we accelerate.

There's a small fishing pond up on the left, so I pull off the road and park alongside it.

I hop off the bike and hold out my hand for her as she steps off. Removing my helmet, she copies me.

"What are we doing?"

"Warming you up." There's a spare thermal shirt I keep rolled up tight under the seat, so I grab it and take off my jacket and offer it out to her.

"I'm really okay, I like the feeling of being cold."

"Well, I don't wanna listen to your teeth clacking in my ear, so put it on." I shake the jacket in front of her, and she accepts it.

Tugging my T-shirt over my head, I catch her checking me out briefly, and I grin. "Thought I wasn't your type."

"Hate to burst your bubble, but I was only looking at your tattoos."

The right side of my ribcage and my right arm and shoulder are covered in a tapestry of skulls, a custom piece by my stepbrother, Logan, woven with a crown, anatomical heart, and Boreas—the God of Ice, to fill the full space. My left arm has a half sleeve consisting of three flowers, one for each of my siblings, including Logan, on my forearm.

Logan's an award-winning tattoo artist with his own shop. He's also got a body piercer who does great work—she did my ladder. I'm ninety percent sure he's got a thing for her, but dude is so tight-lipped he'll probably never do anything about it.

I slip the thermals over my head and pull them down my chest, adding my T-shirt over top. I'm used to being around ice, my body can probably acclimate to the cold better than hers.

"Sure you were."

She zips my jacket up to her neck—thankfully, her hoodie fills it out—and pops her helmet back on.

"You're so full of yourself. Do you jack off to the mirror when you masturbate?"

I bark out a laugh and push my helmet over my head. "How else would I get off?" I say, straddling the bike. She laughs and scoots behind me when I sit down. This time, she doesn't need me to help her, and as soon as her arms are wrapped around me, I pull away from the shoulder.

We've been taking mostly easy roads, but when we get close to sixty miles per hour, a squeak of excitement comes through the intercom, followed by a small giggle. I grab her knee, oddly wishing I could see her expression.

"What's so funny?"

She laughs again. "This is nice. It's very—" She releases a breath. "Freeing."

That's exactly what it does for me. When life's pressures get stressful and I want to drown out all the noise, going for a ride reminds me I'm still alive.

"I come out here when I'm overwhelmed. It makes me feel small, in a good way. Gives me perspective. Most of the time, when I get back home, the other shit doesn't matter so much."

"Thanks for inviting me. I needed this."

"You're welcome." Jordan isn't nearly as tense as she was before, but I wonder what happened that made it a bad day.

We take some of the quieter county highways and enjoy the sunset. I point to a line of trees out in the distance.

"My grandparents used to own all that land. They had a farm with a ton of acreage."

"You come from farmers? And here I thought you were a broken, stuck-up cake eater like the rest of us."

I chuckle. "Oh, *I* am. But my mom had a much humbler upbringing."

"So your father's side is loaded."

It's complicated.

"Kinda. My biological father, Jerry, was an asshole. When my mom divorced him, she had three kids and no place to go. So, my grandparents sold a few acres, and that money was used to give her a fresh start. A couple years later, Mom married Bruce Teller—*cake eater*—and he adopted me and my sisters. He worships my mom and raised us like his own. *He's* who we call dad."

"Do you still talk with your biological father?"

"No, we cut all contact. He died four years ago." *None of us went to the funeral.* I don't need to get into that. I clear my throat and ask what's really on my mind. "That's old news. Tell me about your bad day, what happened?"

She sighs. "It's not so much that it was bad, but I've been dodging calls and visits from Bryan and Veronica all week. I have to go back to the condo, but I don't want to. And I have to find a new place to live, which is a pain in the ass. Guess I was hoping I could hide out at the café and eat scones for a few more weeks."

"So do it."

"I have to face the music. I still have to officially break it off, it's looming over me."

"Eh, let him sweat a little longer. He's losing his fucking mind over it. He texted me that night—raging and pointing fingers. He's been going nuts trying to find who ratted him out."

She groans over the intercom. "I love that his priority is trying to find out the person who gave him away . . . Before my parents left to spend the winter in Monaco, they said I needed to work it out like an adult." She clears her throat. "And I kinda led them to believe we'd be getting back together. So they're gonna be pissed when they find out that's not happening."

"Why would you do that?"

Her shoulders shrug against me. "Peace? I needed to not have them in my ear about it every second of the day. They eased up once I stopped arguing."

They're wrong on this one.

"So, what are you going to say to him?"

She presses to my back as I take a tight turn.

"Why do you want to know so much?"

"I dunno, curiosity?"

"Curious? Or a whore for drama?"

"Can't it be both?"

"Well, first I'm going to return his ring. And after that . . . I wanna hear what he has to say. Not just the stupid messages over the phone. I want to see his face when he apologizes. I want to look in his eyes and see if he's truly sorry. You and I both know Bryan likes his things—especially things he can't have. He doesn't like being told no. And I'm still mad.

"I think he thought this marriage was always guaranteed to him. I can accept having a marriage devoid of butterflies and magic moments. But I refuse to be taken for granted. I'm not going to be humiliated just because he thinks the rules don't apply to him."

Shit, her bar is so low she'd need a shovel to find it. As for Bryan, she's hit the nail on the head. Of course he thought the marriage was guaranteed, he's one of the most entitled people I know—and I know a lot of entitled people. It's a cringy attribute I ignored for much of our friendship. He loves things he can't have, but I didn't think he'd take it this far.

"But you *are* going to end it?" She can't seriously take him back after that.

"I thought about trying to salvage it. However, the thought of going to therapists and counselors, all things he's been promising in his voicemails, we would have *so much* work to do in order to get back to where we were. And frankly, I don't think where we were was that great to begin with. It's not worth it. We aren't a match made in heaven, we're trusting our parents to know what they're doing. But what if they don't? We're both unhappy. I have to trust my gut. As much as these days have sucked, I've started to feel like myself again. Something I didn't even realize I'd been suppressing until I was away from him."

It blows my mind she's being so forthcoming with her feelings. Am I the only person she's had to vent to? I agree with what she's saying. Bryan fucked up, he's left *me* enough desperate voicemails, but I enjoy hearing a man's sob story even less than a woman's. If she's not in love with him, why would she marry him?

"So, when are you ending it?"

"I dunno."

"Set a date, Jordan."

"Ugh, I don't want to," she whines but eventually concedes. "I'll do it this week."

"What day?"

"Fuck, I dunno, Tuesday." She thumps my stomach with emphasis.

"What about Veronica?"

She fidgets, and I realize I've pried too much.

"Actually, do you mind if we stop talking about it? This is fun, I want to enjoy the freedom. Tell me something positive. What are the three best things that happened to you today?"

She thinks *this* is freedom, as if later this week she'll return to captivity. Everyone has kept her in a cage. Even her family pressuring her into this marriage. It's none of my business, but Jordan's a nice girl, she doesn't deserve this lousy arrangement. Worse is that it seems no one's in her corner. The other bridesmaids were all his family members. *Where the fuck are the rest of her friends to support her on this?* Unless he's been keeping her away from them. I hope that's not the case.

"Okay, three good things . . ."

"Yup," she chirps, as if she's already pushed it to the back of her mind. I wonder what else she's pushed back there.

"Well, the Lakes went up in the standings, so that's—"

"Doesn't count. Three things that happened to *you* personally."

I groan. "Fine. *I* made a goal. Next . . . Okay, so now that I'm captain, I've been really working on my aggression on the ice. There was a hit I took in the first period—"

"Yeah, what the fuck was that about?!"

I grin. "You said you only watched the second half."

"Huh. I must have lied."

I clutch her knee again. "Well, after that hit, I could have beat his ass. And the team would have backed me up on it, but I chose to skip the penalty box and take the high road."

"I was wondering why you didn't take a swing." She seems impressed. "I'm sure it wasn't easy."

"Fuck, it was brutal!" I laugh. "I wanted to throw a punch so bad."

She chuckles. "Okay, what's the last thing?"

"Getting to be out on the bike again. I've been driving my car for a month, and I missed this. And the company is . . . well, you're tolerable when you're not whining like a little bitch." I shrug.

She pulls her arm back and slaps my helmet.

"Wow. Risking your safety to hit me? Hope it was worth it."

"It was," she grumbles. "You said you were *curious*."

"Huh. Must have lied," I parrot.

This time when I squeeze her, it's on her thigh. I don't know if I meant to do that or not, but I keep the conversation moving so I don't have to think about it.

"Your turn. What are your three things?"

"Hmm . . .The wedding diet is off, and I've been eating whatever the hell I want, and since I'm an emotional eater, I've already gained ten pounds."

I like that she considers gaining weight as a good thing.

"Well, the ten looks great." Her ass looks even better than before. I can appreciate a thick ass.

"I'm surprised to hear you say that."

I rear my head back slightly. "Why?"

"Aren't you on a constant diet? And don't you usually go for the skinny itty-bitty models?"

"No, I go for *confidence*. Confidence is sexy as fuck. And yes, I diet occasionally for work, but that's because it's part of my job as an athlete, not because I want to fit into a fucking suit."

"Point taken."

"What else is good?"

"Ooh! I've been able to hang out with my dog all week. I missed her a lot, so having her sleep on my feet every night has been a big comfort. She's been my buddy through all this."

"What kind of dog is it?"

"She's an Alaskan Shepherd mix. We got her from a rescue when I was in high school."

"That's cool. What's her name?"

"Chicken Salad."

I nearly choke on my spit. "I'm sorry?"

She laughs and the vibrations against my back make me laugh even more. "I forget how funny it sounds because she's been Chicken Salad for so long."

"So, if you need to tell your dog to come inside, you open the door and yell *Chicken Salad*?"

"I mean, *I* would. My parents hate the name—they call her Sally because it's more *dignified*."

"If she's your dog, how come she doesn't live with you?"

"Bryan is allergic."

Huh? "Bryan's not allergic." Apparently, he's got all kinds of secrets. "He had a bloodhound growing up."

"What?!"

I know we were best friends and all, but Bryan's treated her beyond shitty.

"You didn't know that?"

She shakes her head near my shoulder and mumbles something about him being a motherfucker. "That's good to know." There's a hint of anger behind her words, but it's not aimed at me.

"Are you a cat or dog person?" she asks.

"Dog person. Cats don't have eyebrows, and it freaks me out."

"You're weird."

"You'll never unsee it."

The first stoplight we hit, she keeps one arm around me but uses the other to brace against the gas tank instead of falling into my back.

"Look at you, already knowing where to put your hands."

"I'm a natural." She pretends to flip her hair back.

I grin. "All right, you still have one more, so make it good."

She groans. "Don't let it go to your head—if it gets any bigger, we'll tip over—but probably this. Going for a ride."

"Great, right?"

"Yeah, it's pretty awesome." The light turns green, and we take off.

There's a lull in conversation, but it's not awkward. After a moment, she breaks the silence.

"So, are you going to hold my hand for the rest of the ride or . . .?"

"Huh?" *Fuck.* I look down and my thumb is absentmindedly stroking her gloved fingers, the ones pressed to my stomach. I pull my hand back. *How long has that been going on? Before the stoplight?* "Oh." I laugh it off. "I'm used to fucking the girl who rides in your spot, must be a habit . . . Okay. So, no diet. Wanna grab some food? I ate earlier, but I'm always extra hungry after a game."

"Sure, I could eat."

"You pick."

"Tacos?"

I smile. "A woman after my own heart."

"I told you, Cam . . ." She pats my stomach, and my abs tighten. "You're not my type."

SEVEN

Jordan

My hands are pressed over my eyes as I sit hunched over on the white U-shaped sofa in our condo. The cushions aren't even cushiony. It's like poorly upholstered concrete. I never liked this couch.

After the bike ride, I gained some clarity about Bryan's and my relationship. He wasted my time, my energy, I've defended his problematic behavior to our friends so many times, and he humiliated me at my own bachelorette party. When I hear the click of the deadbolt, I sit up and take a deep breath. *This is it.*

He saunters in, holding his keys in his fist over the kitchen island and opens his clenched palm to let them hit the marble with a harsh clank. He continues his slow stride until he's standing at the edge of the living room and kitchen. He sighs. "I'm sorry for what happened."

I came here to tell him one thing: *We're done*. He's not even taking full responsibility. He's sorry for "what happened," as if their affair was some act of God.

"I've already made an appointment for us to get financials

sorted with the banks. I want our accounts separated. As far as the wedding—"

"No."

Excuse me? Blood fires through my veins. He doesn't get to reject my breakup.

I pluck the engagement ring off the coffee table and meet him where he stands, toe to toe. "You made your choice in Vegas." I hold the ring out for him to take.

His jaw tics. "No. We are going to work this out." Smirking, he takes the ring from me, grabs me by the neck, and walks me to the dividing wall between the living room and bedroom hallway.

"You're hurting me."

"You're hurting *me*," he says. Alarm bells ring. His voice is monotone, but his actions are firm and calculating. Menacing. "Do not try me, Jordana. This marriage is happening. We are walking down the aisle in a month. And you're going to do it with a smile on your *fat fucking face*." He pulls my neck forward and slams my skull against drywall three times to punctuate his last words. "Understand?"

My vision blurs. I want to run, but I can't move. The instant headache has me seeing stars. I roll my lips together and breathe through my nose, trying to stay calm. He's got me standing on my tiptoes. I go into self-preservation mode and nod. Every inch of me is trembling. He moves his hand to the back of my neck.

"Now go get ready for the fundraiser. We're showing up together, and you're going to play nice with me, aren't you?"

Don't cry, don't cry, don't cry.

I nod again; he's not giving me much range of motion. He encircles my shaking wrist and holds it up, offering me a bemused smile. His other hand releases my neck as he holds the ring. *No, no, no*. He shoves the ring back on my finger. It doesn't fit, so he pushes until it scrapes harshly past the knuckle. My brows squish together as I plead with him. It's not only excruciatingly painful, it's like having my old collar put on again. My hand itches to yank it off.

"Obviously, the diet is back on."

A tear escapes, I blink to stop the rest, but it only makes another one fall.

"Don't be sad. Good wife, good life. Remember?" He swipes his thumb over my cheek, and my stomach turns. I resist slapping his hands away. The touch makes me squirm.

My answer is clipped. "Mm-hm."

He smiles, tracking another tear as it cascades down my cheek. "You're ugly when you cry." His gaze returns to mine, and he waits to see if I'll give him more tears.

Nothing. He releases me, and I suck in a breath.

"Get dressed. If you look fat in what I've laid out for you, find something else. Hair down."

He always tells me to wear it up. He must have left marks.

This is the last time I will wear my hair for him. I just need to get through tonight. Wait until it's safe.

A four-piece orchestra plays in the corner while people wander the Safehouse fundraiser for—get this—*domestic violence victims.* The irony makes me want to vomit. I'm such a fraud.

I didn't even realize it was Camden Teller's charity. I knew he was involved but didn't grasp he was the founder. He tried to tell me at the coffee shop, and I dismissed him. I never thought it would escalate to this. Tonight was the first time he put his hands on me for more than a firm grab. I'm so lost and empty inside—ashamed I've put myself in this situation. When did I lose control of my life?

As Bryan parades me around, I put on a happy smile and make small talk. He didn't let me out of his sight for the first hour and a half, or throughout the dinner I wasn't allowed to eat. Now he's lengthening my leash. I want to shove his hand away from my lower back. Every so often, it drifts to my ass, making my skin crawl.

Everything in me says to run, but it's not so simple. Not yet.

I have to be smart. He can't suspect anything. As I was getting ready tonight, I heard him tell his father over the phone that spouses can't be forced to testify against one another. I think his words were in reference to me. I don't know what he's hiding. Does it matter?

For now, I need to focus on getting myself out of this mess.

Every conversation with our acquaintances is more dull than the last. Career successes, real estate, investments . . .

". . . From what I heard, the initial investors did very well. Who have they chosen for the board?"

". . . We summered in Deauville this year. Seychelles has become so overrun by tourists."

". . . Marnie got married in July. He's an orthopedic surgeon. They just bought a beautiful home in Bearpath."

". . .Lorne had everyone out celebrating the merger. Cheers to building solid results in a challenging environment."

Blah. Blah. Blah. Blah.

I want to get drunk, but my head's still throbbing and I'll regret it in the morning.

CAMDEN

Scanning the room, my gaze catches on a gorgeous figure. My jaw nearly drops when the woman turns around—*Jordan.*

I haven't heard from her since our ride the other day. I amble up to her with a smug grin. "Of all the gin joints . . ."

She startles, and I hold up both my palms.

"So it seems," she answers.

Her eyes are . . . empty.

I nod to the shimmering floor-length gown she has on. She looks stunning in it.

"Not used to seeing you without the hoodie."

She offers a tight smile. "Hm." Her eyes convey nothing remotely close to happiness.

"So, which is the real Jordan? The one in the couture gown"—I nod to her dress—"or the one with apple scone crumbs on her baggy sweatshirt?"

She levels me with a hollow stare. "Both and neither."

Out of nowhere, Bryan comes from behind and places his arm around her.

The fuck?

I don't let my eyes react.

"Hey, man. Great turn out. Lots of money to raise tonight, eh?" he says.

I nod. "Hopefully, lots of new sponsors this year."

What the hell is going on?

"Well, it's for a good cause," he replies.

"Excuse me," Jordan interjects, handing Bryan her champagne flute and picking up the hem of her dress. When she reaches down, my eye catches on her diamond ring—the one I removed. *Is her finger bruised?* She pulls away before I can get a good look.

"Good to see you, Jordana," I say, making sure to use her full first name. Something about this situation is fucked.

I scoff. "What's wrong with her?"

"She's not feeling well."

"Shit, I tried out a new caterer. I hope it's not the food."

"No, no. Nothing like that. She's just stressed. Finalizing the last of the wedding plans and all, she's been working herself ragged. Everything's gotta be perfect, you know how it is."

He's lying. He's lying right to my fucking face.

"Oh, things are going well, then? I'm glad it all worked out. I'm guessing Veronica isn't in the wedding anymore, is there someone else I'll be walking down the aisle with?"

"Yeah, we're still working on a few things. I've got a cousin that's willing to stand in for her. You probably met her in Vegas—Georgina?"

He's acting like nothing ever happened. I nod. "I'm impressed. She took you back that easily, huh?"

"It's still a work in progress. But she knows what's best for her. Jordana's very reasonable."

EIGHT

Jordan

I work from home most of the time but have to go in on Wednesdays. So, this morning, I went in like always but took the afternoon off so I could get back to the condo before Bryan came home. I need to load up my stuff and get out of dodge.

I almost told Camden the other night, but I was in a daze, and after seeing how chummy he was with Bryan, I don't know if I can trust him. They were laughing and carrying on like nothing happened. It's not like Cam ever said he wouldn't be friends with Bryan. He just said I shouldn't take him back.

As soon as I unlock the door, my stomach feels uneasy. There's a heaviness in this hallway. The condo feels cold and unfeeling—like a cage. I want to be back on Cam's bike again—free and far away from all this. I want to be with Chicken Salad in my own apartment. My anxiety is telling me to run, but there are a few things I need, and if I'd taken them this morning, it would have looked suspicious.

The first place I go is the bedroom safe that holds financial papers I need. I press my finger to the pad, but it blinks red instead of green. I type in the numerical code. It fails. I run to the drawer in the kitchen for the key, open it, and feel around the back. This is where we keep the spare. It's gone. *Fuck!*

I'll have to worry about it later. I run back to the bedroom, enter the spacious walk-in closet, and pull out a suitcase.

It's not twenty minutes before the front door opens and slams. My heart drops to my feet, stomach rolling, and I want to vomit.

"Jordana!"

I frantically zip the luggage so I can put it back and not look suspicious. Shit, I'll have to try another day. Now that I know he's tracking my whereabouts, the escape plan will need to be adjusted.

It'll be okay. Keep your head on straight.

I shove it back on the shelf and slide over to the connected master bath, in front of the sink, and pinch my cheeks a few times to make them appear flushed.

"I'm in the bathroom." My voice sounds dead. "I think I'm coming down with something."

I know exactly which pointy, square-toed shoes he's wearing based on the way they clack on the tile. He stomps in. "What in the actual fuck? Why are you home?"

He's in his gray suit, his ears are red. He's mad? I'm the one who should be angry!

I splash water on my face.

"I'm not feeling well."

"You look fine."

"Are you allergic to dogs?" I want to slap myself, but something in me wants him to know I know. That all his secrets are coming to light. "I ask because Veronica has dogs." I shouldn't poke the bear, but it's like I can't help myself. This isn't fair. He can't keep me like a prisoner.

"What?! Am I . . . Who the fuck cares if I am or not?"

See, that pisses me off. I pat my face dry with a towel.

"I'm not pleased, Jordana." He advances until he's at the threshold of the room. "You left work without telling anyone, and I had no idea where you went. I was worried."

He's switching tactics. It's creepy how fast he alternates personas. What's worse is how I never realized what a red flag it is. Camden's voice pops into my mind. *"Are you safe with him?"* Do I even know who this man is? Too many times I brushed off those anger issues as immaturity, but now it makes the hair on my neck stand on end. I'm in real danger.

"I just needed to get some rest. I felt ill."

He grinds his teeth as he answers, "You should have texted me you weren't feeling well." His eye is twitching. "For all I know, you've been fucking around with someone else, trying to seek revenge for something you don't even have proof of. Maybe that was your plan all along."

That sends me over the edge.

"Because you're the picture of devotion." I roll my eyes and laugh. "How long have you and Veronica been fucking, anyway?"

"Oh, I see . . ." His eyes gleam. "This is your bullshit attempt to get out of marrying me, is it? You think you can leave me? Use this as an opportunity to sneak away? Do you think it will be that easy?"

I scoff and shake my head. "God, you're such a manipulative mindfuck—you were caught, Bryan! It's over! Everybody can see through you. *I* see through you. We both know this whole marriage was a sham. Neither of us have been happy. It's done."

I've never yelled back at him before, and it feels good. *It feels so validating.*

He wrinkles his nose and sneers. I don't like it one bit. His eyes are dark and empty as he stalks toward me, and I step to the side. I refuse to let him back me up against a wall. *Plan your exit.* I retreat into the closet, which is attached to the laundry room, which is attached to the foyer hallway through a sliding pocket door. *Just get to the front door.*

"You fucking cunt . . . How dare you talk to me that way. You will show me respect."

Cunt, that's a new one. My hand casually moves to my back pocket as I take another step. Keys, *check.*

"You first." I shouldn't antagonize, but every memory of him making me feel small flashes in my thoughts, and I hate him for it.

My phone is in my purse, which I dropped next to the front door when I walked in. I have to get to my phone before he gets to me. *Shit.*

I take a deep breath and hush my voice, staying placid. "We both are not in a good place. You're angry, and I'm going to stay at my parents' house until you calm down."

"I'm calm!" he shouts, and I flinch. "Oh, did I scare you?" His face is getting redder by the minute. "You don't have anywhere to go. So if you want to smooth things over, stop walking away, and let's talk like civilized adults."

Inside the closet, I continue backing up, and as soon as my feet hit the laundry room, he lunges for me. I slam the pocket door, smashing his hand in the process. My eyes bulge. *Fuck*—now I'm in trouble.

I spin on my heel and run down the foyer hallway, snatching up my bag. Keys, phone, purse. *Move.*

Out of the corner of my eye, he comes barreling out of the laundry room.

Run.

Just as I grab the door handle, the clothes iron from the laundry room explodes against the wall next to me at eye level. *He missed.* I don't scream. I don't turn around. *I don't breathe.* I run.

Past the elevator, I throw open the heavy metal door to the stairwell and pray I don't trip in these stupid fucking heels, my feet moving as fast as they can, one after the other.

He's on the stairs now. His strides are bigger than mine. This isn't happening.

Go, go, go.

He's coming for me, and if I don't escape, he might kill me. I'm not sure if the iron he threw at me was to scare, maim, or worse . . . but it would have done the job if he was a few inches closer. I'm such an idiot for even coming back here.

Then his footsteps stop. My spine tingles. Why did he stop? Was I farther than I thought? Did he give up? His feet are no longer slapping the steps behind me. My hand keeps a loose grip on the handrail as I go. Swinging around each landing, I don't stop to take a breath. My legs are shaking, but adrenaline keeps me focused. *Stairs, landing, stairs, landing.* Farther and farther, I descend the tower. How many more levels until I reach the underground parking? I can't tell how much time has passed, and I'm unsure of what floor I'm passing.

Glancing up, I pass a giant seven, but my feet falter and I yelp, clutching the handrail and catching myself from falling and twisting an ankle. Holy fuck that was close.

Slow down! If you trip on these stairs, you're a sitting duck. The goal is to make it out of here, remember?

"Okay, okay!" I say aloud to myself, then pause for a split second on the next landing to yank my heels off. The cold, damp concrete stairs fight against the sweat breaking across my skin. I shake off the cool relief and thank whatever higher power I didn't kill myself trying to get away.

I pace myself, worried I'll stumble again; it wouldn't take more than one slight misstep. Too afraid to look up, my eyes remain trained on the stairs ahead of me. As safely as I can, I race to the bottom. Fate has given me a second chance. I fear it won't be as kind the third time.

After what feels like forever, I hit the lower level, yank open the metal door, and freeze. The blood drains from my face when I see Bryan leaning against the security desk. How can I be so foolish? He took the fucking elevator down. He looks up and smooths his hair over and smiles. His likely mangled hand is stuffed in his pocket. The security guard behind him is unaware of the peril I'm in. I slip my shoes back on.

"There you are, honey. Why did you take the stairs?"

I stay closer to the wall as I near the garage. "Wanted to burn the extra calories," I mumble.

Think, Jordan! If I tell them he was chasing me, he'll convince them I'm crazy. Maybe he already has. A second security guard walks past me, and I grab his arm.

He swings around and stares at me. I clear my throat. "I, um, I need an escort to my car."

"No, she doesn't. She's coming upstairs with me."

Faking a smile, I wave him off. "Relax, babe. I'm just picking up groceries, I'll be back soon." My voice wavers but I remain smiling. "We need milk."

"I'll come with you."

"No, I want to go by myself," I demand.

The officer looks down at me, and I dare to take my eyes off Bryan for a second to make this man see I need help. He must see the desperation in my eyes.

"I don't mind, Mr. Davenport. You can return to your residence. I'll make sure she makes it to the vehicle safely."

His eye does that twitchy thing again, but he nods with a tense jaw while glaring at me. I follow the officer, and I swear I can feel Bryan breathing on me as we walk past him. My knees are shaking so much, I'm worried I'll collapse. I hold my breath, as if my own exhale could tempt him enough to get his hands on me and prevent my escape. When we exit the lower level and enter the parking garage, the cool air hits my face, and I realize how much I'm sweating.

I thank the guard and ask if he would mind staying to make sure I get out safely. He nods, and as soon as we reach my car, I scramble inside, locking the doors. As casual as I can muster, I back out of my spot and drive toward the exit. There's no point in reporting Bryan to him, I'd have to stay and fill out a statement. We'd have to wait for police. I'm not doing that. I'm leaving while I can.

The garage door seems to move in slow motion as I wait for it to rise. I tap the wheel frantically. "Come on, come on, come on . . ."

As soon as the roof of the car can fit under, I hit the accelerator. Sunlight floods the interior, making me squint, and I take a deep breath, heading toward my parents' house. Shit—I can't go there. Now that my parents are in Monaco, the house manager is only there a couple days a week, and I'd be alone at night. I can't go to a hotel, all I have are credit cards. He'd track those too. Fuck!

My hands tremble as I'm overwhelmed with the sensation of dread. *Where do I go?* He knew this would happen. He said I've got nowhere to go, and he's right. I double-check my wallet. No cash.

"How did you let it get this bad, Jordan?"

I can't think and I'm stuck, so I call the only person I

know to call, the one who's basically a stranger. I don't know if I can trust him, but I'm out of options. He said to call if things got rough. I'd say we are well within *rough* territory.

Unlocking my phone, I tap the screen until I see Camden Teller's name and hit the call button.

It rings. *Four rings. Five rings. Six.*

"Pick up. Please pick up," I whisper into the receiver.

It rings eight times and goes to voicemail. "No!"

Sweat beads at my forehead, and I continue checking the rearview mirror every few seconds, expecting to see his red car behind mine.

"Stop it, Jordan, you're fucking paranoid. Focus." Tears threaten to fall as the adrenaline rush wanes. I'll be a sobbing mess in a matter of minutes. Don't give up. You can do this. My phone rings, and I look down to see Cam's name on the screen. I sniffle and clear my eyes, putting a fake smile on my face, hoping he'll be able to hear it through the phone.

"Hey!" I answer cheerfully. I swallow down my fear, trying to sound normal. What do I say?

"Jordan?" He sounds out of breath.

"Sorry, are you busy?" God, my voice is so fake.

"No, I'm just wrapping up with practice. What's up? . . . Everything okay?"

No, nothing is okay. You were right, I'm an idiot. I put myself in danger, and now I can't get out of it. I'm terrified.

My fingers tremble as they grasp the phone. "Yeah, yeah, fine. I just, um—" My voice catches and the tears start to fall. There's nothing I can do to stop it. I pull the car over and hold the phone away from my face, willing myself to be strong. *Get your act together.*

"Where are you?" he asks.

A sob escapes, my fear and loss of adrenaline hijacking my body. I cover my mouth, hoping to smother my emotions, and look to the ceiling, trying to keep the tears in my eyes. I feel so pathetic. I hate crying in front of people. Even though he's not here to see it, I don't want him to hear it either. I feel so weak already.

His voice is calm and slow. "Jordan, take a deep breath and answer my question. Where are you?"

I suck in air and blow out a shaky exhale. Breathing feels impossible. My lungs burn and my chest heaves. Great, now I'm hyperventilating; I'll pass out and Bryan will find me in no time.

"I'm . . . I don't know," I choke out. I take another breath and try to get through my sentence as fast as I can. "I'm driving around, and I don't know what to do."

"It's okay. Are you near any intersections?"

My gaze bounces around, and I catch a street sign. "I'm on Humboldt." I know where I am, but I have no idea how to articulate it, so I name things I see. "There's a grocery store and a repair shop and . . ."

"Do you see a car dealership on the left or right?"

"The left."

"Perfect, that's great. I want you to go to my house. I'm going to give you directions, and once we hang up, I want you to turn off the GPS on your phone and car, then put your cell on airplane mode and shut it down. Understand?"

My hands shake again. *Bryan's tracking me.* He was just a cheating asshole last week, how did this escalate so fast? Now he's a threat to my life.

I nod, even though he can't see me. He calmly gives directions, and his voice sounds like one of those meditation recordings. I scribble down the street names he tells me on the back of an old receipt in my purse. He provides the code to the gate and another code for the door.

"Am I really doing this?"

"It's gonna be all right." His voice sounds so sure. "I'm going to wrap up here. I'll be home soon."

"Can I stay with you for a night? Only a night until I can figure shit out." I squeeze my eyes shut and hold my breath, hoping he'll say yes. *Please, one night.*

He chuckles "Of course. There's an apartment above my garage, stay as long as you want. I've got a few errands still, but help yourself to whatever."

Relief washes over me now that I have a plan. I have somewhere safe to go.

"God, thank you so much, Cam. I owe you. Whatever you want, it's yours."

"Uh-oh. Is that you changing your mind about me not being your type?"

I choke on a laugh.

It may be inappropriate, but he has no idea how much I needed the levity. I appreciate him not pitying me or treating me differently. I sniffle and shake my head. "Not even close."

There's a slight grin in his voice. "It's going to be okay, Jordan. Go to my place and hang tight."

I exhale, and some of the tension leaves my shoulders. "Thanks Cam."

"You bet. Don't forget, turn off GPS on your phone *and* car."

"Okay."

NINE

Banksy

I don't know what the fuck went down this afternoon with Jordan and Bryan, but I swear to Christ if he laid a finger on her . . . And how am I the first person she called? It confirms my suspicions he's been isolating her. It's probably been going on for a while. Veronica is probably the only woman in her life she had. Then he went and fucked her. I'm praying this is only a bad breakup and she's been kicked out and not something more nefarious.

On the way home, I make a couple of stops. First the grocery store to get ingredients for macaroni and cheese, a toothbrush—just in case—a few pints of ice cream, and a six-pack of those hard seltzers women like. After that, I swing by the coffee shop and pick up a half-dozen apple scones and a few pumpkin muffins.

When I turn onto my street, I see her car in my driveway and take a relieved breath. I type my code in the keypad, and the gate slides open. Instead of parking in the center of the garage like usual, I park on the far-left side.

I grab my groceries and enter through the mud room.

"Jordan?" I call out.

"Kitchen." Her voice is more collected than before, but it's hoarse.

When I find her, she's sitting on a barstool by the kitchen island. I set down the groceries on the counter. Her eyes are puffy and red. She looks utterly defeated.

"Hi."

She's clutching a small duffel bag.

"Hey. I'm glad you got in okay. Where're your keys? I'm gonna pull your car in."

She slides them across the island toward me, I grab them, and jog back outside to move her car. I've got a spare door opener around here somewhere I can give her. Meanwhile, I don't want Bryan to know she's here. I will be gone for a couple days while we play in New Jersey—plus the other away games—and I don't want to be worrying about her while I'm traveling.

When I get back in, I unload the reusable grocery bag.

I nod to her duffel. "Were you able to pack some things?"

"No, this's my gym bag. It was left in my car from before."

"I picked up some essentials."

I untie the string around the bakery box and slide it in front of her, and she peeks under the lid. "You got me scones?"

"It wasn't selfless. I was already stopping to get myself a half-dozen muffins." *Yeah. That's it.*

"I'm not hungry." Her shoulders slump. "But thank you for the gesture."

"When was the last time you ate?"

"Um . . ." She peers at the ceiling, and her eyes dart around as if she's mathematically calculating the answer in her head.

"You need to eat something. You barely ate anything at the fundraiser last night." She pushed food around with her fork but never brought it to her mouth. "Food first, talk after."

I open the lid in front of her, and she hesitates but eventually plucks a scone out of the white box and takes a bite, releasing a big exhale through her nose while she chews.

"I told him I was leaving yesterday. We got into a fight." Her lower lip quivers. "He put my ring back on." I steel my expression. Inside, I'm seething. I take the string from the bakery box and turn around to open my junk drawer, pulling out a paper clip. I thread the string through it and push it under the ring.

"I left work early today, so I could go home and pack some things."

I shake my head. "Start with last night." I wrap the string around her finger, like I did at the café, while she gives me a play-by-play.

"Yesterday, I was waiting for him when he got home. He walked through the door and says he's sorry for *what happened*. I told him we had an appointment to split finances, and I tried to give him back his ring."

I want this ring off her. *Now.*

"Then what?" Her hand trembles. *Fuck.* "Jordan, what happened last night?"

She looks like she's on the verge of a breakdown. "He yelled at me and told me I needed to go to the fundraiser."

She's not telling me the truth, but I'm not about to force information out of her. We'll sort it out later. I hold her hand over the counter and grab the bottle of olive oil, letting a couple drops fall on the ring. I rub it around her finger and unwind the string from the opposite side. Thank God it budges.

"I didn't argue. But last night I walked around the

fundraiser telling myself I'd leave work early today and get my things and go to a hotel or realtor office. Somewhere away from him. He came home right after I got to the condo."

Yup, he was definitely tracking her phone. "He made me so mad, he said some things, and I yelled back. I don't even remember everything that was said, but it escalated fast. He came at me, so I slammed the door in his face, and I think I crushed his hand. I don't know. I didn't see. I was scared and ran." Her free hand tucks some loose hair behind her ear, and she stares at the countertop as she recalls the harrowing events of today. "I got to the door, and he threw an iron at me—"

"Wait, he threw something at you?"

"I don't know. He was probably trying to scare me into staying. I can't be sure he was actually aiming *for* me."

What's the difference?

She stares into space, like she's replaying it in her head. "I grabbed my purse and ran. I took the stairwell, and he followed me." Her glazed eyes widen. "No, not follow. He *chased* me."

I blow out a breath. The massive donation he made to Safehouse last night flashes in my mind. *Motherfucker.* Her eyes are wild like a frightened rabbit. I get the ring over her knuckle, and it slips off. I hold her hand out, the purple fades from her finger, save for a blotchy area around the knuckle where she's bruised. She yanks it back and rubs the spot. Did it happen when he shoved the ring on her finger? That couldn't have gone on smoothly.

"I don't know if I've ever been so scared before, but I knew at that moment there was no coming back from it. I couldn't go back."

That's how it was for my mom. That's when she knew it was time to leave too.

"Then he stopped. My feet kept moving, I couldn't get down the stairs fast enough, but he must have left the stairwell and taken the elevator the rest of the way down."

"So, what happened?"

Her hands are trembling as she speaks, and I have to keep my cool. The last thing she needs is to have *me* scare her with my temper. I would never direct my anger at her, but she might not see that.

"It was like we were putting on this little skit for the security staff. Bryan tried to play it off like everything was fine, called me *honey*, told me to come upstairs with him. I should have told them he tried to attack me! Why didn't I tell them to call the cops?"

"You were trying to deescalate the situation and get out of there."

She shakes her head. "I don't know what made the guard do it, but he escorted me to my car and sent Bryan upstairs, and I left."

"That was when you called me?"

She nods.

"You should be proud of yourself. You did great today."

"My parents are going to say I made a mistake, a poor financial decision."

Taking her face in my hands, I peer down at her wide brown eyes. They're so full of uncertainty. I can't imagine what she must be feeling.

"You are not making a mistake. You can do this."

She nods, her lip trembling. I stare at it for what feels like minutes, then drop my hands. "I'll help however I can. Staying here is the safest place for you. It's gated and secure. There's an apartment above the garage, private entrance and everything. It's not massive, but you'll have your own space."

"That's not necessary."

"It is, Jordan. At least for now. Leaving is when you're most vulnerable. I don't care that you're here, really. Stay a few days, at least until you figure out what you want to do."

How could I have not seen what was happening? It makes me sick I was almost the best man at this woman's funeral. I know this shit up, down, backward, and forward. The signs were there, but I ignored them.

"I'll pay rent."

"All I ask is you don't go back to him. He's going to tell you everything you want to hear to make you come back. Don't."

She narrows her eyes at me. "Do women go back to their abusers because they still love them?"

"Sometimes, yeah. Or because they've been made totally dependent on them without realizing it. They've been manipulated financially. Sometimes kids are involved. There're a million different reasons."

She looks down at her scone and picks off a piece. When she glances back up and meets my gaze, her expression tells me love won't be an issue for her.

Was their entire relationship staged? Jordan explained their arrangement was somewhat transactional, but I didn't realize he took it so literally. She was another thing for him to own. Before this mess, I thought he loved her.

"Come on, I'll give you a tour and show you the apartment."

I start with the kitchen since that's where she's sitting. Opening the cabinets and drawers, I show her where all the pots, pans, tools, and other cooking shit are. The apartment space has a kitchenette, but it's bare bones. In the butler pantry, I tell her if there's anything she needs, to add it to the grocery list. I demo by using the smart home assistant to add apple scones to the grocery list.

"I don't keep a ton of food in the house since I travel a lot, but Raquel, the house manager, usually restocks on Thursdays. She's here a couple times a week, don't freak out if you see her around."

She follows me. "Mud room." The spacious laundry room houses two sets of washers and dryers lined on one wall with a deep utility sink and countertops. Two walls are mostly cabinets and storage. A large square island countertop sits in the center of the room. I show her that the second door on the adjacent wall opens a powder room.

"Laundry is on Mondays and Thursdays. Want me to have your clothes added to the schedule?"

"No"—she shakes her head—"I can handle my own laundry. I won't be here too long. I only need to crash until I get an apartment lined up."

I nod, not liking that answer. In the living room, I show her the touchscreen remotes. She has the same ones, so there's no demo needed. "The home theater on the lower level is better for movies. Same A/V system. There's also a bar, pool table, et cetera. Feel free to hangout down there if you're bored." I point to a secluded cased opening off the main living space. "My bedroom is through there."

After showing her the other main level bathrooms, I steer us up the curved staircase.

"Spare bedrooms on this side, and over here . . ." We cross the catwalk to the other side, and I guide her to the short hallway leading to the L-shaped bonus apartment over the garage.

She's hardly said a word the whole tour. I might as well be talking to myself.

"Here's where you'll stay," I say, opening the door. Late-day sun floods the interior through the eight angled skylights running the length of the vaulted room. We walk past the sofa, television, and bookcases in the main space until we reach the corner of the L, which makes up the kitchen. Opening the fridge, there's a few drinks and a bottle of hot sauce. Thankfully, the freezer is stocked with meal kits. That'll get her started.

"Bedroom and attached bathroom are there," I say, pointing to the other end. The bedroom comprises a big bed engulfed in a downy white duvet with matching fluffy pillowcases. Everything is generic enough to give the appearance of a trendy hotel suite. I used to rent it out to guests but stopped after I had some of my gear go missing. I motion toward the metal door on the right. "That's the private entrance you can reach from the garage stairs, so you can come and go as you please."

I double-check she's stocked up on linens, toiletries, and towels. From inside the bathroom, I call back to her. "It's not massive, but you'll have a private kitchenette, bathroom, living area, and bedroom. No laundry, you'll have to do that on the main level." I walk back out, and her hands are clasped as she goes up on her tiptoes, surveying the space. "I'm pretty low maintenance. I promise I'm not as prissy as I look. This is more than enough. It's only temporary."

She looks every bit the privileged princess Bryan made her out to be, but her actions are contradictory.

I nod. "If it's not, that's okay too. Help yourself to whatever you want. If there's anything you need, let me know."

We stare at each other for a moment. Her blonde hair is down, not up like usual, and I like it. Her makeup streaked from tears has some of her freckles peeking through. I wish I could see them all. Even exhausted and puffy, she's beautiful. My fingers itch to haul her into my arms for a hug. I ignore the urge, but it's hard to look away. When the silence grows more awkward, I clap my hands together. "Okay. So, um, yeah. Make yourself comfortable, I'm going to cook some food. I'll be back to check in on you. Take a few minutes to breathe. Or watch TV. Or whatever. Is there anything I can get you?" *Pull it together, man.*

"The towels are in the bathroom?"

"Cabinet on the right."

"I'm going to wash the day off." She sighs. "Might crash after."

I nod and exit the space, closing the door behind me. I haven't had a roommate in a long time. Why am I suddenly so flustered? I don't mind hanging out with her, but we'll barely see each other—and that's fine by me, better we don't. Keep things less complicated.

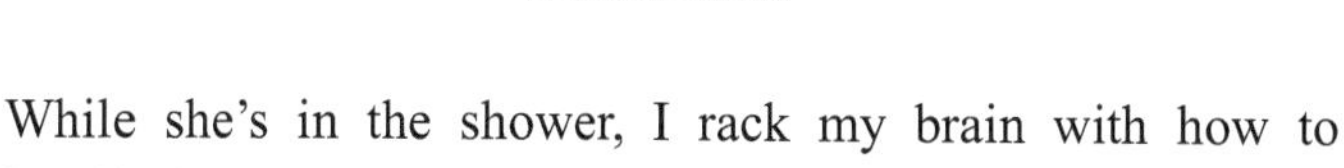

While she's in the shower, I rack my brain with how to handle her ex. If I had it my way, I know exactly how I'd handle him. Bryan fucked up with this one. I plan on dealing with him . . . I just don't know when. If I go after him now, it'll be a dead giveaway to where she's staying. I travel too often, so it would compromise her safety. I can't have him showing up or discovering her location while I'm away. Which reminds me, I should have Raquel get the house codes reset. I don't remember if I ever gave them to him, but I'd prefer to not take any chances.

Back in the kitchen, I get to work on dinner, and my mind drifts to her. I don't need to know Jordan well to know she has a good heart. She's silly, playful, driven . . . gorgeous—not that it matters, but when I think of the words to describe her, it's hard not to place her beauty toward the top. I'm no stranger to pretty girls, but Jordan has me in a trance. She proves my point when she walks into the kitchen after her shower.

When I glance up from the stove, I do a double-take. My whore brain is confused. She looks nothing like the women I go for. She's not wearing a trace of makeup, her clothes aren't skimpy, and yet . . . she's still a showstopper. I'm not a jealous man by any means, but Bryan's had a chance with a woman I can't have . . . and it pisses me off.

There's nothing revealing about what she's wearing, but somehow, it's doing it for me. She's in a matching sports jacket and yoga pants that hug her curves, and those brown eyes, pink cheeks, and freckles? Come on.

I can't look away. She opens the fridge and pulls out one of the seltzers, cracks the top, and takes two big gulps, her throat bobbing. *Jesus fuck.* She plops down on her seat at the counter.

Shaking my head, I turn to the pot of homemade macaroni and cheese in front of me. I stir the contents and resist laughing. It sounds like sex. *What the fuck is wrong with me?* It's like I'm fourteen again.

I clear my throat. "Feel better?"

When she doesn't answer, I look back and she's dragging another gulp from the can, wincing. She nods as she swallows. "Yup."

"Did I get the wrong flavor?"

"No, I always think these are going to taste better than they do." She looks down at the can, turning it in her hand as she studies it. She takes another sip and smacks her lips together. "It's like drinking knives. If those knives cut a lime once—four years ago."

Amen. I have never liked carbonated water, but people lose their fucking minds over it. Makes no sense.

"Fuck, thank you! I think it tastes like your tongue fell asleep."

"Yes!" She giggles, and it makes me smile.

I dish out the corkscrew cavatappi pasta coated with delicious melted cheese into two bowls. When you eat as much pasta as hockey players do, you learn to perfect certain dishes. I make a mean mac and cheese, and tonight calls for comfort food. The trick is starting with a roux, adding cheddar, Monterey Jack, Gouda, and gruyère . . . and folding in Velveeta when no one's looking.

"Okay, enough of this shit." I peel the can from her fingers and set it aside. "How about some wine instead?"

"Wine and cheese, always a classic combo." I may have been a little heavy-handed on the Velveeta. *Which pairs better with rubber cheese-a-like?*

I land on a bottle of chardonnay from under the kitchen island and uncork it, then pour each of us a half glass.

"Cheers," I say, handing her one.

I sidle up next to her at the kitchen island and hold out a fork and spoon. "Choose your weapon."

"Fork," she says, plucking it from my hand. Another thing we agree on. She dives it into the noodles and brings it to her mouth. I have to look away.

Don't look. Don't even fucking look. The more I try to avoid it, the weaker my resistance becomes. In my peripheral, she drags the fork out between her thick full lips, then I glance over, and she's licking them clean. *Goddamn it.*

"This might be the best mac n' cheese I've ever had. Congratulations."

"It better be," I answer, looking back down at my bowl. No more watching her. I spear a cheesy corkscrew onto my fork and pop it in my mouth. While chewing, I contemplate how to ask my next question. "Don't take this the wrong way, because I'm happy to have you stay here, but how come you don't have anyone else?"

She swallows. "I don't have a ton of friends. I mean, I do, but none are close. And you seem to know what you're doing when it comes to my . . . situation." She uses her fork to roll pasta around in her bowl, then sets the bowl down. "When you grow up with a lot of money, it's hard to find true friends. I thought Veronica was mine, but obviously that's no longer the case. It's weird, I almost called her the other day because I needed to talk to someone. It hit me that I lost the only confidant I had."

That fucking sucks.

"Are you going to talk to her again?"

"No."

That surprises me. "No? Not even to yell at her?"

"She fucked my fiancé. I don't owe her anything. Our friendship is over, why should I give her my time too? To make her feel better? Fuck that. She wants him, she can have him. That's punishment enough . . . I don't even want to waste time talking about her now, let's change the subject."

With wide eyes, I wrench my gaze back to my pasta. This is the second time she's shut down a conversation when it got heavy. "Listen, if you ever want to talk about it . . . I may be a dick, but I'm a surprisingly good listener." She's got this weird way of making me feel like we're old friends.

She peers up at me with a lopsided grin. "I'll keep it in mind." Her brows furrow. "Why are you a dick, by the way? In public, I mean. Because you certainly have that persona, but you're not really a jerk, are you?"

I chuckle. "I'm not a fan of most people, and I can get a little protective of the boys on the ice, so there's that."

"I think it's because you don't like yourself."

I scoff and take a bite. "I love me."

She shakes her head and studies me, tapping the back of her fork on her lips as she formulates her thoughts. "I believe you when you say you don't like people. But you're almost never alone, you're constantly immersed with parties and women. So either you enjoy being surrounded by new people —and what you said was a lie—or you hate being alone with yourself . . . Or you're running away from something."

"Okay, Freud." I roll my eyes. "If I don't like myself, how come I'm so confident?"

"You're not confident, you're confrontational. You live your life on the offensive, that's why you're a dick."

"Not always. I'm not a dick to my teammates. I'm not a dick to you."

"Because you trust the boys, they prove to you every day they have your back," she explains with a shrug. I cock my head and stare at her, and she spins away from me. "I think you trust me because I have the same issues you do. Trusting people doesn't come easy for me either. It's easier to keep others at a distance than to have to wonder if they're only trying to fuck you over."

How does she do that? I've never been able to put that feeling into words, and she did it in about ten seconds. It's like she looked inside my brain, took all my thoughts, and organized them into one simple explanation. It's unsettling.

"Hm." I scoot a little farther away. "Something like that." *Exactly that.*

"I thought you were simply another womanizing douchebag at first—"

"Oh, I am."

"Well, you better start working at it"—she scrunches up her nose—"because your nice-guy is showing."

I blow out a breath. "Can't have that, I have a reputation to uphold."

"Don't worry, you can get it back. Just make a few tweaks."

"Such as?"

A smile grows on her face. "For one, you need to talk more shit. You want that come-at-me-bro energy. Be obnoxious but get creative with it."

I laugh and she keeps going.

"Ooh! How do you feel about bumper stickers?"

Shaking my head, I smile. "Nothing says *tough guy* like stickers."

"Maybe an energy drink logo? Something like 'DOES NOT PLAY WELL WITH OTHERS.' One of those Pissing Calvins . . . You get the idea. Really lean into the douchebaggery."

"I could bring an acoustic guitar to a house party?"

"Can you perform a shitty rendition of 'Wonderwall'?"

"No need, I'll figure it out on the spot."

"Alright, alright." She nods along, smirking. "Wanna roll with the big dogs?"

"Obviously," I answer.

"Can you start a fight at the party?"

"Baby, I'll make the cops show up."

Her grin widens, crinkling the corners of her eyes, and she claps me on the back, and her touch makes me sit up straighter. "You're gonna be okay, kid."

We return to our bowls, eating silently shoulder to shoulder.

Who is this girl? How did we get here? After the night I heard him berate her, I formed a soft spot for Jordan, like I do with every victim I meet at Safehouse. If it weren't for that, I would have assumed she was another rich housewife-in-training. But she has this way of understanding me—and doesn't judge me for it. She's not one of those women who thinks they can be the one to change me.

She nudges me with her shoulder. "You're a lot different than I thought you'd be."

I glance down at her focused on her meal.

"You are too," I mutter.

It's a good thing I'll be gone for a couple days.

TEN

Banksy

We're about thirty minutes from landing in Arizona, and I've been watching game footage for the last two hours, hunched over my tray table with a tablet and phone, comparing two games playing on each device. It's become my new process while we fly. First, I go through our team's performance, then our opponent's so I can pick out any weak spots I didn't see before, and finally, I wrap up with footage from my favorite players so I can improve my personal game.

I spoke to the coaches about switching around one of the lineups earlier this week. We have two players who aren't in sync. They can't read each other, but there are other guys we can switch them with to mitigate the problem. I gave them a solution, but they weren't having it. Pissed me off and put me in a bad mood.

I've been focused on this game, but whenever I'm not thinking about the team, my thoughts are on her. Before I left for Arizona, I made Jordan promise she would wait to get her things from her old condo until I got home. I'm hoping she keeps her word. I have seen little of her since we ate dinner together a couple nights ago. She's been focused on work, which she'll be doing remotely for now. I instructed her how to use the VPN so her location isn't traceable on her work laptop.

She's welcome to raid my closet if she needs anything to sleep in for the time being. I suppose I could ask Raquel to pick her up some clothes, but that feels like crossing a boundary. She's a grown woman. I'm giving her a place to crash and helping her get some shit from her ex. I don't have to take care of her every need. That's not my job.

As if she knows I'm thinking about her, a notification pops up at the top of my screen. Since I've left home, my heart has been in my chest every time she texts me. My mind goes to the worst-case scenario. I gotta deal with Bryan so I'm not getting a hit of adrenaline with each ding of my phone.

JORDAN LANDRY

Where's your step stool?

Why?

JORDAN LANDRY

I can't reach the coffee beans.

I smile, picturing her up on her tippy toes, stretching for something out of reach, making her tits look even perkier.

Garage wall, on the right.

A minute-and-a-half passes, and I don't hear back. I open my security camera app to watch her, simply to make sure she's found it. At least, that's what I tell myself when the screen loads. *Fuck me.* Her blonde hair is tied up in a ponytail and she's wearing the yoga pants from the other day, but this time she's ditched the track jacket for a sports bra. Before I get a good look, she marches into the pantry. After a few seconds, she returns with a bag of coffee beans. I take in her curves. She's not toned, her midriff is supple and sexy. My fist flexes, wanting to dig my fingers into her softness. She picks up her phone to text me back, and I feel like an asshole for watching her like this.

JORDAN LANDRY

Thanks!

This is where I'm supposed to go back to my videos of hockey games. Leave the text messaging and surveillance apps and focus on my responsibilities as a captain, but I no longer have control over my lizard brain as my fingers fly over the touchscreen keyboard.

I switch back to the surveillance app, I'm an asshole, after all, and observe her smiling and leaning against the wall next to the built-in coffee system. She's a vision in lime and black spandex.

I took the last chocolate protein bar. Told Jonesy to fuck off when he asked to trade for peanut butter.

It looks like she's laughing, and I smile.

JORDAN LANDRY

Sounds like you're going to make a full recovery.

Thanks doc.

JORDAN LANDRY

You're welcome.

The conversation is over. Let it go.

Is there anything you need before I get back?

JORDAN LANDRY

I think I can manage on my own until Sunday.

You really are low maintenance, huh?

JORDAN LANDRY

More like I handle my own maintenance.

I chuckle.

Can I watch?

JORDAN LANDRY

You're still not my type.

I'm everyone's type.

JORDAN LANDRY

After the game you might want to consider finding a woman to help take the edge off your testosterone before you fly home.

The smile on my face fades. *Shit.* I'm flirting with her. I have four women I could hook up with in Arizona, plus an inbox full of DMs looking for a chance, but the thought of rando-sex doesn't excite me. I'd see a doctor about it except . . . I'm half hard. It's not an equipment issue, it's a Jordan issue. I gotta nip this in the bud, or I'll never get laid again.

I'll be sure to find some women to keep me occupied tonight. Don't worry.

I resist looking back at the cameras to see her expression. Either she'll smile and I'll feel dejected or she'll frown and I'll feel like a jerk.

JORDAN LANDRY

Atta boy.

Good luck tonight!

Thanks.

On the ice, all my problems disappear. This is where things make sense. My objective is clear: put the three-inch black rubber puck into the net on the other side of the arena. Piece of cake.

Arizona is playing well, but we're holding our own. Though it wouldn't be so neck and neck if they tried the lineup switch I suggested. When my shift is over and I come off the ice, I practically fall onto the bench. It's not standard height. Some arenas purposely lower their away team benches. When you sit lower, the lactic acid builds up in your knees and it's harder to recover after a shift. I make a mental note for the boys to hit the bikes extra hard tonight before they hit the bars.

I look up in time to see Matthew Laasko, our left winger, get checked into the boards in front of us.

Barrett leans over and growls, "What the fuck is up with Jorg?"

Arizona's enforcer, Jorgensen, has been gunning it for Matty all night. I threw my arm out at one of the refs earlier, trying to make sure they keep an eye on those hits. They're out of regulation and over-the-top.

I shake my head. "No clue. Think I should step in?"

Barrett narrows his eyes at the asshole in question. "Let Broderick take it."

Nah, I'll take him. Broderick has been slowly replacing me as the new enforcer on the team, but I'm taller and am better matched for Jorgenson. Jordan said I needed to work off that testosterone. Fucking up that guy's face sounds better than taking a bunny back to my hotel room. I already warned the officials once.

We're up 3-2. I anticipate a tight win tonight, but I'm not saying a word for fear of jinxing it. There's always a little superstition during games. After a few more pulls from my water bottle, I stand, ready to swing a leg over the boards. Broderick's shift is up, and he starts back in.

Barrett reads my mind and huffs. "Go easy on him."

"Uh-huh," I say, sweat raining down my face as I jump back on the ice.

Like I knew he would, he aims for Matty again but doesn't get far. I drop gloves and jump in his face. Grabbing his sweater, we swing around in a circle like we're performing some ice-skating duet. He tries to fake a drop to the ice.

"You fucking pussy." I pant out a laugh. "No, we're not done yet."

Cutting my skates into the ice, I yank him up and throw my elbow into the soft spot where his pads don't cover. He leans, and I get a clear shot at his helmet, knocking it off and raising my shoulder to hurl my fist into the side of his face.

"Fuck you, Teller!"

He's gripping the nape of my neck and grabs a handful of hair.

"Harder," I grit out.

"You would like that, you son of a bitch." He cracks me in the jaw, and I shove him against the boards.

His head bounces off the plexiglass when my knuckles connect with his skull—bet that one rattled his teeth. Not a second later, the linesmen are grabbing me under my armpits and hauling me back. The asshole spits blood at me, and I lunge for him, getting in one more shot before they throw us in the sin bin.

The ref escorts me to the penalty box, and I politely remind him I gave fair warning earlier; his checks were not regulation. I flop onto the short bench and smile, folding my arms behind my head and leaning back. "Ahhh, feels good to be home, boys!" I don't get a grin out of the linesman or the penalty box attendant. *Tough crowd.* Whatever, fuck all of 'em.

When I look up, Jorgensen is glaring at me from the opposing penalty box, and I wink back with a smile.

See? I can still be an asshole.

Matty Laasko is a passive dude until he's not. There was no reason for Jorgensen to go after him. Those hits were unprovoked—even Barrett had had enough of that shit, and he's not one for fights. Nothing pisses me off more than watching someone get attacked by some dickbag, simply to exert control. I intervened because I was defending Laasko . . . but as soon as I knocked his helmet off, all I could picture was Bryan Davenport's face.

ELEVEN

Camden

Pulling up to the house, I get a rush of excitement as I anticipate seeing her. *Jesus Christ, it's only been three days.* I walk in and throw down my bag in the mud room.

"I'm back!" I holler, striding into the kitchen to find something to eat.

All our plane food is processed shit. I need something fresh, cold, and crunchy. I could make a salad, but I need something more substantial. I want . . . a sandwich. Yeah, a big fucking sandwich.

Footsteps bound down the stairs and my shoulders loosen. A cozy, relaxed ambiance settles in the room. It's bizarre, I've never had that reaction with a girl before, other than maybe my sisters. It's foreign and strange. I fuck women, but I don't often form friendships with them. *Where the hell is the brown mustard?* My head is still buried in the fridge gathering up sandwich ingredients when she says, "Hey! Congrats on Arizona. Saw the goal, pretty awesome."

"Thanks." I continue digging around.

"Mustard's in the door if you're looking for it."

I almost bark out a laugh. There she goes again, getting in my fucking head. I grab it and spin around.

"What?" she asks with a smile.

"Nothing." I shake my head while constructing my meal at the counter but almost drop everything when my gaze lands on her in one of my shirts. She looks comfortable—*she looks good in it.* Shit, I never want to see her in anything else.

I set everything down and avert my gaze to the counter, staring at the bread, meat, lettuce, cheese, onions, pickles, and various condiments . . . *What was I doing again?* I run a hand over my face. This attraction is getting on my nerves.

I clear my throat and untie the bread bag. "How were things while I was gone? Any issues?"

"Just the high shelves." She leans over the counter on her elbows and rests her face in her hands. "Oh, and I hope you don't mind, but I ground up all your coffee and put it in the freezer."

I chuckle. "Aren't you funny." When I glance down, my eyes stop at her chest; she's not wearing a bra. This is hell.

She peers down at the shirt. "Oh, hope you don't mind I borrowed this? I wore all the clothes I had in my bag and needed to do laundry. You said I could raid your closet."

Finally, I look up at her eyes.

"Yeah, I did. I was just, uh, surprised you found that one, I thought I'd lost it." *Nice save, dumbass.*

"Oh, it was in the drawer on the left, right on top."

I can't let her wear my shit if this is the reaction I will have. *I need some serious boundaries.*

"Funny. Hey, have you been in contact with your parents or Bryan?"

"No." The smile on her face falls. "Every time shit goes sideways, there's a PR person there to pick up the pieces and tie it up in a neat little bow. If I told my parents, they would come home, and it would be this whole thing. I don't want to ruin their time in Monaco. This is my problem. I need to deal with it. Maybe it's because of the way things ended with Bryan, but I really want to come back from this without someone else doing the work for me. I need to stand on my own two feet and say I overcame him."

I can respect that, but she should still communicate what's going on. "Don't you think they should know the wedding is off?"

"Yeah, but it's not only about the wedding. The more I think about it, the more I believe the institution of marriage is a total sham. I mean, look at my parents. They're cordial, but there's no romance. So, what's the point? Money? Status? I have enough money already. I don't need status. I'd rather live happily alone than be like them and live a parallel life with someone under the same roof. Makes me wonder how many other marriages are that way. Am I letting all the love stories in books and movies cloud my judgment? I mean, I've never seen a Nicholas Sparks marriage, have you?"

"Yeah, I have." She pauses and cocks her head to the side and smirks, like she's trying to call my bluff. I continue, "My teammates are obsessed with their wives. Lonan and Birdie. Rhys and Micky. Barrett and Raleigh . . ."

"You're only hearing what they tell you. It's a facade." She rolls her eyes.

"No, it's not." I scoff. "They have the real deal. I've seen it. They love each other when no one's watching."

"And what about your parents?"

I drop the knife back in the jar of mustard and open the container of sliced deli meat.

"My bio dad was an abusive asshole. I've seen what that kind of marriage looks like, but I've seen the other side too. My stepdad, Bruce, and my mom are in love. They're disgusting together. I've never seen two people more into each other. They're best friends. He treats her with respect, he's never told her how to live her life, never raised his voice with her, and he looks at her in a way my father never did. Bruce worships her. *That's* how it's supposed to be, Jordan. Respectfully, your family is fucked up. As trite as it is, they are proof money can't buy everything."

"Traitor. I thought you were on my side." She sits and watches me build my sandwich before getting off her barstool and coming around to my side. "Move over, I want one."

As she extracts two slices of bread, she speaks as if she's defending herself. "My parents are good people, they just prioritize their life differently. Bryan's parents are the same—neither one of us had a healthy marriage to model after. I left, and my life is still a mess."

I drop down to her eye level, and she looks up from tearing lettuce. "But it's less messy. You're in control again."

She nods, a frown on her face.

"It gets easier. Leaving is hard, but it's worth it." And she's so fuckin' worthy of finding true love, whether she believes it exists or not. She's a great girl, there's no doubt in my mind she will find someone who'll give her the book-worthy romance she speaks of. *But it won't be me.*

"I don't wanna talk about it anymore. Tell me something good. What are the three best things that happened to you today?"

Damn, she likes to deflect, but I don't argue. "Hmm . . . three good things . . ."

She struggles to get the lid off the pickle jar, holding it against her chest for leverage. I take the opportunity to admire the way her hard nipples are outlined in my shirt. The cotton rubbing back and forth over them. I sink my teeth into my sandwich. Seeing *that* is definitely in my top three.

I could watch this entertainment all day. After she grunts trying to open it, I wipe my hands free of crumbs and make a beckoning gesture with my hand.

She passes me the jar, I pop the top, and give it back.

"Thanks."

"Okay, first thing, this sandwich is pretty fuckin' dope. Second, I'm looking forward to being home for a few days."

She smiles and puts the lid back on the deli meat.

"Third thing?" she asks, putting all the sandwich fixings back in the fridge. She's really gotten to know her way around this place while I've been gone. I don't mind it as much as I thought I would.

"Real talk?"

She furrows her brow and smirks. "Duh."

"I was relieved to come home and see you here. I worried you'd go back to him. I've seen it happen many times. You've got a good heart, and you're doing the right thing. And I'm glad you're not marrying him."

She releases an exaggerated groan, dropping her arms to her sides, feigning exasperation. "Seriously . . . you're not my type."

I smirk. It's become our little schtick. She tells me I'm not her type, and I respond with:

"I'm everybody's type."

She grins while pulling out one of the barstools, plops down, and takes a bite.

"What are your three good things?" I ask.

"Hmm. One, I also like my sandwich. Two, work is going well. I am finishing up a project I'm working on. By the way, I have to go into the office Wednesday—don't worry, Bryan is gone for a client meeting."

I nod while chewing and hold up three fingers.

"Three . . . Also on Wednesday, I'm going to check out a

few pet-friendly apartments and, if I've got time, stop by my parents' house and see my dog. So, that's something I'm looking forward to."

"Chicken Salad." I laugh and bring my plate to the sink. "Hey, I'm probably gonna lay low tonight and watch a movie. Not sure what you've got going on, but you're welcome to join me."

"Can't. I've got a hot date."

Bracing myself with my palms behind me, I lean against the sink and raise an eyebrow. *With who?*

"Easy, killer. He's fictional. I started a new book last night, and it's *really* good."

"What kind of books are you reading that could be better than watching a movie with me?"

"I mean, there's a lot of books that would be better than that, but in this case, spicy ones." She bounces her eyebrows as she takes a bite.

I roll my eyes and push off the sink, heading to the mud room to grab my carry-on suitcase. I need to unpack. As I pass her on the way to my bedroom, I call back, "Well, if he gets limp dick, you know where to find me." My feet pause when I hear how much it sounded like an offer for sex, and she cackles.

Shutting my bedroom door, I look down. Jordan's got me hard even thinking about it. Or maybe it was her nipples poking through my shirt that did it. Or the way she licked her lips while eating. *No, it's not her. It's the lack of sex. You need to get laid!*

I toss my bag on the bed and unzip it. All I can picture is her lips. Damn it, there's no use ignoring this. I shove the suitcase away and pull out my cock, releasing a sigh. I turn around and drop to my knees. When I close my eyes, all I see is her big brown ones looking up at me. Is she as innocent as she appears, and more importantly, could I corrupt her? I want to see her pretty and depraved. I pant harder and imagine teaching her all the things she didn't learn in her preppy finishing school. Things Bryan could never give her.

"Can you be a dirty slut for me, sweetheart?" I whisper.

I picture her smirk, the way her thighs felt when I squeezed them, how hot her pussy felt behind me on the bike. Her nipples poking through *my* shirt. That does it. Cum fountains out of the engorged tip. Each pump bringing more until I'm finally empty.

Fuck. I needed that.

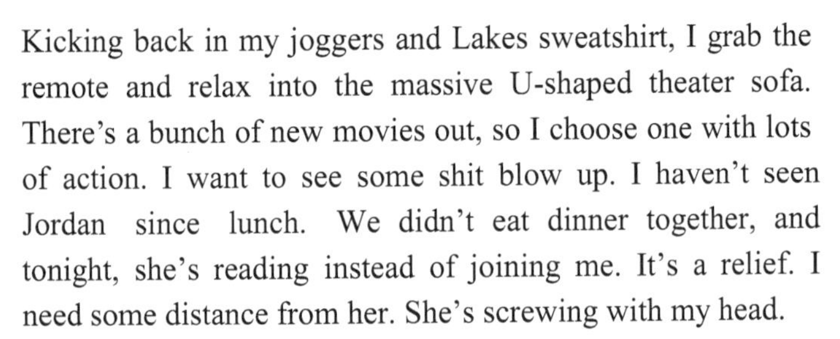

Kicking back in my joggers and Lakes sweatshirt, I grab the remote and relax into the massive U-shaped theater sofa. There's a bunch of new movies out, so I choose one with lots of action. I want to see some shit blow up. I haven't seen Jordan since lunch. We didn't eat dinner together, and tonight, she's reading instead of joining me. It's a relief. I need some distance from her. She's screwing with my head.

Getting off earlier helped, but I need to get laid. By a woman, not my hand.

So, what am I doing at home? I should go out tonight. O'Callahan said something about drinks at Top Shelf. I pick up my phone to text the boys as Jordan strolls in, grabbing a blanket from the overflowing basket.

"What are we watching?" she asks, plopping down adjacent to me on the left wing of the sofa. She brings her hand to the touch sensor to recline. She's still in my fucking shirt.

Then again, it's been a long day of traveling. Maybe I should stick around home and rest.

"What happened to your hot date?"

She scrunches up her nose. "There was some other woman drama, he kissed the wrong girl. Took me right out of it." She laughs. "Shit, even my book boyfriends are cheaters. I must have a type."

"Well, no wonder you aren't into me. I'm not a cheater."

"It's easy not to cheat when you never commit to anyone," she says with pursed lips. My gaze focuses on her mouth, and I gnaw the inside of my cheek.

"It's easy not to cheat, period. Just because I like variety, doesn't mean I couldn't remain loyal if it were my situation."

"And do you think that *situation* will ever be a reality for you?"

I smile and chuckle to myself. "Nope."

She laughs with me. "Exactly. Dude, you're a slut."

I press a hand to my chest. "I'm sorry, are you shaming me?"

"Not at all," she says, grinning like the Cheshire cat.

I shouldn't be checking her out, but it's so easy from this angle. And when her eyes are on the big screen, I can stare as long as I want. The freckles I plan to memorize are on display. They make her appear even more wholesome, which makes my dick twitch. She's not innocent. There's no way. I've seen that mischievous flicker in her eyes, the combination is . . . *damn.*

She's so far away. "You can sit by me, you know. I won't try fucking you. I have self-control, believe it or not."

She gets up and trudges closer but keeps a couple cushions between us and tucks up her legs.

"Seriously?" I scoff.

"What?"

I shake my head and hit play on the remote. We sit in the dark, and I fold my arms behind my head to get comfy. As the movie plays out, the two main characters develop a predictable romantic connection as they try to stop a government coverup. I honestly don't know what's being covered up because I'm so goddamn distracted.

She looks over and does a double-take when she notices me staring at her.

"What?" she asks, with a nervous grin.

"Nothing."

"Why are you looking at me?"

"Because you're looking at me," I say, chuckling. I gaze back to the screen. "You're so weird."

In my peripheral, she narrows her eyes and slowly returns her focus to the movie. How the hell is she not attracted to me? I'm a good-looking guy, it's what the tabloids focus on. At least on a physical level she must feel something. The room is filled with heavy tension and sex. It's so palpable, I'm shocked it hasn't formed into a thick fog. There's no way it's all in my head. It wouldn't feel this strong if it was one-sided. If so, I'm losing my grip with reality.

Doesn't matter, Jordan is the inverse of the women I go for. She's chill and easy to hang out with, and she dishes out as much shit as I do. She reminds me of hanging out with one of the guys. We're becoming fast friends and—

Wait a minute, did she fucking friendzone me?!

Holy shit. That's exactly what she's done.

I've never been on this side before. Well, this sucks—though I don't know why, it's not like I want anything with her. Relationships are complicated, but losing the option of having something more than our friendship leaves me feeling a little empty.

This is stupid.

Shaking my head, I attempt to focus on what's happening on the screen. I'm sucked into the plot until I feel her gaze on me. When I glance over, she quickly looks away. *I knew it.*

I smirk but don't say anything. Over the next twenty minutes, we exchange brief glances twice more. What is happening between us? I have to clench my jaw to keep from laughing. It feels like middle-school shit. Toying with her is so fun.

She seems immune to my charm. Maybe that's where this magnetism comes from. If I fucked her, would this tension dissipate into thin air? One wonders. I've never developed a crush. Sure, there's been women I've wanted to sleep with, but that's all physical attraction, it's biological.

With Jordan, it seems like more, but I can't place it. Not that I'd make a move when she's vulnerable, but there are times I forget about the shit with Bryan and she's simply a girl in my space. She's hot, and I enjoy spending time with her. If she wanted to rebound, I'd be happy to assist. I'm curious what it would be like to have a situationship with someone like her. She's so down-to-earth and intuitive. She's easy to be around. And I like the way her brain works—which is the strangest compliment I've ever given to someone of the opposite sex.

The male actor shoves the woman against the wall, and they start making out.

"Oh, he's doing the wall lean thing. Ugh, that's so hot," she mutters.

I raise my eyebrows, entertained by how captivated she is by on-screen romance. For someone who suddenly hates marriage, she sure enjoys romantic gestures. The background music is right where it needs to be, hot and heavy. The characters move it to the bedroom. This pound-town soundtrack only makes me want to fuck her more. The heated friction between us isn't helping. We get a view of the woman's naked back as she rides him, and she throws her head back—naturally, her hair is the same color as Jordan's. I'm being punished by the universe.

The scene seems to go on and on. I scrub a hand down my face. Once the sex wraps up, we're back to car chases and vehicles exploding into giant fiery plumes. I adjust myself and refuse to look at her for the rest of the movie. First thing I will do after this ends, is take a shower and drain my balls. *Again.*

Finally, the main character saves the day and gets the girl —lucky fucker. The credits roll and she stands up, folding the blanket and tossing it back into the basket of throws and pillows.

She clears her throat, looking like she's about to say something. "Um, so I wanted to apologize earlier. I know I tend to change the subject when we start talking about every-thing, I'm not dismissing you, I really appreciate your honesty and giving me the reminder."

"Anytime."

"And thanks for letting me crash here. It won't be much longer. I've been looking at apartments, and a couple look promising. I've emailed to set up tours. This isn't the most convenient arrangement for you, but I'm really grateful you're letting me invade your space."

She's already found a place? That was fast.

I stand and stretch. "It's fine. Please, take up space, Jordan . . . Are you going to bed?"

"Yeah."

I walk toward the doorway with her. Our hands brush, and she peers up at me. Her gaze drops to my lips, and I'm done for. Electricity rides up my spine, and I react without thinking. I pull her into me, my lips crash into hers, and she grips my shirt with both hands. Her scent permeates the air. I love it. Clean and crisp.

She gasps, and I take advantage of her open mouth to

taste her. I'd do anything to hear a gasp like that again. I swipe my tongue across hers. She tastes like toothpaste and *her.* My hand slides in her hair, then she moves her mouth in tandem with mine. This woman can kiss. Hard nipples brush against my chest, and I walk her backward into the doorframe. Her lips are perfectly matched with mine. She smells like heaven, and tastes just as good. It's not enough. I want her legs around my waist and my cock buried deep.

After two steps, she pushes against my chest, and it's like a rain cloud opens up and douses the embers smoldering between us. Our kiss goes up in smoke.

"Sorry . . . I don't know what happened," she stammers.

The kiss of my life happened.

Realizing she's still holding onto my shirt, Jordan shoves off me like I scalded her. She runs a hand through her hair, straightening it where it was ruffled from my palm.

She covers her mouth and looks around like she's about to bolt.

I drop my arms to my sides. "Jordan—"

Her face is screwed up like she's disappointed in herself. The way she closes up so quickly is disheartening. For a moment, she let go and gave herself what she wanted. She kissed me back with as much tenacity as I had. She was into it. Getting to experience this other side of her felt monumental.

"I didn't mean to. I had wine earlier and—"

"So, you can't kiss me unless you're drunk?" I cut in.

"No, I mean . . . it's not—I can't do that!"

"Jordan, it's okay. I kissed you first. It's on me."

Her fingers press her pink, swollen lips, and she narrows her eyes. "Why the hell did you kiss me?"

I shrug and tell the truth. "I wanted to."

"You can't just go around and kiss people! You have to ask!" Her manicured nail points at my chest. I snatch up her wrists.

My lopsided grin gives away how turned on I am by her feistiness. "I've asked consent for a lot of things, but never for a kiss."

"Well, you should start." She rips herself out of my grasp and storms off with her arms crossed. It wasn't a big deal.

"It's just a kiss, Jordan. Relax," I say as she stomps off.

The lies I tell myself. Kissing Jordan was like nothing I've ever experienced before, and I've experienced a lot. None have made me feel what I did with her.

TWELVE

Jordan

There's no way in hell I'm sleeping tonight. Not after that. I'm pacing back and forth in the kitchenette of his bonus apartment. I feel more alive than I have in a long time. I'm energized and light and . . . *fuck, I'm so horny.* Some kisses you always remember: your first kiss, your first hot-and-heavy kiss, the kiss from your first love, and the one from Camden Teller. Dear god, no wonder women flock to him.

CAMDEN TELLER

Sorry.

I haven't kissed anyone since Bryan. Just caught me off guard, that's all.

Had I known a kiss from him would be like that, I never would have allowed it. Now that I've had a taste of him, I want to feel like this all the time. I want to feel invigorated, feel the blood pumping through my veins. It was cruel of him to make me feel so good, especially when it can't happen again.

CAMDEN TELLER

I'll ask before I kiss you next time.

Why is he making this so difficult? I bring my fingers to my lips again and close my eyes, allowing myself to relive the whole thing. Sparks are firing throughout my body, and I forget to breathe as I recall the way his lips moved against mine. I saw stars. The brief kiss with Cam turned me on more than any sex I ever had with Bryan.

He has to know this was a mistake, one we can't repeat. I wish things were less complicated. . . Damn him, I was fine before! I had no problem being in his vicinity, then he had to say all those nice things during our heart-to-heart earlier today. Honesty is so hard to come by these days. And all the stolen glances. And the kiss. Now what?

There's no next time. I can't get involved with anybody right now.

That fucking kiss. It made me forget every ugly disaster in my life—it was pure bliss. I surrendered to the moment and actually let go for once. He tasted so good. I rummage through the cupboard until I find my precious bag of Sour Patch Kid gummies, then stuff a handful in my mouth. I need to get him off my tongue.

CAMDEN TELLER

Who said anything about being involved?
I'm just talking about a kiss.

We need to keep things platonic. Just friends.

CAMDEN TELLER

Friends can make out platonically.

I can't.

CAMDEN TELLER

K.

My heart sinks a little. I don't want to say no, but my brain says having a repeat of tonight would be a bad idea. My vagina vehemently disagrees. Our kiss was hungry and desperate and overwhelming.

Thankfully, I've already started looking for a new place to live. I need to put some distance between us. This was not supposed to happen. Until I move, I'll lock myself in my room and never come out.

CAMDEN TELLER

What time do you want to get your stuff tomorrow?

Ah, fuck. I have to see him tomorrow. Embarrassing as it is, I'm not chancing going alone. I'll risk my pride before my safety.

Can you meet me there at 3? I've got a couple apartment viewings, but I should be done by then. I'd like to get my things and be out as fast as possible.

CAMDEN TELLER

I'll be there.

I grab another handful of sour gummies and shove them in my mouth like popcorn as I walk to the bathroom. I need a cold shower.

Even as the cool water sluices over me, my body is red hot. I can't get the butterflies to fly away. Twenty minutes later, my phone dings while I'm pulling on some clean clothes. *Ones without his scent on them.*

CAMDEN TELLER

You're a good kisser.

Is he still thinking about it too?

Not my type.

CAMDEN TELLER

You are so full of shit.

Goodnight Teller.

Both hands come up and slap my cheeks. "It's a stupid fucking kiss, Jordan! Get over it!"

I flop onto the bed with my arms open wide.

"I'm so full of shit," I mumble. Fuck.

THIRTEEN

Jordan

There's a mandatory weekly meeting, so unfortunately, no working from home today. On the way to H&H, I pull into a cheap hotel and turn my phone on. I need to check my messages. I've been off the grid for four days and the texts and missed calls make my notifications pop up back-to-back.

There are sixty-three messages from Bryan, the most recent one seems to be an apology, but I ignore the rest. He and I are beyond done. I refuse to open a line of communication with him. Thankfully, my meeting is the same day Bryan has his own mandatory meeting with his father and clients off-site—far away from the corporate campus.

When I arrive, I swipe my badge at the turnstile. Oddly, it flashes red instead of green. I walk through anyway. Alarms blare, but nobody pays attention. It happens at least a couple times a day. With around five thousand employees, there are always a few who forget and/or lose their IDs. Other times, the badge readers are glitchy, like today. No big deal. I swing by the security desk to see the friendly face of a woman I've gotten to know over the years. I'm glad Barb is working today, I like her.

"Morning, Barb, the badge reader is acting up. Are you able to log me in manually?"

"Sure! What's your ID?"

I rattle off my nine-digit corporate ID. "121908603." She types it in and furrows her brow.

"Sorry, give it to me again."

I repeat the number slower this time. She looks up at me with sympathetic eyes.

"Um . . ."

I cock my head to the side. "Is there a problem?"

"Jordan, I'm going to need your laptop and badge."

"What? Why?" There's only one reason you have to turn in your laptop and badge. I just don't want to believe it's happening to me.

"It says you've been terminated."

"But I still have laptop access. I'm in the middle of a project."

She shakes her head. "I'm sorry. I'm just doing my job." I don't want to give Barb a hard time, she's a sweet woman.

"Um, okay. Can I—please, let me send a resignation letter first."

She looks around and bites her lip. My eyes plead with her.

"You can keep the laptop until John shows up, he's on his way down to escort you to gather the things from your desk."

My eyebrows shoot to my forehead, shocked and hurt. "I don't need an escort, Barb."

She glances at the computer and cringes. "You're flagged for it."

He's trying to humiliate me. Hardly anyone gets an escort,

only the most disgruntled employees who they anticipate making a scene. He knew I'd be coming in today, knew I'd show up, then get walked around the campus by security to collect my things like some pathetic parade of shame. *Well, fuck if I'm gonna help him do that.* I won't give him the satisfaction. I mentally inventory the items at my desk. There's nothing I can't live without.

I log into the laptop, thankful IT hasn't pulled my credentials yet. Sitting on a padded bench along the wall, out of sight, I quickly copy the files I want to a flash drive. I'm not ready to give up the project I was working on, there's something off about it. I want to make sure I have copies of the work I did in case he tries to throw me under the bus later on. Once the files are synced, I pocket the flash drive and close the lid. Standing, I slide it—*and my badge*—across the desk to Barb.

"Have security throw out my things."

She winces. "Jordan, I'm so sorry, it's—"

I turn and hold up my hand. "It's your job. I understand. Take care of yourself, Barb. Don't let anyone around here give you shit." I force a smile on my face.

I'm an impeccable employee. I've got a plaque with my fucking name on it for Christ's sake. I didn't deserve this. I'm sure the memo of my termination will be emailed shortly. That'll go over well with my team. We're already understaffed for projects as it is. I can get another job. It was only a matter of time anyway, I couldn't continue working for the Davenports' company, I knew that. I trudge back to the parking garage with my head held high.

I climb back in my car and ignore my trembling hands, reminding myself it has nothing to do with my job performance. My clients love me, my team loves me, I did nothing wrong.

He's a vindictive asshole who wants me to suffer. That's why I was fired.

As I exit the ramp, the gate lifts, and I can't wait to get the hell away from this place. Cut one more tie with the Davenports. The farther I get away from them, the better. This is simply one more step in the right direction. Still, it's strange to think I don't work here anymore. I've worked at H&H Holdings for six years. I started as an intern before I graduated college.

Less than ten minutes ago, my brain was going over the clients I needed to call today, the updates I would give in the team meeting. I was brainstorming a new strategy for the legal project I was tasked with—the one I'll investigate more. And now I'm driving back home because I was fired before I could even walk in the door? I'm in a trance as I drive out of the parking garage. I guess I'll go back to Camden's. My mind goes on autopilot as I rethink every life choice I've ever made.

I'm two blocks from the corporate campus when sirens blare. My rearview mirror flickers with blue and red lights.

"Wunderbar," I say with a scoff as I pull to the side of the street.

Damn it, I probably forgot to use my blinker or something. My thoughts are all over the place. Time to focus, Jordan.

I roll down my window, and when I look up, there's an officer with his hand on his gun. *Really? Is that necessary?* It takes every bit of my strength not to roll my eyes.

"Hands on the wheel."

I do as he asks but turn to glare at him. "What's the problem, officer?"

"ID and registration."

"I'll have to take my hands off the wheel to get my purse."

"That's fine." He nods to the bag in the seat next to me.

I reach for my wallet, unzip the billfold, and slide out the documentation. Oh, I am *so* going to fuck up an entire pan of brownies when I get home. I'd like to submit my official hatred for this day.

"Turn off the vehicle, please."

Again, I follow this stupid Simon-Says bullshit and do as he asks. He returns to his cop car, and within five minutes, he's back at my window. "This vehicle isn't registered to you."

"Yes it is. It's my car."

"This car is registered to Bryan Davenport and has been reported stolen. If an error has been made, we can discuss it later, but for now the car will be impounded and you'll be placed under arrest."

My jaw drops and my eyes nearly bulge out of my head. This isn't happening.

"Officer"—I glance at his nametag—"Bradshaw. Look, my fiancé bought me this vehicle. We broke up, I did not steal the car, you can have it. But please don't arrest me."

"I'm just doing my job," he says with his hand on his hip.

"So they keep telling me . . ." I mutter under my breath.

"Excuse me?"

I shake my head and formulate a new plan. I've never once used my name to get what I want, but it's all I've got.

"Who donated your new fleet of vehicles last year at the fundraiser? The Landry Foundation, right?"

He cocks his head and drops his gaze to my driver's license.

Come on, Gomer Pyle. Two plus two equals four.

"I heard Mayor Campbell cut the department's annual budget last month."

He pauses, narrowing his eyes at me. I release a breath

when he turns off his body camera. "Nearly ten percent," he gruffs.

Now we're getting somewhere. "I'm not great at math, but I'm guessing that's . . . what, about twelve million?"

He looks around as if someone might be watching, then shifts his weight and nods once. "Something like that."

"That must be frustrating. Sixteen is my lucky number. Will I see you at the fundraising gala in a few weeks?" I smile.

The wheels in his head are turning, but it's clear he's conflicted. I wonder if Bryan bribed him to arrest me, and now I'm bribing him not to. Nah, knowing Bryan, he probably threatened and asked for a superior when he made the report of a *stolen vehicle*. You catch more flies with honey.

I relax my shoulders. "Look, take the car. Impound it. I don't care. But don't arrest me, it's unnecessary. This has been a huge waste of your time due to an angry ex-fiancé, and I apologize that it's impacted your day. He can have the car. I'm happy to walk away from it. I think we can agree minimizing this traffic stop will be less paperwork for both of us."

My heart is racing. I cannot get arrested. I will have a mental breakdown on the spot if this guy puts me in cuffs, and that's probably what Bryan requested. He probably told them I was violent when he reported it stolen. He could have said anything he wanted about me. Thank God my family padded the budget for those new vehicles last year.

He's studying me. My luck could go either way.

"I promise, I'm not a menace to society." I give a small chuckle, trying to appear as least threatening as I can, as if to say, "*What a gas! Can you believe this silly little mix-up we've found ourselves in*!"

He nods. "Yeah, that's fine." He opens my door. "The department appreciates your donation, Ms. Landry."

I grab my purse, and he hands me back my ID.

"I appreciate your discretion."

"Can I drive you to the bus station?" He offers.

I'm not getting on a bus; I don't even know how the public transportation system works. I'll take a rideshare.

"I'll walk. Do I leave the keys with you?"

"You can leave them in the car."

"Fabulous." I throw them on the floor of the vehicle and shut the door, stepping onto the sidewalk.

"Have an outstanding rest of your day, officer." My response is dripping with sarcasm, but he lets me get away with it, and the side of his mouth tips up in a smirk. I'm sure he recognizes I'm having a bad day, but there's nothing he can do about it.

"You too, Ms. Landry." As I hoof it down the sidewalk, I find a bench and sit down. Pulling out my phone, I open the rideshare app. "Wonder if I can get my driver to stop at the liquor store first," I say to myself.

A text message flashes across the screen.

BRYAN DAVENPORT

Ready to come home yet?

I pretend I didn't see it and open the rideshare app to request a car.

Payment declined. *What the fuck?*

I switch the payment method.

JP Morgan Reserve. Declined.

AmEx Black. Declined.

Did he deactivate my cards? The problem with ultra-wealthy people is we don't "have" money, because having money costs money. We have assets, liabilities, and commodities. Any transaction is done with an equity line of credit, a loan secured against a financial portfolio. As long as my portfolio returns more than the interest on my credit, everything's copacetic. The downside of this is rarely having any liquid money or cash.

This is ridiculous. As fast as I can, I open my banking app to check my finances.

Password declined. No. No way. Tears well in my eyes. That's *my* money.

"Don't cry. Not yet. Get back to Cam's, then you can lose your shit."

Camden's phone rings and rings, eventually going to voicemail. He'll be on the ice all morning. I can't wait here. It's not safe. I have no idea what Bryan has up his sleeve, maybe he's close, waiting to find me alone on this bench. Okay. How do I get back without money? I grab my wallet and check for cash. None, so much for using paper money to get a ride. I've got coins . . . four dollars and thirty-seven cents worth. Forgetting to clean out my wallet is about to pay off—literally.

Buses take cash, don't they? I google how to ride the bus in Minneapolis. Holy hell. This map looks like someone shat out rainbow spaghetti. The lines blur together. Thankfully, there's a route planner, so I type in Camden's address. I memorized it. Okay, 540 to 6. 6 to 46C. That will get me to the library, which is the closest I can get for the money in my wallet. After that, I'll still have to walk five-point-three miles to his house, but I'll do it. I'll take every goddamn step, because fuck Bryan Davenport.

He thinks I'll give up. That I'll come crawling home because I've got my back against the wall. Never. I'll do it for the sheer pleasure of pissing him off.

"I just need to get back to Cam's. I can do this. I can do this," I whisper to myself.

I can't believe I'm psyching myself up over a bus ride.

I push all the other shit out of my mind and focus on solving my first problem: transportation. My eyes check the time. If I don't hurry, I'll miss the next bus.

I turn off my phone and hustle to the nearest stop. I'm not giving Bryan the satisfaction of watching my location bounce from bus station to bus station or giving away where I'm staying.

As I arrive, a bus pulls up, right on time, number 540. I almost jump for joy, that's *my* bus—and it's here! Exactly like the internet said it would be. I'm annoyed at my privilege, millions of people do this every day, but right now I don't care. It's the first thing that's gone right for me today, and I'm taking my wins where I can get them.

The driver opens the door and two people get on before me, all of them have these yellow cards. Uh oh, do I need a special card?

"Do you take coins?"

The driver nods.

I grab a handful of quarters and feed them into the slot, someone behind me sighs loudly, irritated I'm holding up the line. I find a seat near the window and pay attention to the number of stops and my location so I know where I need to get off.

Two more buses later, I'm standing at the library. The bus departs, leaving me in a cloud of exhaust fumes. I find my bearings and remember the map I made in my head.

Now, I have to walk.

In heels.

Over five miles.

I'm not turning my phone back on to try and call Cam. I'm too paranoid. Instead, I let my mind wander. Unfortunately, it's stuck on one channel, replaying the morning I've had. I'm exhausted.

Even though I don't deserve it, shame clings to me like a gross film on my skin. As if everyone around me can see what a failure I am.

The dam of emotion behind my eyes weakens with each step. This isn't a nightmare I'll wake from. This is happening —*I let this happen.* The tears build in my eyes until they roll down my cheeks.

"You can cry until you reach the next stop sign. Then you're done."

FOURTEEN

Jordan

By the time I hit the halfway mark, my feet throb and the flesh is raw at my achilles. *How am I only half-way?* There were sidewalks in the beginning of my trek, but those ended a while ago, so I've been walking along the shoulder. I look like a hitchhiker. If someone stopped, I'd probably take the ride. It's tempting to turn my phone back on, but with each step closer to Camden's house, the more dangerous that becomes. I can't continue in these heels, they hurt too much. When I peel them off, my feet are swollen and bleeding.

"Shit." I stuff the shoes in my purse, and the cold ground feels soothing. The only way to get home is one damn foot in front of the other. Eventually, my feet will go numb and it won't hurt anymore. *Keep moving.*

As soon as I take the first step, the gravel on the road is hell. Something about that step flips a switch in my brain, and almost instantly my sadness turns into rage. It's as if every dig, every infraction, every *Jordana* from Bryan's lips are tossed in the pile of shame filling my thoughts. I let it build and build until I finally douse the heap in gasoline and strike a match to watch the whole thing go up in a blazing inferno.

He pushed too hard. He took too much. He went too far.

I snap. Now it's my turn. The night he hurt me, all I wanted was to be free of him, but being free isn't enough anymore—he needs to know what this feels like, this hopelessness. I want him to hurt. I want him to *fear me*.

Being a villain sounds like more fun than being a victim.

I imagine his smug smile, thinking he's got me under his thumb. Doesn't he know an animal is most dangerous when cornered? I welcome the dark thoughts in my mind. Camden's right, I don't need to play nice anymore. I will start by making good on that hefty donation to the police department . . . Bryan may have started this war, but I will finish it.

The numbness kicks in, and my feet don't hurt as much. I come up with a list of things he values most: money, reputation, comfort, and power. *I'm taking them all.*

Fuck what I said to Camden in the coffeeshop. I won't rock the boat, I'll sink it.

When my gaze lands on the attractive brick security post of Camden's gated neighborhood in the distance, I smile. After wiping my eyes, I put on a fresh coat of lip gloss and attempt to freshen my face. Last stretch.

My feet are dirty, blistered, and bleeding. When I get about fifty feet away, I slip the heels back on so I can get by the security guard without looking suspicious or in need of medical care. I just want to be alone. I got this far, I can take myself the rest of the way.

I made up some bullshit story to the attendant and showed him my ID. The gate closes behind me, and I smile.

"You badass bitch. You fuckin' did it." I start laughing, which turns into more frenzied cackling. As soon as I tap the code into Cam's gate, I feel like a powerful goddess.

"Your days are numbered, Bryan." I took back my independence today. I didn't give up. That has to count for something.

As suspected, Cam isn't home. I hobble into the mud room and throw one of my legs over the edge of the utility sink.

"Ow, ow, ow!" Wincing when the water hits my open wounds, I brush away the caked dirt and dried blood. I repeat it with the other foot. The first cabinet I open has a pile of cleaning rags, so I wrap my feet in them and limp to the stairs. The extra padding feels like I'm walking on a cloud. As soon as I'm in the safety of my own space, I exhale.

In the bathroom, I strip off my clothes and let them land wherever. My second shower of the day is much longer than the first. I sit on my ass while I tend to my feet again. Sitting for a while, I let the water wash away the dark thoughts. *For now.* After I get out, I put on some workout shorts and a sports bra and enter Cam's room. I find the first aid kit and wrap up my injuries, then dig through his closet to steal a shirt and the thickest pair of socks I can find.

"Poor little rich girl had to take public transportation and walk in her heels," I mutter. "And she's got twelve whole cents leftover! Book the cruise." I have no idea how to fix my life. It's a festering, flaming shitfest. However, I know where I'm gonna start: *brownies*.

FIFTEEN

Camden

I shoot a puck into the sideboards as hard as I can. This is so fucked. We need to switch the lineup. Our next games are against teams who are dominating this season. As of today's practice, there's no way we'll walk away without getting destroyed next week. The coaches are equally frustrated, but they won't listen to me. Their pride is ridiculous. I'm annoyed and sick of their shit.

"Banksy, you coming?" Jonesy calls from the tunnel.

I shake my head. "No. I gotta skate." Really, I'm trying to kill some time and gear up for my fight with the coaches after the guys have left the locker room. We can't go into our next game like this.

The defense coordinator put our defensemen Dean Burmeister and Cory Dopson together in the lineup, and it's been a nightmare since. Cory and Dean couldn't find their way out of a paper bag if they relied on each other. We've tried teambuilding shit, but some guys don't play well together, and you can't force it.

I bag skate back and forth, angrily slapping more pucks into the boards. It's been about a half hour since practice ended, and the longer I skate, the worse I feel. They don't trust the captain to know his own guys, and it pisses me off.

When I stomp off the ice, I smash my stick into the wall, breaking it in half. There. That feels a little better.

I remove my pads and skates in the locker room. Under the shower spray, I play out my argument, anticipating what he will say. I enjoy my shower fights; they always go in my favor. After I towel off and throw my gear in my bag, I stalk down the admin hall to the head coach's office.

I knock on the open door, and the defense coach is leaning against the wall, chatting with him. He pushes off it and stands when I walk in. Good, they're both here.

"Look, I know you're sick of seeing my face. I'm sick of seeing yours too. But we gotta talk about the defense line."

Coach sighs. "Teller. Here to bust my balls again?"

"Hey, if you didn't want me to care, you should've given me *his* job instead of captain." I nod to the assistant coach.

"First off, you need to take it down a notch. You're coming in real hot, and I'm not above swapping captains if you can't keep this attitude in check—"

"Do it. I dare you."

He rolls his eyes. He's used to my bullshit. If it were anyone else, he'd probably can their ass on the spot. ". . . Second, we have coaches who measure skill sets, they have it down to a science. What makes you think you're smarter than them, Teller? Huh? I get you're a fucking hotshot out there, but you still need to respect the role you're in and respect the roles of the rest of the organization."

The defense coach crosses his arm over his chest, getting comfy now that the head coach covered his ass.

"You can measure data all you want, but I'm the one on the ice with them. I'm the one at the bars after the game with them. I'm the one sitting on the plane next to them. I know them better than you *or* your fucking coaches." I point to the secondary coach without looking at him. I want to punch him. He switched up the line so he could try to flaunt his bullshit numbers. Yes, on paper Burmeister and Dopson should work, but it doesn't translate on the ice. "Burmeister needs to defend with Paek."

"And what about Cory?" the other coach interrupts.

I throw my hands up in the air and look back and forth between them. *Seriously?* "Cory Dopson and Elsworth played in college together!" I bark out. "They can read each other like a book!"

Coach hangs his head between his shoulders before looking up at me and rubbing his brow. "Teller," he says, exasperated.

"Hey, you want to prove me wrong so bad? Fucking do it! If I'm wrong, let me eat shit, I'll take the blame. But it ain't gonna happen."

I march back into the locker room, throw my bag over my shoulder, and walk out.

SIXTEEN

Jordan

In the kitchen, I sit on a stool as I mix ingredients and slide a tray in the oven. *Step one, fudge brownies. Step two, get drunk.* I reach into the wine fridge, feeling around for a bottle. My fingers wrap around the neck of the first one I touch, then I pull it out, uncork the bottle, and take three very healthy gulps from the rim.

"I owe Camden Teller one bottle of whatever this is," I announce, then glance at the label. "Ah, a Riesling. Lovely."

Forty minutes later, Cam comes home from practice. I'm three-quarters of the way through the wine and halfway through the nine-by-twelve pan of chocolate heaven. At least, I think it's half. It's not like I've started on one end of the pan and am working across. No, I'm plunging my fork wherever it lands. The whole pan is mine, who cares where I start? He walks in to me sitting on his sofa watching reality TV.

What stage of grief is binging brownies, wine, and RuPaul's Drag Race*? Is it the one before or after bargaining? I can never remember.*

He looks surprised to see me. "Hey. Saw you called. Sorry, didn't have my phone on me."

The silly straw in my wine bottle spins around the rim, and I struggle to get my lips around it for a drink. When I finally take a sip, it makes a sucking noise, unable to reach the wine at the bottom of the bottle. I pluck out the now-useless straw. "Well, that's disappointing," I mutter.

He gets closer and jerks his head back. "Whoa. What happened to you?"

"Oh!" I respond with the most facetious smile I can manage. "I'm having a horrible fucking day! Would you care to join me, sir? It's BYOB." I hold my breath to burp. "Want my straw?" I offer it to him.

He cautiously sets down his gym bag. "Why?"

"Because everything is better with a silly straw!"

"Jordan. Stop." He grabs the remote off the table and pauses my show, then takes a seat on the coffee table in front of me—blocking my view. *Rude*. It was getting to my favorite part!

"Dick! Put it back—they're sissying that walk! It's Mermaid Fantasy Extravaganza. I *need* to see this." I shove another bite of brownies into my mouth and gesture with my fork. "Trixie's our bitch, she's gonna slay this shit," I say with my mouth full. Hopefully, the muffling hides my slurred speech.

He raises his eyebrows, gives a paused blink, and blows out a breath. "How much have you had to drink?"

"Not near enough." I take another pull from the bottle, bummed I no longer have my fun plastic orange straw.

"Okay, tell me what happened."

I hiccup. "Pass."

"No, you're done deflecting. You gotta face your problems."

"I've faced them, Cam!" I throw my arms out to the sides,

wine sloshes inside the bottle as I emphasize my words. "All morning!"

He furrows his brow. "I thought you were at work. And where is your car?"

I raise the bottle of wine into the air victoriously. "At the impound!"

"Why is it at the impound?" he asks with furrowed brows.

"That's what happens when you steal a car," I answer in the same cadence. "Which, apparently, I did."

"Wait—"

"Thankfully, dear ol' dad funded the department for a slew of new vehicles last year. It helped convince the officer to not arrest me. Well, that, and I may have bribed him. Shit, I'm on fire." I almost forgot that even happened. I laugh and take another sip and wipe my mouth with my arm. "I was almost arrested!" I laugh.

He squints at me. "Stolen? So, wait, how did you get home?"

"Buses, baby! I got to the library and walked from there."

He stands and points out the window, shouting. "The library is miles from here!"

Duh, didn't he hear me when I said I walked it?

"I'm aware, thank you." I point to my feet.

He slowly sits again and lifts my ankles, setting my sock-covered feet in his lap. The movement makes me wince.

"Jesus. Got any other good news, Sunshine?"

"Sure do! It gets better. I tried to pay for a rideshare, hence the bus, but he deactivated all my cards—Oh! And I was fired." My eyes burn with tears. "It's been a hoot-and-a-half," I say with a cracked voice.

"*What*?" His hands flex and jaw tics.

The sadness returns as I say the words aloud. I smile, but my eyes are filled to the brim. "I have no money, no job, no car. I'm having a bad fucking day, Cam." I shake my head, feeling the weight of the tears return.

Now, more than ever, I want to sabotage Bryan. One final, *Fuck you. Love, Jordan.*

My voice comes out scratchy and angry. "This is why they stay, isn't it? How do women leave if they don't have anyone? How the fuck do they do it?"

He peels the rolled-up socks off my feet and sucks in a breath. *He should have seen them before, when they resembled hamburger meat.* "Jesus—fucking—Christ."

"Ya know what's funny?" I tap my fork against my lips. "I always thought I was independent. I wasn't. It was a ruse." I treasure another gulp from the bottle, it's mostly empty. "I was so stupid. Bryan's had his claws in every part of my life. This whole time he's been giving me the illusion of control, but it was simply a leash with a long lead. With the snap of his fingers, it was all taken away."

I stab my fork into the pan of brownies, then stuff it in my mouth. I can't imagine what I must look like. At least after today, I know Cam won't be attracted to me anymore. Drunk, red swollen eyes, and hair I never bothered to brush after my shower. That's one less problem on my plate.

"Have you talked to your parents?"

With my shoulders held back, I lock my eyes with him. "No. I'm fixing my own problems this time."

"You're not thinking about going back, are you?"

I think about the taunting text message I saw from Bryan that came through as I was shutting down my phone. *"Ready to come home yet?"*

"No."

"Good . . . you know what you need?"

"To get laid?" I mumble into my mess of brownies. The

pan looks like an excavation site, peppered with random holes.

"Oh, did you finally decide I'm your type? I was gonna say go for a ride, but we can do that too."

I purse my lips and stare at him. "Is a ride on the back of your motorcycle going to help me get a job and avoid my ex?"

He sighs. "No, but it'll take your mind off it for a little while. And afterward, once you've eaten some real food and not this shit"—he snatches my tray of brownies away—"and gotten a good night's sleep, you might be able to look at the bright side."

I bark out a laugh and reach for the brownie pan. "What bright side? En*light*en me."

Ever so slowly, the corner of his mouth tips up. "That this is the best thing to ever fucking happen to you. He's cutting you off." He leans forward, and his intense hazel eyes bore into me. "Let him."

Sitting back in my seat, I stare at him and consider his statement. I didn't think about it that way. When I finally pull my gaze away, I press my palms to my eye sockets, surely smudging whatever mascara is left on my lashes.

"It's like he's trying to start a war," I huff.

"As long as you don't go back, he'll never win. Like *Braveheart*, ya know?" He breaks out the worst Scottish accent I've ever heard. "You can take our jobs, our credit cards, and our Lexuses, but you'll never take our freedom!"

The corner of my mouth tips up. "Hm. I almost forgot about that time when thirteenth century Scotland went to battle for their luxury sedans and corporate careers. William Wallace and I are basically the same person."

"You're way hotter than William Wallace."

I tip my bottle at him. "But am I hotter than Mel Gibson?" I try to take a sip but, sadly, it's empty.

"No, I'm sorry."

That makes me laugh. It's my first, nonmaniacal laugh of the day.

He smiles back, pleased with himself.

"Come here." He wraps me up in a big hug, and I let him.

"You're not my type," I quip.

"I'm everybody's type." With his mouth pressed to my hair, he says, "I guess we're not getting your stuff today."

"Nope. And no checking out apartments . . . No seeing Chicken Salad . . ." Bryan torpedoed all my plans.

"What do you need?"

I speak my truth. "I need my brownies back."

He pulls away with a half grin.

"Okay, Sunshine." He hands me the tray, and I dig in with my fork. They don't taste as good anymore. "Let me get you something for your feet, though."

I hit play on the TV and finish watching the queens roll through their runway looks. As I predicted, Trixie Mattel gets top marks. For the first time, escaping reality isn't as satisfying, but at the end of the episode, RuPaul looks at the camera, and I swear she's speaking directly to me: "If you can't love yourself, how in the hell are you going to love somebody else?"

"Can I get an amen?" I respond monotone.

Cam returns with salve, places my feet in his lap again, and inspects them. As soon as he unscrews the jar, the smell invades my nose, and I turn my head away. "Fuck, dude! *What* is *that?* It smells horrible!"

He laughs. "Yeah, it stinks, but it works wonders. I use it when I'm breaking in new skates."

"Ach! It's gross."

"Your *feet* are fucking gross," he says, rubbing them. *It smells like death, but God, it feels so good.*

"Shut up. After these toes heal, you're going to buy me a pedicure to apologize for that mean remark."

He winks. "Deal."

I gag at the smell once more but let him do the other foot.

SEVENTEEN

Jordan

It's been a week since I lost everything. Cam has been the one by my side to help me wade through the putrid swamp that is my life. I've been trying to be as helpful as possible around the house. Laundry, cooking, keeping the place clean and tidy wherever I can. It's difficult, considering he has people he pays to do those things. I've washed and folded all the shirts I've borrowed. When I go to return them, his bedroom door is cracked. I knock, but there's no answer. I push the door open and freeze.

He's got his headphones on.

And that's it.

He's naked. *Completely naked.* Dropping my gaze to his pierced, Pringle-can dick, I gasp like the wind has been knocked out of me. I press a hand to my chest as if I transformed into a southern belle clutching her goddamn pearls. He's walking across the room like it's no big deal. His eyes reach mine, and he grins.

"Oh my god!" I shout.

Once I'm able to tear my eyes away, I grab the doorknob and slam the door to the sound of him laughing his ass off. I cover my mouth, even though I'm certain my jaw is still on the floor. The whole interaction was only a matter of seconds, but it felt like I was staring at it for minutes. *Fucking sue me. A built, tatted up, hot-as-hell hockey player—you're telling me you wouldn't look at his giant pierced penis?*

"Sorry! I, um, I'm leaving the clothes outside your door. 'Kay, thanks!"

"Sounds good," he chirps, a smile in his voice. He sounds proud of himself. To be fair, he should be. What did I see? *How many piercings was that?*

Just my luck that he's home for the next *four* days. That won't make things awkward. I roll my eyes.

I try not to think about what sex is like for all the women he sleeps with. He had some serious hardware going on. What does it feel like? Is he a generous lover? I've heard big dicks can be selfish, as if the size makes up for their lack of effort. Ugh! I'll never be able to get the image out of my head.

I shoot off an email to my lawyer and financial manager to get a meeting set up. I need to get my finances back in order as soon as possible so I can move out of here.

EIGHTEEN

Jordan

I'm prepping dinner—thought I'd make shepherd's pie —when Cam walks into the kitchen wearing a T-shirt and gray sweatpants, which outline his cock perfectly —*it has to be intentional.* The sweatpants aren't what kills me. It's when he sidles up next to me and flips his baseball cap backward to help with food prep. I'm an absolute slut for a backward ballcap. I press my lips together and close my eyes, gathering my strength. We stand in uncomfortable silence, save for the chopping of our knives.

He's the first one to break the tension. "So . . . I'm off for the next four days."

I nod. "That's nice. Plans for anything fun?"

"I dunno, I mean, you're here. I figured we could hang."

I scrunch my nose. "And do what? I'm a boring hang, and my feet still hurt. You should go out and get some strange."

"Some strange?" He laughs. "Nah. Honestly, I've had more fun here lately . . . Wanna get high?"

I laugh. I don't think I've gotten high since college. *Not since Bryan warned me never to do it again.*

"Don't you have drug tests and stuff?"

"It's legal and not performance-enhancing, and as long as it doesn't affect my playing, they look the other way."

Huh, that's interesting. Well, count me in. I'm enjoying my rebellious streak. "All right, I'm down. Are you an edibles guy, or are we jumping straight into bong rips?"

"I'm old-fashioned, I like to roll my own."

"Fancy."

We chat about his upcoming games next week and where he'll be traveling. I tell him about the companies I've been looking at. This time I want to find a career that's a good fit for me. I've never needed to work, but I like it, it gives me purpose. Which is why it's been so tough since leaving H&H.

After the shepherd's pie is put together and in the oven, he cracks a window in the living room and gets his gear. We sit down on the couch, and I watch him roll us a joint. His skilled fingers are meticulous as they delicately roll back and forth to balance the gram of cannabis in the hemp paper. When he's pleased with the size, he licks across the paper while looking up at me through hooded lids. The dark rings around his hazel eyes are more vivid than ever, and my cheeks heat. He's fucking with me because I walked in on him.

He sparks it, takes two hits, and passes it to me. My drags are much shallower. Based on the smell and how colorful the bud was, he's got the good shit. It's been a while, but I know quality weed when I see it. I'm pacing myself.

After easing into it, my shoulders relax. Time to get the elephant out of the room.

"So . . . Piercings, huh?"

He looks down and laughs. "Yeah."

So many questions roll around in my head. "Did they hurt?"

"A little pain once is worth a lot of pleasure later." He winks.

"Looked like the pain was more than *once*." There were at least five bars.

"It's not only me who benefits from them."

"You're such a whore," I say, chuckling and shaking my head. "Does it really make that big of a difference?"

"Want to find out?" he asks, raising his brows.

He looks away and takes another hit. It was a joke, but it's hard not to let my imagination run wild. He probably knows what he's doing. He's experienced, packing heat, and then there's the piercings . . .

I'm surprised I didn't see a sticker on his dick earlier that read *WARNING: ADVANCED COCK. NOT FOR BEGINNERS. FUCK AT YOUR OWN RISK.*

It might be nice. It's been so long since I've had good sex. *Have I ever had good sex?*

I don't know if it's the THC or the aftermath of the week, but I call his bluff. "Would you?"

His eyes snap back to mine. "Would I what?"

"Would you fuck me? If I asked you to?"

He stares at me for what seems like forever. His gaze travels over my body like a predator sizing up his hunt. "Yeah . . . Yeah, I would fuck you, Jordan. Is that something you want?"

"I mean, I'm a little curious what it's like." Not just the piercings, but what it would be like to have sex with someone who isn't Bryan. Maybe it's time I acted selfish. Besides, I'm not in a relationship. Why should I wait to jump into bed with someone? Bryan didn't. I don't need to justify my wants.

"If you think this is some kind of eye-for-an-eye thing with Bryan, you should know the sex you had with him would not be equivalent to a night with me."

I laugh. "You're very cocky." I reach my arm out, and he passes me the joint so I can take a drag.

"Shhh! That's my secret ingredient. It's what makes it so good."

I hold the smoke in my mouth, letting it cool before I open and inhale. I hand it back and roll my eyes.

He chuckles. "Do you have any piercings?"

"My ears." Another one of my wants pops into my mind. "But . . ."

A smile curves on his lips, and he makes a beckoning gesture with his hand. "Come on, safe space."

"I've always wanted to get my nipples pierced." I run my fingers over the top of my chest. "I hear it's good for sensation. Bryan would never—" I giggle. "Oh God, he was such a prude. He hates body modifications."

"So, I don't get it. Did you guys have sex and stuff?"

My head rears back. "Yeah, of course."

He nods, staring at me and narrowing his eyes. "He's a shitty lay, isn't he?"

"I have no idea."

He furrows his brow. "You don't know? Well, what's it like? I mean, your answer is pretty telling already."

"I dunno, it was . . . *normal*?" I shrug. "But there was this one thing he did, he liked to remind me over and over he was the dominant and I was the submissive—"

"Did you say he's a *dom?*"

"He said it." Bryan would mutter it repeatedly during sex.

"He's not a dom." He chuckles, dismissing the idea.

"How would you know?"

He leans forward. Damn, that backward ballcap is really working for him. His eyes search mine. "Because I'd never treat a partner the way he treated you. It's as much about *your* pleasure as it is his. Did you even like being submissive? Or was that some more shit he pushed on you?"

No one ever asked me if I liked it. Being submissive to Bryan was never discussed, it was something I went along with. *Did I like it?*

"Yes and no. I liked the *idea* of being submissive, I enjoyed the power exchange, but the way we had sex was the same every time. No foreplay, doggy-style, lights off. There was no variety. I always had to use my imagination to picture *other* things happening." Camden's throat bobs as he waits for me to continue. "I'd mentally change my setting, imagine him saying dirty things to me. And . . . ugh, this is so bad . . . sometimes I would even pretend there was someone else behind me." I crumple into my chair, ashamed. "I thought it would be different, you know?"

"Different how?"

"So, the doggy-style thing. We *only* fucked if he was behind me. If I ever made noise, he'd tell me to be quiet because it would mess up his concentration. He never forced me or anything like that, but it felt like pity sex. The sex itself felt fine, but we never had that *intense* connection. It wasn't like the stuff in books."

He shakes his head. "Fuck, Jordan. I'm sorry. That's awful."

I shrug, and he hands me the joint. *Doesn't matter anymore. I won't have to fuck someone like Bryan ever again.*

"So what have you read about? Is there stuff you want to try?"

Right away, a flush rises up my neck, and I giggle again. I take a hit, trying to stall.

He smirks. "Oh, it's kinky, isn't it? Come on, tell me."

I exhale the blue-tinted smoke and rattle off the bucket list I've memorized. "Breath play, blowjobs, kneeling, slapping, spitting, impact play, praise, some degradation, objectification, anal, being watched . . . being shared—I don't think I could actually go through with it, I'm too monogamous at heart, but the idea is thrilling and I enjoy a good *why choose*."

His jaw practically drops, and he laughs with raised eyebrows. He's not mocking me, simply amused.

"That's fucked up, Jordan! Not your kinks—that's great—but it's blowing my mind he never tried to give you *even one* of those things!" He winks at me and tips his chin up. "So . . . is that what you want, Sunshine?"

"Oh, shut up." I steal the joint back and watch the embers burn when I suck the smoke into my mouth. "Your turn. What kind of sex do *you* have?"

I glimpse at his joggers and try not to ogle, but I'm pretty sure this conversation is making him hard. Prying away my stare, our gazes meet again. There's a hunger in his eyes as he watches me. It makes my heart flip, pounding harder the longer he stares at me.

"It depends on who I'm with. I like to be in control, but only when I know she's getting off on it."

The way he talks about sex is so confident. I tilt my head to the side. "Are you good at sex?"

He laughs, but his smile is soft. He's actually trying to be humble for once in his life, which means he's probably gifted as fuck. "I think so." His gaze is so intense. "I bet you're good at it too."

I gulp and break eye contact. *I'm definitely not. I'm in my midtwenties and can count on one hand the number of blowjobs I've given.* "I don't have the experience you do. I don't know what I'm doing."

Cam gives a subtle head shake. "I don't buy it. I see how excited you are about trying new things—that's *everything*. Nothing is sexier than curiosity."

The warmth that spreads through me pools at my center.

"Shit, how the hell did Bryan ever snag someone like you? It doesn't make sense. If you were mine . . ." He shakes his head. "Did he at least make sure you came first?"

I know he means well by that question, but it makes me feel foolish and insecure.

Tugging down the cuffs of my sweatshirt, I curl deeper into the sofa, mumbling another embarrassing truth. "I can't come during sex."

He sighs, sounding annoyed. "Do you want to?"

I scowl in defense. "What the hell kind of question is that? Of course I do!"

"Have you ever had an orgasm?"

"Yes. I have no problem when I'm alone."

"How do you get yourself off?"

I hold up my hand and wiggle my fingers. "Or toys, but they were a point of contention in our relationship."

"He was threatened by a vibrator?"

"Something like that." It's funny when I think about it that way. Big tough Bryan scared of pink silicone penises.

He barks out a laugh and sits up. "Jesus, Jordan, how long has it been since you've been properly fucked?"

A flush rises in my cheeks. It's embarrassment, not arousal. Is it really that bad? A sad smile spreads across my face. *I'm beginning to think I've never been fucked properly.* "It's not that big of a deal. Sex isn't everything."

I pass the joint back to him. He takes a hit and studies my face.

"Let me."

It takes a minute to grasp what he's proposing, and a nervous laugh escapes. "Excuse me?"

"Let me show you what it's like. We're both high, it doesn't have to mean anything."

He can't be serious. "No way." I giggle again, shaking my head.

"What are you afraid of?"

"I just got out of—"

"He's got nothing to do with it. This is only me and you. That's it. It's just sex."

If I slept with Camden, he'd probably laugh at me. The more we've spoken, the more I realize how little experience I have. My skills are limited to my own masturbation and living vicariously through my books. Blowjobs even elude me. The only ones I've given I had to beg for, and they weren't appreciated, which means they were probably lousy. I need to watch more porn before I climb into bed with anyone. Especially someone like Camden Teller.

"I told you how inexperienced I am. You don't want this, trust me. I'm a mess."

"Oh, Sunshine, I love messes. I'll take care of you. Promise."

"Cam—"

"But the lights stay on—I want what he never got to see. I don't want to miss a second of watching you come on my cock."

Damn. Heat floods to my core. My body is certainly ready, even if I'm not. It's a free pass to experience what sex could be. He'd probably teach me a lot . . . It'd help prepare me if I ever start dating. I'm not making a mistake like Bryan ever again. Our gaze pings back and forth, searching each other's eyes. *Shit, I'm in.*

"Okay."

"Yeah?"

"But only because I want to gain more experience. What do I do first?"

He sits next to me on the sofa, his lopsided smile is so striking with that damn backward hat of his.

"Can I kiss you?" I look away, and my mouth curves into a grin. *He asked.* He's facing me, but suddenly, I'm too shy to even glance back. The other night happened without thinking, now all I'm doing is overcomplicating it in my mind.

"Okay."

"Jordan." He takes a hit and sets the joint down. "Let's just have some fun."

His fingers thread into my hair, and he opens my mouth with his, blowing the smoke inside. I inhale and let the high tamp down the noise in my mind. *I'm done caring.* At least for tonight.

He kisses me deeper. It's a rush. Before long, he loops his fingers over the sides of my leggings, and I let him peel them off. He smiles, then goes for my shirt. I do the same to him. I will not be the only one naked. When his shirt is over his head, he studies my body, and I don't cover myself up. I feel pretty when he looks at me like that.

I straddle his lap and continue kissing him, my fingers trail down his abs, appreciating his muscles. He feels so different from Bryan. Opposite in almost every way. His body is hard and firm, his hands calloused. Cam grabs my thighs and shoves my hips down on him, and I grind slowly. Even with his pants still on, his cock is different from my ex's. *So different.* I've seen it with my own eyes. Would he let me give him a blowjob? Would he give me pointers and encourage me through it?

When I'm left in only my underwear, he fills his hands with my breasts and tugs my nipples, sending waves of pleasure through me. One hand skates over my stomach and continues lower . . . His thumb passes back and forth over the damp strip of cotton between us.

"Please," I beg.

He groans, shoving my panties to the side and sliding his thick fingers between my folds.

"Fucking hell, Jordan. You are *so* wet."

Not surprising, this is more foreplay than I'm used to.

He slides one digit in, and I clench around him.

Wow.

"How many fingers can you take in this tight pussy, hm?"

He adds another, pumping them inside me while I enjoy myself. Touching me doesn't benefit him, yet he keeps going. *What is he getting out of this?* It feels incredible. The sound of my wetness fills the space. My arousal practically dripping out of me. He pulls his hand out and wipes it on my nipple, dropping his mouth and sucking it off while he looks up at me. *Oh my god.*

My jaw drops, and I smile at his brazen move. He pops off me and shoves his hand between my legs again. "Why didn't you tell me you tasted so sweet?"

Cam drives two fingers inside, and my eyes roll back. "I didn't know."

He brings our mouths together, swiping his tongue across mine, and I moan as I taste myself on his lips. His thumb hits my clit with the proper speed and pressure, refined after many women, I assume. "Now you do."

My breaths quicken, my core tightens—*I might come.* He probes, tapping the spot inside me I've only ever reached with a vibrator, and I'm sent over the edge.

"Oh my god!"

An invisible wave crashes over me, trickling down my entire body. I grip his shoulders as muscles tense. I'm coming. *I'm actually coming.*

"Thaaat's my fucking girl," he growls. His praise sends me deeper, my vision tunnels as I'm swept up in total pleasure. I stare at him dumbfounded. *A man made me come.* A smile takes over my face. That was incredible. "You have no problem coming."

"Show me how to give a good blowjob," I blurt. He chuckles. I'm too elated to care about humility. I just want more.

He stalls for a moment, and I look up at him.

"Wait, you've never given a blowjob?"

"Of course I have, but I want to be better at it."

The idea has always turned me on, but I never got enough practice, and Bryan wasn't into it, which negated the whole experience. It wasn't fun.

He leans back on the sofa.

"Get on your knees."

I do as he says. He studies me, kneeled on the floor between his parted thighs. He's hard, and I want to see what was rubbing me in all the right places when I was grinding on him. See what I saw when I walked in on him. Cam nods at his crotch. "Go for it, Jordan. Show me."

I push down the gray joggers. His cock bobs out, and I try not to pay attention to the thickness or piercings. They're intimidating.

Using only what I know from experience, I do what Bryan liked. I make myself look as pretty as possible. Running my fingers through my hair to smooth it over and bringing it behind my shoulders. Then I sit up with good posture and open my mouth, taking him inside. The bead of precum hits my tongue with a satisfying saltiness. *I love it.*

I keep my eyes down and focus. In and out. Keep my mouth tight, which feels impossible with his size and piercings. I'm scared I'll let one of them hit a tooth or something. I can only imagine how easily I could hurt him. Clean and disciplined. I gave blowjobs here and there before Bryan, but I was a teenager—and knew even less than I do now.

"A little wider, you can take it."

I open my mouth wider, but it doesn't seem to make a difference to him. He's as quiet as Bryan was. My self-esteem starts to tank. *Fuck, I'm terrible at this.*

"Come on, Jordan, you can suck dick better than this. I've seen those lips work a popsicle."

The only popsicle I had was when he was gone; how did he know that? *Did he watch me on camera?*

"Wetter." I stop swallowing so much and let some saliva pool on my tongue. "Wetter . . . I want to see you drooling for me."

I pop off him and tuck my hair behind my ears again. "I'll look ridiculous, it won't be hot if I'm drooling everywhere."

"The fuck?" He rears his head back. "Did Bryan tell you that?"

I don't answer. This is what I was afraid of. I'm so ashamed. My experience is garbage. Covering my face, I shake my head. "This is so embarrassing. I knew we shouldn't do this. Shit." I drop my hands to the floor and push off to leave, but he holds my shoulders in place.

"Our lesson isn't over. You want to do this, then let's do it. I don't know what fucked-up shit Bryan is into, but forget everything he ever told you. Blowjobs are meant to be wet and sloppy. You suck, slurp, and lick until I fill your mouth with cum, understand?" He leans back on the sofa, cups my face, and brushes my cheek with his thumb. The smile on his face is wicked. "Stop being prim and proper and show me what a filthy slut you are when nobody's looking."

I gawk at him, shocked, speechless, and *soaked.*

"If you want to stop, we can—"

"No!" I shout. I want to make Camden come. I want to

bring him to his knees with my mouth. "I want this."

He leans forward and grabs my chin, getting right in my face. "Then fucking act like it."

Oh my god. The way he speaks in that tone. Flames lick at my neck, and I've never wanted it more.

"Make it wet."

I spit on his length and slide my lips over him. He smiles.

"Be my messy girl."

I've never been spoken to this way or treated like this, and I can't get enough. I moan around him and take him deeper but gag. Before I can feel mortified, his voice cuts through my negative thoughts.

"Ugh, I love that sound. It's okay if you choke a little . . ."

If that didn't deter him, I've got nothing to lose. His encouragement spurs me on, and I go all in. I stop worrying about what he might think. All the little rules from Bryan go out the window. I take him deep, letting myself drool around his erection, swirling my tongue under the ridge. Exploring him with my tongue. It's everything Bryan would hate—which makes me love it even more. The uncouth slurping sounds, the gagging, the spit, all of it. It's freeing. I can do what I want.

He growls. "Oh fuck, Sunshine. You were holding out on me." He sucks air in through his teeth and grunts. "Ugh, this is my fucking fantasy. Look at me."

When our eyes meet, it's like I can't control myself. His are dark and filled with lust, as if he's warring between anger and ecstasy. It's the greatest aphrodisiac seeing how turned on I can make him. It's my fantasy too, being with someone who's as into it as I am. It's empowering.

"Oh, you're a fucking pro. Goddamn it, Jordan. Why were you hiding this side of you?"

I let his words wash over me and build my confidence.

The piercings aren't as scary as I thought they would be, they're fine as long as I keep my tongue on them, where I know they're safe.

"Grab my balls like this . . ." With his hand over mine, he wraps my hand around the base and tugs, and when he lets go, I repeat the movement, and he groans while letting out a laugh. "Fuck. You're doing so well." His hands thread into my hair and push the strands away. He stares down at me, stroking my cheeks.

"You sure are easy on the eyes, aren't you? Yeah . . . you know you are." He goes quiet, and he looks down on me like *I'm* the one being worshipped. His eyes appear entranced as he stares. "So fucking beautiful," he whispers, though I'm not sure he even realizes it. He leans back on his hands, his head tilted to the side, giving me room to work.

He's a great partner, and knows exactly what I need to keep going. I whimper, and he smiles big. The sound snaps him out of the sex haze.

"Hearing you enjoying yourself drives me wild." I moan, and he cups my cheek, smiling. "This is still your blowjob, *you* are in control."

I've never had this before. It's rewarding as hell to make him hard, feel him twitch in my mouth. See the sharp inhales, the way his jaw clenches and relaxes. Watch his head loll to the side as he regards me with reverence. No one has ever looked at me the way he does, and my skin buzzes all over. I get to choose how much pleasure to give him. I have the power.

He wraps my hair around his fist. "Do you like how this feels?"

I nod.

"Yeah? I'm going to pull a little bit. If it feels good, make a noise telling me you like it. Too hard, and you tap my leg."

I nod again. As soon as he adds tension, I hesitate. My eyes find his, and they're filled with trust. Suddenly, my scalp prickles, and it shoots straight to my core. It's rough and commanding, but in a different way than I've experienced. His watchful eyes are studying my reaction. The firmness increases, and it's a mixture of pain and affection. He's not trying to hurt me. He's not Bryan. I moan, and he tightens his hold. The more pressure he adds, the greater the sensation. The trust between us grows with each strained tug. I love it. Humming around him until it starts to hurt more than feel good, I tap his leg.

"You like it rougher than I thought you would."

He works my scalp and alternates between stroking my cheek with a feather touch and pulling my hair. It's magnificent. It's like feeling real pleasure for the first time. Unfortunately, my jaw is getting sore. He must sense it because he smiles and asks, "Do you want a break?"

I nod and pop off him. This is thrilling. I felt powerful, desired, wanted, all the things I'd been missing. He strokes himself while watching me. I bite my lip as I watch the erotic scene taking place.

"Jordan, you did such a good job. If you want, we can try again later or try something new."

Seeing him touch himself and smiling while I watch, gets me wetter by the second. "I want to try again." I need my mouth around him. I already miss it.

He grins, with a sparkle in his eye, as if he's proud of me. "This time, I'm going to try and set the pace by holding your head. If it's too much, you tap my leg like you did before, okay?"

What does that mean? "Too much?" I ask.

"If you need to take a breath, or don't like it, or want to

end. Remember, you don't need a reason to stop other than simply wanting to stop. Got it?"

"Mm-hm." I love that. I can stop any time, just because.

"Open up for me," he instructs. I do, looking up through my lashes and feeling sexy as hell. His mouth opens with mine. Like he's trying to convince me to eat. He slides between my lips, and my eyes roll. "Oh, you like this, don't you? There you go, Sunshine. Just like that. . . *Fuck.* Your mouth feels so good." My self-esteem rises even higher. "I'm going to guide you."

He fists my hair into a ponytail and sets a gentle pace. I'm panting, relishing the loss of control. It's like he's using me to get off. *I like it. It's exhilarating.*

"How's this?" he asks.

Needing more, I move my head side to side, trying to push him deeper. I want all of him. I relax and turn my hands into fists and swallow him farther than I ever have. His piercings firmly press into my tongue and feel foreign at the back of my throat.

"Fucking Christ!" He roars, then grunts. "Do it again, baby. Exactly like that." He's begging *me*. It's the first time he's called me *baby*. Normally, it's my name or *sunshine*. I repeat the move, and he groans, tossing his head back.

"Oh, you are so fucking precious . . . Eyes, Jordan." I glance up to his. "Do you have any idea how many times I've thought about this? How many times I've gotten off to fantasies of you on your knees? Those beautiful brown eyes looking up at me while your pouty lips take every inch . . . You like that? When I talk dirty to you?"

I moan. I can't get enough. It turns every bone I have to jelly. Makes me feel valued and wanted. *Cherished.* He clutches my hair and pumps into me.

"Good. I like it too."

I suck and swallow, letting him push to the back of my throat again, and he becomes more erratic with his movements and control. His piercings skitter across my tongue as he invades my mouth. It almost tickles.

"Fuck, you're a fast learner . . . I'm gonna come. I don't want you to swallow it. Hold it on your tongue. I want you to taste me." His panting turns into curses, and I lavish every second of watching him fall apart. When his cum hits my tongue, I resist the instinct to swallow, though I desperately want to. As soon as he's finished, he drops to his knees in front of me and grips my chin to open my mouth, checking to see if I followed directions.

His fingers slide between my legs. I tremble, needing his touch. Needing friction. The second his thumb hits my clit, I melt.

"Don't swallow."

Breathing through my nose, I salivate with his climax behind my locked lips.

His fingers push inside me, and I lean into him. "Do you like your mouth filled with my cum?"

"Mm-hm." It coats my tongue. It's my prize, I earned it. *I made Camden Teller, sex extraordinaire, come with my mouth.*

I can hardly take it. My body is on the cusp of another orgasm. Crushed against him, he snakes a hand around my waist to hold me up and whispers in my ear, "Everyone thinks you're so demure, graceful, and elegant. Do you have any idea how fucking sexy it is to watch the sophisticated Jordana Landry transform into my *perfect* cum slut?"

I groan and shiver. His fingers are relentless, and the corner of my mouth leaks with him.

"Hold it," he warns, pressing the heel of his hand against my clit.

I'm panting through my nose, and my knuckles whiten with the grasp I have on his arm and shoulder.

"God, I love corrupting you. You're such a pretty little thing all flushed and flustered. These sweet hips are grinding so hard. Are you embarrassed by how needy you are? Watch this." He removes his hand right as I'm about to explode. My legs shake and twitch. Every muscle in my body is engaged.

"Mmmmm!" I panic, trying to keep my lips sealed. The sensation of my climax slips further away, but as soon as he stuffs his fingers back inside, it's as if it never left.

"See? You need it, don't you, Sunshine?"

The moniker warms me from the inside out. He attempts to pull out again, but I grip his arm and hold him in place as I hum every moan. I've never come more than once, but if anyone can make me, it's him. His forearm muscles flex against my palm as he brings me to my peak.

"Tsk, tsk. What would everyone say if they knew the real Jordan loved getting finger-fucked with a mouth full of cum? Always wanting more." *The mouth on this man. Holy shit.* "I can't wait to pin you down and fuck you," he growls. "Swallow for me."

My eyes squeeze shut as I swallow and gasp for air. He keeps rubbing my clit through the orgasm. Euphoria washes over me as I come on his hand for the second time.

He smiles and crashes his mouth to mine, swiping his tongue inside, no doubt tasting himself. I feel the biggest rush of vulnerability.

"Unreal," he says, awed. Camden offers his hand, and I take it. "My turn."

NINETEEN

Camden

After leading her to my room, I set her in the middle of my bed and let my eyes take in her sinful body. She's gorgeous. This woman's got an ass built for back shots but a face made for missionary.

"I need a minute," she says, still coming off the last one. She's not something to rush through. I love taking my time with her. After I finish, I usually don't care to keep going, but she's making me want to savor every moment. She's not a virgin by any means, but the pleasure is new to her. It makes it that much more rewarding when her face flushes and eyes roll back.

And her willingness to try new things? Goddamn. Her blowjob had me coming harder than I ever have before, not because of her technique, she's still learning. What got me was opening her eyes to true pleasure and seeing a sex-starved demon staring back at me. Jordan is the exception to all my rules with women.

And now I want to taste her. I want her pussy. I want to lick and suck on her clit until she cries big swollen tears. I want to wreck her.

"I'm ready. Do I need to do anything?" Jesus Christ, after

all this, I don't know whether to kill Bryan or thank him for letting me show her how it should be. I want to erase every memory of him from her mind and body.

"You enjoy yourself. Stoplight system. If you don't like something, say yellow. If you want me to stop, say red."

"'Kay."

She lies back on the pillows, and I shove one underneath her backside, propping her up. I plan to eat her all the way to her ass. Grabbing her panties, I peel them off. She's glistening. I kiss her ankles, knees, and inner thighs; occasionally nipping her flesh, inching higher. Her scent is addicting, and I need it on my tongue. She hisses with each love bite but sighs when I lick it all better. When I reach her pussy, I look up at her and lap at her arousal. She's so wet. Her head falls back, and she drops her mouth open.

"Oh my god," she whispers.

"So fucking delicious." I lick again and crawl over her. "Come here." With a thumb pressed to her chin, those soft lips part, and I sweep my tongue over hers. She blushes and I grin, returning to my home between her thighs, where I could live out the rest of my days with a smile on my face. I spread her open wide, licking each side and up the center, picking up every trace of her on my tongue. I don't want to spare any of it.

She threads her hand into my hair and scratches my scalp with her nails. I groan. "Greedy boy."

Well, look at who has some dirty talk of her own . . .

I chuckle and slide a finger inside. "You have no idea how fucking selfish I can be."

Watching her carefully, I add a second finger, and she grinds against them. "That feel good?"

Her only response is a moan, and I chuckle. "You're

cute when you forget your words." I pump in and out, bringing my lips to her clit and sucking.

Her back arches off the bed. "Cam . . ."

She doesn't even know what that does to me, whimpering my name like that. She tightens her grasp on my hair and tugs. I grunt and suck harder.

"Oh my god. Oh my god, it feels . . ." I look up at her between her thighs, and her gaze snaps to mine with wide eyes. Her mouth drops open, and her cunt grips my fingers while she grinds against my face. *Hell yeah.* I keep the same rhythm, not changing a thing, I want her orgasm drawn out as long as possible. She props up on her elbows. Tears swell at the corners of her eyes as her legs quake. I remove my hand and thrust my tongue inside, enjoying the way she pulses around it. When I get my fill, I shove my fingers back in, stroking the spot she loved earlier. Her head falls back as another one hits her.

"Jesus, Jordan, you are so beautiful when you come, baby. Keep coming, you're doing so good. You deserve this, let yourself have it." I dive back in and suck her clit again. After one more loud cry and arch of her back, she slowly comes down.

Her muscles eventually relax, and she wipes at the tears on her face. She sniffles, and a huge smile spreads across her lips as she peers down at me between her legs. "Can we do more?"

I laugh and nod. "Absolutely." She's fun to play with. "You ready now?"

"Yeah. Show me what else I've been missing."

"Tell me you're on birth control."

"I am."

I kneel between her thighs, spreading her wide open for

me. She's plump and pink, and I've never seen a pussy need to be fucked by me so badly. I spit on her clit, and her mouth drops open.

"You spit on me."

"Yeah, I did." I smirk, and the corners of her eyes wrinkle with a grin.

"Do it again." *She's like every wet dream coming true.*

I prepare to spit between her legs—her lips part in slow motion. She gapes at me like she doesn't want to miss it. Those big dark-brown eyes are dancing with curiosity and lust. I push her legs wide but snatch her throat with one hand. She grabs my wrists, and I pull her up and spit into her surprised mouth before dropping her back down.

Her fingers press to her chest. "I can't believe you did that," she says, almost laughing.

I chuckle, sliding between her legs again. "Did you like it?"

"I *shouldn't* like it."

"Nobody gets to tell you what you should or shouldn't enjoy." Her thighs part, and I smile. Grabbing behind her knees, I lean forward and push my forearms against the back of her thighs, spreading her until she winces, putting her on full display. I smile and take in how pretty she is like this. My well-mannered little heiress is about to find out how dirty she likes to be fucked. She squirms, and I can't get enough of her eagerness.

I slap my cock against her clit, then rest it at her entrance. I want to fuck her hard. Show her *exactly* what she's been missing while she's been in the wrong man's bed. I want to see her shake as every rung of my ladder is stuffed inside.

As soon as the crown breaches her pussy, I'm in trouble. It's different. The freckles on her nose. The depth of her eyes.

The way she's breathing. All of it. She will not be a one-and-done.

It's not like me to admire the woman I'm fucking the way I do Jordan. I rarely have repeats with someone, twice tops. This was supposed to be a one-time thing, a fun activity while we're high. I'll admit I wanted to erase Bryan and his fucked-up idea of sex . . . I'm sure it was easier to fuck her if he didn't have to see the hurt in her eyes. I won't do that. Ever. But tonight, it's not the high that feels intense, it's Jordan. She intrigues me like no other, has me curious. She's exciting. I know after the first thrust, *once* will never be enough with her.

Shit.

"Cam . . ."

"Huh?" My eyes snap to hers, and she looks worried.

"Are you having second thoughts?"

Yes. I'm having straight up regrets. I should pull out. I realize I've been staring this whole time instead of actually fucking her.

"What? No. Never."

I shove the rest of me inside, and her breathing stops. She freezes.

"Holy—" Her lips tip up into a smile.

I pull out and thrust again, getting an eyeful of her tight pussy swallowing my thick dick so well—all of me at once. Feeling the thrum as each piercing fits inside. It's impressive. Her legs quake under my palms. She turns her head to the side and breathes out slowly.

The third time I sink into her, something seems off. It's like she's avoiding eye contact.

"What are you looking at?"

"Nothing."

"Look at me."

"No, thank you."

What the actual fuck? "Why?"

She clears her throat, still facing away. "Can you do it from behind?"

I choke, trying to swallow. "Excuse me? No, I'm not fucking you from behind!" I snap, that pisses me off. I'm not taking her like he did, the thought disgusts me. "Why the hell would you want that?"

"I'm not used to eye contact," she says.

"That's not my problem. Look at me while I'm fucking you," I growl back.

"Cam!"

I grab her chin and turn it toward me. "What is it, Jordan?" I ask, rubbing circles into her clit.

"Fuck . . ."

"This too much for you?"

It's too much for me too, but it's not enough to stop me from filling this darling girl with my cum and watching it drip out. I want her well-fucked and sated—covered in smudged makeup and bite marks. I need her sweet and filthy.

She covers her face with her hands. Her voice chokes on a sob, "Yes!"

Too fucking bad. She needs to be reminded this is different. This is for *her*, and she's going to stay with me through this.

"Use your safeword."

She shakes her head.

"You're always in control, Jordan."

With one hand, I grab both her wrists and pin them directly above her head. With my other hand, I grab the back of her neck and crane her neck forward.

"Look down. Watch me fuck you."

She sniffles and opens her eyes.

"Do you want me to stop?"

She stares for a moment. "No." Her voice is breathy and seductive.

"Then we're not stopping. This is your fucking baptism, Sunshine."

She nods. Every piercing hitches on her tight opening, and it makes me throb harder. She releases a sexy desperate sigh as we watch together.

I release her neck. "Such a good girl . . . Now I want you to look up."

Her eyes are swimming with tears, I can't help but press my lips to hers. I hate him for breaking her like this. He should thank his lucky stars I haven't shown up at his doorstep. Yet.

I drop her wrists, and she brings her soft fingertips to my jaw and kisses me back so hard I think she's sucking my soul out of me. She's an enigma. So powerful and submissive at the same time.

I've never wanted to ruin and resurrect something more.

"You're stronger than you think. Show me how good it feels."

A smile shoots across my face when her eyes fully focus on me. She's been in such a fucked-up relationship for so long, she doesn't yet know her own strength. When she rises like a phoenix from that pile of ash, she'll be a force to be reckoned with, and I'll be here waiting to tame her when she's ready.

This is only the beginning of her transformation, and I want to be the catalyst. I'm fascinated by Jordan.

Her body tightens, and I lean down, biting her nipples. She cries out, and I reward her, licking each like a balm to the sting.

"Do you hear those sexy sounds you make? Goddamn, I want to devour you."

She seizes the back of my neck, pulling the hair at the nape. *Shit.*

Her nails scratch down my back, mauling me. If she keeps it up, the guys will think I've been fucking Wolverine. I hope she never stops. I want her to mark me as much as I do her. My hand snakes between us and up toward her neck. When my fingers wrap around her throat, she tilts her chin up, giving me more access. It's *so* submissive.

"Fuck." Her lips part with a slight grin.

"Sweet Jordana Landry from the big house on the hill. Always following the rules, behaving like a sophisticated socialite. Prim, proper, and pretty as can be. So lovely." I lick across her lower lip, she opens up, and I spit inside. Her eyes fill with fire, and I smile. "But when you tilt your head up like that for me, I know you'd rather wear my hand around your neck than anything from Harry Winston. You need someone to worship and fuck you the way you deserve. Because deep down, you're a needy little whore, aren't you?"

Her eyebrows push together, and she nods.

Good god. "That's my perfect fucking girl." I drop my mouth to her ear. "Maybe I should tattoo a diamond necklace on the back of my hand . . . that way I can dress you up whenever I want."

When I sit up, her eyes are nearly black. Any sign of her innocent, angelic nature has been replaced with a succubus. Sitting back on my heels, I open her knees, gazing down at her with a smirk, appreciating the way she takes each inch, with parted lips and sexy moans while trembling under my palms. I grip and grope her thighs like I can't get enough.

"You're getting close," I comment as her body slowly closes

in on me. Her panting grows more desperate. My thumb finds her clit and rubs small circles. She props herself on her elbows with parted lips, looking down, as if she wants to see it as bad as I do.

Reaching under her arms, I drag her on top of me. She lets me lift and drop her on my dick over and over. With her nails in my shoulders, I cup her chin in one hand and bring her right in front of my face. "You are such a pretty girl. Why don't you show me how pretty you are coming on a big, fat cock."

Her mouth opens on a silent scream, and then it hits.

It hits like a fucking hurricane.

She twists and writhes, her hips rolling on me. "Please, please, please . . ."

"You learn those manners in finishing school, princess?"

"Uh-huh." She nods again. "When do I say thank you?"

I grab her neck and squeeze with one hand while pinching her nipple with the other.

"Open your mouth." She does, and I spit inside. "*Now* you thank me."

She throws her arms around my neck and rides me, gasping and panting. "Fuck, Cam—" She groans. Her body erupts, and she throbs over my length; it feels incredible.

"That's it." I smirk, feeling proud as hell. She's a shaking mess. Her claws dig into my shoulders, and it sends chills up my spine.

"Come for me, Jordan. Only for me," I growl.

She's mine now. I haul her ass closer, pounding up into her. I pull back and see tears streaming down her face. The overwhelming pleasure has her raptured. It's breath-taking. I roar as hot ropes of cum shoot inside her over and over. *This* is the release I've been waiting for.

We collapse against each other.

"Thank you," she murmurs.

I laugh; she's so sweet. "Fuck, Jordan. You're fun."

Her breaths are heaving against my chest. Nipples hard, flush tear-stained cheeks, freckles, and hooded bedroom eyes. I can't take my gaze off her. She's mesmerizing.

Jordan sucks the air right out of my lungs. "Wow," I mumble.

"Yeah." She drops her head to my shoulder and sighs. "That was amazing."

Amazing doesn't even cover it. She rocked me to my core. Guys talk about magic pussy, but I figured pussy was like pizza. Each woman is different, but it's all good. The variety's what made it great.

I was wrong. Fuck variety.

Bryan always wanted the best, well, he fucking had it and only fucked her from behind. He missed the desperation and need that sparkles in her eyes right before she comes. The way her plump lips part and the fucking symphony that comes out of her mouth when she's submitting to the blinding pleasure. She's irresistible. Whether she wants to admit it, I *am* her type. No question, I'll be taking her again. I'll be setting goddamn records.

She sits up like a rocket. "Oh my god!"

"Fuck, what? What?" I shoot up.

"We have shepherd's pie!" A huge smile grows on her face. "I'm so fucking hungry!" Jordan scoots toward the edge of the bed and grabs her clothes, pulling them on and hopping toward the door.

I laugh and fall back onto the pillows.

"Stoner."

I can't move. I'm still in shock. We were in sync the entire time. One look into her eyes tells me exactly what she needs. I'm glad he never saw her like that. She deserves far more than Bryan Davenport. Hell, she deserves more than me.

TWENTY

Jordan

The next morning, I roll over in bed and am instantly reminded of the night before. I'm sore. Everywhere. My throat, breasts, and mostly between my thighs. Cam gave me a deliciously painful workout. Hopefully not the last of those. It was amazing. Passionate and exciting. I didn't know sex could feel so intense. With Bryan, it was a chore. Hunched over, waiting for him to finish. Only twice did we have sex facing each other, and it was early in the relationship. After that, it was always the same way, and after a while, it became emotionless.

My eyes finally open to see the sun's position high in the sky. I slept in. *When was the last time that happened?* I grab my phone off the nightstand, hardly remembering plugging it in last night. After the sex, I ate an absurd amount of shepherd's pie and crashed. My hand brushes a piece of paper, and it falls to the floor. Leaning over the edge of the bed, I snatch it up and flip it over, squinting to read.

Went to get your things.
Stay put.
—C

Shit. My arms thrash as I throw off the covers, the aches even more apparent after moving my major muscle groups. After I get to my feet, I open the bedroom door and hobble out, colliding head-on with about ten garbage bags of stuff. *My stuff.*

I rip into the first bag; he got my clothes! I drag the bag to the small kitchen table and begin folding and stacking the pieces.

"Underwear!" I raise my arm in triumph. Oh, hell yeah! I've been washing and rotating the same three pairs for way too long. I don't even care he's seen all my lingerie. He saw a lot more last night anyway.

The next bag is filled with sweaters and jeans. Next, winter coats. Not all my shoes are here, but the ones he took are the most versatile. Smart man. After that, purses and jewelry. Makeup. He even grabbed my toothbrush. I have my things back!

How did he already get all this accomplished this morning? I grab my phone and text him.

I don't know how to thank you.

CAMDEN TELLER

Last night was great for me too. My dick says you're welcome.

You know what I mean. When did you have time to get my things?

CAMDEN TELLER

This morning. Saw one of his cousins post on Facebook they're out of town to take care of family business. Timing worked.

Who saw you? They let you walk out with all my stuff?

CAMDEN TELLER

Bryan never took me off the guest list. Used your keycard to open the door, filled up the bags, sent them down the trash chute, and loaded them up in the alley. Not the first time I've done this.

Clearly. For a sister? Or maybe a woman he's helped through Safehouse?

Wow. That's pretty clever, buddy. I owe you big time.

CAMDEN TELLER

No need. But if you insist, I can think of a few ways... 😉

I mean, it's only fair.

CAMDEN TELLER

Glad you agree.

I thought you didn't sleep with the same girl more than once? 🤔

CAMDEN TELLER

I decided that doesn't apply to you.

Somebody must have been a good student...

CAMDEN TELLER

She was a very good student.

I smile. Why does him talking about me in the third person make my thighs tingle? I've got kinks coming out of the fucking woodwork after last night. A decent person would feel guilty about having sex so soon after breaking off an engagement. Not me. Guess I'm not a perfect angel. *My villain era is well underway.*

Humans aren't meant to have quiet, boring, faceless sex. It was passionate and wild. He lit a fire in my soul. I woke up physically weak but emotionally empowered. The opposite of previous relationships. There is so much of myself I've ignored or suppressed over the years, but I got a taste of freedom last night. Sex the way *I* want it. How can one person teach me so much about myself?

No matter what comes of us, I'll never regret my night with him. Camden isn't available; he doesn't do relationships—which I respect, but it's hard not to feel a slight disappointment. When I'm ready to start dating again—*if* I date again—I want someone who will consume me the way Cam did. I shouldn't get involved with anyone, but . . . knowing such a chemistry exists in the world is enough to give me hope for a chance at something great.

After years of numb intimacy, I could finally *feel* again. The sex was emotionally charged, and our connection was terrifyingly powerful, but he made me feel safe when I was most vulnerable. It was the first time I've been face-to-face with someone in a long time, and even then, it's never been like that. He seemed to feel it too. Does he feel that with every woman he's with? Selfishly, I want it to be exclusive to me, which is a dangerous seed to plant.

He didn't let me take the easy way out when I got scared. I didn't know it, but it was exactly what I needed.

I'm never sacrificing my own sexual pleasure for another man again. From now on, sex is on my terms. I want someone who will call me a slut because he knows I enjoy being objectified, not because he thinks I'm fucking someone on the side. Have him whisper filthy things that send waves of ecstasy down my spine instead of fear. I want him to bite, spit, and pull my hair because it brings me pleasure, not pain.

Camden opened so many new doors last night but made sure I entered by my own volition. Whereas, Bryan shoved me inside and locked it.

Perched on the laundry room countertop, waiting for the last load of clothes to dry, I get caught up on my to-do list by sending cancellation emails to each of the wedding vendors. Ironically, that's when a text comes through from Bryan. Camden helped me get the VPN set up on my phone, so now I can use it without worry.

The only reason I haven't blocked him is to keep a record of his hostility in case I need it for evidence. Usually, I ignore his texts, but curiosity gets the best of me and I open the message history. There are so many. They oscillate between rage and remorse. Yells at me in one, apologizes the next.

BRYAN DAVENPORT

Where are you?

I'm sorry.

Jordana, please answer me.

You've made your fucking point. If you thought I was mad before, just wait. You better be home by the time I get off work. You don't want to fuck with me.

WTF??

Where are you???

You're going to regret ever walking away from me after I get done with you.

Tomorrow, I want you to remember that you asked for this.

Ready to come home yet?

That was the day I got fired.

Look, come home and everything will go back to normal. I'm sorry about the thing with your job, but I'm willing to reverse everything if you come home. Do you see how much I love you, Jordana???

At least respond to my texts.

SILENT TREATMENT??? REALLY? GROW UP!!!!

Do you really plan on never speaking to me again? How about you act like an adult and quit being such a fucking coward.

I fucked up, okay?! What the hell do you want from me?

Is this about Veronica still? She is nobody. You're the one I want.

I said I was sorry. WHAT THE FUCK IS WRONG WITH YOU????

STOP BEING SUCH A FUCKING CUNT, JORDANA!! ANSWER MY TEXTS!!!PICK UP THE FUCKING PHONE!!!!

I'm only mad because I love you and I care about us. I'm sorry if I flew off the handle, but you're scaring me. I don't know how I could go through life without you. Just call me back. Let's work this out. I'm willing to get a counselor if that's what you need.

We can fix this. We just need to set expectations of each other.

A smirk spreads across my face. *He's losing it.*

And *expectations?* Give me a break. Should I *expect* he's going to fuck my friends on the side? Hit me when he's angry? I want to text back, but I feel like he would use it against me somehow. He's already destroyed the normalcy in my life, I won't load the gun for him too.

Now that I've got my things, it's time to make it official. The wedding date has been creeping closer, and I need to tell my parents before they catch wind from the wedding vendors I've already canceled.

I check the time, 6:00 p.m. in Monaco. I click their name, and it rings twice before my mom picks up.

"Jordana!"

"Hey, Mom . . . we need to talk."

TWENTY-ONE

Camden

After collecting Jordan's things this morning, my anger was about to boil over. I dropped them off in her room, then had to get out of there. I've spent the last two hours at the gym and am still seething. I saw the hole in the wall from the clothes iron.

The lengths Bryan went through to cut off her resources . . . It takes everything in me to resist going back to the condo and waiting for him to return. After he threatened, terrified, and turned her life upside down, nothing would please me more than to play the role of karma.

I hit the showers after my workout, then find a secluded hallway at the training center and call my stepdad. He answers on the second ring.

"Hey, Camden, what's up?"

"Dad, quick question for you."

I sweep my foot over the artificial turf under me.

"Yeah?"

"I need you to loan out one of the cars in your fleet."

"That's not a question."

I roll my eyes.

"You want to borrow one of the cars," he repeats. "Is this for Safehouse?"

I pinch the bridge of my nose. I should refer Jordan to my foundation and let them handle it.

"Kinda, yeah."

"How come they aren't giving you a referral for a vehicle?"

I pause, unsure how to answer, because there's no reason I shouldn't be following Safehouse protocol. Jordan isn't mine to take care of. My stepdad is a good man, but if I told him the car was for Jordana Landry, it would only raise suspicion, and I'm already clueless regarding my behavior toward her.

"I'm handling this one differently."

"Alright . . . Everything okay?" There's a twinge of concern in his voice.

"Yeah, yeah. It's fine. Just need a car temporarily," I answer as casually as possible.

"Okay. I'll get something couriered over tonight. Which center do you want it dropped off at?"

"You can drop it off at my house. I'll be there to sign for it."

"Uh-huh." He's quiet, hoping I'll fill the air with more details. He's not getting any. Not today at least.

"Thanks, I appreciate it. I gotta get going, tell Mom I love her. Talk to you later."

I hang up and drop against the cold concrete wall.

"What am I doing!?" I shout, angry with myself.

"Getting in the fucking way," Rhys answers, turning the corner. "I need to sprint."

Rhys is finally coming out of his shell, and it's a good thing too. After how quiet he was his rookie year, I was wondering if he didn't possess a sense of humor. Now that he knows he's got a solid spot with us, he's loosened up a bit.

I'm glad he's working on his sprints; it's an area that needs improvement.

"Who says I'm not using it?" I ask.

"Give me a break, you're too old to sprint."

"A break?" I smirk. "If I gave a shit, I wouldn't give it to you."

He laughs. "Well, if I gave a fuck, I'd give it to your mom."

It takes me a second to register his chirp.
"Unfortunately, my mom would probably love that. She's a freak."

"Must be where you get it from. Now, may I?"

"All yours." I pick my bag off the floor and head out. I'm almost to the door when Coach stops me.

"Teller. A word."
I blow out a breath and stride over. *Tell me good news, old man.*

"We're gonna give your lineup a shot. If it falls through, it's on you."

"Hell yeah." Finally, something I want to hear. "It's going to pay off."

He nods and heads back to his office. I walk backward toward the exit with a big-ass smile on my face. "You won't regret it."

When I leave the training center, a crisp breeze blows through my still-damp hair, and a few crunchy orange leaves skitter across the parking lot. I love fall. Today would be a great day for a ride, and it might help me find some peace. I could use it.

Driving home, memories from last night sink into my thoughts. What is it about her that made last night seem different? I've had orgies before, but none were as hot as showing her how to spit on my cock. I've always pictured

Jordan as a good girl but didn't realize she could be such a *good girl*.

Teaching her how to give a decent blowjob? Normally that would have been a turn-off. Any woman who wants to put her mouth on my cock better know what she's doing before she even drops to her knees, but Jordan? *Fuck.* It satisfied my corruption kink like no other. Pretty sure it's some weird ego thing. Every blowjob she gives from now on will be *my* blowjob—the way *I* taught her. *You're fucking welcome.*

Now that she's discovering and trying out her fantasies—she'll never be the same. She's so eager, I want to show her everything. And her pussy? *Jesus Christ.* I've never had an issue blowing my load early, but last night came close. She made an adorable cream pie.

If she wants to explore, I'd rather it be with me. The only risk is her catching feelings. If she's discovering this about herself for the first time, her emotions could be right under the surface. Not to mention, she recently got out of a relationship. I would need to know she could separate them. Because we can't be anything more than physical. I don't date . . . but I wouldn't be opposed to a friends-with-benefits situation if she was down. I enjoy her company either way.

I need to lay down some ground rules and have *the talk.* She can't catch feelings and live under the same roof, and I want her to stay, she's safer with me than she would be anywhere else. Besides, I want to sleep with her again. Last night, I watched Jordan regain her power while I was balls deep in her. She seemed carefree and excited and . . . *alive.* Those brown eyes had a sparkle I've never seen before, and I desperately want to get her there again.

The back of my bike, you pervert.

JORDAN LANDRY

I'll get my coat.

TWENTY-TWO

Jordan

Partially bare trees cover the old country roads on both sides, and the fallen leaves fly up on each side of us as we ride through them. The sky is blue, temperatures are perfect.

I understand why he loves his bike so much; the freedom and openness are unmatched. All the noise in my head is drowned out when I'm on it. Someday, I'm going to buy one. I'll take lessons and learn how to ride, or maybe Camden could teach me? For now, I'm happy to be his backpack, where we can just *be*. I sense Camden is experiencing his own version of these feelings . . . needing to let go.

"Hey, I wanted to talk to you about something," he says, his voice coming through the speaker in my helmet.

"What's up?"

"The sex last night? I said we could do it again, but—"

Oh God, please don't change your mind.

I think quickly to convince him I won't be a problem.

"But you want to make sure I don't get attached? I'm not going to turn into some clingy bunny. And I appreciate you teaching me some new tricks. I don't want to be embarrassed with the next guy—hey, you'll keep the things I've told you about my relationship with Bryan confidential, right?"

"Of course."

I exhale a sigh of relief. I trust him.

"After that engagement, the last thing I should entertain is another relationship. Like you said, we're just having fun. Don't worry, buddy, you're still not my ty—"

"Whatever." He scoffs. Whether he's my type doesn't matter, because he *can't* be.

"Oh, I'm sorry, did you want me to change my relationship status on Facebook?"

Is he mad? I'm trying to reassure him I'm okay with this.

"Nope, just making sure you know it's only sex." His voice is clipped and cold.

I swallow hard. It's true. This is sex at face value. No strings. It's Camden, he's a terminal bachelor and not someone to tangle with when it comes to feelings. I will not let another man hurt me. I'll learn to separate my feelings from what we do behind closed doors, because I need this friendship.

"You're a fuckboy," I say, patting his stomach where my arms are wrapped. "Lucky for me, that's exactly what I need."

He laughs. "So you're using me? I should be offended by that." He smacks the side of my thigh.

"We're using each other. Just 'til I get my own place, then it's done. I'll be gone before you know it." *Will I?* The hesitation I feel is all the more reason for me to move out. We will never be a thing, the more distance I have, the better.

He's quiet for a while and clears his throat. "I've given that some thought . . . You should stay with me."

I bark out a laugh. "And you're telling *me* not to be clingy?"

"Hear me out, from a security standpoint, he's going to find out where you are."

"He'll discover my location eventually, regardless of where I sleep. It's only a matter of time. And I'll get a VPN like you have. I can't always be on the run."

"Yeah, but once he finds out, I won't be there to back you up."

I smirk. "You sure this isn't because you want to extend your time in my pants?"

He covers one of my arms with his. "This is serious, Jordan. You need to keep yourself safe. You want your freedom back, I get that, but at least be prepared. I know how these things progress. You said he's been texting, but I would bet anything that in a week or so he stops messaging altogether. He's going to make you think he's gotten over it so you come out of hiding."

"Fine, I'll take some self-defense classes or something."

"Stay until you know it's safe. In the meantime, I've arranged for you to borrow a car, it'll be delivered to the house tonight."

I huff. "Thanks. I appreciate you setting up a temporary vehicle for me. However, when it comes to where I live, that choice is mine."

He's being too nice. If we continue living together, will I be able to maintain our emotional separation?

He sighs, and we ride in silence. We were having fun, but now Bryan is in the center of everything, and I'm letting Camden tell me what to do. I'm irritated with him, my ex, and myself. Am I being an idiot by sleeping with Cam, losing focus on what I need to do? I don't regret the sex, but perhaps it was a mistake. I shouldn't bring him into my chaos anyway. "On second thought, maybe we shouldn't do this."

"What?"

"Sleep together . . . God, this was supposed to be a fun ride. All you're doing is reminding me I'm some fucking victim in hiding."

He reaches back and squeezes my thigh, and it feels different after our night together. Too intimate.

"I'm just making you aware of the risks."

"Yeah, out of one cage and into another," I mutter. "Which is why fucking you is a bad idea."

He flips his blinker and pulls off the road. *Why are we stopping?* Cam gets off the bike and climbs back on, this time, facing me. He flips the visor on his helmet so I can see his eyes and wraps his palms above both knees, clutching me tight. I'm thankful he can't see my flushed cheeks. "Is it a bad idea for me to touch you like this?"

"Yeah."

"How do you *feel* when I touch you?" He rubs my inner thighs, his fingers climbing higher and higher. My breath catches. "What's going through your mind?"

I avert my gaze. "That we shouldn't keep doing this."

"I hate being lied to. So, this time when you answer, tell me the truth. *What are you thinking*?"

My eyes stare into his; he's so intense. It's as if he can see me through the black glass visor.

"I never want you to stop." I exhale. "Your touch is . . . everything. It's exciting, sexy, fun . . . It makes me forget about my past. I feel wanted and powerful. It's the first time a man's touch has felt like my decision, like I'm still in control."

His jaw tics. "What about *any* of that is bad, Jordan?"

"My life is a mess. And you're his best friend."

"You know how I feel about messes." He flips my visor up, exposing me. "I *was* his best friend. But now I'm the man who enjoys making his fiancée come on my cock . . . and she's fucking gorgeous when she cries my name."

I am? My breath whooshes out of me, and I'm sure he's getting a good look at the blush burning my cheeks. His eyes crinkle with a smile, satisfied he's hit his mark, based on my obvious physical response. I glance away. *This is all a game to him*, making me pink and flustered. He doesn't understand how deeply I'm affected by his words. He can't say those things to me and not mean them. "Don't be a dick—"

He pries my helmet off and holds my chin in place. "You're gorgeous all the time, but when your eyebrows push together and your mouth opens with those big brown eyes, begging me to push you over the edge . . . *fuck*, I'm powerless against you."

My lips part, and memories of that night flood my thoughts. The cocky smirk on his face like he knew exactly which buttons to push and levers to pull. The rush of every time he brought me to climax. Blood surges through my veins, causing my heart to hammer. My teeth bite into my lower lip.

"Do you like the way I fuck you, Jordan?"

I can barely hear him over my pounding pulse. This has to stop. I snatch my helmet back and put it on.

"That's what I thought," he says.

I narrow my eyes at him but don't deny it. My lip slides out from under my teeth, and my eyes drop to where his lips are behind his helmet. Good thing we have a barrier between us, if he kissed me right now, I'd be a goner.

I like the way he kisses and the way his hands roam my body when he does it. The way he presses the small of my back and cups my neck. I suck in an inhale and break eye contact, flipping my visor down again. Watching him leer at me like I'm his next meal is a bad idea.

He gets off the bike, then mounts it, facing forward this time. I put my arms around his waist, and we take off without saying a word. I'm so turned on and frustrated by him. He must be having the same thoughts as I am, right? A few minutes later, I can't stand the silence. "You're thinking about it, aren't you?"

"I never stopped."

I groan. "Why is it so good?" Sex with Bryan never came close to the way it is with Cam. I don't get it.

"Because our sexual chemistry is off the charts. You don't have to be involved with someone to enjoy sex with them—we can use each other for pleasure without the romance. Friends with benefits isn't uncommon."

"I'd say we're more like acquaintances-with-benefits." That's a lie, but I feel too pathetic to admit he's the closest friend I have.

"We're friends," he says. I smile. "Stop being a brat."

I inhale, about to retort, when music blasts through the helmet speakers and he revs the bike, shooting us forward. I wrap my arms tighter around his torso, my thighs tensing as I cling to him, and roll my eyes.

He's not my type. He's not my type. He's not my type.

Across from me sits my financial manager, Robert, and my lawyer, Sean. The ride with Cam earlier today was a wake-up call. I still have business to take care of, so I can't lose focus of my priorities. When we returned, I set up a meeting at

Robert's office to give them all the information I have at the moment.

I'm being issued new credit cards, and we've fixed the password issue from Bryan. I've cashed out some of my investments to tide me over and get money together in case I need to come up with a security deposit. The more I can pay in cash, the better. Even though Bryan's name has been forcibly removed from my accounts, leaving a credit card trail makes me uneasy.

I can press charges and report domestic violence—*but with no evidence?* I'm not doing that. They'd ask why I waited until after he fired me to make the accusation. It's a bullshit system, but I can't risk losing any credibility.

Bryan ruined my life, not only on paper, emotionally too. But outside of the abuse, there's not much I can charge him for. Technically, he didn't steal any money from me. H&H's official position on my termination was unrelated to Bryan, which we both know is bullshit. Minnesota is an at-will state, anyway. My car was reported stolen because he lied about ever switching the title into my name when he bought it.

He knew exactly what he was doing every step of the way.

He's always been sneaky like that. He destroys people without having to face repercussions for his actions. Sure, I can put in place an order of protection, but I'd rather not attract any attention from law enforcement at the moment. Sean, my attorney, is not happy about my decision. He pinches his brow and lets out an exasperated sigh when I shake my head for the third time.

"Jordana. I strongly suggest you take my advice."

I need to fly under the radar. If I press charges, I don't want to know what he'd do to get me to drop them. Corner me at the grocery store, a gas station, local park—no, thank you. I want him to think I'm hiding, scared—even if it is partially true. I'll give him a false sense of security while I figure this out. I can't let him suspect retaliation.

"I will—when I'm ready. I promise." I have a few calls to make first.

TWENTY-THREE

Jordan

The project I was assigned to before I was fired was for a company H&H was absorbing, named Bluetower. I managed contracts on the healthcare side of H&H, but Bluetower was IT. I questioned it but was told it was given to me and to push the contract through. It was a small tech startup with some new technology they were working on. Something seemed off, but I couldn't tell what it was. I never finished researching the project to find out.

Unfortunately, my access is limited to the documents I downloaded to the flash drive the day I was fired, and no one from Bluetower will return my calls. So today I am taking a little field trip.

The parking lot is empty. I double-check the address. This is the place. The building says Bluetower in big bright letters, but it's the middle of the day and my car is the only one here. I see no security cameras, so I park and get out to take a peek. The windows are wrapped in full-coverage decals that match the website branding, blocking the view inside. I search LinkedIn, employees are listed but even the photos don't look right. They're too perfect. They're *all* pretty. I don't mean to stereotype, but what are the odds of an *entire* team of tech geniuses looking like they stepped out of GQ?

I dial the number for Bluetower one more time. It's an automated line, but no one answers and all the extensions seem to go in circles. Looks like I will have to bust out the big guns.

I get back in my car and drive to the only payphone left in town and pull out my quarters. Every billionaire worth their salt has *a guy*. Seven is my family's *guy*, and I need him to come through for me on this. I've never met him, probably never will. He's not exactly on the up and up, but it's not my business. His number is on a piece of paper my parents instructed me to keep in my wallet in case of *special emergencies*. This emergency is more of a Hail Mary.

It rings twice before he answers. My eyes sweep the surroundings for people. I don't need anyone eavesdropping on what I'm about to ask.

"Jordana Landry. To what do I owe the pleasure?"

So creepy. I take another glance around and furrow my brow. "How did you know it was me?"

"A good magician never reveals his secrets."

I don't even want to know the secrets this guy holds. If someone told me he knew the nuclear launch codes, I wouldn't blink an eye.

"I need a favor."

TWENTY-FOUR

Camden

"Christ Almighty, Conway, what are you looking at? Game is that way." I point in front of us from the bench.

This dumb motherfucker has been staring up at the WAGs box all night. It's grating on my nerves.

He shakes his head. "Man, you gotta get your attitude under control."

"The fuck are you talking about?"

"I dunno, you're on edge. You got some personal shit going on?"

Yeah, I went for a ride with Jordan, which was great until she told me she wanted to get her own apartment. It's not the right move, and I don't understand what the hurry is. I brought up the sex we had, and she put me in my place by telling me I'm a fuckboy, which kinda irritated me, and I'm annoyed because she's right. We are friends with benefits, that's it. The sex we had was *just* sex.

"I'm fine," I snap.

When I look over, Barrett's gazing toward the box again. It's like I'm talking to myself.

"Does Raleigh have her tits out or something? Why do you keep looking up there?"

"Look, you dead-hearted asshole, my wife is pregnant. So, when I'm not on the ice, I'm gonna keep an eye on her."

I knew something was up before he even announced the pregnancy, he's been overly protective of Raleigh and Arthur, more than usual.

Taking a deep breath, I shake my head. Love makes people lose their minds. I cross my arms. "My heart isn't dead, it's sleeping. Besides, my dick pulls the weight around here."

"I'm sure it does—with all the fucking hardware you have shoved through it. That thing probably has a tow hitch."

"It does. I towed your mom to my place last week." I wink.

"Finally break that dry spell of yours, eh?"

How does he know I had a dry spell? Operative word being *had*. Damn it, my thoughts are back to Jordan.

"I'd rather have a dry spell here and there than be saddled down with one pussy for the rest of my life. Haven't you ever heard variety is the spice of life?" The words taste sour in my mouth.

"Yeah, you've got a spicy life all right. So much you've lost your palette." He hangs his head between his shoulders and laughs. "Young and dumb. Someday you'll have a woman up there and you'll get it."

I laugh. "Ha! Doubtful."

No way in hell will that ever be me. I brush it off, but what he said about the WAGs box gives me an idea. Jordan should come to a game so she can meet the wives. To say her social life is lacking would be an understatement. Building up a group of safe friends would benefit her. I'll suggest it and see what she thinks.

"Okay, old man. For now, can you at least pretend to focus. Jesus Christ."

He slaps my stomach with his glove. "Shit, Lonan's gonna get this one." We rise to our feet. Sure enough, a second later, Lonan Burke sends it in. Guess he was paying attention more than I gave him credit for.

"Fuck yeah, Burkey!" I yell from the bench. One last squirt of my water bottle, then I'm back on the ice.

Coach sends out Burmeister and Paek together, and I grin. *This is it*. The previous line was like trying to fit a square peg in a round hole. As soon as the staff gave it a shot, it was night and day difference. Practices have been going smoothly now that we've implemented the change, but this will be our first time trying it out at a game.

During their shift, Paek and Burmeister pass and move around as if they can read each other's mind. I resist jumping up and down. I knew they would be great together! Their strengths complement each other so well. I feel on top of the world.

Coach gives me a slap on the back when Paek does an absolutely beautiful, filthy deke to Burmeister, but I don't look back at him. He and I both know it wouldn't have happened on the previous set up. I don't care to say I told you so, I'm just pleased it's working and we have our solid defense back.

JORDAN LANDRY

Congrats! I'm going to celebrate your win with an ice cream sundae.

I'm sure. And what were you going to do if we didn't win?

JORDAN LANDRY

I was going to grieve your loss with an ice cream sundae.

Thought so.

JORDAN LANDRY

I'm assuming you'll be out late. I'm going to use the theater to watch a movie, but let me know if you're coming home with a friend and I'll make myself scarce.

Does she honestly think I'd bring home a girl while she's living there?

Whoa, what if I want ice cream too?

JORDAN LANDRY

Do you?

Not really.

JORDAN LANDRY

Thought so.

See you laterrrrrr.

On the stationary bikes, Shep shouts, "Top Shelf, who's in?"

A few of the boys cheer, but I remain silent. It feels weird leaving Jordan home alone. Besides, I've been spending so much time with practices and Coach that a quiet night kinda sounds nice.

"Banksy, you're buying the first round."

"Nah, I'm gonna skip this one."

Wilder rears his head back and stops pedaling. "Dude, it's Halloween!"

I can't tell them why I'm skipping out, they won't understand. It's not like me, and Halloween is like puck bunny Christmas.

"I'm beat."

"It's Hallo-fucking-ween! Do I need to remind you every hot woman in the city is going to be out, in costume, and looking sexy as fuck?"

Jonesy walks up and puts the back of his palm to my forehead like he's checking my temperature. I slap his hand away.

"Fuck off, I'm just tired. Can't a guy take a night off? Shit."

Normally, after a game, I find someone to blow my load with. All that testosterone needs an outlet. Lately, though, I prefer Jordan. I know what I'm getting with her, and what I'm getting is a stellar bare pussy that clamps down like a fucking vise. I'd take her in a baggy sweatshirt over a bunny in a sexy nurse costume any day.

After the press box, we depart in our suits and duffels. Half of us are leaving for Top Shelf, the other half going home to women. My situation isn't like theirs, but like everybody, I'd like to get laid tonight.

When I walk through the mud room, the vibration of bass in the theater below hums under my feet. Toeing off my shoes, I head downstairs, hoping I haven't missed out on too much of the movie. The closer I get, the louder the unsettling background music becomes. Which can only mean she's watching something scary. *Of course, it's Halloween.*

As I get closer, I see the silhouette of her against the movie screen. The camera pans around a corner and she tucks her legs up. A jump scare is coming, and I can't resist the opportunity. I sneak up behind her and bring my mouth right behind her ear.

"*Boo.*"

She screams and leaps out of her chair. When she spins

around, she clutches at her chest, then bounds toward me and smacks my bicep.

"You asshole!" she says between laughs. "You scared the shit out of me! What are you doing home?"

She crouches with her hand on her knees, catching her breath. I smile and reach down to grab the remote, pausing the horror flick. "Movie sounded better."

"Better than getting laid?"

"Eh, I figured I could get that here too." I wink and dodge the pillow she chucks at my head.

"See if I ever sit on your dick again."

"You will, you can't resist."

She rolls her eyes. "Whatever. Are you going to make me back it up all the way to the beginning?"

I point at the screen, the ticker shows she's barely fifteen minutes into it. "You just started it! How about you make me an ice cream sundae while I get caught up?"

"Ugh, fine. But only because I don't want to watch the opening scene again."

I smile as big as I can and fall into the leather bucket seat. "Thanks, dear."

She holds up her middle finger as she walks out, and I kick up my feet. I'm about to rewind the movie when her phone lights up next to me. I glance down in time to see a new text message flash on her screen.

BRYAN DAVENPORT

This isn't over. Where the fuck are you?

I pluck her phone out of the cupholder as another text comes through.

BRYAN DAVENPORT

You can't hide from me.

And another.

BRYAN DAVENPORT

We aren't done. I'll fucking find you.

I swipe to unlock her phone, but it asks for a passcode. Damn it. She told me he was texting apologies, so what the hell is all this? With her phone in hand, I head up to the kitchen. She's putting the ice cream back in the freezer when I get there.

"Impatient much?"

"What the hell is this?" I ask, holding up her phone.

"My phone?"

"Bryan texted you."

Her head lolls to the side, then she steps closer and snatches it out of my hand.

"Don't go through my phone. He used to do that too."

"I wasn't going through your phone, the messages showed up on the screen. You didn't tell me they were threats."

She unlocks it, and I don't take her phone away, but I hold her arm up so I can read too.

She texted him. I specifically told her not to interact.

Stop contacting me. We are done. Regarding wedding plans, I've already spoken with the wedding planner and additional vendors to cancel. My half is done. You can tell the guests.

I'm proud of her for putting it out there—I'm sure that message took a lot of courage to write, but the snippets from him make my blood boil. I sigh and release the gentle grasp on her wrist, speaking as calmly as I can. "We need to get you a new number."

Jordan stuffs her phone in her back pocket and hands me the bowl of ice cream. I don't even want it anymore.

"I'm sorry," she says, looking defeated as hell.

"Why are you apologizing?"

"Because you're mad at me for texting him!"

"What?! No! I'm mad at *him* for texting you!" I grit my teeth. "Fuck!"

Maybe I should have gone out with the boys tonight. There's a thousand pounds of aggression built up inside me. and I need to let it out. I take a deep breath.

"I'm sorry, I shouldn't have yelled. I want to be clear; I'm not mad at you. But he can't talk to you like that. Nobody can talk to you that way. I wish you would have told me it was happening so I could help."

Her face pales. "Camden, I need you to stay out of this. I'm dealing with it in my own way, it's something I need for *me*. Just give me time."

I dislike the sound of that. "I don't think—"

"It doesn't matter what you think about my past relationship. How I end it is my own business. Please, Camden. Stay out of it."

"I will for now. But if this escalates, I need to know."

"Fine!"

"Okay . . . Ready to go watch the movie?"

She purses her lips, shifting her weight from one foot to the other before she slowly spins on her heel—heading in the wrong direction. "I'm going to bed, I'm not in the mood anymore."

"Jordan, I'm sorry. Come back down and let's start over. I want to hang out. Please."

She pauses on the steps and trudges back down, and I pull her into my arms for a hug. It makes me feel a hundred times better, and I can only hope it's doing the same for her. I don't want her to think I'm mad, and I don't want to ruin her night.

"Forget the ice cream, let's watch the movie." I sigh.

She nods against my chest and takes a deep breath.

"I'm going to change into something comfortable and meet you down there." We had a press box interview after the game, and I'm still in my suit, and she's wearing some soft sleep shorts and a loose shirt. All I want is to wrap her up in my arms and keep her close. Where she's safe.

Back in the theater, she settles into her seat. *Nah.* I grab a blanket from the basket and crawl over the back of the couch, pulling her back to my front as I settle in behind her.

Her neck cranes to look at me. "What are you doing?"

I nuzzle the back of her neck and breathe her in. "I'm watching a movie."

"You've got me trapped between your thighs."

"Friends can cuddle and watch a movie together . . . If you don't like it, then move."

She leans against me, and I smile. I'm sure she's rolling her eyes. "By the way, that goal in the second period? Phenomenal passing."

I smile. She's talking about Paek and Burmeister, and she's right, it was. They anticipated each other's moves so naturally. All of us on the bench lost our shit when they made a goal. The new line is killing it, and I'm filled with pride.

"It really was."

I wrap my arms around her, and she melts into my chest, letting me tighten my bear hug. Her soothing scent surrounds me. I love the Viktor & Rolf perfume she wears, but there's an underlying natural Jordan fragrance that's sexy and cozy. She lets out a sigh when I press my lips to her neck. I do it again, hoping for another noise, this time closer to her shoulder. The exhale is thick with longing, this woman holds such power over me.

“I want to kiss you,” she murmurs.

My tongue tucks into my cheek as I try to tamp down my smile. She’s just as affected by me, and I love it. Angling her chin, she twists in my arms, and I loosen my hold on her. Her trusting eyes gaze into mine before dropping to my mouth. Cupping her neck, I brush my lips over hers, and the breathy sighs are my tipping point.

With her hands planted on my shoulders, she rotates in my arms until she’s straddling me. I palm her ass and bring her closer. My tongue skates across hers, it’s sensual and charged. She’s overwhelming my senses. “He never deserved you,” I mutter against her mouth. The tang of salt hits my tongue, and I open my eyes to see a wet streak down her face. Someday soon I will get my hands on Bryan and make him pay for her tears.

My thumbs stray under her shirt and stroke her waist. She grips the hem and drags it over her head. I groan, noticing she’s wearing nothing underneath. My tongue trails down the column of her neck, and she rises to her knees to give me better access to her breasts. *Goddamn.*

I peel her cotton shorts and underwear down her thighs, and she lifts one knee at a time to let me slip them off her body. Once naked, I allow my hands to explore from her shoulders to her thighs. Her move. Jordan's lips dance with mine while she tugs at the joggers I’ve changed into, and my hard cock springs out.

“What do I deserve?” she whispers.

I deepen our kiss. She deserves far better than me, that’s for sure. I had no expectation of fucking tonight, but I’ll let her use me for whatever she needs in this moment. My palms skim up the back of her thighs, over her ass, higher to her back and shoulders before traveling back down. My fingers slide between her cheeks and lower; she's hot, wet, and trembling.

She moans when I nip her neck. I wrap an arm behind her lower back and use my other hand to knead between her legs. She's already so wet, and I wonder how anyone could skip this foreplay. Her body is so receptive to every touch, hearing her sounds and feeling her shake are the greatest rewards.

My palm grinds against her clit as I stuff my fingers inside her. Her kiss is frenzied, and she moans against my mouth until she rips her lips away to breathe. Her arms wrap around my neck as I work her over.

"What do you want, Sunshine?"

"All of you." Her voice cracks, and the sorrow in it destroys me.

I nod. "Spread those pretty thighs for me."

I scoot forward and glide my cock through her folds until I'm coated with her, then wait at her entrance. I've never wanted to take away someone's pain more than right now. Her jaw falls as she settles onto me. *Jordan is a knockout.* It takes two tries before she fits every inch of me inside her, and I can't stifle the guttural sound that escapes my throat. Our bodies are made for each other.

My lips find hers again. Kissing is effortless, our mouths fit so well together, perfectly in sync. Grinding against me, she rocks, and my piercings ruggedly massage her from the inside. She settles hard on my lap as if there's an itch she needs me to scratch. I love being inside her when she's so greedy, but this grind isn't doing it for her. Her adorable, frustrated whine causes me to grip her waist and bounce her on my cock.

"This how you need to be fucked, baby?"

She whimpers my name, and begs not to stop.

"Let go. You're safe with me." I lock in on her dazzling brown eyes and jiggling thick thighs. "Goddamn, you look absolutely perfect."

She gives me more of her weight as her muscles clench. My jaw tics as I focus on her. Her orgasm hits, and I fuck her through it, stealing every sweet sound with my lips, and claim my own release.

It's not long before our panting slows, and her soft smile is a massive comfort. I slip away to the bathroom, returning with a washcloth for the cleanup. After, we each put our clothes back on in silence and return to the movie as if nothing happened.

Jordan snuggles into my arms again, but this time her scent is mixed with sex and me, and I like that even more. I kiss the top of her head as we continue the movie where we left off.

What happened tonight was simple, she had a need, and I took care of it. Because that's what friends do.

TWENTY-FIVE

Jordan

I move a load of clothes from the washer into the dryer and turn it on. For whatever reason, I stand there, staring at the clothes tumbling around behind the circular glass door. The hum of the dryer is comforting.

Today was supposed to be my wedding day. The day couldn't be more perfect for a wedding. Blue skies and soft breeze on an unusually warm November day. When I walked outside this morning, the bright sun made the orange, red, and yellow leaves glow. However, the feeling inside me doesn't fit what I imagined I'd feel walking down the aisle. Because today, I'm happy.

I'm also twenty-six years old. I never wanted to be married on my birthday. Looking back, I wonder if it was one more way for Bryan to take something that was mine and make it his.

This will be my best year yet. I can feel it. I'm living my life for me, doing what I want, when I want, how I want. I'm being reckless and irresponsible, and it's the most fun I've ever had. All thanks to Cam. He's shown me it's okay to be selfish once in a while. I'm allowed to be the main character in my own life.

Camden Teller is misunderstood. People love his demeanor; they remember the things he does that fit the playboy narrative. They talk about all the fists he throws, but they forget to mention that the guy he was punching tried to go up against a much smaller player. They write about how much money he makes, how he's one of the top paid players in the league, but they don't say he gives away nearly half of that to charities and domestic violence survivors.

Yes, he takes home a lot of women, but he's honest about it being a one-time thing from the start. I've been around a fair share of people praised for being "family men" only to watch them turn around and have an affair.

Everybody talks about Cam, but nobody really knows him. With the exception of his teammates, I presume. He would do anything for those guys. He's fiercely loyal and protective of the people he cares about.

Movement in my peripheral snaps me out of my staring contest with the dryer. Cam sidles up next to me.

"Is there anything good on?" he says, staring ahead at the clothes getting tossed around. "This channel always plays the same old shit."

I smile and nudge him as he hoists his duffel over his shoulder.

"Heading to the arena?" They have a game tonight, and I've noticed he likes to get there extra early.

"Yeah. I left you something upstairs. When you're done with your television show, you can go check it out."

"How come the press writes you as this wildcard player?" I blurt out.

He furrows his brow, and his lips tip up on the sides.

"How come the press writes anything? To make money."

"Does it bother you?"

"I don't care what they say about me. I know who I am."

A smile spreads across my face. He says it with such confidence and certainty. It's sexy. Really, really sexy. Bryan seemed to only care what people said about him. Reputation was everything, but Cam is the opposite. He lets the press go on a rampage and doesn't even blink.

"Good for you."

He clears his throat. "You okay?"

I chuckle and walk backward toward the hall. "Yeah, sorry. Just a lot on my mind today or something." He nods, and I lift my hand in a wave. "Good luck at the game tonight."

"Thanks. See ya later."

I spin around and head back down the hallway, and the door leading to the garage shuts, echoing behind me as he leaves. The house falls silent, but it's peaceful. Silence used to stress me out, it meant tension, but that's not the case anymore. When I get back to my living space, I immediately notice the jersey on the table in the kitchenette. As I get closer, I pick up the notepad, scrawled with Cam's handwriting. There's a ticket underneath for tonight's game.

Dear Sunshine,

You were supposed to be wearing a wedding dress today.

Instead, I'm offering you this. It was the jersey I wore when I scored my first goal with the Lakes. It's special to me. Kinda like you. Don't look too far into that. And don't spill beer on it.

If you're not busy—and I know you aren't, because you never leave the fucking house—come to the game tonight. Some of the WAGs will be in the seats next to you, Birdie, Micky, and Raleigh. They're nice girls, you'll like them. It's time for you to get out and meet people.

–C

I smile. As if I needed more convincing that he's got a kind heart. He's such a terrific friend. Probably the best friend I've ever had. I pick up the jersey and press it to my nose, it smells like him.

I get to the arena early and find my seat. My knee bounces while I wait. This feels like a blind date with friends, which seems even more pathetic.

I repeat the names in my head. Birdie, Micky, Raleigh. God, what if they're like stuffy hockey Stepford wives? No, Cam said I would like them. I don't think he'd set me up with them if he didn't think we'd get along, no matter how badly I need friends.

I try to look busy, and find myself texting Cam.

How hard is it to get red wine out of jerseys?

CAMDEN TELLER

That better be a joke.

Only time will tell... Thanks for the ticket btw.

CAMDEN TELLER

No problem. I fuck harder when you're watching me, thought I'd see if it works for playing hockey too. 😉

My eyes just rolled across the arena. If you see them on the ice, will you pick them up?

CAMDEN TELLER

You're lucky you're wearing my jersey...

Why's that?

CAMDEN TELLER

Because if you weren't, I'd rip off your clothes later and punish you for being so snarky with me before a game.

Promises, promises...

CAMDEN TELLER

I keep my promises. I'll push your face into the pillow and make you mine if you're not careful.

It was all fun and games until he used the *M word*. He can't throw it around so loosely.

Shut upppp. And quit texting me, I'm waiting for the girls. Nervous.

CAMDEN TELLER

Don't worry, you'll like them and they'll like you. Just remember to be Jordan, not Jordana.

K.

CAMDEN TELLER

Good luck.

You too.

I tuck my phone back in my pocket, and not two seconds later, a blonde, brunette, and redhead—*like a bad joke*—head down the stairs toward my seat. I'm three rows up from the glass, right next to the tunnel. I've never been *myself* around new people, and I have no idea how to act with them. *Be Jordan, not Jordana. Be yourself.*

"Hey!" they say, almost in unison.

"Hi! I'm Jordan." I paste on a smile. We make introductions, and I figure out which name goes to which woman and who their husbands are.

"Banksy told us you're new to the hockey scene. You're a friend of a friend?"

"Banksy?"

"Yeah, you know, Teller?"

"Oh!" *Wonder why they call him Banksy?* "I've watched a lot of hockey but haven't been to many live games. And yeah, we're friends."

"I've never seen him with a girlfriend before," Micky says. "Normally, he flips through women pretty fast."

Birdie and Raleigh both smack her legs. "Mick! What the fuck!"

I laugh. "No, you're right. It's no secret he gets around."

"I mean it in a good way! Like she's special to him!"

"It's special to me. Kinda like you."

Micky wraps an arm around my shoulders. "And see?! She knows, it's fine!"

"Oh, I'm not his girlfriend."

Raleigh puts her hair up in a ponytail. "Well, you must be something to him, Barrett said he's never invited a girl to a game."

I try not to let that sink in. It's not like that for us, we'll only ever be friends, and that's the way I like it. It's not like he put my name on the WAGs box, he gave me a ticket for seats, and I appreciate that the girls are sitting down here with me.

"Just a friend, really. I wouldn't want anything more anyway. Men are too much work," I explain. "I hope you aren't missing being in the WAGs box on my account, but it's really nice to have the company."

"Not at all. We got sitters!" Birdie shouts, holding up her hand for Raleigh to high-five. "This is where all the fun is. We normally sit up there because we've got kids in tow. They're much easier to manage in the box. But tonight is girls' night!"

"Whoa, *we*? *You* all have kids, not me," Micky says. "Don't lump me in with your overactive ovaries."

"Except for Micky, but she sits up there because we're there," Birdie says.

"Okay, I'm gonna grab a soda. Want me to get a round of beers for the rest of y'all?" Raleigh asks. I notice she has a slight southern accent. She looks at me. "Do you drink?"

I chuckle and nod.

"Perfect, you already fit in!" Birdie says. "What else do you like to do?"

"I read a lot. Travel. Normal stuff."

"Oooh, we went to Hawaii during the offseason, and it was amazing," Raleigh adds. "It's Barrett's last season, but after he retires, we plan on spending more time there."

We go back and forth for a while, getting to know each other, and I realize quickly that *Banksy*, as they call him, made a perfect friend match for me. I'm glad he got me together with them because these women are awesome. Before we know it, the warm-ups have begun and the ice is full of players. Cam's eyes land on me almost instantly, then he smiles and winks.

I wink back.

When we finally get to the puck drop, excitement explodes in the stands. Though the girls next to me seem more excited to add another to their troupe than watching their husbands play. I suppose this is normal to them. For me, it's thrilling to watch hockey up close like this. I cheer along with the girls who root for the different players on the team—mostly for their husbands. I follow their lead, but mostly keep my eye on Teller, number forty-six.

Cam is playing great. He retrieves the puck and flies down the ice with it, passing back and forth to other teammates. A puck battle breaks out, and everyone stands. He recovers, gets a shot, and it bounces off the goalie's skate, pinging into the net. I'm instantly jumping, screaming, and high-fiving strangers along with everyone else in the crowd. I've been catching a lot more televised games since moving into his apartment above the garage but seeing the lightning-fast action right in front of you is a thrill!

A few guys slap his helmet, then he heads back to the bench, and the coach claps him on the shoulder, but his eyes are still on the ice. Cam looks at me over his shoulder again and smiles. Micky nudges me, and I nudge her back like we're in middle school.

"Maybe she's his lucky charm . . ." she says to the group.

"Nah, if anything, it's his first goal jersey." I pluck the thick material.

All three stare at me.

"What?" *Do I have something on my face?*

"He gave you that jersey?" Micky asks.

Raleigh points at what I'm wearing. "That's his first goal jersey?"

"He didn't *give* it to me. It's just to borrow for the game," I explain.

"Oh girl. Come on." Birdie's mouth tips up on one side as she smirks at me.

"No, it's not like that." I shake my head adamantly.

"No, girl it *is* that. Plain and simple," Raleigh says. "He's probably got a mountain of jerseys at home, all the guys do. If it didn't mean anything, he would have given you one of those. But to give you *that* jersey?"

Birdie's jaw drops. "Holy shit, hell must have frozen over. Banksy's crushing!"

"No, no, no." I wave my hands. "I promise, he's still Banksy."

"Yeah, okay!" Micky laughs. "I'm calling it now. He's into you."

They can't give me false hope like that.

"I got out of a serious relationship not long ago, the last thing I need is to get involved with somebody."

"Too late for that!"

I laugh. "I swear. Besides, it's complicated."

"Oooh-ooh! Are we playing the *whose-relationship-is-more-complicated* game? I love this one, I always win. Okay, let's hear it!" Raleigh says.

I narrow my eyes at them. I don't know these women. Can I trust them?

"You first," I reply. I gotta know that my story isn't going up against something like *he forgot our anniversary once* or some shit.

"We had a one-night stand. I got pregnant, tried to contact him. He tried to contact me. We lost contact for five years. I thought he'd abandoned me, I hated him. But he didn't even know he had a child because I raised Arthur, *that's our son*, by myself, until he showed up at one of my work events and wouldn't leave me alone until . . ." She wiggles her ring finger and clicks her tongue. "Now we're finally back on track and getting our happy ending."

I stare wide-eyed. Guess mine doesn't seem so bad.

"Yeah, you win."

She smiles. "I know."

"You gotta tell us yours!" Birdie says.

Might as well be dramatic. "I was supposed to get married today. Camden was my ex-fiancé's best man."

The others cover their mouths in shock. "Holy shit. *Today*?"

I nod.

"Damn!" Micky exclaims. "Strong contender, you might have Raleigh tied."

It's not the place to discuss the whole thing, but I make Raleigh promise she'll tell me more about hers later.

I explain he's only taking me in because of my crazy ex, and he founded a charity that specifically helps women in my situation. Yes, we've developed a friendship, but he probably would have done this for any woman that needed a place to go. That's the kind of person Cam is. I leave out the sexual stuff between us—and some of the uglier parts about Bryan—though I'm sure they can read between the lines.

Birdie sighs. "God, the poor puck bunnies are gonna be devastated."

I groan. No matter how much I try to clarify why nothing

will ever happen between Camden and me, they still seem convinced we're destined.

"Oh. No. What ever will we do?" Micky says deadpan in a staccato rhythm.

"Please. Stop. I can't take it," Birdie adds.

"Hey, as a former *bunny*, they will not be devastated. There's always fresh meat to go after. Well, except he *is* the pretty one . . . Okay, they'll be devastated." Raleigh concedes, throwing her hand to the side.

"We'll have your back in case they decide to attack."

"Nobody is going to be attacking me because he's still a free agent who is welcome to take home whomever he pleases."

They give me puppy-dog eyes, and I laugh. "Come on, let's watch them play. I promise it's way more interesting."

Not long after, the game heats up again and Camden scores a second goal. He's on fire tonight! Seeing how talented he is in person is so different from watching it through a screen. He carries the puck with such skill and can turn on a dime. His skates are simply an extension of himself.

After the first period, they're winning 2-1, both goals from Cam. They walk through the tunnel, and we sneak a peek at each other.

TWENTY-SIX

Camden

Seeing Jordan in the stands does something to me. And yeah, I play better when she's watching. *What's up with that?* I'm a cocky son of a bitch, but those goals even surprised me. If I get a hat trick tonight, she will definitely come to more games.

I adjust my gloves while sitting on the bench and squirt my water bottle in my mouth. I glance over my shoulder to see her, and she's laughing with the other women. Her eyes wander over to me.

Having fun? I mouth.

She presses her hands to both rosy cheeks with a smile. *So much fun.* She gestures to the chatting wives, and mouths, *Thank you.*

I wink, and she winks back. Damn, she's gorgeous. Seeing her in my shirts at home is one thing. It makes me want to fuck her. But seeing my name across her back? It makes me possessive. *Makes me want to keep her.* This is why the boys walk around with hard dicks whenever their women wear their number. What a messed-up phenomenon.

Not that Jordan's my woman. Whatever she and I are, it's

our own unique thing. I don't need to label it. She's a nice girl who's become a good friend, and we're using each other for sex. We share this bizarre yet comforting camaraderie. I like who she is as a person, and she's so effortless to be around. In fact, she's one of my favorite people.

It started as a way to keep her safe with me, but now I'm the one who feels safe with her. And we enjoy each other. Why should it be any more complicated than that? I try not to think about the things I do for her that I wouldn't do for other women. The way I treat her is different, I'm aware, but Jordan's special. She's my friend. I'd never let just any girl wear my first game jersey, but today was going to be a big day for her, and I wanted her to wear something meaningful —I just didn't realize how meaningful it would be for me to see her in it.

I'm up next. I spray water in my mouth from my water bottle and spit it out again.

"Teller!" Coach yells.

Colby skates in, and I swap with him, pounding the ice to get into position. One quick look at her in the stands is all I need. I feel good about this. *She's gonna give me my hat trick.*

The puck drops, and I steal it the first chance I get. After a sharp deke to Conway, I shoot from where I am. It soars through the five-hole. Luckiest shot in the world. The fans lose their goddamn minds. I skate by and point at her. *You.*

TWENTY-SEVEN

Jordan

When the game wraps up, the guys win 5-1. A clean sweep. The energy in the arena is electric, everyone is high-fiving and talking about *Banksy's* hat trick. I'm having a blast with the other women. I swallow the last of my beer and stack the empty plastic cups.

"They'll be out celebrating tonight," Birdie says, pulling out her phone. "I'm going to have to text my mom and let her know we're going to be back late."

"Barrett and I will probably head home. This pregnancy has me wiped out."

Micky leans over and faces me. "I have a question." She's direct, but her kind eyes and smile keep her from being too intimidating.

"Shoot."

"Okay. So you say nothing is going on between the two of you—you're wrong, by the way, but whatever—if you had your druthers, would you *want* there to be something between you and Banksy? Girl code—you gotta be honest and nothing leaves the circle."

I think for a moment. The sex is good. Who am I kidding? The sex is out of this world. It's hot, frenzied, intense, dirty, and unhinged. I fucking love it. However, it's Camden Teller. My last relationship ended with my fiancé cheating on me with my best friend. Even though in some ways it was a relief and helped me dodge a bullet, it still hurt and left me with fears about future relationships.

If I couldn't see it happening with my own best friend, it would be even easier for it to get past me if it was with a bunny or one-night stand. I've seen the way the women are around him. He's obviously plenty experienced, but I would worry, and that's not fair to either of us. When I'm ready for a relationship, I want to be stable and ready for something like that.

"No."

"Why not? You know, I know the tabloids give him a bad rep, and I said what I said, but the guys really vouch for him. He's a good captain. He's dependable and loyal."

I smile, it pleases me to know other people understand how great he is.

"I like Cam, he's a great guy, but I'm done with relationships for the time being, with anyone. I'm not sure I could be mature enough to handle his . . . *following*. Besides, I'm in my man-hater era. But Cam is an amazing friend who watches out for me, and I appreciate that."

The players skate toward the tunnel and step off the ice. I reach for my purse on the floor but startle at the loud bang next to me.

"What the hell was—" I look up to see Cam, he hooks his arms over the side of the barrier with it digging into his armpits. Fans around us clamor to get a puck, stick, or autograph, anything. The security below is talking him down, but he's ignoring them completely. A few of the other players stand gawking, one of them being Barrett Conway. He's ignoring everything around him.

"Hey, birthday girl."

"Hi?" I laugh. *How did he know it was my birthday?* My eyes glance to the security below, instructing him to get down. His coach yells his name, but he doesn't respond. "I think your coach wants you."

"Come here," he says it so casually. I scoot closer, and he high-fives a starstruck young boy sitting behind me.

"Teller! Let's go!" one of the coaches bellows from the other side of the plexiglass.

"Cam, what are you doing?"

"Kissing you."

He grabs the back of my neck and pulls me in, doing exactly that. His mouth presses to mine, and he slides his tongue over my lower lip. It takes my breath away. After that, he drops from the board onto the padded floor below. The coach smacks him with a clipboard.

"Jesus, Teller. The fuck is wrong with you? Lockers, now!"

He looks up at me and winks again, and I press my fingers to my lips. My cheeks flare red and nervous laughter bursts out of me. *What the hell was that about?*

"I fucking called it!" Micky shouts. She turns around in her seat. "Did I not fucking call it? You heard me, right?" she asks the person behind her—who happens to be the young boy Cam high-fived seconds ago.

"Sorry," the rest of us say in unison to the parents, apologizing for her use of the word *fuck*.

Camden didn't do it to be romantic, he did it for the thrill of getting in trouble and maintaining his heartthrob reputation.

My friends laugh, and I shake my head, they don't know him like I do.

CAMDEN

Coach takes a minute to yell at me for my little "publicity stunt" as he calls it. Do I fucking care? Not even a little. Let the org fine me and move on. Jordan was in the stands wearing my jersey and I got a hat trick. I kissed her because I wanted to, and I don't regret it.

The boys are stripping their gear when I walk in from my ass chewing from Coach, they all start clapping. I take a bow.

"What the hell was that all about?" Barrett asks, laughing.

Shep holds his arms out. "You stop going out with us after games, and then *that* happens? Who is she?"

"That's Jordan," I answer.

"Yeah, but are you guys dating? Is she a bunny or—" Burmeister adds.

"Easy . . ." Barrett warns, his wife was a former bunny, and he's not a fan of the term.

Shaking my head, I look up while unlacing my skates. "Nah, she's not like that. She's the opposite actually. We're friends."

"Bullshit," says Lonan.

I chuckle. "I mean, we've messed around, but—"

Jonesy cuts in. "The slut comes home to roost!"

Are they even listening to me? I said we're only friends.

"Was that some fucked-up way to pick up more pussy? You know they caught you on the jumbotron, right?"

Good. Now everyone will know she's mine. The thought pops into my head before I can stop it. It's a new development in my feelings and likely a dangerous one I need to get control of.

"It's not like that, really. She's going through some shit and we're hanging out."

"Holy fuck, I never thought I'd see the day. Figured the only way you'd ever get hung up on a girl was if you were doing some kinky rope shit." Lonan laughs.

"Who said we haven't?" I grin at him, tugging off my socks that smell like something died. They think I'm dating her, which is ridiculous. Sure, I'd rather fuck her than take home a bunny, but it's not like we're in a relationship.

"Where did you meet?" Rhys asks.

"Remember that wedding I was the best man in?"

"Ohhh, shit, Banksy bagged himself a bridesmaid!" Shep shouts.

I shake my head and smirk. "She's the bride."

TWENTY-EIGHT

Jordan

Banksy, as I'm learning to refer to him as when around the players or their wives, invited me to Top Shelf for the postgame celebration. I fit right in with my Lakes jersey. I wanted to wear something fun for my birthday, so I dressed it up with a miniskirt and my favorite knee-high boots. The ones Cam rescued from the condo.

While waiting for my drink, I sit facing the room with my elbows propped up on the bar top behind me. The energy in the room is chaotic and fun, everyone is smiling and having a good time. It's nice to be partying with no dress code, other than the team colors. Nobody is gossiping or talking about stock prices or leveraged buyouts.

Cam is a hit. I watch him interact with fans across the room. The women know him well, and it makes my stomach twist even though it shouldn't. *And the touching!* Every time a woman walks by, she's touching his shoulder, his arm, his leg, his ass. He smiles his megawatt smile at each of them, and it grates on my nerves.

"Don't worry about them," Micky says, taking the seat beside me.

I furrow my brow and spin around, waiting on my cocktail. "I'm not. There's nothing between us. It was just a stunt after the hat trick. I'm fine. I told you I didn't want anything to happen between us anyway, remember?"

"Me thinks the *friend* doth protest too much . . ." she says, pushing off the bar and heading out to find Rhys.

The bartender finishes making my second martini and slides it over to me. I hand over my card, but the man shakes his head and points to a guy at the end of the bar. "He took care of it." I smile and lift my drink to him. He lifts two fingers off the bar and grins. He's attractive, and I'm a buzzed birthday girl.

He leaves his chair and strides toward the one Micky was sitting in a moment ago. I glance up at Cam, his eyes are on the man walking toward me. His gaze meets mine, and he shakes his head. I roll my eyes. *What's his problem?* A strange woman puts her arms around Camden, and he shakes her off. He told me I should meet new people, so that's what I'm doing.

"Hi," the deep voice says beside me.

"Hi, I'm Jordan."

"Brett."

"Thank you for the drink," I say, raising the stemmed martini glass. I can feel Cam's glower from here. It makes my skin hot. Out the corner of my eye I see him advancing toward me.

"You're welcome. So what do you do for a living?"

Why is that always the first thing people ask?

"I'm a contract manager." I'm not used to saying unemployed yet.

Camden's cologne wafts from behind me. He's practically breathing down my neck.

"Where at?"

A woman squeals behind me on my left. "Banks. Long time. Wanna buy me a drink?"

"Maybe some other time," he grumbles. It's unpleasant to think of him with other women, but he said *some other time*, rather than *no*. It's another reminder that he's a forever playboy. The last thing I need is to get involved with someone like him in the spotlight who can't handle temptation.

I bring my focus back to the guy in front of me.

"I was at H&H Holdings, but I'm looking for something new."

He nods. "I've heard some funny things are going on over there lately. I'm over at Wrenbury." It's another equity firm in the area. Not nearly as big as H&H, but they have a reputation for having strong ethics.

Camden puts his arm around me and holds his hand out to the guy. "Camden Teller."

The man I'm talking to stares at him for a moment and reluctantly takes his hand. "Brett Anderson."

I shrug off his arm, and Brett looks at me with his head turned slightly away, like he's unsure of what's going on. His guess is as good as mine. "Camden is a friend," I say, for the hundredth time tonight.

"Can I talk to you for a minute?" Cam says, taking my hand and pulling me off my barstool.

What the fuck?

"Don't worry, I'll return her to you shortly," he growls at Brett, who's probably thinking I'm more trouble than I'm worth.

Camden leads me to where the rest of the team sits, he has them move out, so we can slide to the center of the large U-shaped booth.

"What the hell is wrong with you?" I snap, under my breath. "You said you wanted me to meet people!"

His voice drops, and he speaks against my neck. "I was talking about the WAGs. I didn't teach you how to give a blowjob so you could go practice on somebody else."

"Actually, that's exactly what you were doing, whether you realized it or not."

"You know that wasn't my intention."

"I don't mind *sharing*," I sneer.

"Oh, you want to be shared, now?"

I shrug. "He might be into it, should I ask him?"

I look down to see him unzip his dress pants. "He might, but I'm not. Pull up your skirt." My mouth drops open. If anyone heard him, I'll be mortified, but thankfully, everyone around us seems preoccupied by the game highlights on the big screen. His hand covers mine and he brings it to his lap, under the table. His dick is out, and he's hard. *Holy shit.* My fingers explore his ladder, enjoying the way his piercings feel.

"No way."

"Do it now, Jordan, or I make a scene and fuck you on top of this table for everyone to see. I already have a reputation, no one will be surprised by it. You, on the other hand . . . Well, your secrets won't be so secret anymore, will they?"

"What secrets?"

He hauls me into his lap and leans close to my ear. "That you love being a slut for me. That I'm the only one who gets to see how wet you get misbehaving. Maybe everyone else wants to see. You like that idea, don't you?"

I grit my teeth. "I might have been a slut for that other guy too," I mumble. He twitches under me. "Cam, we can't."

"Yes you can. I'll be discreet if you're nice about it. You think they're gonna find out?" He gestures to his teammates.

"Yes, they're going to find out if you're fucking me," I

say through clamped teeth. "I think that'll be obvious." He can't be serious.

"Push your panties to the side, Jordan. I know you're fucking wet."

I'm not wet, I'm drenched. "Forget it."

"Safeword is ordering another drink."

Do I dare call his bluff?

The ESPN highlights are rolling on the giant televisions over the bar. The guys watch as they're about to show Cam's hat trick replays. They show the first goal, everyone cheers, and he shoves up my skirt, pulls my thong to the side, and spears himself inside me. My jaw drops and I gasp.

Lonan looks over at me. "I know, I still can't believe his fucking luck with that shot. Unreal."

I blink back at him, my face burning. "So crazy," I answer. Lonan's oblivious of the true reason for my gasp. He returns his attention to Birdie at his side.

Cam barks out a laugh. "Oh my god, that was perfect," he mutters in my ear, amused by how well that worked for him.

Birdie leans forward to look around Lonan at me. "Hey, we're getting nachos, what do you guys want?"

His knee bounces, thrusting himself deeper, and my legs fall to either side. "Come on, Sunshine. Tell them what you're hungry for."

"Yes," I answer.

Birdie cocks her head and furrows her brow at me. "You want nach—"

"Uh-huh." I'll say whatever to get the attention off me. "Get two orders."

"Two for you? Or two for the both of—"

"One for you, one for me!"

Cam shakes with silent laughter behind me. He squeezes the back of my thighs, and his husky breaths warm my neck. "Deep breaths, lean back." He smells like Doublemint gum and cologne. *The signature scent of fuckboys everywhere.*

Once the shock of him being inside me fades, the burn around my entrance throbs. "I think your ladder tore me in half."

"Want me to kiss it all better?"

I jab my elbow into his ribs. "You're a dick, you know that?"

"*Everybody* knows that."

"How many times have you done this to women at this table?" I immediately regret asking, I don't want to know what number in line I am for his under-the-table pussy play.

"You're the first . . . How come you didn't tell me it was your birthday earlier?"

How did he even know? Did he go through my wallet?

"Because it's none of your business. It's just a birthday. After twenty-one, birthdays don't matter."

There's a pause. "Your birthday matters. I got you a present."

I roll my eyes. "Let me guess, I'm sitting on it."

He chuckles and spreads my thighs wider. *Oh fuck.* "You'll have to wait and see . . ."

I lean across the table and reach for a drink menu. Needing something to have open in front of me. He runs his hand up my spine and grips the nape of my neck, pulling me against him.

"So pretty," he says into my hair. "I can feel the pulse in your neck. Is there anywhere else I can feel it?" His hand slips under my thigh and presses hard against my clit. "Found it. Pretty easy when you're throbbing. What a soft pussy you have."

I take a sip of his beer, trying to act natural while he warms his cock inside me.

"Sully!" Everybody yells when the giant hockey player steps closer.

"Assholes. Ladies." He nods to everyone.

"Captains sit together," Jonesy shouts.

Sully rolls his eyes. "I'm not Captain Sullivan anymore," he grumbles.

Lonan grins slowly. "Oh, would you prefer Hero of the Hudson?"

"Fuck off, Lonan," he responds.

He whispers in my ear, "Remember your safeword."

His fingers circle my clit. I'm so wet it's probably audible, but luckily, the bar is loud and most of its patrons are well on their way to drunk.

Lonan and Birdie scoot out, letting Sully slide up next to us. *Fantastic.*

Cam drags his hand from me, wipes it across my thigh, then shakes Sully's hand with it. *Is he deranged!?* I slap his leg, and he chuckles while chatting with the former captain. His hand slides back under the table, and he goes back to rubbing circles around the tight nub, making my entire body tense up. I could stop this, I *should* stop this. All I need to do is order a drink, but a wicked part of me doesn't want to. I want him to keep it up. *This is so fucked.*

He adjusts me on his length, and his piercings rub against my G-spot while he chats up his friend.

"Oh . . . Sully, this is Jordan. Jordan, meet Sully. He was the former captain of the team." *I know who Lee Sullivan is, thank you.* We make introductions and are interrupted when a server comes to the table. While Sully orders a beer and a water from the server, Cam gets next to my ear. "Talk to Sully about his retirement."

"Can I get anyone else anything?" the server asks. She

looks at the half-empty beer in my hand. "Would you like another?"

He does that thing where he adjusts his knee, bouncing me once on his lap. "Yeah, honey, do you want another drink?" His voice is dripping in condescension. His fingers work me over while the other hand caresses my thigh with his thumb. *The audacity.*

"I'm good for now, thanks." I can only imagine the smug look on his face.

His voice is in my ear again. "Go on, ask Sully what he's been up to." He pinches my clit—*fuck, that's nice*. "Don't be rude, Jordan. Talk to him."

"How's retirement, Sully? What have you been up to?"

"Good girl." I hear in my other ear. *Holy hell.*

"Not bad, trying to keep busy, I'm in the process of building a house, so there's that."

How do I keep the conversation going while he's doing this to me? He'll pay for this later. "Where are you building?"

"I found a lake lot west of the cities that I recently made an offer on. It's a gorgeous property. Lots of evergreen trees for privacy."

"I like trees." *Did I just say that?* "I mean, they're good for what you said, privacy . . . and good for the earth too." *Seriously, stop talking.* "What architect are you using?"

Cam murmurs little praises into my neck, and it's nearly impossible to concentrate.

"I'm actually designing it myself, but Mead & Brandt will manage the build. They work in sustainable architecture."

"Wow, that's impressive. You must stay busy."

"It's not too bad. Still got to play a lotta golf last summer, and I flew to New York to visit some friends."

"How was that?"

Cam flexes inside me, and I swallow.

Sully continues, "Traveling solo feels strange, especially after being with the team for so long. Might have to start taking Barrett with me once he's done. I need a travel buddy."

I fake an amused laugh. "Ha! Yeah. Well, I'm sure there's a line of women that would want to." *That's worse than the tree thing.*

His breath is on my neck. "You're doing so well, keep going." He adds pressure and rubs a little faster. I clear my throat. "You keep pulsing on me like that, I'm gonna come early."

"Yeah, not so much luck with women," Sully answers.

I dig my nails into his thighs as hard as I can.

Cam's voice is in my ear again. "You think you can hurt me? Joke's on you, sweetheart. I'm into that shit. Come on, break the skin. Make me bleed."

"How . . . where, uh, wh-where would you like to travel?"

Sully looks at me with a grimace. "Are you okay?"

Cam feigns concern. "Yeah, Jordan, are you okay?" He slaps my clit.

"Fine!" I say way too loud. *Shit.* "I'm fine. Lost my train of thought for a second," I say between nervous laughter. "Probably had too many of these." I lift the glass. Noticing my hand trembling, I set it down. It feels like a bomb is about to go off inside me.

"I guess I'd like to spend some time in Greece someday."

My cheeks burn, and I do everything I can to calm my voice. "It's beautiful there. My family has a place in Santorini, I highly recommend it. May is gorgeous."

"I'll keep that in mind. Do you do a lot of traveling?"

Cam leans forward. "That's enough, cut him off."

Oh, now I'm talking too *much? God, Camden! Make up your mind.*

"Not anymore."

"Jordan . . ." Cam urges.

I squirm in his lap, and look at the TVs, thanking higher powers when the ref makes a bad call. "That ref was an idiot." I point up.

The rest of the table joins in, taking over the penalty conversation when his hot breath is at my neck again. "Ready to come?"

"I don't want to do it here, what if it goes—"

He sits up, adjusting, somehow pushing even deeper while he works my clit with his hand. "Almost there, aren't you? Does this turn you on? Knowing you're shoulder to shoulder with a table full of hockey players and about to come all over their captain's cock? They might find out. You're getting wetter just thinking about it. You've drenched me, Jordan."

"Yes."

"You wanted to try something new. So, how is it?"

"I'm not . . ." *What am I trying to say?* ". . . pleased." *Words are hard.*

"Don't lie to me, angel." He slaps my clit harder than before, and the pressure is too much for me to hold back.

Without trying, my hips rock on him, and he pulls me back so my head rests on his shoulder. "There you go, now was that so difficult?"

I turn into his neck while I come, pretending to whisper back, but it's a cover for my face and to hide as I pant against his skin. My knuckles are white as I grip his thighs and slowly breathe in and out through my nose.

"That's my special girl . . . Your pussy is so sweet milking me like that." One quiet grunt later, his hot cum fills me up. My eyes widen. Oh my god . . . it's a lot. Shit, what do I do?

"You came," I mumble, stating the obvious. *How am I going to handle this?*

"I did. Look up, someone is trying to get your attention."

When my gaze lifts, I see a waving hand across the room. It's Brett, from earlier, waving me over. *No, no no no.*

"Go on. Why don't you go flirt with that guy across the bar again? I want to watch you talk to him while my cum leaks down your leg."

"I'm absolutely not doing that," I say through gritted teeth.

"Yes you are." His voice raises so the rest of the table hears. "Don't you know that guy, why don't you go say hi?"

"I don't know him."

"Yes you do." He looks at his teammates. "You guys mind sliding out so she can go say hi?"

The left of us clears out, and he lifts me off him, snapping my underwear back in place, and I flatten my skirt under me, trying not to make a scene. Thankfully, by the time I make it to the other side of the U-shaped booth, everything's back to normal. Minus the cum I'm desperately trying to hold inside me. I stand and look back at Cam, who's wearing a big-ass grin. I mouth, *I hate you.*

Sully shakes his head. Shit, he might be onto us. I hope I never have to face him again.

I feel Camden's gaze on me as I make my way toward the man who bought me a drink earlier. Jesus, my brain is so scrambled I can barely remember his name. *Brett. His name is Brett.* The poor guy smiles as he meets me halfway.

"Hey, I wasn't sure if you were coming."

Oh, I came.

"Yeah, sorry, had to catch up with a friend."

"That's cool, are you close with the team?"

Shit, his cum is leaking. I cross my thighs and lean against a barstool, trying to look natural. From across the room, Cam's eyes are locked on me while he takes a swig of beer. That cocky son of a bitch.

"Yeah, sort of a family friend." It's beginning to run down my leg. "I'm really sorry, I'm not feeling well and need to head home. But it was really nice to meet you."

"It was nice to meet you too. Can I get your number?" I'm about to decline, but I look at Camden, and his smug smile sets me off. See how he likes playing his own games.

"Sure." The guy pulls out his phone, and I make a show of taking it from him, typing it in, then hand it back. "Have a good night, Brett."

"You too, Jordan." He smiles.

I'm not interested in going out with him, and I feel like a bitch for giving Brett false hope, but when I see the way Cam's jaw is locked up, it's worth every ounce of guilt.

I wave goodbye to Brett and head toward the exit, opening up a rideshare app.

The brisk air hits me with a blast, and I shiver. I swear if it were any colder, there'd be a cumsicle frozen to my inner thigh. The sunny sixties temps from this morning have settled into the low forties. Thankfully, my car will be here in two minutes. *Why didn't I stop in the bathroom first?*

The two minutes is all I need to overthink everything. Was it wrong to let him do that? I liked it—*a lot*. I've been wanting new experiences, wanting to let loose, and that's exactly what I did tonight, and I loved it. I didn't know it would feel so exhilarating to throw caution to the wind and be impulsive. Be risky. But did I allow him to mark me so other guys wouldn't have the chance?

I'm sure some other woman is already sitting in his lap. He'll take her home and be discreet about it, meanwhile I'm waiting for a ride with cum running down my leg. Shame sneaks into my thoughts, and I push it back. I liked what happened, but without Cam next to me on the sidewalk, it makes me feel . . . used.

The car arrives, and I step to the curb, but another hand darts out to open the door. It's Cam. A wave of relief crashes over me.

"What are you doing here?" I ask.

"I had to close our tab first. The way you darted out of there had me nervous. You okay?" I nod and sit down. He shuts the door and walks to the other side, climbing in.

"It said one passenger," the driver states.

"She meant two," he answers, shutting his door.

The driver gives me a cautionary look in the rearview mirror, and I nod my agreement. He'll get a good tip for that. We pull away from the curb, and the car is shrouded in darkness. Orange light filters in and out as we pass streetlamps.

"You're a dick," I mutter under my breath.

"You can call me all the names you want, talk to whoever you want, but at the end of the night, we leave together. I leave with you. You leave with me."

He squeezes my hand, then produces a wad of napkins from his jacket pocket and turns toward me, spreading my legs. His eyes stay on mine as he sweeps between my legs. His touch is tender and affectionate. He stuffs the napkins back into his pocket and threads his fingers in mine. It feels like crossing a line. I clamp my legs together and turn away from him, gently shaking off his hand. This isn't anything more than friends with benefits. I can't let him do nice things like that; it confuses me.

After a few minutes, his voice cuts through the silence. "Why did you give him your number?"

I look over at him and smile. "In case we ever want to add a third."

"Hm," he hums, but something about it tells me we're not done with this conversation.

After a minute, I glance back at him over my shoulder, and he's staring out his window with a tense jaw. *Shit.*

As soon as we get home, he tips the driver, and we make our way inside. I kick off one shoe and hobble around, trying to pull off the other. I'm going straight into the shower. He's behind me, still not saying a word. Something is up with him.

"In case—*we*—ever wanted to add a third." I internally cringe.

"Is there a problem?" I fake a smirk. "If you're not up for it, I'll bet one of his friends is. No big deal." I wave him off and head toward the stairs. It's harsh, but I'm saying it for myself. *I need to remind myself this isn't more.*

He catches up to me and wraps his arms around my stomach. "You want to know what it's like getting fucked by two men at the same time?"

I shrug with a smile, egging him on and secretly hoping he doesn't call my bluff.

"Okay." He nips at my neck. "Let me show you what you've been missing out on."

My heart stops. "What? No, that's okay."

"If you want to know, then let's do it."

I shake my head. It's not a fantasy I need to fulfill, by any means, but it's fun to read about in books. Besides, I don't think I'm in a mental space that would allow me to handle more than one man, I only trust Cam.

"I was joking. Just trying to get a rise out of you."

"You got a rise out of me, baby."

I scoff. "Baby?"

He nods. "Tonight, you're gonna sleep like a baby."

"Babies don't sleep, they cry all night."

"I know. Get your toy, Jordan. The one he hated most."

TWENTY-NINE

Camden

She smiles—*really fucking smiles*—and it relieves some of my worry. Things were weird after she walked out of Top Shelf. It also eases my frustration. Truth is, I shouldn't even be angry. I have no stake on Jordan. She's not mine.

"Yes sir."

I swallow. *Fucking hell.* I am really enjoying this arrangement. She stalks off, and I scrub a hand down my face, mentally reviewing the list of things she said she was curious about. I committed them to memory the second the words left her mouth. Being watched, spitting, slapping—*tread lightly with this one*—impact play, praise, degradation, objectification, breath play, anal, being shared.

She said she was too "monogamous at heart" but was thrilled by the idea. Her silence in the car on the way home gave me plenty of time to come up with a happy medium I think she'll enjoy after she brought up being shared—and a way to do it without actually sharing her. Because after that Brett guy spoke to her, I saw red.

I've had threesomes, sharing women with both sexes, but

I'll never invite another person into what Jordan and I have. She's too important to me. Anyone else would ruin it.

When she returns, she's wearing skimpy pajamas. I remember those well when I packed up her things.

"Don't you look cute."

"Thank you." She's got a hand behind her back, and I hold out mine to see what she brought. What was Bryan most threatened by?

She hands over a sparkly pink dildo with a suction cup, and I almost laugh. "This is what intimidated him, huh?" *What a little bitch.*

"It was another dick." She lifts her shoulders.

My fingers encircle her wrist, and she trails behind me to my bedroom. She heads toward the bed, but I lead her off that path, crossing to the other side of the room. "Not yet."

I toss the toy on one of the navy high-back chairs as I walk by. She follows me to the dressing platform near the windows. The raised floor is met with an oversized three-panel wardrobe mirror mounted to the wall and a clothes valet. I take off my suit jacket from the press box interview and place it neatly on the stand. Rolling up my sleeves, I step down and spin to face her. "Strip for me."

I want to see every side of her get naked in that mirror.

"Here?"

"Yes."

And she does.

Slipping the spaghetti straps on the mini silk nightie down her shoulders, she cups her breasts in her hands.

"Turn around." She spins, facing herself in the mirror.

Shimmying out of the nightgown, it falls from her clutches and pools around her ankles. The thong she wore earlier felt like cotton—this one is lace.

"Now face me."

She's amazing at following directions. When she makes eye contact, and I see the flicker dance in her eyes, it's on. I stride over to the chair and grab the toy. My hands twitch as I step up on the platform next to her, I bend down low and slap the suction cup to the mirror.

She stares at it and looks back at me. I nod.

"You want me to . . . Will it hold?"

I drop to my knees in front of her, loop my thumbs in her thong on each side and drag it down to the floor, then press a kiss to her pussy.

"It'll hold." Standing, I stuff the underwear in the pocket of my dress pants.

"I've never done it that way."

She means she's never *masturbated* that way, but she's had plenty of experience in that sex position. Just not while someone watches her from the front.

"I know how well your cunt can grip a dick. Show me how you like being fucked. Keep your eyes on mine the whole time. He may not have enjoyed watching you, but I do. And tonight, you're the main attraction. Understand?"

She nods and bites her lip. It excites her. A flush creeps into her cheeks, and I cup her face, pressing a kiss to her lips. "Come on, Sunshine. Show me what a slut you are for this."

She kneels, facing away from the mirror. There's a shy sweetness to her that has me watching with rapt attention.

"O-okay." Her voice is shaky, I find it endearing.

Crawling backward, she aligns herself with the dildo and presses against it. There's a light smacking of wetness, and she spreads her legs, adjusting to better accommodate the size. That cunt is soaked.

Her lips part as she pushes against it, impaling herself on the glitter silicone cock. *Holy hell.* The sound of her arousal is killing me. I'm throbbing behind my zipper for her. I love watching.

My voice comes out gruff. "There you go."

She pulls it to the tip and pushes back. I want to take my dick out so bad. Fuck, I will never forget tonight. A soft moan escapes, and I smile. That's that good stuff. Her tits swing and bounce with each movement. She's perfection.

Her big brown eyes leave mine, only to drop to my groin, where she sees my cock trying to spring free. "Do you want to fuck me, Cam?"

Want? No. I *need* to fuck her. *Christ, woman.*

"That what *you* want? A second guy?"

She nods, and the corners of her mouth tip up. I walk to the mirror, and she leans forward, the toy sliding out of her. I wrap my hand around the dildo and adjust its position on the mirror. Her wetness coats my palm, and I lick it off, savoring her.

"Spin."

I drop to my knees behind her and unzip my pants, stroking myself. She's so primed and ready for me. We watch each other through the mirror's reflection for an extended moment before I remember what I'm doing. "Let's make this more fun." I loosen my necktie and place it over her eyes. She holds it in place while I knot it behind her head. "Bringing in a person would require a much lengthier conversation, but for now, we're going to pretend. Safewords are still in place, but I want you to slap the floor if you want to stop."

"Okay."

I guide her mouth to the toy, slick with her own arousal and my cum from the bar. "Suck."

She leans forward, taking it in her mouth, and I grin.

"Lick it clean," I instruct, slapping her ass with my wet

palm. Does she realize how fucking incredible she is? Gripping her bare hips, I pull her onto me, and her moans are muffled by a mouthful of pink silicone.

"How do you taste?"

She moans again and I chuckle. "What's the matter, is your mouth full?"

I carefully watch how she responds to my taunting, but the way her body pulses tells me everything I need to know. She likes it, and I reward her with another spank. Each snap of my hips pushes the dildo deeper into her mouth. "Just because I'm taking you from behind, doesn't mean I get to miss out on how pretty you look like this. You're breathtaking, Jordan."

She moans, and I close my eyes, committing her sounds to memory.

"You took me down your throat with all my piercings, this should be no problem for you, right?" Inching closer, the toy is pushed deeper. I brace one arm on the mirror above her head so I can lean forward and wipe the drool from her mouth with my thumb. "Show me how well you take a cock in your throat." I lightly slap her cheek.

Another clench. *Goddamn, she's a dream.*

She gags and retreats.

"Relax." I graze my palm down her spine and over her ass. She exhales through her nose and lets her shoulders droop slightly. Then, like a fucking pornstar, she wriggles her head side to side as she forces more down. I thrust inside and push forward, grunting.

"Tap the floor if it's too much."

As her face pinkens into a purple, my erection throbs harder. A tear slips below the blindfold, and I melt at the image of this sweet girl being so depraved and loving every second. I slide out and slam back inside. Her pussy pulses, the orgasm building and building. I stare in awe as I fuck her with long strokes. Another tear rolls down, and I grab her hair and pull.

She's making me a little nervous. "Slap the floor when you need a breath," I remind her. "You're too precious to let suffocate." It's no use, Jordan's sacrificing her oxygen for her climax. *So fucking sexy*. She whimpers from the back of her throat.

"Fuck, you're close." She's impossibly tight. If I pulled out, I'm not sure I could get back in. With one hand fisting her messy hair, my other slaps her ass, and her back arches. *Damn*. Her hand strikes the floor. I yank her back to give her air, and she comes.

"Deep breath for me, Jordan. Deep breath—"

She gasps.

"That's my girl," I praise, kissing her shoulder. She's a slice of fucking heaven as she constricts around me.

She coughs, splutters, and makes the sexiest sounds, the redness fading from her face. With a runny nose, drool leaks from the side of her mouth. *Daddy's little princess is a mess*. I peel off the necktie and clean her up with it.

"You did amazing," I say. She surprises me every day. I withdraw, and she whimpers, sitting up on her knees.

"I want more."

"Okay, Sunshine . . ."

"I call shotgun on your pussy," I say, unbuttoning my shirt and shrugging it off. I find the bottle of lubricant from my bedside table, kick off my pants, and lay them on the valet before I sit facing the mirror. I want to watch her ride my cock from behind.

"Take a seat."

She straddles me, sinks down, and I groan. There are pussies, and then there's Jordan's pussy. The way it hugs me . . . Fuck.

"Lay your chest on top of mine." She leans forward until her tits are pressed against me, and I glance behind her, seeing her ass in the mirror spread wide for me. Feels good to be the luckiest motherfucker in the world. I lube up my finger, her ass, and the toy.

"Ready?"

She nods against my shoulder. "I'm going to stretch you out first, but I want you to pretend it's someone else touching you. Remember how you used to imagine someone else fucking you from behind? Just like that. Except it's me and whoever you want—as long as it's not Brett." As I push inside, knuckle deep, I turn my lips into her hair and press a kiss to her temple, whispering, "He's so fucking hard for you."

Her breathing turns shallow, and she moans. Her internal flutter tells me she loves it.

"I think you're ready. Still doing okay?"

"Yes," she pants.

This sweet cunt is all mine. Goddamn, this girl is the greatest. I smile as I whisper in her ear again, "Be my sweet fucking girl and let him fill up your ass."

I chuckle and bring the sparkly toy to her rear entrance. She's tight, but the lube helps it fit. She pushes up onto her elbows and bites her lip. Her gaze stays on me as she takes every inch.

"Any pain?"

"In the best way . . . keep going."

"Breathe through it. You're doing incredible."

I'm so proud of her. Thank god she doesn't have a monster dildo, or this wouldn't work, she's almost too tight as it is. A soft moan leaves her lips, and her walls close in around me as her ass is filled. It feels great on my end too, sliding over my cock buried inside. I'm itching to thrust. I need to fuck her, and it's taking every ounce of patience to stay relaxed. I gotta take my mind off it.

"So, who's part of our threesome?"

"Dean Winchester." At least she didn't say Big Bird or some shit. I like kink, but I draw the line at puppets.

I laugh. "Sure, I'd rub dicks with him."

She laughs but sobers quickly when I speak about her like she's not even here, trying to feed her objectification kink. I want to check off everything on her list, be all her firsts.

"Fuck, I love this pussy. I bet her ass is just as tight as it looks . . . *I knew it.* You should see the look on her face, she loves this."

She searches my eyes and gawks at me.

"Our little sub's so stuffed she doesn't know what to do." It's bizarre talking to an imaginary person, but it makes her grip me so hard, I can't stop.

"Oh my god," she whimpers.

Her fingers grasp my shoulders, and she rocks back and forth. Here we fucking go. A rasp slips out, and I squeeze my eyes shut. *I love that sound.*

"Doesn't she have a pretty voice? See if you can get her to make that noise again." I glide out half the length of the dildo and push it back inside her again. It works, the sexiest moan leaves her lips, and I bite my lip. Her forehead dips to mine, and she looks me right in the eyes. I smile back and keep up the charade.

The blissed-out expression on her face melts me.

"Fuck, look at her take it. She's doing *so* well." She smiles bigger. I let the toy sit in her ass while I delve one hand into her hair and rub the thumb of my other hand over her lips. "Yeah, she's such a sweet slut," I whisper. My lips press to hers, and she sucks in a deep breath through her nose, writhing against me.

"More."

I wrap one arm around her waist and slide her up and down my cock in time with the toy.

"I could fuck you forever."

She mewls, her inhales and exhales becoming more desperate. She's going to come.

Grabbing the toy, I pull out and thrust it back inside her, harder than before.

She gasps. "Again."

"You like getting fucked and shared?" I slap her cheek and kiss it. "Letting two men fill you up at the same time."

She grinds and backs into the pink toy, making me grin.

"The things you crave go much deeper than you let on. And at the bottom, you want to be degraded and praised and used. It's as if you want to bring me to my knees—well guess what, Sunshine? You fucking do."

Another slap. She groans, it's desperate and aggressive.

Her thighs shake against my sides.

"You poor thing, never having anyone fuck you like the dirty girl you are . . . I'll take good care of you."

She drops her mouth open. She's struggling so hard. Her knees knock my ribs as she trembles.

"Relax for us." Her arousal is sliding all over. I look behind her. "Should we make her finish? She's so pretty coming. You gotta feel how tight she gets, it's unbelievable."

She grits her teeth and whimpers, trying to keep it in.

"Feeling you clamp down on me is the greatest. Show him how tight you are when you come. Milk our cocks until we're empty."

I pump the toy in and out of her asshole and bring my

other hand to her throat, lifting and forcing her to look at me. She claws at my chest, and I see the fire in her eyes. The real her, bare and exposed like it's the first time she's let it out. She shivers and moans on top of me. Her choked sobs are intoxicating, like she can't take a breath. Every spastic snapping of her hips has me reeling.

I pout and patronize her with a mocking voice. "That's it. Oh, it feels so good, doesn't it?"

She tightens, and it leaves me breathless. Her hips flex, and she rides me like she was built for this—built *for me*. I love watching her fall apart. "Fuck, Sunshine." I lick up the side of her neck, and she trembles. Her grinding becomes erratic. She gasps and clenches down on me.

And *screams*.

Her cries of pleasure ignite an inferno in my chest. "Fuck!" It takes every ounce of concentration to continue deep long strokes with my cock *and* the dildo as she pulses around me. It sends me over a cliff, and I haul her against my chest as I come inside her with a grunt, filling her with my cum for the second time tonight. "Christ, Jordan. You did so well . . . You were perfect, I'm so proud of you, baby."

Her pussy throbs, still twitching from the orgasm. With a heaving chest against mine, she sobs. She's doing something to me. I relax, even though my mind is panicking. *I want more.*

"I've got you." Sliding her hair to the side, my fingers trail up and down her bare back with a feather touch while I plant soft kisses on her scalp. "You're okay." We lie together, coming down from our high until silence surrounds us.

After a bit, she sighs with a big exhale. "Oh my god. I-I can't believe . . ."

I smile. "Did you like it?"

Her giggle makes my shoulders relax, then she breaks into a full laugh. We crack up together. I'm relieved she's okay. I love that smile and the sound of her laughter.

"Fuck, you are so hot. How are you feeling?"

"Terrific." I like feeling her breathing settle again.

"How about a shower?"

"Mm." Her hair sticks to my neck as she nods.

"Say goodbye to Mr. Winchester." Carefully, I remove the dildo from her ass, set it aside, then roll us to the side and pull out.

"It feels so weird," she murmurs. "I feel so . . ."

"Empty?"

"Yeah."

I stand and hold out my hand for her to take. She stands on wobbly legs.

"You look like a baby giraffe." I scoff. She's quite cute after she's been thoroughly fucked.

"You try getting taken in two places at the same time and tell me you wouldn't walk like this."

Laughing, I stride past her into my en suite bathroom and turn on the shower, letting the room fill with steam. I open the medicine cabinet, grab a painkiller, then pass it to her with a glass of water.

"Drink the whole thing."

I stand back and watch, her throat bobbing as she finishes it and hands me back an empty glass.

"Good girl." I smirk, and she smacks my arm.

I sit on the bench in the walk-in shower and motion for her to take a seat next to me. Goose bumps rise on her arms, and I slide my palms up and down her chilled flesh.

"You did really well. You're strong as hell, you know that?"

The corner of her mouth tips up. "Really?"

"Yeah, you jumped in the deep end tonight. I loved having my cock in you while you took that toy up your ass . . . though, not gonna lie, I was a little jealous."

"Is there a reason you didn't want to fuck my ass?"

"It was your first time, my piercings would have torn you up."

"Can we still try it sometime?"

She says all the right things.

I massage her shoulders and dig my thumbs into a knot in her back. "Of course." I kiss her spine. "Anything you want."

This is aftercare, that's it. Nothing more, nothing less. I don't catch feelings—*bullshit.*

My thoughts turn on me.

I've been saying I'm not into her romantically for weeks, but even I don't believe myself anymore. My actions say differently. I don't know what I want with Jordan, but fuck it, I want something.

"Do you want to stay with me tonight?" I ask.

"Um," she hesitates, her voice dimming. "No, I'll go back to my bed."

My hands freeze. *Ouch.* I didn't expect it to go that way, and I didn't expect it to sting so much. I've never invited a woman to spend the whole night with me, and if they do, it's never in my bed. The first time I offer and I'm turned down. *Maybe I'm really not her type.*

"Works for me, birthday girl," I answer flippantly. With my arm wrapped tightly around her, I secure Jordan to my chest and swallow down the lump in my throat.

Shit.

THIRTY

Camden

I drew a line in the sand last night with her. Zero thought went into it, it was pure reaction. I didn't like seeing her with another man. If she needs to be fucked, I'll do it. If she wants to practice flirting, she can practice with me. She wasn't getting birthday sex from anyone else.

And what was that shit about *birthdays don't matter*? I did a little research early on and found out her birthdate, couldn't believe it was the same day as the date on their wedding invite. I couldn't give her the present yesterday because I was gone most of the day with pregame prep. Who the hell made her think her birthday doesn't matter?

I had to run a couple errands this morning to get her gift ready, and when I get back, she's sitting in the living room with one of her romance books. She's in her baggy sweatshirt and leggings, messy bun, and no makeup. It reminds me of the day I ran into her at the coffee shop.

"Hey, cover your eyes."

She narrows her eyes at me like I'm about to play a cruel prank on her. "Why?"

"Because I want to give you your birthday present."

The corner of her mouth curves up on one side. "You *really* got me something?"

"I *really* got you something. Now cover your eyes, or I'll blindfold you again."

"Sounds like a win-win to me," she says, covering her face with her hands.

"Another time. Okay, stay there. No peeking, promise?"

"Yeah, yeah, promise. Hurry up, I'm in a good spot in my book."

Creeping backward toward the mud room, I keep an eye on her to make sure she stays true to her word. As carefully as I can, I pick up the clumsy, heavy-ass surprise—I didn't realize it was so big until I showed up to transport it. Thankfully, it's size is mostly due to its thick fur. This thing is gonna shed all over my house.

"Are your eyes still closed?"

"Yeh-es," she singsongs, sounding almost bored. "But if you tell me to reach into a box, I don't want it."

All it took was her voice for the dog to leap out of my arms and bolt toward her. She opens her eyes right before she's clobbered by the thing. She squeals, and so does the damn dog. Well, I don't know if the noise the dog is making is so much a squeal as it is a happy scream. *Is that normal?*

"Chicken Salad!"

What a ridiculous name for a pet. I roll my eyes and try to wipe all the dog hair from my shirt. I told that hairy motherfucker to be cool, but apparently, she was equally excited to see Jordan.

With her arms wrapped around the dog, her eyes turn glossy. "Cam! You got my dog!"

"Thought you could use some company while I'm gone or

traveling or whatever." And for my own comfort. I like knowing there's a dog around when I'm gone. A big dog. Not sure how much of a guard dog Chicken Salad is, but hopefully, she's protective enough to bark if she hears something strange. "Besides, it's your dog. I cleared it with your family—oh, and updated the address for the dog groomer your family has *on retainer*?"

"I can brush my own dog."

"Good, because this thing sheds worse than you do."

She laughs. "I don't shed!"

"Tell that to the hair I found wrapped around my nutsack . . ."

Her jaw drops, and she tries to hide the shocked smile.

I shake my head. "A dog groomer on retainer." I still can't get over that. "You are such a princess."

She stands and scoffs at me, Chicken Salad right at her heels. "Shut up. I'm not a princess." Her arms open to offer a hug, and I pull her close.

"Oh, you're definitely a princess." Without a second thought, I cup her jaw and press my thumb to her chin to open her mouth for mine. My tongue sweeps across hers, and she kisses me back with those plush lips I find so addicting. I like the way she sucks in a breath and holds it for a second, then releases it on a soft sigh. Like she's as lost in the kiss as I am. *Is she?*

The dog howls, then she steps back. We stare at each other.

"Thank you. For Chicken Salad, I mean. This is one of the most thoughtful gifts I've ever received."

Before Jordan, I never kissed a woman I didn't have the intention of fucking right after. But this wasn't a kiss because we were having sex or fooling around. It wasn't even a kiss with the hope of something more. I did it because when her face lights up, it warms my insides and puts me at ease. Seeing her happiness is a natural high I never want to end.

"Happy Birthday, Sunshine."

Then I get the hell out of there so I don't need to think about the feelings expanding in my chest.

THIRTY-ONE

Camden

"I need to FaceTime my parents," she says, sitting at the kitchen island with an apple scone. She's picking at crumbs instead of inhaling the whole thing like she usually does. "They saw the hockey game kiss."

From behind, I rub her arms to ease her tension.

"What do I tell them?"

"Tell them whatever you want."

She nods, biting a nail, and wraps one arm around her stomach.

"Do you want me to do it with you?"

She spins in her chair, her eyes big and appreciative. "Do you mind? I really don't want to talk to them alone."

My chest expands with pride to know she seeks comfort in me when she's anxious. I thread my fingers in hers. "It'll be okay."

"Let's get this over with."

This will be slightly awkward, considering I've never actually sat down with the Landrys before. Even when I arranged to take Chicken Salad, all correspondence was done through their house manager.

She unlocks her phone and taps the video conferencing app. It rings once and Mrs. Landry answers.

"Jesus Christ, Jordana! What the hell is going on over there?"

Mr. Landry steps into view, and I take a seat on the stool next to her, placing a palm on her thigh. She sets the phone on the island and pushes it back so we both can be seen in the frame.

"Mom, Dad, this is Camden Teller."

"Oh," the woman says, putting her proverbial mask back on. "Hello, Camden, nice to unofficially meet you. You have to understand, this is quite a surprise to us, and we didn't realize you and Jordana were *involved*."

"Last we heard, you were the best man at her wedding, not the *groom*." Her dad chuckles.

"She's been staying with me while she gets on her feet again."

Jordan smiles and her shoulders relax. "Camden has been a good influence on me."

Mr. Landry speaks up. "Do what makes you happy, kiddo. But you should've given PR a heads-up so they could get a spin on it early. You've kept us in the dark for a while now. We've been worried. I think it's time we come home to the States."

It sounds like Jordan's sent more calls to voicemail than she originally led on to.

"I'm sorry," she says. "But I needed to take time to fix things. I didn't like who I was with Bryan. I'm finding myself again, and part of that process is dealing with this on my own. I wanted to show you I could handle it solo."

"And have you?" he asks.

"Yes. But, until things blow over, I'm staying with Cam."

Mrs. Landry interjects. "Until things blow over? What—"

"Look, I'm really happy. That's all that matters, right? I'm taking time for myself, that's all." She's sticking to her guns and is practically glowing. I lick my lips, kissing her is all I want to do. Instead, I squeeze her thigh.

"I'd like to speak with Camden," her dad says.

I tilt the phone my way. "Nice to meet you, sir."

"I know about you, you have a solid playing career, but from what I hear, you like to party, you're a playboy and I don't want—"

I chuckle. "You don't need to worry about that. Jordan's been a good influence on me too."

He nods, and her mom steals the camera. "Please have Jordan step out of the room for a moment."

My hackles are already up, annoyed by another person trying to tell her what to do. They handle Jordan with kid gloves when she's strong and capable of making her own choices—far more capable than people give her credit for. She's no weak prima donna.

"Out of respect for her, I'm not going to do that."

That'll go over well. It's bad enough it's the first time I'm meeting the Landrys, but they're also rich as fuck and probably not used to hearing the word *no*.

"This is nothing against Jordana." Her mother placates. "But I'd like to speak candidly with you."

"I'd like to stay and hear it," Jordan cuts in.

"With all due respect, it's Jordan's decision, and I'm going to honor it." I shrug. "I'm doing things differently than the last guy. If it makes you feel any better, I can promise my answers won't be dependent on whether she's in the room or not."

Her dad's lips curl up in the corner for a split second. He purses his lips and leans back on the sofa. I might be winning points with him.

Mrs. Landry pastes on a stiff smile. "Fine. I need to know you aren't playing around with our daughter. Like Frank said, you have a reputation."

"We've learned a lot about ourselves as we've gotten closer over the last couple months, there's been a lot of change—for both of us. I think we've brought out the best in each other. She's a wonderful person, you should be very proud."

Her dad pipes up. "Our friends have been asking about you. Obviously, they know the wedding didn't go through, but what would you like us to tell them?"

She rolls her lips together and laughs. "Tell them I found a better man. The *best man*."

"Jordana."

"Oh, come on!" She crosses her arms with a big smile on her face. "There's no other chance I'll get to use that joke. It's solid gold. And it's true." She glances at me, and my heart thumps harder.

Mr. Landry nudges his wife, and they smirk. "She's happy, Patricia," he says to his wife.

"I guess it's good she's making jokes again," she replies, pleased.

"You don't need to come home early. I'm happier than I've been in the last couple years, and I'll get better about staying in touch."

Her dad looks back at us. "We need to know you're all right. We worry about you. You're no longer engaged to your fiancé, you're living with his best friend . . . this is strange."

"I get it, it looks bizarre from the outside. But really, I'm in a good place." Jordan sits back, satisfied. "I will ask for help when I need it."

"Promise?"

"I promise."

THIRTY-TWO

Jordan

I'm staying up to watch the game. The Lakes are playing in California, and they went into overtime. It's a nail biter; I've got the chipped polish to prove it. The camera lands on Camden a few times, his chest heaves, and sweat rolls down his forehead, dripping from his brows. He squints when he blinks. His eyes look tired, but I know he's focused.

I scurry over to the kitchenette in my apartment, tear into a fresh bag of anxiety-relieving Sour Patch Kids and leap back onto the couch in front of the TV, tucking my legs up under me as they begin the second shootout. Chicken Salad whines at my side.

"These are mine. You won't like them, they're spicy," I lie. As if she's a child asking me to share my snack. California gets one on goal, and my shoulders fall. *Shit.* She hops off the couch and paws at the door, whining again.

"I'll take you out, one second. I gotta see if they make it."

Cam's up, he shoots, and I hold my breath. The goalie blocks it.

"Nooo! No, no, no." Ugh, that shot is probably eating him alive.

Chicken Salad barks at me, and I stand, slowly walking toward the door while I keep my eyes fixed on the TV. I grab the leash and attach it without looking down. I can't peel my eyes away.

A right winger for California takes the next shot, and it gets by Strass.

"Fuck." My heart sinks for him and the rest of the team. They've played their asses off tonight. "Okay, pup. Ready to go outside?" I ask glumly.

With Chicken Salad leashed, we head downstairs. I don't feel like crossing the house to get my jacket from the laundry room, so I grab one of Cam's from the closet in the foyer. She impatiently circles while I slip on his slides in the entryway.

"I know, I'm sorry I made you wait."

When I open the front door, the crisp, cold air makes me wish I had on something longer than these pajama shorts, but Cam's jacket smells like him and provides warmth from more than the cold temperatures. *Like when his arms are around me.*

Chicken Salad wanders the frost-covered yard, looking for the perfect spot to pee. "Any spot'll do . . . I'd like to give a friendly reminder that you've got fur pants, I don't."

My phone buzzes in my pocket, and I wonder if it's Cam. He must be so disappointed. When I dig it out, I see the text across the lock screen.

BRYAN DAVENPORT

Keeping his coat warm... how about his bed?

The hair on the back of my neck stands on end, and I jump when Chicken Salad releases a low, deep growl. My eyes frantically scan the front yard, then I see his car on the other side of the gate. Lights are off, but it's his. Actually, it's *mine*, the one he gave to me as a gift. The one I was driving when I got pulled over after he reported it stolen. I wonder if that's how he got past security at the neighborhood entrance? Did they think the license plate was me?

"Okay, we're moving to the backyard."

I stuff the phone in my shorts, and it buzzes again. I ignore it, the last thing I'll do is give him the pleasure of seeing fear on my face while I read his creepy messages.

"Come on." I tug the leash, but she steps toward the car, still growling. "Let's go. Now!"

She obeys me this time and allows me to lead her inside. When I glance to my apartment above the garage, the flicker of the television is seen, clear as day. How long was he watching those windows—watching me? Hurrying inside, I lock and flip the deadbolt. With my back flush to the wall, I peek outside. The headlights turn on and the car drives off quietly into the night.

My heart is racing. He found me. Fuck.

I walk out the back with Chicken Salad. Thankfully, she goes right away, and we haul ass inside. Now *I* have to pee. I suppose being terrified does that. After hanging up Cam's coat, I retreat to my living space and turn off the television. Though, it's pointless trying to hide it when he already knows where I am.

My phone rings, and I nearly jump out of my skin. I don't want to answer it until I see Cam's name on the screen. Breathing a sigh of relief, I answer it and level my voice. The last thing I need to do is get him worried.

"Hey, I'm sorry about the game."

"Yeah. Where are you?"

"In my room, why?"

"Bryan sent me a weird fucking message. Asking if I was renting my apartment above the garage."

I can't lie to him.

"He was here."

"What!" he shouts, loud enough for me to pull the phone from my ear. "You let him in?"

"God, no! He was outside the gate." I recount what happened. "He left after I went inside."

"Fuck."

"I'm sorry, I didn't mean to make you worry. He was trying to scare me." *It worked.* "The doors are locked, deadbolts and all."

"I hate that he can look at a fucking game schedule and know when I'm away and when I'm not. We don't fly home until Wednesday. I'm going to reach out to a security firm and see if we can get someone to watch the house at night."

"That's unnecessary. I'll keep an eye out and stay inside. You've already got the alarm system. It'll be okay."

"Jordan, he's a stalker. I want you to call the police and file a report."

"That'll just piss him off. You said my reactions are what keep him going, I'm not going to engage."

"He showed up to the house. We're passed that. Call the police."

THIRTY-THREE

Jordan

He's been home for two days and won't stop pacing. It's driving me nuts. After Bryan's scare the other night, I called the police, gave my statement, and filed an official report—per Cam's insistence. I contacted my lawyer, who was happy to get the ball rolling on a protective order, and a temporary filing was put in place yesterday and will hold until it's finalized. I haven't heard any update yet.

When I enter the kitchen, Camden's stirring a pot on the stove, whatever it is smells amazing.

"Whatcha making?"

"Marinara."

"Hey, aren't you supposed to be at the gym today?"

"I had a virtual meeting with my trainer this morning and did my workout at home," he mutters, placing a lid on the pot and turning down the flame on the burner.

"Camden."

He spins around and leans against the counter, his eyes fixed on mine. "Jordan."

"Stop. You're overreacting. After he showed up, I realized I don't care about revenge anymore, I simply want him to go away."

He looks at me funny, and I realize this is the first he's hearing of my plans. *Oops*.

"Whether you wanted it or not, you got your revenge. You're happy without him. He underestimated your strength. You were the best thing he ever had, and it kills him to know you're no longer in his control. But it also means he's got nothing to lose."

His phone dings. His fingers swipe across the screen, and he holds it up to show me the security camera outside. My stomach drops. "Overreacting?"

I freeze. Bryan's face is on the screen, he's at the gate, tapping the keypad. I look out the window, almost not believing he's here. I look back at his phone screen. He's still pushing buttons.

"Does he know the password?"

"I changed it after you moved in. I can't understand how he got past the security station at the neighborhood entrance."

"It might be the car. He's driving the one I used when I first came here."

"Shit, I didn't think to notify them your vehicle changed."

The speaker on his phone pipes up with Bryan's voice, and it forms a knot in my throat. He looks directly into the camera with dead eyes and a smile. "I know she's here."

The blood drains from my face, Cam's face does the opposite. His temples bloom red. He pulls the phone back, taps the screen, and heads toward the foyer.

I follow behind his heels. "Did you let him in?!"

"Wait in the house, Jordan."

Moving quickly, I get in front of him and grab his arm. "Don't! Tell him to leave. He plays dirty, Cam." He delicately pries my fingers off him and looks down at me.

"So do I."

We regard each other for a moment, and he swallows. It's a mix of compassion, rage, and protectiveness. I've never seen him like this. Yet, even with all that anger, he's still so gentle with me.

"Stay inside," he says calmly before walking out.

I'm too afraid to look. I stand staring at the backside of the entryway. When I hear voices, I put my ear against the door to listen.

"I know she's here."

"Yeah, she is. What I want to know is what the fuck you're doing here. And what you were doing here the other night."

"I'm taking her home."

"Wrong."

"You need to stay in your lane. This is between her and I," Bryan spits. "By the way, I saw the game. I saw what you did."

"That's nothing. You should have seen what else I did that night."

The smile in his voice is audible, even through the door. He's baiting him. Why is he being so stupid? This isn't the time to be cocky. He's going to make Bryan even angrier.

"Jordana is my fiancée," he snarls.

Based on the footsteps, Camden crosses the porch and steps onto the brick driveway. Closer to Bryan, I assume.

"If she's your fiancée—" He laughs. "Then why was I the one kissing her on your wedding day? . . . And fucking her on your wedding night?"

I grit my teeth. What an asshole. Blood rushes through my ears with a mix of embarrassment and fury.

I hear a thud. Then a grunt. More thuds. Another. I open the door and can't move. I've never watched a fight outside of hockey. Never up close, bare-fisted, and no gear on.

It's not a movie, it's happening in front of me. It's ugly and gritty and . . . *I like it.* It's satisfying to see Bryan's body get pummeled, taking hit after hit. I enjoy watching Camden throw his fists into the man that put his hands on me.

"Go fuck yourself." Bryan grunts.

Camden straddles his chest and throws a fist into his jaw, spraying blood across his pastel polo. I slap my hand over my mouth. I've never seen violence like this up close, but it's terrifying to think how close I came to being attacked by Bryan.

"Why would I when I have your ex-fiancée to do it for me?" Cam says through gritted teeth. I nearly gasp.

"Cam, stop!"

"Hey, Sunshine . . ." He swings, Bryan blocks it, and he throws another, this time it connects. His voice is calm but winded as he wrestles with Bryan. He holds Bryan's arms to the side and looks up at me. "Can you please stir the sauce on the stove, baby? I don't want it to burn." He's clearly the stronger opponent.

I blink and step back as I process his request. He's like a cat playing with his prey, keeping Bryan in place so he can bat him around—*for amusement.* It's as if everything is happening in slow motion but too fast at the same time. Something is wrong with me, because watching him use his strength to hurt the man who hurt me, makes me wetter than ever.

Chicken Salad barks at the window, and it makes me jump. I slowly retreat inside to make the extra noise stop. *What am I supposed to do, wait for him to kill Bryan?* I walk back to the kitchen and pace. I don't want to call the police because it's obvious who is taking the harder hits. Shit, this could ruin his career. I hurry out of the kitchen; I'll pull him off Bryan myself if I have to. Before I can get there, the front door opens and slams shut.

Cam stomps through the foyer and over to the kitchen sink, I can't tear my eyes away from the blood on his hands. His knuckles are cut and swelling. I run outside, half expecting to see Bryan's lifeless body on the lawn, but he's nowhere in sight. I check the driveway to make sure his car is gone, and on my way back in, I notice something on the ground. *A tooth.*

What an idiot! I can't believe he would be so reckless, it makes me want to punch him too! I pick it up and run back inside.

"You lost a tooth?!"

He laughs, looks back at me from the sink and runs his tongue over his teeth. Cam smiles at me, blood stains the corner of his mouth where his lip is split. "I didn't lose a tooth." He shrugs. "Bryan must have forgotten it here. Remind me to mail it to him."

"Are you okay?"

He turns off the water and inspects his hands. "Fine. Nothing broken. Did you stir the marinara?"

"Who cares about the goddamn sauce, Camden! The cops are probably going to be here any minute, but yeah, let's worry about fucking spaghetti sauce." *How can he act so cavalier?*

"It's marinara, it's different. And no, they aren't. Calm down." He grabs the wooden spoon and stirs, the sauce hisses as he tries to scrape the charred tomatoes off the bottom of the pan. Cam turns off the stove burner. "It's okay, I think we can salvage it."

My jaw drops. I'm nearly shaking with an equal combination of worry and anger.

"Has anyone ever told you to *calm down* before?"

He smirks. "Only at every game I've ever played."

"Then you know it has the opposite effect! Why don't you think the cops are on their way to arrest you for battery?"

"You filed a report for stalking the other night, remember? They're going to be watching him. The temporary protective order is in place. He's not going to risk saying he came back here. And if he's dumb enough to do that, I've got him on camera typing on the gate keypad. They can't tell that I opened the gate for him. On video it looks like he was breaking in. He threw the first punch, I was defending myself."

"You baited him."

"Maybe a little."

"And what if he still presses charges?"

"Let him."

"You're being reckless!"

This time when he spins around, all his anger rises to the surface. "No! What *he* did was reckless!" he booms.

I startle and raise my chin to him as he stalks closer. "This isn't like hockey, you can't beat people up like that!"

He scoffs. "What the hell are you talking about?"

"I've seen your games, you love throwing punches! Before you were captain, you spent half your time in the penalty box for slugging it out with the other team. I'm not an excuse to fight."

He stabs his finger into his chest. "I'm an enforcer. That's my job. It's my job to protect my team on or off the ice."

"Exactly! I'm not one of your teammates! I'm—"

"I'm protecting you because I care about you, Jordan!" He scrubs a hand down his face. "Fuck!"

He walks away but turns on his heel until he's right in front of me. His still bleeding hands are shoved into my hair, then he crushes his lips to mine, walking me backward. "I'm sorry if I scared you, but the thought of him getting close to you terrifies me. I need to know you're safe."

The only thing that scares me is Cam getting injured. I wish things could be different between us. Why did I have to be engaged to such a monster? Why couldn't it have been us the whole time? *Why can't I have him?* He tugs at my pants, and I pull my shirt over my head, then unzip his fly, and grass and dirt stain the knees of his jeans.

His hand dives between my legs, and he groans. I'm so needy for him. He swipes his tongue over mine, shoves my back against the wall, and kisses me like I've never been kissed before.

I'm a feminist until the day I die. I've never wanted to play the part of a weak, helpless woman. I'm no damsel in distress. But seeing his torn-up knuckles and thinking about the way he protected me today has turned me into a puddle.

He presses himself against my entrance before plunging deep. I gasp as his piercings rub my inner walls just right.

"You know that rush when I first push inside you?"

I nod as he thrusts. *It's my favorite.*

"*That* is worth fighting for. It's worth bloody knuckles. I will never make you feel the way he did. I will never try to control you or own you. But when my cock is inside you . . . I can't help but feel like you're mine."

Instant butterflies. I wrap my arms around his neck and bring him close as I swallow down emotion. His gaze brims with the most affectionate possession. When his fingers press into my sides and he works me up and down his length—he's not fucking me, he's worshipping me. At this moment, I want to be his more than anything.

He pumps inside me, and I can barely hold myself together. I squeeze my eyes shut, feeling the prick of tears.

"You're shaking," he whispers.

I'm unsure how to respond, so I don't. He kisses my neck

and works his way back to my lips again without once missing his rhythm. Every thrust is ecstasy. I love the way he makes me feel.

"Wrap your legs around me." I lock my ankles behind his back, and he carries me to his bedroom.

Laying me down, he pulls out, kisses up my stomach, then unhooks and chucks my lace bra across the room. His forehead presses to mine while he sinks inside me. My mouth drops open, and the sounds of our bodies moving together is snuffed out. My world goes silent when his eyes bore into mine. Every second pushes me closer to the finish line, and my muscles pull taut.

"I'm going to come."

"I know, Sunshine, me too."

His hand slides up my neck, into my tresses, and his tongue skates across my lower lip. I sigh into his mouth. A hand snakes between us, and the way he's rubbing my clit, his fingers don't seem to be slowed by the injury to his hand.

"That's it, baby. Let me have you. Cry for me."

And I do. For the next ten seconds, I surrender to him. Emotionally, physically, spiritually. It's the most intense orgasm I've ever had, it's enough to make me jackknife. He pushes me back down on the bed and wraps his hand around my neck. The exchange of power is filled with raw vulnerability. I willingly hand over what Bryan always took without asking. I trust Camden. Irrevocably.

His eyes darken as he holds me still while driving in and out. A smile forms on my lips as I focus on the sensation. He growls and thrusts hard, emptying himself and pressing his chest against mine. Our bare skin touching sends shivers down my spine. *This is us.*

My arms fall to my sides when I let go of his shoulders—

and the emotional tether between us. I'm exhausted after releasing all the stress from Bryan's unwelcome visit.

Slowly pulling out, wet and warm, he leaks out of me. He spreads my legs, admiring his handiwork. "Mm." He pushes his thumb inside me and grabs a tissue to wipe away the excess. *Damn.*

"You wear my cum beautifully."

He lifts the comforter and slides me underneath, climbing behind and wrapping his arms around my stomach, hauling my back to his chest. Thick, cotton sheets cradle us. His lips find my favorite spot between my neck and shoulder, and he rests them there, licking the small sensitive area. He knows exactly what I like.

"The things you said back there—" I say, wanting to know where he stands.

"Let's not talk about it."

"Why?"

"I got carried away."

A long, drawn out silence sits between us. *He regrets it.* He got lost in the moment, coming off an adrenaline rush with Bryan, and I took it for more than it was. I lie there awkwardly. Not knowing how to respond.

"Come home with me for Thanksgiving," he mumbles against my skin.

What the hell? No.

"I'm not going to meet your parents."

"Why not? They're cool people."

I push out of his grasp and crane my neck to look back at him. *He won't talk about the things he said twenty minutes ago but now wants me to go home with him for Thanksgiving?*

"Because it would be crossing a line."

His arms circle my body, and he rolls me on top of him. I rest my cheek on his chest, not wanting to look into his eyes—it's overly personal for how fragile I am in this moment.

"All I'm saying is it's safer this way, I can enjoy my Thanksgiving dinner without having to worry if Bryan shows up while I'm gone."

Oh.

He doesn't press me for an answer, so I don't give one. I'm not completely opposed to it, it's logical. However, our arrangement may be too difficult to maintain. Lines are blurring. Perhaps it's better to put an end to this before it's too late. I have to stop looking for something that isn't there.

Friends with benefits are all we'll ever be.

Eventually our breaths even out and the sound of his steady heartbeat lulls me to sleep.

THIRTY-FOUR

Jordan

"I can't believe you talked me into this. What if your parents think we're in a relationship?"

He continues singing along with the radio.

"Cam."

"Huh? Yeah, they know you're staying with me."

"That's not what I asked." He's too distracted with the damn song. Whatever. I shake my head and lean back in the passenger seat, staring out the window and watching the mostly bare trees go by. "Why did you invite me?"

"I invited you . . ." His gaze captures mine for a moment, and I'm hanging on his words. *Tell me we're more.* His stare dissipates, and the corners of his eyes crinkle as he smiles. ". . . Because I want to watch you eat a whole ass turkey leg."

I lean back in my seat, staring out the window. The mood in the car turns stale. I want him to be serious with me for one second. "Well, prepare to be disappointed."

"If you're not hungry for turkey, I've got another suggestion . . ."

"I'm scared to ask." My voice is flat.

He places his hand on my thigh, and I cross my arms. "If you gobble me tonight, I promise you'll wobble tomorrow."

This is all you'll ever be to him. Either shut down your feelings or walk away before you get hurt. I choose the former and relinquish hope, so we can fall into our usual banter.

"You're the worst."

"I have to tell you something." He reluctantly drags his hand away and places it on the steering wheel. A shred of anticipation rises within me. "Jordan . . . I'm *fowl-ing* for you."

Even though it's not intentional, the joke cuts deep. I sweep aside my foolish wishes.

I rattle my locked door handle. "Would you mind pulling over and letting me out of this turkey pun nightmare?"

"They say tying the legs together keeps everything moist."

I groan. "Is there a safeword for this conversation?"

His palm lands on my thigh again, and this time he squeezes and gropes until I'm fidgeting in my seat, pressing my legs together.

I turn away and brush him off. "I'm going to close my eyes for a bit."

Being friends is better than being nothing because Cam is the truest friend I've ever had. We have fun together, share the same humor, even enjoy the same food. My attraction to him is a *me* problem, one I can fix.

I mentally tick off reasons we wouldn't be good together . . . It would jeopardize our friendship. He travels a lot. He can be possessive and bossy. He's probably a better friend than a boyfriend. He snores sometimes. He says things he doesn't mean—which brings me to the number one reason: *he doesn't like me that way.*

We're staying at his parents for the weekend, which seems silly since they live less than an hour away. And especially because he'll be gone all day tomorrow for a home game. Apparently, he always spends Thanksgiving weekend with them, game or not. Which means so do I.

Monday he'll fly out and be gone for back-to-back games in Canada. He's arranged for me to stay with Micky. I'm tiring of being babysat every time he's out of town. After he gets back, there's supposed to be somebody new starting at night to watch the house. I don't see how this living arrangement even makes sense anymore.

Without a job or something to do during the day, I'm getting bored. I thought I'd be fine with my books, but even that's getting old. I'd like to find something I'm passionate about. I enjoyed being a contract manager, but it wasn't a fulfilling career, by any means. *I want to make a difference in someone's life.* Like how Camden has Safehouse. Maybe I should start a charity or philanthropic organization.

"We'll be there in a couple minutes," he says, snapping me out of my daydreaming.

I sit up in my seat, adjusting the cuffs on my sweater and smoothing my hair.

"You look fine. Stop messing with your outfit. My parents don't care about that stuff, I promise."

"I'm not messing with my outfit."

"*Okay.*"

We pull up to a house on the steep river bluff, it's close in size to the one I grew up in, but that's the only similarity. Where my parents' house is more traditional with classic colonial columns and symmetrical windows. His parents' is welcoming with warm cedar shakes and round dormer windows. It's massive but nestled in pine trees gives it a cottage appeal.

"Did you grow up here?" I imagine a young Camden.

"Yeah," he says, as we open our car doors and get out. "We're staying in the boathouse out back."

I cock an eyebrow. The house isn't so much on a river bluff as it is a cliff. "Please tell me there's a tram elevator."

"There is, you princess. Don't worry."

I roll my eyes but am deeply thankful I don't need to descend down a million stairs with a suitcase. I open the rear passenger door, and Chicken Salad jumps out.

"I'll introduce you to everybody and bring our bags down after."

I nod and follow him to the front door, mentally repeating the names of his family members in my head. *Mom, Linda. Stepdad, Bruce. Sisters, Alexis and Hailey. Stepbrother, Logan.*

We enter and are met with the delicious scents of roasted turkey and pumpkin pie. His mom strides toward us and wraps her arms around me and introduces herself.

"I'm so happy you're joining us, Jordan! I'm Linda."

"Thank you, I really appreciate you opening up your home to me."

"And who's this pretty girl?" she asks, scratching my dog behind the ears.

"Pretty girl? Sounds like Cam's here!" a woman shouts from the kitchen—I'm guessing one of his sisters.

"This is Chicken Salad. Thanks for letting her come along too."

"Of course!"

While she hugs Cam, I slip out of my boots and take in the space. The river side of the house has an incredible view. Cold, black waters flow below on a gentle current, and the bluff on the opposite side features beautiful rocky ledges. A few patches of yellow and orange peek out of the pine trees covering the side, showing off the leaves that haven't yet fallen. I bet the sunsets here are extraordinary.

We follow Linda into the kitchen and are introduced to the rest of his family. His stepdad, Bruce, pauses from peeling potatoes to shake my hand. His sisters, Hailey and Alexis, are huggers like their mother. Both are very sweet, though I'm certain I heard Alexis call Cam an assface when she hugged him.

All of my Thanksgivings have been prepared by chefs or caterers. It's fun to see his whole family involved in making their own feast. His older stepbrother, Logan, is microplaning orange zest into what appears to be muddled cranberries, he looks up to give me a curt nod before returning to his task. The sleeves of his beige sweater are pushed up to his elbows. One forearm features a brightly colored tattoo sleeve, the other is blacked out.

If it weren't for the tattoos, I would get a different impression of him based on the sweater, ruffled hair, and black-rimmed glasses. He's attractive in a dark, brooding sort of way. He looks up and swallows just as another woman enters the kitchen smiling. She's my age with gorgeous, silky black hair and the best wingtip eyeliner I've ever seen.

"Hey, Kelly," Cam says, giving her a hug. "I didn't know you were joining us. Sorry to hear about your dad."

"Yeah, I have a feeling Logan has adopted me for all future holidays."

Cam nods and introduces me. "Kelly, this is Jordan. Jordan, Kelly. She works with Logan at his tattoo shop."

"Oh, are you a tattoo artist?" I ask.

"I'm a piercer for now but am in my tattoo apprenticeship."

"That's awesome, you must be quite an artist."

"I'm not terrible."

"She's exceptional," Logan interrupts.

I'm guessing Kelly was the one to do Cam's piercings, based on how familiar he seemed with her. I make a note to thank her later for doing such great work.

Hailey cuts in and hands me a glass of wine. "I hope you drink. I'm sure you could use one after being trapped in a car with Cam. He didn't sing, did he?"

I smile and take the glass. My lower back hurts, probably from sitting in the car funny or something. I'm hoping it will numb the dull ache. "Only the entire time."

"Oh God, you poor thing," Alexis says. "Wine may not be enough, Hails. We should break out the good stuff."

"On it!" she replies, ignoring him and grabbing a bottle of Tito's. Cam laughs. "Fuck both of you."

His mom puts a hand on her hip. "Cam, language. This isn't the locker room."

"Yeah, Cam. It's Thanksgiving. Don't be so crude." Alexis snickers.

He narrows his eyes at his sisters and scratches his temple with his middle finger. Stepping behind me, his hand brushes my lower back as he leans down to my ear. "I'm going to bring our bags to the boathouse"—he raises his voice—"have fun with Frick and Frack over here."

"Good one," Hailey says dryly, adding some pumpkin puree to the cocktail shaker.

"God, can't you guys get along for two seconds?" Linda asks.

All three crane their necks to face her, confused. "We do get along!"

She shakes her head and says she's going to bring up a couple bottles of wine from the basement. "Bruce, will you help me?" He smiles and stares at her ass like he wants to do a lot more in the wine cellar than choose a chardonnay.

I was worried this visit would be stuffy and formal, but it's quite the opposite. Cam and his sisters' love language is giving each other shit, but there's affection under the playful digs.

Hailey hands me a creamy bronze cocktail with crushed graham cracker on the rim. I take a sip and smile. She makes a fuckin' mean pumpkin-tini.

Kelly is enthralled with Chicken Salad and offers to take her for a walk. She convinces Logan to go with her. Once they leave, I'm left defenseless with his sisters in the kitchen.

"So, what's the deal with you and our brother?" Alexis asks, her eyebrows bouncing.

I furrow my brow. "What do you mean?"

"I mean he's never brought a woman home. Ever. For anything. Are you *together*?"

My forced laugh seems to disappoint her. "No, we're not dating. I recently got out of a bad relationship. He's giving me a place to stay until I get back on my feet." It's the truth.

"Wait, are you—"

"Yeah. I was engaged to Bryan. It was kind of an ugly split."

They nod, with understanding in their eyes. I wonder how much Cam has told them.

"Bryan always gave me the creeps," Hailey says.

"I wish he'd had that effect on me . . . Doesn't matter anymore, it's over now." *Though Bryan doesn't seem to think so*. Either way, I'm desperate to change the subject. "Camden has been a lifesaver. He's a smartass, but deep down . . ."

"We give Cam a hard time, but he's a good guy. He watches out for his people."

I take a sip of the martini and nod with a tight smile.

"Okay, give me something to do. I feel weird standing here and not helping."

They hand me green beans to wash and snip, and I get to work. It goes by quickly with easy conversation. I like his family.

THIRTY-FIVE

Camden

My sisters have had their eye on me since we sat down to eat. My gaze continues to land on Jordan, and they notice. Not sure if it's happening because I want to look at her or because I'm trying *not* to. Like when someone tells you not to think about pink squirrels, but suddenly, there's a million of those little magenta bastards hopping around your brain.

Hailey and Alexis study me as if I'm some freak experiment. They're scrutinizing every interaction I have with her. Cutting their eyes at each other every time I'm caught staring or giving her the girlfriend treatment. I see it but can't explain it, nor can I stop.

This all began because I offered her refuge from a bad situation. When did I forget she's simply a girl I'm helping? Did it happen the day I invited her on the back of my bike? The night we got high and first had sex? The next few times after that . . . Was it the night I kissed her at the game, or all the birthday festivities that took place after? *Shit.* Her feelings haven't changed toward me, she's still on that page, but I'm not. *Who even am I anymore?*

"Can you pass the mashed potatoes?" my dad asks.

I glance up at her, she nudges my mom, laughing at some joke she made. My mom tries, but she's not funny. My sister cheers glasses with her over something else. Everyone is falling for her charm. Well, everyone except Logan, who apparently has tunnel vision with Kelly—who also seems to enjoy Jordan, or at least her dog.

"Cam?"

"Huh? Oh, yeah." I grab the bowl and pass it down. "Here you go."

She's got us all under her fucking spell. I gotta pull back, it's the only logical choice. Let her move out, get her own space, have everything return to normal. She'll be like the Facebook friends you meet at a concert and never speak to again. We shared an experience, but now it's over.

That's the best course of action. The problem is, I don't want to. She's too tempting. Why should we stop? I'm interested in finding out what would happen if we made it something more. It's a unique arrangement. I like Jordan. I enjoy her company, and I want to know more about her for reasons outside of sex.

It doesn't need a label, but it needs to be exclusive. After seeing her flirt at Top Shelf with another man, it made me want to throw up, and I realized I'm not willing to share her with another person.

Fuck, why am I even thinking about this? I return focus to the table conversations and listen in on my dad and Jordan discussing some investment opportunity that landed on his desk.

"Wait, did you say Bluetower?"

"Yeah," my dad answers, smiling. "You heard about their expansion?"

Jordan sits back in her seat and slowly nods as she chews. "Who presented the offer?"

"H&H sent it over."

"Hm." She furrows her brow and blots her mouth with a napkin. "Did you accept?"

"Considering it."

"Let's chat after dinner," she says to my dad, and they nod as if they're communicating in some secret code. Whatever's going on, it doesn't sound good. Now I'm curious. If it has to do with H&H, the Davenports are involved.

Jordan makes eye contact with me, and we stare at each other for a moment until she looks away. I can tell she's bothered.

Jordan and my dad are in his study, so I wander in and take a seat on the leather sofa, my arms stretched over the back as I eavesdrop.

"They don't have the assets to make an expansion like that, certainly not one to have such a high return. There's no way." Sounds like there's some shady shit going on. "Have you ever seen a guaranteed return like this? In this timeframe?"

"I mean, Bluetower hit record speeds with their new wireless development. I saw the reports."

I have no fucking clue what they're talking about, but I'm not about to get in the middle of this.

She smiles. "Who supplied those reports?"

My dad scratches the back of his neck.

Jordan continues, "The tests failed at the demo. They aren't supposed to be retesting until next spring. The technology isn't there yet. And based on the data I saw, it won't be for years." They go on for a bit more, speaking techno-babble and going way over my head.

"What are you trying to say, Jordan?" I ask, point blank. They spin around to face me, then she looks back at my dad.

"I'm saying *don't* invest. There's no way Bluetower is going to generate a return with those numbers. But—and this is very important—I need you to keep all of this between us. Politely decline the offer, say you're going with NexTech or something. That's been on the rise lately."

He furrows his brow. "Yeah, I bought some of their stock last week. You know your stuff . . . Okay. I'm going to go out on a limb and trust you. I'll reject the proposal . . . You're sure about all this? One hundred percent?"

"I'd bet my life on it."

"Okay." He sighs. "I'll cancel the meeting."

She releases a deep exhale, and her shoulders relax.

"Thanks, Jordan. I appreciate the heads-up."

"You're welcome. I appreciate your delicacy on the matter."

"Understood."

She smiles and claps her hands. "Alright, I'm going to grab a slice of pie before I rain on any other parades."

I track her with my eyes until she leaves the room. Dad tilts his head toward the kitchen.

"That the woman you wanted the car for?"

I nod.

"Hm."

"What's *hm*?" He stares at me like he's trying to read my mind. "Just ask me, old man."

"You like her?"

My head falls back, and I groan. "Why does everybody keep assuming that because I brought her home, we're together? I invited her to Thanksgiving because her family is in Monaco."

He laughs. "It's got nothing to do with bringing her home, it has everything to do with the way you look at her. So if you want to make a move, you better let her know your intentions. She deserves to know if the guy who's giving her a place to stay is actually crushing on her."

"She just got out of a bad relationship."

"So did your mom when I met her. You want my advice?"

"I have a feeling my answer to that question is irrelevant."

"I love you, kid. But let's face it, you have a reputation. You're going to have to wise up if you want anything to do with her. That girl's too smart for asshole hockey players with commitment issues—and she knows it too."

Ugh, I know she does. She's my newest addiction. I used to think hooking up with different women every night was the best. Zero commitment, zero responsibilities, and now . . . *zero appeal.* And I like it that way. Whatever it is that we make each other feel should be protected, not thrown out the next morning.

Would I miss the other women? Would I tire of monogamy? I think about the way her eyes sparkle after I kiss her or her smile when she's reading a spicy book scene and thinks no one's watching. *Never.*

I clear my throat. "I don't know what you're talking about." I've only admitted these feelings to myself, it's hard to say them out loud.

He stares at me like he's waiting for me to break. Well, this was fun. I stand and limp over to the doorway, still sore after our most recent game.

"You got it bad for her, huh?"

"Yeap."

I turn to walk out the room.

"She's good for you. Don't lose that one."

I won't.

THIRTY-SIX

Camden

The Thanksgiving weekend game was horrible. I don't know if we were still all slow from the fucking turkey or what, but we played sloppy. No one anticipated passes, including our goalies Strass and Kap. We lost 2-7. It was a joke.

The locker room is quiet as the ass whooping we received sinks in. What's worse is knowing my family and Jordan were watching from home. Probably cringing since the first period.

JORDAN LANDRY

How are you doing?

Shitty. Got our hat handed to us.

JORDAN LANDRY

We saw. I'm sorry.

You had a great third period.

Yeah. Ready to come home.

JORDAN LANDRY

You could probably get a pity blow from one of the bunnies.

I know she's trying to cheer me up with a joke, but it pisses me off.

Stop.

JORDAN LANDRY

No good?

Rather have your pity blow.

JORDAN LANDRY

Yikes. That would be a pity.

Quit with that self-deprecating shit. Wanna know something?

JORDAN LANDRY

What?

No bunny's lips have ever made me come as hard as yours did.

I wait a minute . . . no response.

...you gonna say anything?

JORDAN LANDRY

Why do I miss you?

I don't know.

But I miss you too.

The guys talk about wrapping up bad games and wanting to go home to their wives and girlfriends, seeking comfort. I never wanted comfort when we lost, I wanted an escape. An escape by inviting a new face into my bed. Tonight? She's all I want. I've been away for not even twenty-four hours and miss her.

And it's not the sex—though it is great. I want to see Jordan wrapped up in that ugly, grungy hoodie and spend the night watching a movie, or talking, or telling her the three best things about my day.

THIRTY-SEVEN

Camden

"Cam," Jordan whispers. It takes a minute for me to remember I'm in the boathouse. I didn't get back to my folks' place until almost midnight after our loss and the grueling press box that added insult to injury.

"Yeah?" I croak out. My voice is still sore from shouting at last night's game.

"Can I get the keys? I need to run to the store."

I crack open one eye. "Jesus, the sun isn't even up yet. What do you need from the store?"

"I just need to pick up some things." She holds her hand out, gesturing for me to give them to her. "Where are the keys?"

I roll over, my voice is muffled against my pillow that I'm planted face-first into. "Whatever you need, we probably have it here."

"No, you don't. I got my period. Funny thing about periods, if you don't have a tampon, it's kind of a time sensitive issue."

Fucking hell.

I groan and sit up. "Go take a bath. I'll run to the

store." She opens her mouth to speak, but I cut her off. "Don't argue with me, it's too fuckin' early. Just do it, Sunshine."

When she exits the room, it's not long before I hear the bathtub filling up, and the corner of my mouth tips up.

I throw on a pair of joggers, a baseball cap, and grab a jacket. On the tram, I enjoy the view. Fog hangs above water on the river, and frost covers the fallen leaves on the ground. Shit, I need a cup of coffee. I stop in my parents' house, in case either of my sisters have something.

I stick my head into Alexis's room first.

"Yo. Wake up. Do you have a tampon?"

"Fuck off, it's too early," Alexis says, shoving a pillow over her head. *Somebody's got a wine hangover.*

I try Hailey's room.

"No, I use a cup. Oh no, did Jordan get her period?"

"Yeah, I'm gonna make a store run."

There's a loud thud from the room next door, and Alexis stumbles out, squinting with her hand in the air. "Did you say you're going to the store?"

"Yeah, you need something?"

"No. You're going to the store. To buy tampons. For your '*friend*.'"

Christ, this again. She's dissecting my life as if it's some show on Bravo for her to pick apart. "Yes?"

Hailey's smile spreads ear to ear, then she looks at our other sister, then back to me. "Holy shit. You like her."

I roll my eyes and turn to leave. "Don't even start. It's way too early for your meddling-sister bullshit. I'm heading out. Text me if you need something."

Alexis grabs my arm and pulls me back. Older sisters are such a pain in the ass. No matter how much taller or bigger I am, they will always see me as their baby brother.

Hailey brings her covers up to her chin like she's cozying up for story time. "Fuck, you're serious about this one."

"Do you need anything, or can I leave?"

"*I need* to know more about what this thing is between you two!" Alexis says.

I don't even know what it is, how can I explain it to my sisters? "None of your fucking business is what it is."

Alexis crosses her arms. "You stole your best friend's bride, then fell in love with her—this is so rich it *must be* fattening."

Hailey's hands rise to her cheeks. "Omigod. Can this be my Christmas present?"

I roll my eyes.

"I never liked Bryan," Alexis adds.

"I know, right? Such a douchebag—"

"I'm not in love with her!"

"Uh-huh," they say in unison. *Goddamn it.*

Alexis puts her hand on her hip. "Well, it's the closest you've ever come to love. Do you know what kind of tampons to buy?"

No fucking clue. I figure if I buy a large enough variety, one of them should work. "Leaving now."

"For what it's worth, I like her," Hailey calls after me.

"Me too," Alexis adds.

And myself makes three.

"Stop crying."

"Shut up," Jordan says, sniffling. "It's a period cry, it doesn't count."

After grabbing half a dozen boxes of tampons—and all the other shit my sisters used to get when they had their periods: pain meds, chocolate, potato chips, four kinds of dip, ice cream, and men's sweatpants—Jordan grabbed all the bags into her arms and sobbed.

"You even got bath bombs! You are-are-are s-such a softie."

Soft is the last thing I am around her. The hair on the nape of her neck is still wet from the bath and she's wearing the same stained sweatshirt she was wearing at the coffee shop. She really ought to have a Lakes hoodie by now. *One with my name on the back.*

"Whatever. Are you taking a nap with me or what?"

"It's not even ten a.m."

"You had me up at the ass crack of dawn after a game night." I yawn and head for my bedroom.

"Was it scary having a gun held to your head?"

"Jesus Christ," I grumble, kicking off my shoes and throwing my hat and shirt into the corner of the room. I collapse onto my bed like falling timber. "Get in here." The sheets are cool and soft, perfect for napping, but it would feel better if she was cuddled up next to me.

She trudges in behind me and stands awkwardly next to the bed, shifting her weight from one foot to the other. "I might head up to the house. Logan said he was making hash browns this morning. I was kind of hoping for another peek at his tattoos."

I crack open one eye and capture her waist, hauling her into bed. "Did you forget what happened last time you flirted with a guy at Top Shelf? If you wanted me to fuck you, all you have to do is ask."

She rolls her eyes. "Did *you* forget I'm on my period?"

"No."

She spins in my arms to look at me. Her raised eyebrows are all I needed to see. *I'm definitely fucking her.* I've never done it before; the opportunity hasn't presented itself. But when I was looking up things that relieve cramps, sex was near the top of the list. *Sold.*

"I'll give you all the orgasms you want, but let me get a couple more hours of sleep first. There're apple scones in the bag if you're hungry."

She sniffles again and pulls out of my arms. The sound of paper bags crumpling tells me she's digging them out. More sniffling.

I roll onto my back, chuckle, and drape my arm over my eyes. "Stop crying over pastries."

"They're my favorite."

I need her to stop talking so I can go back to sleep. "I know, Sunshine . . . Eat up, then come to bed."

When I wake up, I'm much more well-rested. I smile at the warm ball of sweatshirt and sweatpants next to me. She's facing away, curled up in the fetal position, e-reader tucked in her hand. Her hair is all over the place, only half is being contained by the elastic band. "Nice hair, I hope you win."

"You're one to talk, hockey hair."

I chuckle under my breath and nuzzle the back of her hoodie.

"Sweetheart, top-drawer lettuce shows my commitment to the game and is a sacred hockey tradition." *But she's right, I need a haircut.* "How are you feeling?" My voice is groggy.

"Meh. How are *you* feeling? You're grumpy when you're tired."

"Maybe I've got my period too."

Reaching behind, she slaps my leg. "You couldn't handle a day with a vagina."

"I'll happily handle yours all day long to prove you wrong."

She swipes the screen, flipping the page in her book. "You're a pig."

Smirking, I pull her close to me and hold her wrist up so I can read the page she's on. She tugs back, but I keep it steady. I thought romance novels had poetic language like stalks, petals, and other floral-genital comparisons. Not these books . . . Damn, this is *explicit*. There's no mistaking what stuffing a cunt and fisting a cock are.

"What the *hell* are you reading?"

"It's a romance," she says, laughing.

"No, sweetheart, it's porn. Give it here. I want to read."

"Fine, but then you read it out loud."

I smirk. "I think we've established I'm not shy about talking dirty. What's this about, anyway?"

The blush on her face makes me weak. She's so innocent on the outside, but she has a greedy mind and even greedier pussy. For whatever reason, she's been waiting for me to let it out—and fuck if that doesn't get my dick hard.

"It's about this hockey player who—"

"A hockey player!" I almost can't contain my laughter. "Why are you reading about it when you could have the real thing?"

She tries to snatch the e-reader back from me, but I hold it out of reach. "For the *romance*. It's not *all* about sex."

Well, what the fuck? I can be romantic. I think. I bought tampons, didn't I? I flip a couple pages, skimming the words. It's spicy, but I'd love to act it out on her. I read to myself as the man in the story porks his girlfriend. Cliffs Notes: he leaves hickies under her tits, rubs figure eights into her clit, puts her legs on his shoulders, fucks her till she screams for mercy, then professes his undying love to her.

Piece of cake, I can do that. Well, except for the last one. Oh, and maybe skip the eye-darkening thing—whatever the fuck that means. The only way my eyes *darken* is getting in a fight and walking away with a black eye. Also, this dude growls at her a whole fuckin' lot, so I'll have to take some liberties there.

When I finish the chapter, I hand it back to her. She wants a hot hockey player, I'll give her one. "You know . . . orgasms are supposed to relieve cramps. That's romantic."

"Cramps? These aren't cramps. This is my uterus so pissed off I haven't put a baby in her womb room that it's decided to rip out the insulation in all four walls and attic. The last thing I need is your bulldozer of a dick getting in there and *helping*. Cramps he says . . . Unbelievable." She shakes her head and stares at me for a second. "Sorry, I'm feeling slightly agitated."

"It might help . . ."

"Do you have any idea what kind of mess that would make?" *She knows I love messes.* "I'm in the middle of a good part. Go back to sleep."

I smile. "How big of a mess?"

"You know that elevator scene in *The Shining*?"

Sitting up, I push her legs apart and loop my thumbs at the top of her sweatpants. She lifts her ass for me to pull them off.

"You think I'm scared of a little blood, baby?" I point to my jaw, a butterfly bandage holding together a cut from a scuffle on the ice last night.

The soft pads of her fingers brush over the healing laceration. "Did it hurt?"

"It stung." I massage the backs of her thighs, and she relaxes into the bed. "Have you ever had period sex?"

"No."

That makes me happy. "Me either . . . Let me take care of you. I'll be gentle."

She stares at me for a few seconds, then concedes. "I'm going to get a towel, but I've got to deal with some things first."

"Whatever you gotta do."

She hops out of bed and enters the bathroom, closing the door behind her, and I harden. The water turns on and off a few times.

I'm not even sure if this will work, but I'm more than willing to try it out. All I have to do is make her orgasm, right? Should be easy enough. The bathroom door opens, she's lost the sweatshirt, wearing only a soft pink sports bra and a towel around her waist. She crawls into bed, and I untie the towel and spread it out. *God, I love seeing her naked.*

She covers her stomach. "I'm bloated."

My dick's so hard that when I shove down my joggers it slaps my abs. "Does it look like I care?"

She laughs and looks away. It's nice to see her smile.

I rub circles into her clit. Her soft moan has me pressing against her opening. Slowly, probably slower than I ever have before, I fit inside. She grits her teeth and hisses. I pull out and spit on my cock for extra lubrication, but when I enter again, she winces at the discomfort.

"What hurts?"

She props herself up on her elbows. "Actually, I think it's the piercings. It just doesn't feel good like it usually does. We can skip this." She tries to wrap the towel around her waist again.

I sit up on my heels and slide out, unscrewing the bars one at a time, then setting them on the bedside table.

"You're taking them out?"

"Yeah, you said they hurt. If this doesn't work, we'll figure out something else."

When the last bar is removed, it feels oddly smooth. I much prefer the balls sliding over my palm, but what my girl wants, my girl gets. I spit again and push inside. This time she hums with a soft smile and falls onto her back, resting comfortably. "Much better."

Fuck yeah. I could always get her off by rubbing her clit, but the urge to be inside Jordan is too great. And when it comes to her, I'm even more selfish than usual.

I grab the little reading device and hand it back to her. "Enjoy your book."

Her teeth sink into her full lower lip as she takes it from me. I keep my eyes on her while she reads, occasionally catching a sight of my cock leaving her swollen pussy. Jordan has painted me with streaks of pink and red, and it makes me feel like a caveman.

Knowing she's offering herself to me when she's fragile and depending on me to make her feel better, makes my chest swell. I get her in ways others haven't had her. I get her in ways I've had no one else.

"What part are you on?"

"Foreplay."

She reads the section I've already read. I push up her sports bra to suck under her breasts. She locks eyes with me when she realizes I'm acting out the scene. I wink at her, and she smiles with her tongue tucked into her cheek. I nip underneath like the author described. She moans, and her hand falls on my shoulder while delicate nails caress me. I've felt how hard she can scratch, but she's soft with me today. I don't mind it, those fingertips have me hypnotized. I crave her touching me like this.

Her chest rises and falls harder. I lick between her breasts and raise my gaze. "Read aloud for me."

She recites from the book, and I grin. Sitting up on my heels, I plant my palms on each of her bent knees and push them apart, and she stammers through the sentence. Now it's a game for me.

My thumb rubs eights into her clit, and her breath catches. I quote the male character with her as she reads. "Such a pretty pussy." She covers her face. I lean down and pry her hand away to whisper in her ear, "You have such a pretty pussy, Jordan."

She shakes her head and returns to reading with rosy cheeks. It's adorable.

She pulls the book away for a moment to watch me, and her blush fades as she's lost in the moment, her hips rise to meet me. "Fuck," she whimpers. Her voice is breathy and sexy as hell.

"How's the pain?"

"Better."

Nothing feels greater than taking some of her hurt.

"Good. Keep going."

She continues the story, and I slide my hands under her calves to bring them to my shoulders. Rising to my knees, I wrap an arm around her legs and raise her up with me, thrusting deeper.

Her sentences are flustered and punctuated with moans, cries, and the occasional swear word. "Cam, there's no way I can keep going with you down there. I can't focus."

"Try. You want to come don't you?"

"Yes."

I turn my head to kiss the inside of her knee. "Then I guess you better keep reading."

My thumb returns to her clit, and her thighs shake. "You're being so good for me." I freestyle that part.

I grip her legs, holding her tight as I thrust in and out. Each time I push back inside, it's harder than the thrust before. She's so tight, right on the brink of falling apart.

"*His pounding is relen—relentless, I'm on fire. His gaze scorches my skin as he offers his heart. 'I'm so fucking in love with you,' he growls. I come instantly. Afterward, he drops me down and he snuggles behind me, holding me. And in th-that moment I'm certain my feelings mirror his.* There. Done." She wraps up the chapter and tosses the device aside, grasping the sheets.

The way she grinds against me, she needs more friction. I lower her legs to the bed, leaving the head of my cock notched inside her. I cross one of her legs over and drop to my elbow, rolling her to the side so I can spoon her from behind and push inside. She reaches back, hooking her hand behind my neck for leverage as she rolls her hips. I cover her hand with mine, and my thumb rubs reassuring circles over hers, and she moans my name. Ugh, I love it when she does that.

"Say I'm your type."

"What?"

I halt my movement. "Say it."

"You're not, Camden." I hear the sadness in her voice, and it kills me. She's lying.

"I *am*. You've never been fucked the way I fuck you. And you're not allowed to come until you admit I'm *exactly* the type you've always needed."

"I don't want to," her voice quavers.

"But it's the truth, isn't it?"

She shakes her head.

I ease in and out, and it's agony for both of us.

With a patronizing voice, I mock, "What's the matter, baby? You want to come, is that it? Are you so tense you can hardly stand it?" I add pressure to her clit, level my eyes with her and growl, "Tell me you've felt this with another man. Lie to me, I dare you. I can feel your pussy trying to suffocate me. You fucking love this."

She stills.

"Admit I'm your type, and I'll make you feel so good."

She swallows and shakes her head. That pisses me off. *Why won't she say it?* We are great together.

"It's not up to you anymore." If she won't accept I'm her type, I'll prove it to her with the best orgasm she's ever had.

I let my fingers work her clit the way she needs to get off. I know what she likes; I've studied her body, her movements, her sounds, everything. I can bring her to the brink in less than a minute.

I sit up on an elbow and turn her chin toward me. "Look at me."

Her eyes open, filled with darkness and desire and tears. In the back of my mind, I'm screaming at myself to pull away, to stop. She's under my skin, burrowed into my soul, and I hate it. *Goddamn it, Jordan! Let me be your type!*

I can't wait. It's as if she can hear my thoughts, because finally, *finally,* her lips part.

"You're my type," she whispers.

My lips crash to hers, and I come like a fucking firehose. Every thrust is so satisfying.

Her body quakes as she whimpers my name over and over.

"Fuck, Sunshine. Where have you been all my life? I should have gotten with you a long time ago. It would have saved us both a lot of trouble, wasting all our time fucking the wrong people." As soon as the words leave my mouth, I regret them, it's too much, too fast. Thankfully, my audible stream of consciousness is drowned out by her pleasure. I ignore my admission and draw her close, and she collapses against me. I thread our fingers together and hug her body to mine from behind. Only stopping to lift her hand and press my lips to her knuckles.

We lie in silence for an amount of time that isn't long enough, but eventually, she gets up and we clean each other off in the shower. I help dry her off, then she pulls on a baggy T-shirt and the men's sweatpants I bought earlier. I wash and slip my piercings back in before we crawl into bed. Normally, I'm not one to lay around all day, but I can imagine nothing better than spending today in bed with Jordan, watching the black waters outside rush by. I'm perfectly content with her proximity.

Her fingertips trace my jaw line as she looks up at me, resting her chin on my chest. Damn, I could get used to this.

"Three good things," she says.

I smile and slide my hand through her wet hair. For whatever reason, that question makes me weak.

"Taking away your pain with my dick? Pretty awesome . . . Seeing my family fawn over you was something. And . . . this." I pull her up and lock my lips on hers. This time when I kiss her it feels different. It's not intense like last time after Bryan left. It's gentle. It's comfortable and safe. It's familiar. *It's Jordan.*

"Could you see us as more than friends?" I ask.

"What?" She closes on me.

"Dating, being exclusive with each other."

She tucks a hair behind her ear. "I did at one time . . . but I respect your stance on keeping things casual. I don't want to tie you down. I'm happy with what we have now. This is better."

Fucking figures. I finally find a woman who I can see myself with—who I *want* to tie me down—and I've already convinced her we can't be more. I talked her out of a relationship with zero foresight into what *could* be. What a fucking idiot.

"I know, I just—"

"Wait, is that what you want now? To be in a relationship?" She detaches from me and sits up. Shit.

"I don't know."

With wide eyes, she puffs out her cheeks and plants her hands on her hips before exhaling. "What the fuck, Cam? Seriously?"

"I said *I don't know*. I wouldn't be opposed to trying it out."

"The sex is great—no, the sex is *phenomenal*—but what I needed from a relationship previously isn't enough now. I can't ask you to be the man I need. That wouldn't be fair."

"I see. So what do you need?"

"I don't want to worry about what happens when I'm not around. I need someone who will kneel at my feet and let everyone know I'm theirs. I need to be their one and only. I'm finally in a good place. I can't give up my heart for something you want to *try out*. Especially not with you. You're my closest friend. It's too risky."

It's like a knife to my chest. She thinks I won't be faithful to her? That I wouldn't cherish what we have? I'd never hurt her that way.

I swallow the lump in my throat, doing my best to brush off the rejection.

"Okay." I grin, trying to feign amusement at her rebuttal.

"I'm sorry," she whispers.

"Why? For telling the truth? It's fine, Jordan. Let's keep the good times rolling, then. It was just something I threw out there. No big deal."

Dropping to an elbow, she snuggles up to me again.

"You're okay just keeping it physical?"

I nod. "Definitely."

What's my alternative? Saying no and losing everything? The friendship we've formed, her safety, the comfort I feel when she's next to me. I'm not chancing that. Somehow over the last few weeks, Jordan's become my best friend. She understands me. She's my favorite person.

When she drops her ear to my chest again, it's not long before she's napping in my arms. I scrub a hand down my face.

Fuck.

THIRTY-EIGHT

Jordan

I'm staying with Micky. Which feels way too similar to a babysitter, but I get it. It's as if Bryan is still controlling me from afar. He'll be back because he thinks I'm weak and hiding. I'm not hiding, I'm plotting.

Camden has introduced me to my villain era, and I've never felt more in control than when I'm planning chaos. After speaking with Cam's father at Thanksgiving, I knew it was time to assemble. *I sure botched the rest of the Thanksgiving weekend though.*

I stare out one of the tall windows of the Kucera loft and watch a plane pass by. At this exact moment, the team is flying over Canada to play back-to-back games, and it'll be days before I see him again. What the fuck is wrong with me? He asked me if I could ever see us as more, and I should have said yes.

But I didn't.

Because I'm an idiot.

It's been weighing on my mind. He can be so hot and cold. After he beat Bryan to a pulp, we had sex and he said all the right things—but then took everything back. I tried to get information out of him the day we drove to his parents', but he kept joking around. Then, after some seriously emotional period sex, he put himself out there, and it freaked me out. I was so caught up in my own hormonal feelings I couldn't tell if he was being earnest. Was it a legitimate opening for us to be more? And if so, would he just change his mind later? What if he decided monogamy wasn't for him?

A tear slips down my cheek. Our day in the boathouse was magical—which is not a word I've ever used to describe a day on my period.

However, after a night of sleep—in his arms—I know without a doubt it's the only place I ever want to be.

THIRTY-NINE

Camden

Last night we played in Calgary, and now we're off to Vancouver. I feel better about this long travel stint now that I know she's staying at Rhys and Micky's while I'm gone. He showed up at my house after the temporary protection order was put in place, so he's already shown he won't be deterred by a piece of paper.

Part of watching out for her is getting her what she needs most—and she needs some fucking friends. Jordan had a blast at the game with the WAGs. The guys have solid women who would be good for her.

Motherfucker had her on a short leash for a long time, so she needs some fun. I added her name to the WAGs box so she can hang with them at more games. Not that she's a WAG or anything . . . but this way she has a place to see them regularly.

I throw my bag in the empty row of seats on the charter plane. Rhys sits across the aisle from me, and I give him a nod.

"Thanks again for letting Jordan stay at your place. You

and Micky don't have kids, it seemed to make more sense until I set up something permanent."

He chuckles. "Permanent?"

"You know what I mean," I say, unwrapping a protein bar. "I want to make sure she's settled. Somewhere I don't have to worry about her damn ex showing up."

Rhys furrows his brow. "So, tell me again why it's better for her to stay with you rather than some building with top notch security?"

"I don't trust him. I feel better that she's with me."

"*With* you?"

"Fuck off."

"Dude, quit fooling yourself. It's fine that you've found someone you click with, but at least own up to it."

Lonan, who's sitting in the row in front of me, points at Rhys. "What he said. We know you had this playboy persona you leaned into, but it's okay to grow out of it."

"It's not like that."

"It is," Barrett says, laughing. "You may have not admitted it, but your actions speak volumes. I saw you watching her talk to that guy at Top Shelf. Looked like you were about to blow a blood vessel."

"Don't forget he rejected those other bunnies," Shep adds.

Why the fuck is everybody ganging up on me? I shake my head.

"First of all, that guy was a douchebag—"

"The girls like her," Lonan says.

"Freya certainly does." Rhys holds his phone out to me, showing a short video clip of the two girls cheersing with wine glasses, and the dogs laying in a pile next to them. *Wait a minute . . .* I grab his phone.

"Why's your dog only have three legs?"

"He was a rescue, we were told he was hit by a car as a puppy. She's got a thing for the busted ones."

"Explains why she latched onto you," I mutter.

"Fuck you too."

I take in the rest of the photo. Seeing Jordan so immersed with one of the other wives on the team warms my heart. I've been waffling back and forth about what we are for a while now. Shit's starting to keep me up at night. This was only supposed to be sex, but the guys are right . . . there's something there. I've been settling down without even realizing it. The problem is, it seems one-sided.

"She's cute, right?" I ask, unable to take my eyes off the photo.

"Don't talk about my wife," Rhys says.

I roll my eyes and hand the phone back. "I meant mine."

"There it is!" Barrett shouts from his seat, and Rhys looks up at Lonan with a huge grin like he was in on it.

I grab the Lakes tablet from my bag. "Jesus Christ. Okay, fun's over. Conway, let's go over plays." Their happiness agitates me. They don't realize I've offered myself to her, and she turned me down.

Rhys slides his headphones over his ears with a smug expression. *Asshole.*

Outside of discussing our upcoming games with Barrett, I don't speak to anyone for the rest of the flight. I need to focus on my job. I'm the captain of the team, and we need this win to make up for the ass-kicking we had over Thanksgiving. This is more important. She's not into me, anyway, so there's no use thinking about it. Maybe I should have her move out, but the thought of losing her companionship leaves me feeling sick.

When we get to the hotel that night, I find my room and kick my feet up. I've spent most of the plane ride going over game footage. I need a break.

A few minutes later, Jonesy pounds on the door. "Uber's downstairs. We're going to a club. Let's go."

I stare at the door for a second but don't answer.

"Banksy. If you're not down there in two minutes, we're leaving without you."

Opening my suitcase, I grab my toiletries and set them in the bathroom.

"Another one bites the dust," O'Callahan shouts, slapping his hand on the door. Their footsteps grow quiet as they walk away. A few minutes later, another knock on my door.

"Yo." *It's Barrett.*

I open the door. "What's up?"

"A few of us are headed to the hotel bar. Wanna grab a beer?"

With the hockey husbands? No thanks.

"Pass. I'm gonna check out the gym."

"Suit yourself."

He pushes off the doorframe, and I close it on him looking at me with pity.

The workout room is decent, though smaller than I was hoping. I'm in my third set of squats when the guys walk in with a couple six packs of beer.

I slide my headphones off my ears and throw my arms up. *What is it now?*

Lonan cracks open a beer and rests his back up against the mirrored wall. "Figured we'd bring the party to you. Ya know, now that—" The other guys lounge on the floor with him.

"Now that what?" I dare him to say it.

My cocaptain smiles. "Now that you're one of us."

I hold up my middle and ring fingers, pointing to the bare finger. "Am I the only one thinking about tomorrow's game?"

Barrett points at me. "Which brings us to why we're here. You're acting weird, and it's gonna manifest into something on the ice if you don't deal with it."

"You gotta come out with that shit. If you're anything like the way I was with Freya, it's eating you alive inside," Rhys says.

That's an understatement.

"Ever since that kiss in the stands shit, you've been over-compensating with studying game plays and working out." Barrett stares at me. "You know I'm right."

"I'm the captain. It's my job."

"Come on, man. Get it off your chest!"

They cross their arms and get comfortable, then wait, laid back, taking sips from their bottlenecks. My weights fall to my sides, and I rack them. Lonan hands me a bottle.

"I brought her home for Thanksgiving."

"You like her," Barrett says.

"I like her." I exhale, and it's filled with relief. Damn, it does kinda feel good to say it out loud. Lonan fakes a spit take, and Rhys shakes his head with a shit-eating grin.

I laugh. "Oh, shut the fuck up."

Lonan leans forward. "Look, we know how this shit affects your game if you don't have an outlet for it. You need to get your house in order." He gives me a pointed look.

He's right. At the time, I didn't want to admit it, but a big part of the Thanksgiving game shitshow was being distracted by thoughts of Jordan with my family and how well she fit in. She's the first girl I've ever introduced to them, even if she was introduced as a friend.

"This the first girl you've brought home?"

I nod.

"You scared?"

I furrow my eyebrows and cock my head back. "Of Jordan? No."

"He's impossible," Rhys says to Barrett. He gestures to me. "How do you deal with this?"

Barrett laughs and turns back to me. "You trust us with all the other shit on the ice, but you have to learn how to lean on your teammates for the off-the-ice stuff too. You don't talk to people about women unless it's fucking them. And now you actually have somebody you're taking an interest in. That's a big fucking deal for someone like you—no offense."

None taken. I haven't discussed it before because I don't want it to interfere with my captain duties. Besides, I talk to Jordan. *Just not about my feelings for her.* They look at me, seeing right through my bullshit. I groan and take another sip. "This is the dumbest episode of *Intervention* I've ever seen."

"Does she know you're into her?" Rhys asks.

"I've only been into her a handful of times."

Rhys scrubs his hand down his face.

"I dunno! Yeah, I've hinted at it. We fuck?"

"You fuck everybody," Lonan says.

"According to Freya, Jordan thinks the only reason you invited her to Thanksgiving was because of her ex." They already knew she went home with me for the holiday. That would explain this ridiculous bromance ambush. "So you may want to tell her that it meant more."

"She's not interested. When I invited her to Thanksgiving, she shut it down right away. I had to convince her to even go with me. When we were there, I brought up being more, but the feelings weren't mutual."

Rhys cringes. "Sorry, man."

"Did she say anything?"

I take a deep breath. "She basically said she needed somebody who she knew wouldn't be a hoe away from home, which really fucking sucks because she trusts me with other shit. But apparently thinks I'll be unfaithful like her ex. She acts like being with someone is giving up autonomy. Her relationship with Bryan was so dysfunctional. I think she's worried she'll be a doormat, but I'd never let that happen."

"Then show her. Make it black and white and see what happens. At least you won't get stuck wondering and you can move on. The unknown of it all is taking up too much space in your sex-addled brain," Barrett says.

It is. Maybe it's time I tell her it's exclusive or nothing. Not only because I'm possessive, but because I want to see what real dating is like. We're basically there anyway, but I've changed my mind about labeling it. Not knowing is driving me up the wall.

"Do you love her?"

"Are you serious?"

"Yeah," they all say in unison.

I'm not answering that for two reasons. One, I don't know the answer. And two, the fact I don't know scares the shit out of me. I take a sip of my beer and change the subject. "You aren't supposed to have open bottles in here."

Barrett narrows his eyes at me. "You were cooler before you became captain."

The other two assholes nod.

I suppose I could tell her I want to be exclusive fuck buddies. She might agree to that more easily than asking her to be my girlfriend.

"Jordan's something else, man. Such a cool girl, but always stuck in my head."

"Welcome to the club, brother." I tap the neck of my beer against his.

"Your club sucks," I say, taking a drink.

"It gets better."

My lip curls. "You sound like a fucking anti-bullying campaign."

"God, you're a dick." Lonan shakes his head.

"It's just because I can't have her."

Barrett smiles into his beer and takes a swig. "Dude, you're so full of shit. You know you've caught feelings for a girl and it's freaking you the fuck out because it's never happened before. I bet you can count on one hand the number of times you've fucked the same girl more than once."

"She's fucked her way into your heart," Rhys adds. He tips his beer. "That's how they do it."

The door to the workout room opens and a woman walks in. We all look up. She pauses, sees our little Girl Scout circle time, and slowly backs out.

"Okay, so what am I supposed to do now?" I stretch my legs to keep my muscles from locking up on me before tomorrow's game.

Their eyes grow big. Lonan leans all the way forward, pointing at me, and shifting his eyes from Rhys to Barrett. "He didn't even check her out!"

I crane my neck around. "Was she hot?" I turn, but she's already gone.

"She was *your* version of hot," he replies.

Impossible. Only Jordan is my version of hot.

Barrett narrows his eyes at me and smirks. I purse my lips, glaring back at him, and shake my head. *He better not tell the guys.*

"He added her to the WAGs box list."

"You motherfucker"—I point at him with my beer bottle and a stern look—"I told you that in confidence."

Like a coward, he leans away from me and looks down,

holding up both hands. Rhys and Lonan slowly turn their heads to me.

"Fuck all of you," I say, laughing and shaking my head as I lift the beer to my lips.

"Okay, okay," Barrett says. "Here's what you do—"

"Uh, no offense, but you're a fucking simp. I'd like to poll other members of the jury, thank you very much."

He rolls his eyes at me.

"Be straight with her and tell her you wanna do more than fuck." Rhys shrugs. "It's not complicated."

My phone buzzes in my pocket. It's a text from her, and my heart rate quickens like it does every time her name shows up on my screen.

JORDAN LANDRY

Micky and I are going to be sister-wives.

I grin, it fills my chest to hear she's bonding and making friends of her own. And yeah . . . I like that it's with some of the WAGs.

The fuck you are. You stay away from Rhys. He's too young.

JORDAN LANDRY

He's the same age as me.

Exactly.

JORDAN LANDRY

You're ridiculous.

I'm a goddamn delight, and according to my second grade teacher, a joy to have in class. You like me.

She doesn't respond, and I'm okay with that. Silence is better than denial.

FORTY

Jordan

"Do you think they like each other?" I ask Micky as our dogs "play" in Micky and Rhys's uptown loft, smashing into furniture like two clumsy beasts, all seven legs skittering across the floor—Chicken Salad four, Craig three.

"Right? Do you want something to drink?"

"Sure, I'll take some water." I take a seat on the couch, then bounce on the cushion twice. Comfy. "I like your sofa," I say, as she returns to the living room with a glass of sparkling water.

"IKEA."

"Nice." I take a sip of the water and lean back. "Thanks for letting me crash with you."

She takes a gulp of her water and folds her legs up under her on the couch. "Okay, sorry, I'm nosy and this is driving me nuts—what the hell is going on with you and Banksy? I've been hounding Rhys, and he can't figure it out either."

"Uhhh," I say with a nervous giggle. I shrug. "I don't really know, if I'm being honest. Things have gotten more intense. I like him. Is that weird though? So soon after breaking my engagement—the engagement where *Cam* was the best man?" He's shown me how to stand on my own two feet. I like being my own person, creating my own life with my own friends and responsibilities. I didn't realize how trapped I felt with Bryan until I was set free. I'm eating up my independence. *The new Jordan don't need no man.*

"Okay, I want you to take that whole mess out of the equation. For now, pretend Bryan didn't exist and Cam was a stranger you met on the street. Now how do you feel about him?"

A smile creeps onto my face. "He's perfect."

She smiles even bigger than me. "That's your answer. Don't let the public drama fuck with what you and he share privately. If you like him, you like him. And it sounds like you're the first person Banks has ever gotten close to, which means he definitely feels *some* way about you."

Micky makes it seem so easy.

"We're in a weird spot. I think he wants more, but I'm not ready to make the leap. Does he even realize what he would be giving up? You've seen him, he keeps women like secrets."

She scoffs. "But you're essentially living together. So what's your endgame?" she asks, turning on the TV and switching the channel to the game in Vancouver.

There are times we look at each other and I see the strong attraction in his eyes. The closest he came to acknowledging it was in the boathouse. He's never been in a real relationship before. What if he decides it's not for him and wants to continue to play the field? I'd be left crushed and alone. I reacted poorly, but this is a big deal—for both of us. It's not something we'd be able to dip our toes into and walk away from unscathed. If I take down that barrier between us, I'd fall hard, and it scares the hell out of me. Cam is my best friend. He knows me on a level deeper than I've allowed anyone else to go.

"You're right. Unfortunately, I acted like an idiot over Thanksgiving. I pushed him away when I should have pulled him closer."

Her nose scrunches. "Why the hell did you do that?"

I cover my face. "I don't know, I panicked or something. It was so stupid."

Doesn't mean I can't undo it. Shit. I don't want to wait too long and lose the opportunity. My hands fall to my sides. "No. You know what? I'm gonna tell him. Tonight. After his game, I'm going to call him. Fuck this no-talking bullshit."

"Hell yeah!" Micky holds her drink out to cheers with me. Yeah. This feels good. I will get it all off my chest, and he can take it or leave it. But not knowing feels so much worse.

"Ooh, we need snacks!" Micky hops up and hurries to the kitchen to grab a bowl of popcorn.

There's a subtle bass in the floor from the live music below us at Sugar and Ice, the cocktail lounge Micky owns. "Hey, how's business, by the way? Sounds like it's hopping downstairs."

"It's going really well! We're partnering with Citra brewing, and they have a couple guys who have been awesome mentors for me."

"That's so great! Sounds exciting."

"It is! What are you doing for work?"

I sigh and lean back, folding my legs in front of me. "Nothing yet. I've been thinking about volunteering with Safehouse, Cam's project, until I figure it out. I gotta get out more."

She nods. "Well, what do you like to do?"

I cringe. "I'm trying to figure that out. Most of my life has been a certain way. My hobbies were chosen for me," I say, thinking of all the equestrian and piano lessons. "And now I'm late to the party trying to find myself. After the engagement ended, I realized I've never really been in control of my own life. So I'm looking for something . . . new. Something fulfilling that benefits other people. It's gotta feel right, ya know?"

She swallows her drink and nods. "Absolutely. Sugar and Ice is my baby, and if I didn't have it, I'd be lost. Speaking of, do you want to go out tonight? I mean, if you want, we can go downstairs and get free drinks," she says, pointing at the floor.

I purse my lips and cock my head to the side. "Are we still doing brunch with the girls tomorrow?"

"Bottomless Bloody Marys."

"Nah, let's stay in and watch the game."

She holds her fist in the air and grabs the remote, turning up the pregame show. "I'm secretly relieved you said that." She ties her hair up into a messy bun and rolls her eyes. "The finance bros tend to take over Thursday nights, and they'd be trying to suck our dicks all night."

I laugh and take another sip of my sparkling water. Cam's headshot splashes on the TV as the hockey analysts discuss his new role as captain. They talk about him like he's the team wildcard, and maybe he is, but they don't know him like I do.

Once the game starts, I smile. Every time he makes a swift pass, steals the puck, or outmaneuvers another player by quickly switching directions, I'm left in awe of his skill and ability to anticipate moves of other players. He's talented as hell.

Micky decides we need to up the ante and whips together a few cocktails. They're delicious, and before we know it, we're three drinks in, and it's not even halfway through second period. My whole body is fuzzy and warm. We've become more belligerent and animated as the game goes on. The Lakes are in their element.

"Fuck yeah!" Micky yells, holding her hand out to me.

I give her an aggressive high-five, and we take another drink.

I hiccup. "If we keep drinking every time they score a goal, we aren't going to make it to third period. We might die. They're on fire tonight."

"They're spanking Vancouver! Hey, wanna get some food? This is so fun, it's like a sleepover. I never get girl time anymore since Birdie and Raleigh insisted on reproducing." She tosses her hand in the air.

Laughing, I nod. "Oh god, it's been forever since I've had girlfriends to do stuff with."

She scrunches up her face. "Really? Why?"

I lift my shoulders. "Don't have a ton of close friends." I avoid saying that rich people don't often have many real friends because it makes me sound like an enormous tool. "My former best friend fucked my fiancé. It's been a dry spell for girl time lately."

Ever so slowly, she turns her head to face me with wide eyes.

"What. The fuck. Go get your pajamas on. I'm going to refresh our drinks, and then you're going to tell me everything."

I laugh, and she snatches the mostly empty glass from my hand. This is fun.

When we have our sweats on—*both of us in Lakes gear*—I tell her the story. All of it. It surprises me when I get emotional. I've never talked about it beginning to end before, it's a massive release. Like pouring out my guts, but I only put back the stuff I want to keep, the good parts. Parts of me that are healing and strong, parts with Camden. Letting go of all the bad memories.

Bryan didn't break me. And after hearing about Bluetower from Cam's dad, I'm going to balance the scales.

Micky wraps her arms around me. "Does Banksy know all of that?"

I nod. "Most of it. I didn't tell him about the night he laid his hands on me."

"So what are you going to do?"

I give her a pointed look.

She narrows her eyes in understanding. "You're going to fuck Bryan up, aren't you?"

I smirk back and nod into my drink. That's the plan.

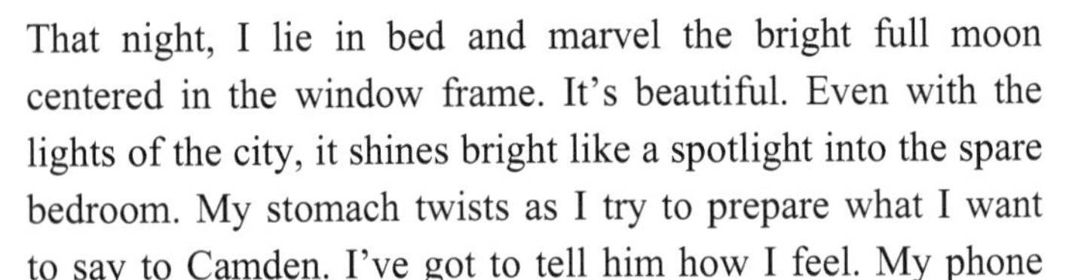

That night, I lie in bed and marvel the bright full moon centered in the window frame. It's beautiful. Even with the lights of the city, it shines bright like a spotlight into the spare bedroom. My stomach twists as I try to prepare what I want to say to Camden. I've got to tell him how I feel. My phone dings, and I grab it.

CAMDEN TELLER

Hey

Hey!

CAMDEN TELLER

Miss you.

I miss you too.

CAMDEN TELLER

I was talking to Chicken Salad. How is she?

I smile and reach down to scratch her behind the ears. She's lying on my legs, as usual.

She and Craig are thick as thieves.

CAMDEN TELLER
Good to hear. Did you girls watch the game?

The football game?

CAMDEN TELLER
Sass me again. I dare you.

Double dare me...

I wait for his response but there's nothing. I need to hear his voice. I hit the phone icon next to his name, and it rings a couple times before a woman answers his phone. It's noisy in the background. "You've reached Banksy's Pants . . . Banksy's not in his pants right now, can I take a message?"

My stomach sinks. *Shit.*

"Hello?" She giggles.

Blood drains from my face. I panic and end the call. *What the fuck was that?*

I swipe at my eyes. This is why I shouldn't be considering anything with him, he's not ready for something more than friends. Maybe I'm not either.

God, and after everything I said to Micky? She'll ask how our talk went tomorrow. This is so humiliating.

I wait for him to call. To text me. To say it was a joke or there's some misunderstanding, but he doesn't. I want him to tell me it's not what it sounded like. In a desperate attempt, I dial him back, but it goes to voicemail after two rings. He dismissed my call. It's over. After hours of conjuring images of Camden with other women, I eventually fall asleep with wet cheeks.

CAMDEN TELLER

Did you try calling me last night?

Butt dial.

CAMDEN TELLER

K. Sorry we couldn't talk last night, had some stuff to deal with.

I swallow the lump in my throat. "*I'm sure.*"

Micky said she can drop me off at home. You don't have to pick me up.

CAMDEN TELLER

I'm picking you up.

Micky ties her combat boots while I slip on a pair of wedged boots. I'm still antiheels since having to walk five miles in them. I glance over at the dogs sleeping in a pile. We woke them every time we jumped in the air with a goal, which riled them up and quickly wore them out. Last night was great. *Until it wasn't.*

"I'm sure she was nobody. Probably some drunk fan."

"It's fine. We weren't exclusive. He can do what he wants." I shrug.

She looks at me with eyes full of sympathy, and her pity makes it worse. I fake a laugh. "Don't look at me like that. I'm okay, Micky. Really."

She nods and gives me a hug. "Men are so fucking dumb."

"Yeah." That's why I'm done with them.

We meet Raleigh and Birdie at brunch, and they wave to us from a table in the corner.

"Hey!" They give me a hug. "We already ordered a round."

"Bless you. Micky and I were up way too late watching

the game." I was up late imagining Cam with the woman that answered his phone.

Raleigh slaps her hand on the table. "They played so well! I'm so happy Barrett is getting a great final season. They're high in the standings."

I nod.

"These are delicious," Micky says, pulling out the piece of bacon from the Bloody Mary and biting off the end. "Tomatoes and vodka bring out the best in each other."

Raleigh raises her Virgin Mary. "To hockey widows." She winks at me. "You're one of us now."

I'm definitely not.

"Hockey widows!" the other girls say, though Micky is less enthusiastic than the others. She grips my hand under the table, and we all clink glasses.

"Micky?" A gorgeous woman stops at the table, and Micky's eyes get big. "Oh, shit. Ken! What are you doing here? Everybody, this is Kendra. Kendra, these are my girls, Raleigh, Birdie, and Jordan. Wanna join us? We've got room."

"Can't, I'm meeting with a few people, just had to stop by and say hi."

Micky thrums her fingers on the table and bounces her eyebrows. "Producers? Are you finally making a reality show about my life?" She smiles sweetly.

"Ha! No, sorry. But I am meeting with a couple creators to discuss the show."

Birdie and Raleigh get caught up on kid stuff, and I eavesdrop on the conversation between Micky and Kendra while I browse the menu.

"What do you mean he dropped out?"

Kendra shrugs. "Yeah. Can you believe that shit? So now I'm on the hunt for a new bachelor. I've got to come up with somebody soon, or they'll scrap the show. So if you know of anyone . . ."

Camden Teller comes to mind.

"What about Rhys's old captain? Lee Sullivan?"

Kendra frowns and raises her eyebrows as she considers it. She shifts her weight. "Would he be interested?"

"I'll have Rhys talk to him. Do you have a card?"

Kendra digs one out of her purse and hands it to her. "Okay, my team is here. Thank you so much. Let's talk later!"

"You got it! Good luck."

She nods. "Good to see you, babe."

"Okay, who's hungry?" Birdie asks.

"Me," Raleigh says, opening up a menu. "Swear to God, if I have to eat another bowl of Cinnamon Toast Crunch for breakfast I'm going to start intermittent fasting. I can't do it."

FORTY-ONE

Camden

When I pick up Jordan and Chicken Salad from Rhys and Micky's, she's slightly buzzed. I appreciate that Micky didn't get her bombed at brunch. It was bad enough I was the sober cab for a bunch of drunk hockey players—last night was a fucking disaster.

Colby got in a fist fight with some guy at the club after partying a little too hard, then between breaking up the scuffle and getting back to the hotel, I realized my phone was gone. Still don't know if it fell out of my pocket or if it was stolen. While waiting for our flight this morning, I spent an hour at a carrier store in the airport getting it replaced. Ugh, it was a goddamn nightmare, especially since I'd been looking forward to coming home to her since I left the ice. Now all I want to do is take her home and crawl into bed. "Hey, Sunshine," I say, kissing her cheek. "Ready to go?"

She pulls away, putting distance between us, and nods. We take the stairs down to the curb where I'm parked. I load her suitcase in the car, along with all of Chicken Salad's stuff. This dog needs its own luggage. Jordan climbs in the passenger seat and puts her seatbelt on. When I get in and drive away from the sidewalk, I ask her about her weekend with Micky. Every answer is short and clipped.

"I missed your face."

Turning to face me, her temple cushioned against the headrest, she gazes at me with a sad smile that doesn't reach her eyes. "Nice try, but I'm not into you."

I scoff. "Again, I was talking to Chicken Salad, but congrats on having such high self-esteem."

"Stop lusting after my dog. She's not into you either."

"She will be when she sees that I brought her a"—my voice crescendos—"*squeaky toy*!" Reaching into the driver-side door pocket, I wrap my fingers around the stupid plush team mascot from Vancouver and squeeze it. It squeaks, causing Chicken Salad's massive ears to stand up. She wedges her big fluffy head between us on the center console, pawing for it.

Holding it up, the furry monster takes it from me more gingerly than one would expect for a dog of her size.

"Tear it to shreds, Chicken Salad," I say, winking at Jordan. "Good girl."

She turns away from me. My fingers itch for her. I want her affection. Her kiss. Her touch. *Anything.* I was expecting a warmer reception when I got to Micky's, but she seems distant. The closer we get to home, the more my mind wanders with all the ways I want her.

When I pull into the garage and turn off the car, she unclicks her seatbelt. Before I can do the same, Jordan reaches out, flips my hat backward, and turns me to face her. Her gaze drops to my lips, and my fingers sink into her blonde locks. I yank her into my lap. *Fuck, I missed this woman.* She always knows exactly what I need. I want to be what she needs.

Wanting more, I lean forward, but she shoves me back. At my shoulder, she draws out excess length from the seatbelt strap and holds it across my neck. We regard each other for a moment, the way she's taking dominance over me. Physically and metaphorically. She has me in a chokehold, controlling me more and more every day. The longer we're away from each other, the more I crave her.

She pushes the strap against my neck, glaring at me, and I swallow. Her lips crash to mine again, and I groan and grip her thighs like she's my fucking life source. Jordan's my oxygen. She's all I need. Her lips are commanding and greedy. And punishing.

What the fuck happened while I was gone? This is a different Jordan.

She withdraws, and when my eyes find hers, sadness flickers in them. "Don't play with me."

I blink back and swallow, not liking the sound of that one bit.

She pops the handle on my door and climbs off my lap, leaving me with a massive hard-on and a million questions.

Chicken Salad squeaks the toy, and I spring off my seat. Forgot she was back there. I remove my seatbelt and exit the vehicle in a daze, opening the rear door for the dog to jump out.

"What the hell is going on in your mom's head?"

She was a relationship girl when we met. Did I get so wrapped up in corrupting her, fucking her in all the ways she's never had, that I pushed her too far? That she'll consider nothing more with me? I'm not great at admitting when I'm wrong, but when it comes to Jordan, I was an abso-lute fucking idiot for telling her we could never be more.

I'd planned to bring it up on the drive home, but she

seemed so detached, I got cold feet. It's time for me to step up and become the man she deserves.

After chatting with the guys in Vancouver, it's been rolling around in my brain, and I've come to the conclusion that I'm as bad as Barrett—I'm a total fucking simp for her. And I want to do everything I can to make her happy enough to stay. Forever.

FORTY-TWO

Jordan

I'm in my room responding to emails, mostly documents against Bryan, screenshots of his text messages. My lawyer is asking for information regarding the way our funds were shared. We've got a meeting later today with Robert, my finance manager. Bryan and his lawyer are being difficult, getting him removed from my bank accounts was a pain in the ass. He's not making anything easy.

I didn't tell them about Bluetower, the company H&H took on, the one they've been touting to investors with lucrative returns that aren't possible. It's my golden ticket to fucking up his life. Unfortunately, the way I obtained my information isn't exactly on the up and up—and Bryan has always been good about covering his tracks. He's brazen but always has a backup plan. So I'm leaving no trace as well.

The next order of business is getting my own place. Now that I've got money in my account from some of my investments, and lawyers are in place to get the rest, it's time I sit down with Cam and explain that I'm safe enough to move out. This isn't the time for us. Maybe someday we'll get our chance.

As I hit send, there's a knock on my door. I open it and see Cam standing there shirtless with a pair of scissors, clippers, and half a head of cut hair. Oh god.

"Can you cut hair?"

As a teenager, I used to cut my grandfather's hair when he was in hospice, but that was a decade ago. I cross my arms and lean against the doorframe with an amused smile. "What happened?"

"I got an email from PR, they want us cleaned up for some photoshoot later this week. I was feeling lazy and overestimated my skill level by about two and a half barbers."

"Come on in." I push off the door. Stealing a chair from the table in the kitchen of the apartment space, I place it in the bathroom in front of the large mirror. It's a tight fit for him to sit down, but we make it work.

I place a towel around his neck, and my fingers skim his shoulders. It reminds me of all the times I've grabbed his shoulders before.

"So, what are we doing today?" I jest.

"You're giving me the best haircut I've ever had."

I scrunch up my nose. "Let's set some realistic expectations."

"I'm getting a haircut from the hottest stylis—"

I turn on the clippers, drowning him out. He bites his lip, and my cheeks flush. First, I even out the damage he's done and clean it up. My gaze bounces back and forth from his reflection in the mirror to him in front of me, focusing on making sure everything looks uniform. Except for the times my body betrays me and we make eye contact. Because he won't stop staring.

His gaze makes every inch of me feel alive, and I hate it.

It makes my heart ache. My masochism wins out, I know I can't have him, but I still want his attention, no matter how much it hurts. My stomach twists. I turn off the clippers and set them on the countertop, then pick up the scissors.

"How long do you want it on top?" I hold up some hair between my index and middle fingers. "About here?"

"Yeah, that's good."

Normally the silence between us isn't awkward, but it feels so heavy now. I can't stand it.

"Oh, I meant to tell you, I've decided to spend the holidays with my parents in Monaco."

"You are?"

"Yeah, I spoke with my mom this morning. They're staying in Cape Martin for a few more months. It doesn't really make sense for me to stick around here."

He hums. "Oh. I guess I'd assumed you would come with me to my parents' again . . . But I understand you wanting to spend it with your own family. How long will you be gone?"

"Three weeks."

"Three *weeks*?!"

"I might as well, it's not like I'm rushing back to a job or anything. You've got a lot of away games coming up anyway, it makes sense to stay in Cape Martin."

He nods hesitantly.

Standing in front of him, I wet his hair. When I begin trimming, there's such little space that I have to keep one of my legs on either side of his. We're uncomfortably close, his scent surrounds me and causes a lump to form in my throat. Camden doesn't seem to mind our proximity. He cups the back of my knees, and his gaze trails higher as his palms roam up the sides of my thighs until he reaches my hips where he decides is a good place to rest them. I don't react, even though the heat from his touch bleeds through my jeans and is doing its damnedest to distract me. I feel his eyes on me.

"Look straight ahead, not up."

He's basically eye level with my breasts.

"Happily," he says.

I give him a small slap on the cheek with my comb.

He turns up the corner of his mouth. "Brave girl."

His hands push my shirt up, and he leans in and bites my stomach, I jerk back, hitting the countertop. I attempt to grab the surface for balance, but he pulls me down so I'm straddling his left thigh. When I look at him, he's got his tongue pressed into his cheek with a smug look, and I ask the universe why he has to be so attractive. The longer we continue to sleep together, the more difficult it is to compartmentalize our "situationship." Especially if I'm not the only one sharing his bed.

Clearing my throat, I use his shoulder for leverage to stand.

"I had scissors in my hand, I could've cut my finger off. Don't bite me. I need to finish your hair, or you'll look like a rooster for your headshot."

"At least the carpet will match the drapes."

I crack, he gets a laugh out of me, and I shake my head. "I hate you."

"You love me."

The awkward silence returns, expanding from wall to wall. *It's deafening.*

I continue trimming, hoping I appear more unaffected than I am, but his hands find me again, and I gulp. My eyes burn, and I'm too scared to look down. I didn't fight my way to my new bad-bitch self to be taken down by Camden Teller. It's hard enough that I've developed this attachment to him. I don't think either of us thought we'd become such close friends. And I'm guessing nine out of ten therapists would agree that jumping out of the frying pan and into the fire isn't a healthy strategy.

Stepping behind him, it's easier to breathe. I comb his hair to check my progress. My fingers slide into his hair, and he shivers.

I draw up the hair with the previously cut strands and trim the length to match, cutting into the ends to make it look as natural as possible for his photo.

"Why have you been pulling away from me?"

His question causes me to freeze.

If I don't pull away, you'll reel me in again, and my heart will attach itself to something that doesn't exist.

"We're literally touching."

"You know what I mean."

I blow out a breath. "I'm protecting my space. The lines feel like they're blurring between us."

"Blurring into what?"

I purse my lips before I go back to trimming. *He knows what.*

"I like you, Jordan."

Forcing a smile, I return the sentiment as casually as I can. "I like you too, Cam." *Which is why this sucks so much, because I really, really like you. And hearing another woman answer your phone gutted me.*

Migrating to his other side, I trim around his ears using the comb and shears.

"No. Stop for a second." He huffs out a breath and tugs me close. "I *like* you."

Nope, nope, nope. I say the first thing I can think of. "Okay." *What an articulate response, Jordan. Those communication credits are finally paying off.*

He's staring straight into my soul, making me flustered.

"Will we be arriving at your point in the near future, or should I pack a lunch?"

His grin grows; he's got a terrific smile. "This isn't working for me anymore," he says.

The floor feels like it's dropped out. I knew we had to stop our arrangement as soon as I heard that girl through the phone, but hearing him end it first hurts more than I expected. I don't let an ounce of emotion show. Instead, I nod. "I get it. Let's go back to being platon—"

"No." He cocks his head at me, and his brows knit together. "I need more than friends with benefits."

"I don't think that's a good idea."

"Why?" Hurt flickers in his eyes, and I wince.

"I don't want to risk our—"

"I swear to God, if you say friendship, I'm gonna lose it."

"It's true!"

He scoffs at me. "You're being a coward."

I gape at him. "I'm trying to set a boundary! I was fine being your plaything—but I'm done now. Because I like you and I'm not going to compete with other women for your attention. I don't think you realize the things you would have to give up. Have you ever even been in a relationship?"

"I mean . . ."

"See?"

He removes the comb and scissors from my hands and sets them on the counter, wraps his fingers around each of my wrists while his thumbs brush my pulse. "What can I do to change your mind?"

I laugh.

"What's so funny?"

"It sounds like some shitty sales pitch. *What do I have to do to get you on this penis today?*" I exaggerate my voice.

"Why do you keep going reducing our relationship to what

we do in the bedroom?" he sneers.

I flinch at the severity of his voice.

"This is the second time you've chalked up what we are"—he gestures an imaginary circle between us—"to sex. And while we're on the topic, don't ever cheapen what you mean to me by calling yourself a *plaything*." He's angry, and I can't help but become overly aware of how much bigger and stronger he is.

I bite my lip and nod.

His shoulders relax and he continues, "The sex is great—fuck, it's *amazing*—but we enjoy being around each other. You understand my thoughts better than anyone. You have this weird knack for reading me. And I've been trying to get to know you more, but every time the conversation shifts to something heavy, you deflect or shut down. I'm not going to pretend to know what you were like with Bryan, but I would bet a signing bonus that you were just as closed off to him as you are with me. So, before you start saying I don't know how to be in a healthy relationship—with all due respect, Sunshine—*you first.*

"Our past relationships don't matter, I'm asking for the future . . . We'll work at it. Jordan, you're my favorite person to be with, and I like that you hold me accountable. You couldn't care less about my money or fame or want anything from me other than my company. And that's all I want from you. All my life I've been pushing my limits to get a rush, to *feel* something—sex, fights, drinking, speeding, buying material shit I don't need. Since you've been around, I've never felt more content. You are my rush."

"Until I'm not there, then you get your rush from someone else."

"I would never do that to you."

I curl my lip in disgust. "You already did! The woman you

were with last night answered your phone, Camden. I called you and *another woman answered.* She said you *weren't in your pants*. It was humiliating. I even called you back and you declined it. Do you have any idea how that feels? I'm not going to be some side piece. Which brings me to another point, I think it's time I move out."

His eyes widen. "I lost my phone last night. I wasn't with any girl, I swear."

I roll my eyes. "That's such a lame excuse."

"It's not an excuse! Whatever you think happened, *didn't happen*. Is that why you've been so weird since I got home?"

"I'm not being weird, I'm taking a break from this." My voice cracks as I gesture between us.

He drags me closer. "I don't want a break. Jordan, we're good together. Look, this is me laying it all out on the line for you, I have never shared my feelings like this with anyone. Know why? Because you're a safe space for me. Let me be that safe space for you."

"You are my safe space," I assure him. He's the only safe space I've ever had.

"Then stop pulling away every time shit begins to feel real—our connection exists whether you want it to or not, we owe it to each other to at least *see* if there's something here." He slumps into the chair and rubs the back of his neck. His hand drops to his lap while he waits for me to respond.

He's not wrong. About any of it. He's got me pegged, and I'm ashamed of the accuracy. I am closed off. It's why I can't figure out what to do with him.

"Who was the woman that answered last night?"

He retrieves his phone from his pocket and dials Barrett, putting it on speakerphone. I notice it's slightly different. Maybe an upgraded model . . .

"I see you got your new phone working," Barrett answers.

Cam points at the phone as if to say *see?!*

"What happened last night at the bar?"

Barrett scoffs. "Right?! That shit was nuts. Thanks for helping me pull Colby off that guy. It's shitty you lost your phone in the process."

"I think you were right when you said it was stolen, Jordan said some woman answered it last night."

"Probably those girls sitting behind us."

"Maybe. Hey, who did I share a room with last night?"

"Me . . ." Barrett answers. "Oh, shit, does Jordan think you had a girl over? Jordan if you can hear me, I swear Cam only touched my balls once and it was because I asked him to."

"Charming. Bye." He ends the call and stares at me. "Sunshine, there are so many things I like about you. You are strong and fearless. You handle the worst challenges with grace. You're smart and observant. You can read me so well, it's spooky. You're funny, playful, wild, and sexy. Not to mention drop-dead gorgeous." His head lolls to the side, and he shrugs. "You make me fucking crazy. Why would I want anyone else?"

I blink at him. "I'm sorry I didn't believe you." I swipe under my eyes, and he smiles.

"You can cry around me, you know."

"You're a really good guy, Cam."

He groans. "But?"

I raise my eyebrows and shake my head. "But nothing. I wish you would let more people see this side of you."

"I don't need anyone else to see it. It's yours."

But I don't want it to only be mine. I don't want to be a secret.

"If I say yes to this, I *want* people to see it."

I vowed that the next man I get involved with will treat me like a queen, and Camden Teller is no exception.

"What do you mean?"

"I'm not going to be some quiet girlfriend on the side that other women think they can step over to get to you. I don't want to be yours behind closed doors. I'm not a delicate princess—I'm a fucking queen. If you want me, that's how you're going to treat me. Leave your ego at the door, I want everyone to know that *you* kneel at *my* feet." I cross my arms, waiting for his response, and mentally pat myself on the back for demanding my worth.

"Yes, Your Highness." His grin spreads across his face until he's beaming at me. "I'm so goddamn proud of you."

My arms fall to my sides. "Thank you."

He pulls me into his lap, pressing my chest to his. His mouth finds my neck, he sucks on my skin and bites. I let out a small moan, and he whispers behind my ear, "But in the bedroom, you kneel for *me*."

I wrap my arms around his neck. "I can agree to that," I mumble against him.

He holds me to his chest, and I rest my head on his shoulder, breathing in his clean scent. I didn't think I'd ever hand my heart over to another man, but this is Cam. He makes me feel alive. He draws down one of my arms and presses his lips to my wrist before kissing me.

"You're my best friend," I say.

"You're my best friend too."

"Our families will talk."

"Let them."

I smile and sit up, cupping his cheeks and bringing his mouth to mine.

"Are you still going to Monaco?"

Sigh. "I told my parents I would. They want to see me . . . I'm sorry."

He nods, and his hands travel under the hem of my shirt. "Don't apologize. Just know you can always come home early if you need to." His fingers slide behind my bra clasp.

"Wait, wait, wait!"

He stops kissing me and blinks.

"I have to finish this haircut."

He rolls his eyes. "Topless." He finishes unhooking my bra and peels my shirt over my head. "Much better." He sucks a nipple into his mouth and pops off. *Fuck.* "What are we doing after this?"

"Actually, I've got a meeting with my lawyer and financial adviser in an hour, after that, I'm all yours."

"Good. We've got nearly five days to make up for, and I haven't been able to stop thinking about all the ways we're going to do it."

Sean, my lawyer, stands, stuffing papers into his briefcase. We had a successful exchange with Bryan's lawyers, he's starting to cooperate, even my attorney is suspicious.

"Okay, well, as long as your financial status is back in order, do we have any other business?"

I look over at Robert, my portfolio manager. "I need to withdraw more money."

"Sure. How much?" He places his hands on the keyboard and begins typing.

"Twenty thousand in cash . . . Also, I need a sixteen-million-dollar anonymous donation to Minneapolis PD."

Robert's typing ceases, and Sean's head falls backward,

and he stares at the ceiling before slowly dropping his gaze to me. He tosses his hands in the air. "What the fuck?"

"It's unrelated."

"Ha!" Sean laughs without a trace of humor and stands. "I'm leaving before I hear something I shouldn't. Jordana, reach out when you're ready to press those assault charges."

I nod. After he leaves, Robert stares at me for a moment, then rolls back in his chair. With steepled fingers against his lips, he looks me head-on.

"Jordana, my job is to manage your money. But this . . .? It's not my place to ask, but is there something going on I should know about?"

"I like you, Robert. You've worked for my family a long time, but you're right, it's not your place to ask."

We have a miniature stare down before he sucks his teeth and returns to the keyboard, making the necessary wire transfers.

FORTY-THREE

Jordan

Blue skies greet me when I step off the plane, I already miss home—or maybe I just miss Camden. After a forty-five-minute drive from the airport in Nice, I'm dropped off at my parents' private estate in Monte Carlo. It's decked out for the holidays, complete with fake flocking on fake trees and perfectly constructed garlands draped across the Belle epoque architecture of my parents' villa. Happy ostentatious holidays. Fa-la-*la-di-da.*

I pull out my phone and text Cam, he's probably just waking up.

I'm here.

CAMDEN TELLER

I want proof of life.

I send a photo of myself with the dusky Mediterranean behind me.

CAMDEN TELLER

Damn . . . that's a view.

Sea isn't bad either. 😉

eyeroll

CAMDEN TELLER

How many days until I see you again?

20.

CAMDEN TELLER

That sucks.

You'll be so busy, you'll hardly notice I'm gone.

CAMDEN TELLER

Oh... I meant sucks for YOU. I'll be fine. But are you really going to last 20 days without my good looks and charm?

Probably not. How ever will I forge through the long-suffering loneliness without you?

CAMDEN TELLER

It's going to be a marathon of misery and gloom.

Tis the season.

My parents welcome me with open arms and hugs.

"We're so happy you're spending Christmas with us," my mom coos, and the three of us are seated at their favorite restaurant, Le Louis XV.

I smile. "Me too, Mom."

Truth is, I'd rather be celebrating Christmas with the Tellers. Every Christmas I've ever had has been flawlessly curated. From the exquisite private-chef menu to the tree I wasn't allowed to touch. It's always been *perfect.* I assumed that's the way it was for everyone, after all, that's what's shown in the windows of Fifth Avenue and holiday advertisements. Christmas is a spectacle meant to dazzle and amaze.

It's not that I don't appreciate the splendor, but I'd like to be a part of it, rather than have it done for me. I want to pick out my own tree, one that isn't perfectly coned. In fact, I want it misshapen and disfigured. With dead spots. I want to decorate it with ornaments that don't come from Bergdorf's.

My parents aren't showy people, they're simply oblivious. They always hire a company to "do" Christmas for them, which results in flamboyant decorations and traditions. It's all so . . . artificial.

I bet Camden's family will cook their own Christmas dinner, wrap their own presents, and decorate their own tree. They probably watch Christmas movies, bake their own cookies using family recipes, and maybe even build a snowman or two. Chicken Salad will be with them on Christmas. She's staying with Kelly, Logan's friend/piercer/apprentice while Cam travels. My dog will be well cared for, considering how obsessed she was with her over Thanksgiving.

I left a couple presents in his closet. One for Chicken Salad and one for him. Chicken Salad is getting a new rope toy, and Camden is getting a hat. It's not the greatest hat, but it was something I knit by hand after finding a pattern online. And I even found out how to knit his number, forty-six, on it. On the inside, I added a small C, for captain. Not sure if he'll even wear it, but I wanted to give him something heartfelt.

I wish he was here . . .

"Jordana?"

"Huh?"

My thoughts are brought back to reality when I realize the sommelier is waiting on me.

"Oh, my apologies. Whatever you suggest for the red mullet."

The sommelier nods and departs from us. I'm left looking at my parents.

"Jet lagged?" Dad asks with a smile.

"Yeah, sorry . . ." That's not true. "Actually, no. I was thinking about Camden," I blurt.

"Oh?" Mom asks.

"I really like him. I want you to meet him."

I told my parents about us.

CAMDEN TELLER

Oh yeah?

Yeah.

CAMDEN TELLER

What do they think about you officially hooking up with the best man?

It was a little awkward at first, but I told them how great you are.

CAMDEN TELLER

Must have been a long conversation.

It was, actually.

CAMDEN TELLER

Anything I should be worried about?

Nope. I think they liked you after the video chat when you stood up to my mom. They want to meet you in person after they return to the States.

CAMDEN TELLER

I'd like that.

Really?

CAMDEN TELLER

Of course. We gotta make this legit. How many days until YOU return to the States?

16

CAMDEN TELLER

Merry Christmas, Sunshine.

Merry Christmas!

CAMDEN TELLER

I love my hat.

I'm glad you like it. Tell your family hi for me.

CAMDEN TELLER

Same to you.

Can I open your package yet?

CAMDEN TELLER

Yes.

I pick up the box I wasn't allowed to open until Christmas and tear into the cardboard package. Inside is a signed hardcover of the hockey romance he read me over Thanksgiving weekend along with a bag of Sour Patch Kid gummies. The smile on my face grows. I never told him that's my comfort snack, but he obviously figured it out.

You're the best. Thank you. ♥

CAMDEN TELLER

How many days?

12

Can I call dibs on next Christmas with you?

CAMDEN TELLER

That's a year from now, you sure you want to do that? If you say yes, I'll hold you to it.

Absolutely.

CAMDEN TELLER

Then I'm all yours.

"Cam says you should be riding your bikes, not letting them collect dust," I say, standing next to my dad in the custom motor shop. We're picking up the newest one he's adding to his collection to take home. It was a Christmas gift from my mother.

"Tell Cam I like my dust collection just fine."

"Beautiful bikes should be ridden, not hidden away."

"Did Cam tell you that too?"

I grin. "Maybe . . ."

"Lovely."

Congrats on your game against Jacksonville!

CAMDEN TELLER

Thanks. Wish you were here to celebrate with me.

How would we celebrate?

CAMDEN TELLER

I can think of a few ways...

Only one week left, can't wait to see you.

CAMDEN TELLER

No shit, I'm putting a moratorium on any future three-week vacations I'm not a part of. It's too long.

CAMDEN TELLER

Three good things?

1. I went for a walk today solo. It was relaxing and I got a lot of thinking done.

2. I am signed up to volunteer with Safehouse when I return. I'm looking forward to doing something with myself.

CAMDEN TELLER

I'm so proud of you.

3. Only 4 days until I go home.

You?

CAMDEN TELLER

1. Only 4 days until I see you.

2. Made two goals against Colorado.

3. Only 4 days until I see you.

That doesn't count...

CAMDEN TELLER

Yeah it does.

ETA 10:10pm

CAMDEN TELLER

I'll be waiting.

FORTY-FOUR

Camden

The last few weeks without her have been hell. I check the incoming flights and watch as the arrival board showing NCE to MSP flips from

EXPECTED 10:10 PM to LANDED.

She's home.

I check which baggage carousel her luggage will come from and make my way over to the nearest security checkpoint. The sooner I see her, the better. Her absence has eaten me up; I want her in my arms again. I pace with my fingers threaded over the hat she knit me. Fucking love that she gave me a handmade gift, it helped me feel closer to her while she was away.

Ten minutes go by with no sign of Jordan. *Where is she?* People trickle through, then I see her blonde hair piled on top of her head in a messy bun and she's wearing one of my sweatshirts. My heart hammers behind my ribcage.

We lock eyes, and she quickens her pace with a growing smile. When we get our hands on each other, I'm astounded by the instantaneous comfort. I wrap her in my arms and dip my face to her neck, breathing her in. I can't get enough. We rock back and forth. *This is my girl.*

"Fuck, I missed you." My voice is muffled against her shoulder.

"I don't want to be away from you that long again," she whispers.

"Let me take you home."

She squeezes me tighter and sighs. "I already am."

FORTY-FIVE

Camden

I'm still surprised she asked for this. I figured it was a *someday* bucket list thing. But here she is, with a huge smile on her face, gripping my hand and tugging me into Logan's tattoo shop to get her nipples pierced. I don't want to show my bias in case she changes her mind at the last minute, but I'm equally enthusiastic.

We get inside, and I grab Logan's newest portfolio of artwork and sketches. I flip through the drawings and marvel at his talent. The stuff he creates blows my mind. Jordan taps her foot next to me.

"Nervous?"

"A little. Will it hurt?"

"Nothing you can't handle."

She nods. "A little pain now is worth a lot of pleasure later, right?"

I chuckle. "You got this."

Her hands ball into fists on her thighs. "I got this."

My phone dings a few times, it's the team group chat. I can't figure out what the hell they're talking about. Something about a woman named Kendra, a dating show, and Sully?

"Hey, who's this Kendra chick the guys are talking about?"

"Oh my god! Kendra, as in Micky's friend? Does this mean he's doing it?"

I'm trying to make sense of these texts, but I'm not following. "I don't quite get it, what's going on?" The texts are coming in too fast for me to catch up.

"Kendra's creating a new reality dating show—the youngest woman to ever produce a show like this. I met her at brunch, she seems cool. Apparently, her original *bachelor* dropped out last minute because—*get this*—he got engaged right after confirming the cast."

"Oh, shit."

She nods. "So, Micky threw out Sully's name as a possibility. If she doesn't have a guy, the whole thing will fall apart. Does this mean he's doing it?"

I scroll through some of the texts. "Sounds like he's agreed to meet about it. Huh, the quietest, most boring motherfucker on the team is getting his own goddamn television show." I shake my head. "Good luck with that."

She gives me a nudge.

"That's the kind of guy she needs though. She wanted someone who was normal and in it for love. Someone who wasn't a cocky prick looking to get his fifteen minutes."

"You mean like me?"

"Exactly!" She smiles big and plants a kiss on my cheek.

"So, how's it work? Is it like *The Bachelor*?"

"No, I think it's kinda techy. Micky tried to explain it to me. It's like a dating experiment to see if we can use AI to create a formula for love . . . or something."

"Oh, God. I cannot wait to watch this trainwreck."

She rolls her eyes. "It might be good for him."

None of this is adding up. I furrow my brow. "Hey, is Kendra attractive?"

Her eyes grow big. "She's gorgeous. A doppelgänger for Taryn Delanie Smith."

I laugh and shake my head. I doubt it will make it past production.

"What's so funny?"

I level her with my gaze. "Sunshine, I've played with Sullivan for years. He was captain until his retirement. I know the way he operates. If he's doing this show, it's because your producer friend sweet-talked him into it somehow. He hates technology and hates reality television."

She rears her head back. "Wait—you think he's doing it for Kendra?"

I shrug and suck my teeth before flipping another page in the tattoo book. I have a sneaking suspicion that's exactly what he's doing.

"Well, I hope he finds love and it's a smashing success," she says matter-of-factly.

Of course she does, she wants the best for everyone. I wrap an arm around her and continue to peruse the book while we wait for Kelly to finish up the appointment before ours. The next page is filled with some celestial sketches, including a sun that reminds me of Jordan.

The buzzing in the studio closest to the waiting area stops. I hear no talking, which means it's probably Logan finishing with someone. My stepbrother is not a conversationalist by any stretch.

"I'm going to get a tattoo," I say. "Want to get one with me?"

She laughs. "Seriously?"

"Yeah. Let's do it."

No matter how our journey ends, I want a piece of her with me always.

"Okay, I'm in," she says, chuckling. "What are we getting?"

I stab my finger on the sun in the book. "This."

"Why?"

I kiss the top of her head. "Because you're my sunshine."

Jordan pulls back and blinks. "Wait, really?" She bites her lip.

Her gaze falls to the book of tattoos. She presses her finger to the moon. "Then I want this one." She tilts her head to the side, tucking a lock of hair behind her ear. "Yeah . . . it's fitting." Her beaming smile warms me when she looks up. "You have this pull. Like the moon does with tides. You've helped me through my highs and lows."

I like that. *A lot.*

Logan steps out from behind the studio wall and peels off black latex gloves, followed by his client.

"If you want something that matches, I can turn them into an eclipse," he grumbles, speaking and signing at the same time. He has a lot of deaf clients, like the one he's signing with. The man pays and nods to us as he leaves.

"My last session had to reschedule, so if you want to do it, I can fit it in." He sounds annoyed, but it's simply his resting bitch voice. He's like a permanently pissed off storm cloud, as if any joy he has is used up on his creative genius.

"I love the eclipse idea," Jordan says, looking at me.

I agree. "Eclipse it is."

"I'll sketch it up during your session with Kelly," he says, disappearing behind the wall again.

"Did we make him mad?" she asks with a hushed voice.

"No, that's just the way he sounds. Where do you want yours?"

Her back goes straight, and she looks down, holding out her limbs and turning them as if she's taking inventory of her body parts to make sure nothing's missing. I've already got mine figured out.

"You can think about it while you're getting pierced, but keep in mind you'll need to have the body part you choose face up and you won't be able to lay on your stomach with fresh piercings."

"I suppose you've been around the block a few times."

"Once or twice." I gesture, holding out both arms.

"Where are you getting yours?"

I pat my hand over my heart. *I haven't told her yet, but Jordan's my first love.* She inhales deep through her nose, and I thread our fingers together.

"You choose my location," she whispers. "I trust you."

My eyes snap to hers. *She's letting me choose where to permanently ink her body.* "Okay."

Kelly walks out with a client she's finished with. She goes over the care instructions with the customer, and I knock my knee into Jordan's leg. "You ready?"

"Yes. You're coming with me, right?"

"Of course." She visibly relaxes. "I'd never miss a chance to see your tits."

She narrows her eyes at me, and I stare back until Kelly interrupts. "Hey, where's my dog?"

Jordan chuckles. "We left her at home, she's afraid of needles. But if I'm ever out of town again, I'll let you know."

Hopefully, that won't be for a long while.

"Just say when, I'd love to. Chicken Salad was an excellent house guest at Christmas." Kelly ushers us to her corner of the shop. "So, how are you feeling? Excited?"

Jordan nods. "How bad is the pain?"

Kelly scrunches up her nose and shakes her head. "I've had mine done, it's not bad. How's your pain tolerance?"

Jordan shrugs. "I'm not sure."

"It's high," I blurt, leaning forward and resting my elbows on my knees. I have intimate knowledge that this woman can handle pain.

Jordan removes her top and the front-zip sports bra she wore in preparation. She chooses a delicate barbell piercing, and I resist biting my knuckles.

"These look like yours," she says, waggling her eyebrows at me, then looks over to Kelly. "Great work by the way."

Kelly chuckles. "Thank you! Are you enjoying them?"

"Very much so."

"Sharing isn't always caring," Logan shouts over the wall.

Jordan laughs and holds her hand out to me, and I sidle up next to her. Kelly goes over the piercing process, and next thing I know, she's got her nipple clamped in a forceps.

"Deep breath."

Jordan breathes in and squeezes my hand. I squeeze back, and she looks over at me with a smirk. Her eyes remain locked on mine, she doesn't so much as flinch when Kelly shoves the fourteen-gauge needle through her nipple.

"Great job. One down," Kelly announces, screwing on the end of the barbell. "How was the pain?"

"Not bad."

I kiss her knuckles. "Thatta girl."

JORDAN

I've had a smile on my face all day. I'm happy. Not just happy under the circumstances, truly happy without reservation. I had my nipples pierced—*cross that off the bucket list*—and now I'm about to get my first tattoo. Camden's next to me, laid back in the chair getting his chest inked. When Logan asked him where he wanted it, he didn't say chest, he said, "Over my heart."

Telling myself our relationship was nonexistent, did nothing. Saying it was *just sex* is laughable. No question, he's got me under his spell, but I've got him under mine too.

I'd been suppressing my feelings for so long, not realizing they'd been spreading like wild vines around my heart, quietly winding until I was ready to admit how I felt. As they grew and matured, so did we, and now there's no looking back.

"How does it feel?" I ask.

"Good." He smiles up at me, and my heart thumps. "How does it look?"

"I'm just finishing up the foreskin," Logan mutters.

"Oh! So you do have a sense of humor, you simply *choose* to be a cantankerous killjoy. I see," Cam says. I smile, amused by their bickering. He's never said it out loud, but it's clear Camden admires his stepbrother. Which is impressive, considering Cam mostly admires himself. And me.

Logan finishes and sits up straight, taking one last sweep across it with some kind of wipe. He begins disassembling the ink gun, tossing out the old needle, and swapping new latex gloves. Camden sits up and checks the mirror. "Thanks, man." He walks over to the counter and opens the drawers, grabbing a few supplies, like he's done it a hundred times. He rubs a salve over it and covers the fresh ink with a large clear bandage.

"Where are you getting yours?" Logan asks.

Cam hasn't told me yet, but I know wherever he decides will be perfect.

Together we learned how to fervently trust each other, and our hearts—which is the greatest lesson—and why I'm handing over sovereignty of this. He's changed my life; saved me, not just from Bryan, but from myself. Shown me how to stand my ground and live unapologetically. Without him, I wouldn't have found the happiness I have today.

"Top front of her right thigh." His eyes find mine, and he nods once to check with me. I nod with a smile.

"How big are you thinking?"

"Same as his," I respond.

"Easy enough." Logan wipes down the tattoo chair to sanitize it. "Climb on and push your pants down."

"You usually say that in the opposite order," I mutter to Cam. He winks at me. Logan smirks and shakes his head, prepping the tattoo gun. I hop on the table and wiggle my jeans down. He wipes down the area, places the stencil, and has me inspect it after it transfers.

"I love it."

The buzzing begins and when the needle hits my skin, it feels different than I thought it would. Sort of like a scratch. Cam stands above me and brushes hair off my forehead. He pulls up a roller chair and settles in next to me.

"You good?"

My smile grows. "So good. Today is a great day." I'm in seventh heaven.

"It *is* a great day."

I don't know how much time passes. An hour? Not much is said between us. It mostly consists of Cam checking in on my comfort level. My thigh is mostly numb from the vibration. He glances down at Logan's progress. "It looks good."

"Yeah?"

He nods and kisses my cheek.

Kelly pops her head in. "I'm heading out, Logan."

He stops tattooing and sits up.

"Alright. Hey, how's your fake skin practice going?"

"Fine. I left a couple pieces in your office to look at if you get a sec. One of them sucks."

"Nothing you make sucks, you're being too hard on yourself. Look at it after a night's sleep and decide if you feel the same way. You might realize you actually love it, if not, we'll find a way to fix it. Or you can save it for coverup practice later on. But I'm sure it's beautiful."

Cam and I are practically gaping at him. It's the most I've ever heard him speak at once.

"Meh. We can go over them tomorrow," she replies.

"Night, Kel."

Logan doesn't look back down until she disappears. *He's definitely got a thing for her.*

Cam looks between the door and Logan. "Jesus Christ, Blabbermouth Betty. Did you want us to leave so you could fuck her on the counter?"

He raises an annoyed eyebrow, wipes the tattoo, and leans forward again, switching the gun on. "Shut up," he says, going in again with his eyes transfixed on my thigh.

I get the side-eye from Camden and press my tongue into my cheek. *Be nice,* I mouth.

"We appreciate you staying late for us," I add.

Logan nods and continues working. When it's about finished, he pauses, studies it, then adds a little more until he's satisfied. "All done."

He sits up and stretches. The guy looks beat.

"Thank you, Logan. You do incredible work." I sit up and marvel at the ink on my pinkened thigh. I love it so much.

"Thanks, man. I can cover it for her, and we'll get out of your hair." Cam pulls out his wallet and hands over several bills. Logan strips off his latex gloves and takes the money to count it.

"Need change?"

"No."

He nods and takes the cash up front toward the register.

Cam sanitizes his hands, then adds a thin layer of ointment before ripping off the back of the bandage and setting it on top.

"You're the coolest person I've ever met, you know that?" he says.

Smiling sweetly, I bat my eyes at him. "Everybody knows that."

He kisses me softly and nips at my lower lip before helping me sit up. I spin ninety degrees in the chair before standing. Cam drops to his knees and raises my jeans back into place, I suck in my stomach so he can button them, and he kisses my leg on the center of my new tattoo.

"You're my girl. Let's go home and get you fucked into bed."

At home, Cam gets me a painkiller. My sex drive has shot to the moon since I've been getting it regularly. Now that I've experienced true pleasure, I can't get enough. Who knew sex could be as amazing as it is in books? *Not me.*

"Go lie down in my room. I'll be there in a minute."

I try not to skip the whole way there. Stretching out on his bed, I close my eyes. I'm in awe of how every day seems better than the last since we've given ourselves a chance at a healthy relationship.

There are times I think I should forget about Bryan, let the court sort out the money stuff and enjoy this new adventure with Camden. Then I remember how bad it hurt when he slammed my head into the drywall. They say the best revenge is being happy, and, well, ruining his life will put a smile on my face. However, this isn't just about vengeance. Every abusive fuck's reign has an expiration date, and his is long overdue. He's been given too much power, I'm simply rectifying the inequity.

After a bit, Camden returns with an armful of stuff. *Snacks.*

"These are for later." His gaze trails from my head to my toes and back again. He grimaces. "Why are you still dressed?" His disappointment is cute. He crawls over me, boxing me in with his arms. "One of these days, I'm going to get your heart-shaped ass bent over for me, but for the sake of your healing process, I'm going to be a gentleman and fuck you missionary."

I laugh. "Excuse me?" Heat pools in my stomach.

"You want to know what it's like to take my piercings up your ass? Let's find out how much pain you can handle, Sunshine."

Holy hell.

"Yes, please."

"I can't wait to see your body swallow each barbell. Tonight, you're going to cry for every rung on my ladder."

I bite my lip. *Fuck.* The way his lips curve into a wicked smile slays me. I've been waiting for this. His palm grips my waist when he lowers his lips to mine.

My hands hook into his gray sweatpants, then I push them down, running my fingers over his erection, and counting the piercings. All seven, each nearly an inch apart. *All* that *is going in my ass*?

Penises are not something I've ever described as *pretty*, but that's exactly what Camden's is. "You have a gorgeous cock." It's thick, velvety, and firm. Not to mention all the shiny hardware he's added. "Has it ever considered modeling?"

He chuckles as he peels off my clothes, heeding my new tattoo and piercings. Once I'm naked, he pushes my knees up and spreads my legs. Dipping down to lick up my center. A sigh leaves my lips. I love the comfort he brings me during sex almost as much as the pleasure.

My eyes catch the bottle of lube on his nightstand, and he drips it over both of us. I ignore the thought of how many other women have had the same lube used on them; because I was the last girl he used it on—*and I'll be the next too.*

He rubs his fingers over my clit and slides two inside while his dick rests its tip on the tight knot. He pumps faster. I squirm as he sits on his heels, smirking, entertained by my struggle. I gasp for air as he brings me to the edge of orgasm. He's gotten so familiar with my body he can push me to the brink almost instantaneously. I fist the sheets beneath me, and my ass clenches.

"Oh, Sunshine, you need to relax for me."

How? I'm too close to coming, my muscles are as tight as a drum. "I can't."

He picks up speed and frowns at me. "Aww, what's the matter?"

I can hardly see straight. "You're going to ma—make me come."

"Not until I say so," he says. "Do you *hear* that?"

Noticing the wet slapping sound between my legs, I blush. I'm drenched. "You have to slow down." I shake my head with a tense jaw. "Cam, it's too . . ."

Camden pouts while nodding, taunting me as I try to gain control. "Poor thing."

I hate when he does that condescending voice, it only

turns me on more. As if his hands weren't doing enough to stimulate me, he has to light up the pleasure center of my brain like goddamn Rockefeller square at Christmastime.

His demeanor turns commanding. "Fight it, Jordan," he warns.

"I don't want to." I groan.

He shakes his head. "Your first time coming tonight is going to be with my cock in your ass. Now *relax* or I'm going to start playing with your clit too."

With a deep slow inhale, I close my eyes and loosen my shoulders, trying to ignore everything happening below the waist. A few more deep breaths and I'm able to rein in the orgasm.

"Very good. Don't forget your colors," he mutters. The pressure on my ass goes up. My jaw drops open, and my shaky breath exits as he forges ahead. "That's it . . . *Eyes*."

I blink open, his gaze overflows with pride, but it's more than that, it's *respect*. The sensation overwhelms me. Our connection seems to throb between us. My heart explodes, and emotion leaks down my face.

"Talk to me, Jordan. You okay, baby?"

I nod emphatically. "Green."

His smile grows as the first piercing pushes inside. "Ask me nicely for another."

"May I have another rung?" I whimper.

He pushes deeper before pausing again, waiting on me.

"More?" This feels nothing like the toy did.

Another inch.

My lashes flutter at the fullness. "Please?"

His jaw tics. "Fuck," he groans through gritted teeth. Watching a man who exerts as much control as Camden Teller reveal his weakness, is thrilling. *Especially when that weakness is me.*

I have to ask for each barbell before he gives it to me. Every piercing adds a layer of salaciousness. I'm gorged with him.

"It's a lot," I hiss.

"Did you think that was all of it?" His dark chuckle makes my eyes widen. He adds more lube. "What's wrong, princess? Can't take it?" His torment is so sexy.

"I'm not a princess. I'm a queen, remember?"

"Queens take all of it."

I smile. "Then give me all of it."

A lopsided grin forms, and he pushes my bent knees to my shoulders, so far it burns, then shoves the rest of himself inside. I gasp while he growls. *He gave me the crown, that's for sure.*

"There you go," he soothes, caressing me with his thumbs. Reaching under the pillow, he pulls out a small vibrator about the size of a battery. "Now let's get you to come, hm? Give me what's mine."

He positions the pulsing toy on my clit and covers it with his palm, pushing down, holding it—*and me*—in place as he drives in and out. My back arches, creating a new sensation of being filled with him. He adds more lube, his ragged heavy breaths match mine. I'm almost there.

"Oh my god!" I writhe, my shoulders lift off the bed as abdominal muscles I didn't even know I had fold me in half. He brings a hand to the base of my neck, forcing me back down. "You may be the queen but look how easily you're ruled under my hand."

That does it.

Bright-white light explodes behind my eyes as I come. The ecstasy of reaching climax after his edging is bliss. "Cam! Fuck!"

He removes the toy as I clamp down and swallow him

even deeper. He pants and blows out a slow breath, like he's trying to concentrate, as he snaps his hips, shoving himself and all seven bars over the sensitive nerves. "Christ." His voice sounds angry. "I'm not gonna last like this."

My lips curl into a mischievous grin. "Aw, what's the matter, babe? You going to come?" I return his heckling, and he shakes his head at me. He grabs the toy and places it back on my overstimulated clit and pushes down.

I scramble to push it off, but it's no use, he's too strong.

"Wait! It's too much, Cam! Too much!"

"How do your words taste?"

As painful as the vibrations are over my twitching, jerking body, I want to smile; his punishments are delicious, and it makes me crave them more.

"It's agonizing!" *Sweet, sweet, agony.*

"You want to act like a snarky little brat, then I'm going to fuck you like one." Cam grips my chin, parts my lips, and spits inside. Flames lick across my flesh when he lovingly slaps my cheek. "Come on my fingers and say you're sorry," he demands.

The climax takes me by surprise. I bow to him despite my attempts to rebel. *Good god.*

"I'm sorry, I'm sorry!"

"Those are mine too," he says, gesturing to the tears streaming down my face. He tosses the toy aside. "Goddamn, Jordan," he growls.

Bracing himself over me, he drops to his elbows. "You are the most beautiful woman in the world. And that's not even the best thing about you." His lips brush mine, our kiss is tender and sweet. One hand cups the side of my breast, and he sweeps his thumb across the underside, mindful of my new piercings.

When our kiss ends and gazes meet, I'm so overcome

with euphoria I can hardly think. I'm on an existential plane of happiness. All I see is Camden. My heart is on fire, and the inferno consumes me. I study his face, in awe of how much better my life is with him in it. Funny how living with this man has taught me how to live for myself.

Am I in love?

"Look at all you've done today . . . new piercings . . . a tattoo . . ."

Letting go of my inhibitions and trusting people who deserve my trust. My chest floods with affection.

I skate my fingers across the clear plastic bandage over his heart. "This is mine," I whisper. *All mine.*

He clutches that hand and brings my fingertips to his mouth, pressing them to his lips, then threads our fingers together and slows his thrusts. His eyes bore into me, and he nods.

"Come with me."

I bite my lip and suck in a breath. His hand snakes between us, and he rubs circles while each pair of beads on his length continue plucking my rim like guitar strings. My sore body pushes through the aches, and I squeeze his hand as he increases the pressure on my clit.

Our lips meet, and he swipes his tongue across mine.

"Now."

I let go, the orgasm exploding from me. Behind the pulse in my ears, I hear him moan, and it fills me with satisfaction. Every sound is so rough, deep, and masculine. We crumble into each other, my chest heaving as I attempt to catch my breath.

"I've got you. You did so well, Jordan.." He showers me in tender kisses. I'm hit with an intense surge of euphoria; a mix of joy, pain, lust, compassion, and vulnerability . . .

I burst into tears. Oh god, what is happening? I'm having a crygasm. I'm crymaxing.

"I know, baby. I know." He holds me tighter, and presses a kiss to my forehead.

"I-I don't know what's wrong with me." My pulse races, panicking that I'm unable to stop the tears.

"Nothing's wrong with you. You're perfect," he whispers.

After carefully sliding out, he lies on his back and pulls me close. One nipple is pressed to his side; it's sensitive but doesn't hurt. He cups behind my right knee and drags it higher. My cheek rests on his chest, and I listen to his heart-beat, the sound settling me.

His fingers brush over my tattoo bandage, and I rest my palm on his. We will always have this.

The overwhelming sensations mix and bloom in my chest like ink in water. It fills all my colorless voids with bright plumes of pigment. I didn't know it could feel like this.

I'm in love with him.

FORTY-SIX

Jordan

Micky and I sit near the glass while Raleigh and Birdie watch the game from the WAGs box with the kids. I could be with them because, as it turns out, my name is on the list. Right there, next to the wives, read: *Jordana Landry*. We both have our alter egos, Jordana and Banksy. He gets my Jordan, and I get his Camden.

Seeing him play tonight is different. He insisted I wear his old jersey today; said he needed extra luck tonight. Must be working because he's playing well. Cam knocks on the glass twice and smiles at me. We're about to go into the second intermission, and he's drenched in sweat and looks cocky as ever when he winks at me. He'll never be anyone but Banksy on the ice. And I'm okay with that. It works for him.

Before he exits the ice, I point to a little girl in the front and mouth, *Puck* to him. She's been cheering for the Lakes all night. Okay, it's not so much *cheering* as it is shouting like a drunk frat boy at a beer pong tournament. She can't be older than eleven, but she's got more passion than half the boys nearby. He nods, aligning himself opposite her, places a puck on his stick, then flips it over the glass.

Her face lights up, and she spins around, proudly showing the whole section her souvenir, which is met with cheers. The female fans "Aww" over his gesture as he walks back through the tunnel with the rest of the team. *God, he's so handsome.* Micky leans into me, and I lean back. She sighs. "What's it like fucking a guy with piercings?"

I chuckle. "Have you ever driven over rumble strips on the side of the highway? It's like that, but in your vagina."

"Can you have your people talk to my people?"

"You got it," I say, grinning. "Hey, do you wanna get anything to drink?"

I stand, but she yanks my arm down. "No way am I standing in those lines."

"We could go up to the box and get a drink?" I offer.

"I wanna watch the intermission show. God, I love it when grown men get a chance to shoot a puck and miss. It warms my heart."

I laugh and sit back down. Not a minute later, I'm being tapped on the shoulder. I glance over, surprised to find one of the arena's security staff.

"You've been randomly selected for the Lucky Pucky shoot off."

"Oh my God!" Micky yells, shaking my shoulder. "Lucky Pucky! You have to do it!"

"What?" I shake my head. "Can I give it to someone else?" I don't wanna play *Lucky Pucky*.

He shakes his head.

Fucking Camden. I observed the Lakes practice the other day, and he missed a goal by a long shot, which is a rarity, so I gave him a hard time about it the rest of the day. I'm sure he set this up to get back at me for trying to have a little fun. I roll my eyes and grudgingly stand from my seat. Randomly selected. *Right.*

I follow the staff member up the stairs and over to the section with ice access. A peewee team is coming off the rink when I step on. Jesus, I can't imagine playing with this many people watching, especially when they're screaming at you the whole time. I have even more respect for Camden and how well he works under pressure.

A thin, narrow carpet is laid from here to center ice, where it's met with a large rug displaying the Lakes logo. Lucky Pucky is the intermission game where the goals are covered up with boards with three small openings at the bottom. Fans get a chance to shoot a puck and get it into one of the holes to win a shirt or something. I'm halfway to the Lakes rug when Cam skates up alongside the carpeted walkway.

"I've got it, Tim. Thanks." He nods to the guy who was making sure I didn't fall, and the guy turns around and heads back.

"Hey!" I say, surprised to see him. "Is this because of the other day?"

He laughs. "Yeah." *I knew it.*

Cam escorts me the rest of the way to the rug, a hockey stick laid on the ice next to it. He takes my hands and turns me with my back to the goal.

"Jordan."

I laugh nervously. "I can't believe you're making me do this."

He drops down on both knees, and we're put under a spotlight. The screaming fans are deafening.

No, that can't be what he's doing. There's something else going on.

"Oh my god . . . Cam. What are—"

He tugs off his gloves and looks up, grinning. "Don't worry, I'm not proposing—but I have a few things I want to say to you. I—"

I look around to see if this is a joke. All I see are camera flashes in the stands. Literally everywhere.

I interrupt. "Why are you doing this?"

When he's silent, I stop questioning and listen.

He begins again, speaking up so I can hear him over the crowd. "I like being around you when I'm home and I miss you when I'm away. I've learned love is more than the butterflies in my stomach when I look at you. It's more than seeing you in my jersey. More than needing you close to me all the time. Love is a quiet trust. It's familiarity and knowing someone, *really knowing* who they are deep down. You know me better than I know myself, and I think I know you pretty well too. You admit your faults without fear and accept mine without question. I'm in awe of you every day. I want a life with you in it, not just because of how you make me feel, but because of who you are. Jordan, you are my everything."

My hand covers my mouth as he opens his heart in front of a nearly sold-out arena. Though, I'm thankful he isn't mic'd up. He's showing his devotion publicly, but his words are mine alone.

"Someone once said that you know you've found that person when you're willing to put the other person first no matter what. Jordan, you will always come first." He pauses and winks.

My voice is shaky. "Camden, why are you on your knees?" *If this isn't a proposal, then what the fuck is he doing? Because it sounds like a fucking proposal.*

He wraps his palms behind my calves and squeezes. "Because I kneel for *you*." A smile spreads across his face, and I swear I melt into a puddle. "You wanted people to see this side of me, so that's what I'm doing. I'm leaving my ego at the door. You are my queen, and I will kneel for you every day. You aren't a quiet girlfriend on the side, you're center ice."

Oh my God.

My eyes are swimming with tears. This can't be real. He pulls out a ring box, and I swipe at the tears on my face. "You said this wasn't a proposal. What the fuck is going on?"

He opens the ring box, revealing a Ring Pop. I start laughing, and he chuckles along with me. "Come on, Sunshine . . . When are you finally going to admit I'm *exactly* your type? That day at the coffee shop was the beginning of our journey, and little did I know it would lead to where we are now. But I'm so happy it did."

I sniffle and nod. "You're *so* my type." He slides the candy ring onto my pinkie, it's the only finger it fits on, and rests his hands on the sides of my thighs. The memory of Cam removing my old ring in the coffee shop flashes in my mind. I told him I'd rather Bryan had proposed with a Ring Pop than the massive diamond. It makes my heart clench thinking about us exchanging real rings someday.

Tell him.

"I love you," I say.

The thumb caressing my thigh stops, and he grips my leg, not letting go. The seconds tick by like hours as he stares up at me. I desperately want him to say something. He releases my thigh and blows out a breath.

"I love you too." He stands and leans down to kiss me. It's not a shy kiss. *It's passionate*. It's hot and heated and fills the arena with cheers. "I love you so much."

I smile like an idiot when he withdraws, my brain scrambled by his lips.

Someone from the bench calls his name. "I gotta go, I'll

see you after the game." He bends down to grab his gloves and tucks them under his arm.

"Okay, but you gotta help me get off the ice."

He shakes his head and leans down to whisper in my ear, "You still have to play Lucky Pucky. Maybe next time you'll think twice before you decide to give me shit about my skills at practice." He kisses my cheek, winks, and skates off.

I glare at him with a smile. *Motherfucker.*

An attendant sidles up, gives his congratulations, and hands me a puck. I suppose anyone watching from afar assumes we're now engaged.

I drop the puck on the ice, shoot, and don't get remotely close to the net.

When I look back, Cam's standing at the edge of the tunnel with the thumb and index finger half-an-inch apart. *So close,* he mouths. *Uh-huh.*

I laugh. I couldn't care less about the shot, I just want to return to my seat. Micky's probably losing her mind. A woman escorts me off the ice, and she also congratulates me, then I'm passed back to the same security staff member. Another congratulations.

"Thank you, I can find my way from here."

"Actually, you're supposed to go up to the box. Mrs. Kucera is up there with your things."

Mrs. Kucera—Micky. I laugh at the formality, especially with how *informal* Micky is.

We get up to the box, and I thank him for the escort. When the doors open, I'm met with balloons, streamers, and a couple of handmade banners that read: *BANKSY'S MEMORIAL SERVICE* and *REST IN PEACE*. The other women cheer and a champagne bottle pops.

I freeze. "Holy!"

Micky rushes me and wraps me up in a hug. "Congratulations!"

"It wasn't a proposal!" I laugh.

"We know, but you took down the biggest player on the team, and that's worth celebrating."

The game ends with us winning 4-2. Barrett made an amazing goal in the third period.

I follow the wives through the maze of hallways that lead to the locker room exit. My stomach isn't filled with butterflies, it's more like thirty raccoons fighting over a footlong hot dog. We said the L-word tonight.

When the guys begin to filter out the door and he sees me, his smile is brighter than ever. *Damn he looks good in a suit.*

"Hey, Sunshine." He drops his bag, picks me up with his palms under my ass, and pushes me against the wall.

I open my mouth to speak, and he kisses me with everything he's got. *Sigh.* I can vaguely hear Micky and the girls leaving.

"Congratulations, Jordan!" is followed by laughter. Barrett cuts in. "Close your eyes, Mini Bear. Uncle Banks is trying to play Lucky Pucky with his new girlfriend."

Players filter out of the locker room, but this moment is ours. When his lips leave mine, we lock eyes for a moment. *I love him so much.*

"Great game," I whisper.

He laughs with big eyes. "Oh, we're going to talk about the game first?"

"Why? Was there something else that happened?" I say, cocking my head to the side and feigning ignorance.

"Yeah, you missed a goal by a mile. How embarrassing for you."

I slap his shoulder. "I can't believe you set me up for that!" I laugh. "Rude."

"I'll show you rude," he says, smirking.

"I'm still sore from the last time you demonstrated your rudeness."

He chuckles and nips at my bottom lip. "I love you."

"I love you too."

He reaches down and hoists his bag over his shoulder, keeping one hand on mine. "Let's go home."

I bite my lip and smile.

FORTY-SEVEN

Camden

When I wake, I roll over and smile seeing Jordan's hair fanned on the pillow next to me. Her shallow breaths are slow and relaxed. She's beyond stunning.

Even though it wasn't a real proposal, my hand still shook when I slid the candy ring on her finger. A rush like no other. I wonder if she knows deep down there's a part of me asking for her whole future. The thought must have crossed her mind.

Wrapping an arm around her, I pull her close to me and tuck my face into her shoulder to breathe her in. I drop kisses down the column of her neck, and she stirs, sighing softly. She lifts a hand and wraps it behind my neck. I feel the smile on her face.

"I need to wake up." Her voice is tired and scratchy.

I smile. "Let me do it."

Peeling back the sheets, I get between her legs and drag her panties down. As soon as I spread her legs, she tries to grab the blankets. "Can I have my covers back?"

My palms cover her thighs and place them over my shoulders. She'll be overheated before she knows it.

"It's freez—"

I lick up her center, flattening my tongue, and repeat it until she turns boneless and sinks into the mattress. I love the way she tastes. Dipping my tongue inside, I take more because I'm self-indulgent when it comes to Jordan. But how can I feel bad about it when her pussy was made for me?

She's resting comfortably with her eyes closed and an arm draped over her forehead. I nip at her thigh, her eyes pop open, and I chuckle. My middle finger delves into her tight opening, and I stroke as I lick. Her sweet moan makes me smile, and I wrap my lips around her clit and tug on it while sucking.

Her back arches, and she gasps when I add another finger.

"*Wow.*"

"Mm-hm," I say against her dewy flesh, my voice muffled.

She threads her hand into my hair and claws while letting out the sexiest sounds, she's a siren. Her stomach waxes and wanes as she pants.

"More. I need more."

I sit up, look down on her, and stuff a third finger inside. She winces as I stretch her. My other thumb ghosts over her swollen clit.

Frowning, I cock my head to the side. "More what?"

"More of you."

"I think if you beg a little more sweetly, I might be convinced," I suggest.

"I'm not good at begging."

"All the more reason to practice."

"Please . . ."

I smile. "Please what?"

"Please fuck me?"

"Hmm . . . No."

She sits up on her elbows and drops her mouth open. "You can't do that."

I chuckle. "I can do whatever I want."

Pushing up to a sitting position, she swallows as I force my fingers deeper. She pulls her top over her head, and when I see her piercings, my dick twitches.

Blowing out a breath, I groan. "Goddamn, Sunshine . . . Those look so good on you."

She pushes her breasts together, and I avert my eyes. I'm in control, she won't exploit my weaknesses. I'll show her she's great at begging.

"Oh god," she mewls as I bring her to the edge.

Her jaw is clenched, and she's grinding against my hand. *There she is.*

"You ready to play nice?"

She falls back on the bed, and her tits bounce. I remove my fingers and drop to my elbows again. The tip of my tongue brushes her clit. She squirms, and her thighs come up. I have to use both hands to hold them open.

She's shaking. "Cam, I'm begging for it. Please."

"So beg harder."

A tear slips down her cheek, and I smile. I've learned that sex is an emotional experience for Jordan, I love that about her.

"Aw, are you going to cry about it?" Another lick, and I curl my fingers inside her.

"Please . . . please, fuck me."

I enjoy hearing her whine like that, it shows her desperation. I suck her clit into my mouth and immediately pop off it. "Again."

"I want it . . ." Her whimper is so pathetic, I smile. I grind into the bed, chasing my own friction.

"Please, Cam . . . Make me your slut. I'll be a good girl. I need to come on your cock, *sir*."

Shit.

I spit on her clit and sit up, keeping her still by pressing my hand to her stomach, pushing inside her and feeling it through her abdomen. It's such a turn-on to feel her getting fucked under my palm.

She cries out and opens her legs for me.

"You can't get enough, can you?"

Her head shakes back and forth, and she holds her knees apart.

I thumb her clit again. "I love making you my slut. You *are* being such a good girl for me, spreading your legs like that. Now ride me so I can see exactly how you get yourself off with my cock."

She smiles and I roll us, putting her on top. Her pierced nipples are killing me. I won't tug on them yet because they're still tender, but in a week, I won't be able to keep my hands off those little barbells. She rises to her knees, and I glance at the healing tattoo on her thigh that matches the one over my heart. She drops down and moans.

My sweet girl has come so far into her own. "I'm so proud of you, Jordan." Her eyes soften, and she leans down to kiss me before sitting up again with a smirk, then grinding over me. My phone rings on the bedside table, and she freezes.

"Ignore it," I tell her.

Her eyes are locked on the screen. "It's Bryan."

At first, I'm angry, but my features soften, and I smirk. "Hand it to me." Jordan leans over, plucks my phone off the nightstand, and passes it. She begins to dismount, but I hold her in place. "No, you're going to bounce on this dick and keep fucking yourself on me until you get off."

She nods, and I answer the call. "Who's this?"

"You know who the fuck it is." I grin ear to ear. "You aren't going to marry her," he barks.

My fingertips travel up and down her back. I look her right in the eye as I respond. "I have every intention of making Jordan my wife." It's the truth. I'm all in with her.

She stills, and I hold the phone away slightly. "Don't stop."

Her hips gyrate again, and I smile, biting my lip. *How did I ever get so lucky*?

"That's why I'm calling. I have an offer to make you," he says, calmer now.

My eyebrows shoot up. "What kind of offer?"

"Name a price."

He wants to buy *her back from me?* I laugh incredulously. I'm disgusted by him for even suggesting such a thing. "She doesn't have one."

"Yes, she does. You just haven't thought of a high enough number yet."

"There's no number," I grit out. It makes me angrier that he's arguing. "You had your chance and you fucked up. You have no clue how to treat women, certainly not one of her caliber. She's done with you."

"I gave her everything!"

"You gave her bruises and a fucked-up sense of self-worth! And you should thank Jordan that I haven't killed you yet, because I promise, she's the only thing standing in my way."

I take a deep breath, he will not rattle me. I smile and pull the phone from my ear and hit speakerphone.

"Do you seriously think I'm going to step aside and let you eat my lunch?" he says.

"I already have . . . I can still taste her on my tongue. *God, she's sweet.*" I groan and slide a finger under her clit. Her eyebrows soften as she whimpers. "You can't put a price on happiness."

"You can, actually."

Jordan's eyes twinkle with rage when she realizes the nature of his call. "Then, tell me, Bryan . . . why are you still so *fucking* miserable?" she interrupts. "The best thing you ever did was fuck my best friend, the best thing I ever did was fuck yours. The only difference is I love Camden. You only love yourself, and that's why you'll end up alone. When are you going to realize that everyone in your life is simply putting up with you?"

She's hot when she's angry.

Her hips snap, and she's right on the edge. I smirk. She's getting off on taking back her power from him. I set the phone on my chest and clutch her throat with one hand.

"That's it, Sunshine. Tell him how good I make you feel." I rub her clit faster, and her eyelashes flutter as she rocks into me, her voice hitches.

"You lost, man. It's over," I say. "Eyes, Jordan . . ." She blinks open and her body clenches. *Christ.* My smile stretches ear to ear. "That's my girl."

With hands planted on my chest, she rolls her hips as she comes. Her breathy cry is so fucking sexy. If I didn't know any better, I'd think she was putting on a show, but the sounds she makes when she orgasms are this sensual every time.

"That's what it sounds like when she comes. Thought you'd want to hear it since you never got to experience it yourself."

"Both of you can go to hell."

"Wait, before you go, I want to give my sincere thanks for giving me the opportunity to show her how priceless she is." I smile. "But we need some privacy while we get settled, we have a lot of planning to do—*you know how it is*."

"You're going to regret the day you ever left me."

"No, Bryan," she says, her voice eerily calm. "You're going to regret the day you ever underestimated me." She gazes at her new manicure and sighs. "I'm not to be trifled with."

"You're a—" I cut him off before he insults my queen.

"Say goodbye, Jordan," I tell her.

"Good riddance," she mutters, smiling and leaning down to kiss me. I end the call and toss my phone to the side.

Sitting up and cradling her back, I bring her lips to mine. "What a good wife you'll be." Her sigh tells me she's ready to go again. She pushes me to the mattress and grinds, then braces a hand on my neck. She's earned my submission this morning.

I grab her other hand and place it overtop, wrapping her grip around me. "Now squeeze. You have all the power, baby." A smile creeps onto her face.

Her muscles tense and she groans. Clutching her hips, I fuck up into her. I won't last like this. Her cunt has an iron grip. *Shit.*

"Just like that. Milk my cock and show me how much you love my cum."

Her lips are parted on a silent scream, her body shakes, and seeing her pleasure, makes me so happy. The way her pussy convulses over my length is unbelievable.

"Fuck, Sunshine." My ass clenches, and my balls draw up. I explode into her, cum spilling out of her as I thrust through my climax. I don't know if I've ever had that much volume before, but seeing her hold her ground and take control, made me feral. She's my every desire rolled into one and has me wrapped around her finger. She will forever have my heart.

"I'm so in love with you, Camden."

I flip us, drop to my elbows, and kiss her with everything I have. She's worthy of so much love. I plan to give her double.

FORTY-EIGHT

Camden

Jordan and I sit side by side while we finish dinner. "When your parents get back, I think we should take them out for a proper introduction. Do they have a favorite restaurant?"

"They'll probably want to go to Demi."

"I'll make a reservation."

She waves her hand while she brings her plate to the sink. "Don't worry, they have a table."

They have a permanent table? I snort. "Well, excuse me, Miss Monopoly."

She stalks toward me with a smirk and gives me a shove. I stand and catch her around the waist to carry her over my shoulder. While I stride into the living room, I fish my phone from my pocket and video call my parents. Mom's been blowing up my shit since I dropped to my knees for Jordan at center ice. I dump us on the sofa while it rings and pull her into my lap. She tries to scramble away, but I hold her flush to my chest.

"You can sit on me. Don't worry, the *poors* aren't nearly as formal."

She laughs. "Oh, fuck y—"

"Hi, Mom!" I shout as her face fills the screen. Jordan clamps her lips together.

"Camden!" my mom squeals. "Congratulations! Show us the ring!"

Mom knows it wasn't a real proposal, but she's still excited that I've fallen in love with Jordan. She's been swept up in our romance ever since I let her know about my plans with the Ring Pop.

Jordan presents her empty finger. "We're getting it resized at Wonka."

I nod, but the truth is, there *is* a ring. Jordan will see it when the time is right.

Mom's face grows serious. "I assume Bryan knows at this point?"

"Just spoke to him this morning, actually," I say with confidence. Jordan clutches my knee off camera.

"And?"

"His thoughts hold no value over the matter. We're together, and he's not allowed near Jordan. We're letting the lawyers figure it out."

"That ugly, huh?"

Jordan cranes her neck to face me and whispers, "You didn't tell her?"

I shrug. "It's not my story to tell." Though if anyone would understand, it's my mom. She was in a situation like hers for far too long.

Jordan gives an appreciative smile and relaxes into me, and I dip my chin and bite her shoulder. She blushes and smacks my leg.

"Camden! Don't bite her!" my mom scolds.

"What? She likes it!"

Chicken Salad trots over, wagging her tail like we're about to start playing. Jordan covers her reddening face. "Oh my God. I'm so sorry." She apologizes for my public display of affection.

"I'm not sorry." I tighten my forearm around her and haul her back.

My mom smirks. "It's okay, his stepdad's a biter too."

"*Eugh!*" My lip curls in disgust. "Jesus fuck, Mom! Don't say shit like that!"

Jordan cackles.

"Well, good! I hope you're as uncomfortable as your poor girlfriend. Sorry, Jordan, I tried."

"Thank you, Linda!"

"Okay, I think we're done here."

She rolls her eyes. "Your sisters are right, you love to dish it out, but you can't take it."

"Yeah, do me a favor and tell Alexis I pissed in her shampoo in seventh grade after she filled my conditioner with Nair." I had the best hockey hair on the peewee team until that point.

Jordan's jaw drops.

"Cam!" Mom gasps. "That better not be true."

I neither confirm nor deny. *I totally did though.*

"By the way, we're having dinner when Jordan's parents return to the States. I'll send you an invite when I have a date."

"That sounds nice, I look forward to it."

"Yup! Love you! Bye!"

My mom laughs and shakes her head. I blow her a kiss and toss my phone across me onto the sofa and kick my feet up. "There, now that *that's* over with, we can get back to what we were doing earlier."

“What were we doing earlier?”

“I don’t remember.” I pull her on top of me and smile against her lips. “But probably sex.”

FORTY-NINE

Jordan

My hands are shaking. I received an email from Bryan this morning with an attached document. It's the financial funding approval he received to move forward with his offer to purchase the Minnesota Lakes franchise for one-point-one billion.

I've grown up around corporate contracts all my life and worked with them at H&H. It's legit. Bryan's dad is the billionaire, not Bryan. And I doubt Mr. Davenport would buy a team. That's not his style. I'm not sure how the hell he managed this, but I have an idea.

I fumble with my phone, loading up a call recording app before I dial his number.

"Miss me?" His voice makes my skin crawl. I noticed the other day his voice was slightly different. He probably had dental work done after Cam knocked his tooth out. Hearing the new whistle-lisp he's gained is the only silver lining of this phone call.

"No."

"Well, considering you're calling me, I'm guessing this

has something to do with me becoming the next owner of the Lakes hockey team. Have you told Camden yet? I'd love to tell him myself."

"How the hell did you even swing this? One-point-one billion?"

"Good investments."

"I'm sure." I roll my eyes. "Do you have any idea how volatile NHL franchises are? For your sake, this is a bad purchase."

"Don't talk to me like I'm an idiot. We both know I don't give a fuck, it's not about the return. If it succeeds, great, if it doesn't, oh well, it bankrupts. Like you said, *so volatile*."

"How do I make this go away?" I ask, gritting my teeth.

"I don't want money."

I move closer to the bathroom. I might actually throw up.

"What do you want?" He wants *me*. *I* make this go away.

"You."

Why did I ever get involved with Bryan? *How could I not see how unhinged and cruel he is?*

"You cheated on me, Bryan—you didn't even want me when you had me! Why can't you let us go?"

"Just because I fuck Veronica doesn't mean I don't want you. You and I make a strong alliance. We were meant for marriage. It looks good."

Makes him look good. He means my financial status, being tied to the *Landry* name.

"What happens if I don't?"

"I submit the paperwork and get the ball rolling. The finances are in place, all I have to do is sign the dotted line and your fiancé's career is over. Either way, I win."

"This is about Camden. It has nothing to do with me." He makes me sick. "You're unwell, you know that?"

"I've got to go, Jordan. I've got a board meeting. Busy, busy," he quips. *Asshole.* "Looking forward to hearing your decision."

"Wait!"

"Yes, dear?"

"If I do this, you're never going to lay your hands on me again. If you ever slam me into a wall or put your hand on my throat again—" I choke out a sob. "God, Bryan, why are you ruining my life?"

"Aww."

My nose sniffles. "How do I know you won't marry me and buy the team?"

"You have my word."

"You're joking, right?" I scoff. "If I do this, I want an airtight contract that you will never purchase *any* NHL team. Drafted and in my email by the end of the week."

"Are we done here?"

"No, one more thing." Now I've got the tears going. Sniffles, snot, hoarse vocals, and all. *I should get an Academy Award for this.* "I get to tell Camden."

"Deal. You always were a reasonable girl." He hangs up, and I wipe my face, clearing my eyes. Step one, complete.

There's a vetting process for owners, so how the fuck did Bryan get a green light? I grab my laptop and start doing some research. The NHL uses one firm to check out prospective owners. Robux & Holt out of NYC—the same firm H&H uses. *Fancy that.*

Doesn't matter. He'll also need approval from the NHL Board of Governors. My father looked into purchasing teams about five years ago. Once he saw the numbers and returns, he decided it was too "hands on" for him. There's so much more than the game that goes into ownership. It's all about expanding the business, and a lot of that depends on the value of the team rather than the revenue. It's a reselling game, and there are too many variables that fluctuate year to year. It's unstable.

Fuck, I'm angry! I'm running out of time. I've been carefully watching his location since he showed up at Cam's that night. I slam my laptop shut and pace the floor. Then call the one person I said I'd never speak with again. *Veronica.*

She answers almost immediately, apologizing profusely over and over.

"Jordana? I'm so sorry! Oh my God, I never should have risked our friendship." I roll my eyes.

"Stop talking."

Her whining voice trails off. "Are you still mad at me?"

"Veronica, I'm going to marry Bryan. We're getting back together. And this time, you're not going to interfere."

"I th-thought you were marrying his best man? Th-that hockey guy?"

"Bryan has made it clear he still loves me, and we've decided to make it work."

"Oh."

I sigh. "So here's what you're going to do. While I'm ending things with Camden tonight, you're going to invite Bryan over to your house for dinner and tell him you're done sleeping together. This is *my* marriage and this affair you two have is over. Got it?"

"Mm-hm," she mumbles between sobs. Her remorse sounds genuine.

"Because if you don't, I will make your life beyond miserable. Do not misunderstand me. You are *done* being a homewrecker."

"Okay, okay. Jordana, I'm really sorry. Truly . . . Do you think we could ever go back to the way things were?

Would you like to go out for coffee sometime? We could talk about your wedding plans. I still value our friendship.

"Maybe someday. But I'm not ready yet."

"Sure . . . I understand." Her voice is soft.

"Thank you."

I hang up and wring my hands. This needs to work. Bryan better be ready to have his whole world flipped upside down.

Don't fuck with the queen.

FIFTY

Camden

I swing by Uncommon Grounds to pick up a couple coffees—and an apple scone for my girl. It's only been a week since we dropped the L-word. The guys gave me shit at practice today, but damn, I love being in love! And it's Jordan. How I landed a showstopper like her is beyond me. She's the entire package. She deserves the world, so I'll work every day to deserve her.

When I arrive at home, I step inside with my hockey bag over my shoulder, a coffee in each hand, and a bakery bag wedged somewhere in there.

"Jordan, where ya at?" Silence. "Brought you an apple scone!"

Still nothing. The car she's using is here. *Where is she?*

I hear footsteps, and she walks down the stairs, talking to someone on the phone. "Maybe someday. But I'm not ready yet . . .Thank you."

Cocking my head to the side, I furrow my brow. She ends the call and stuffs it in her pocket. She runs her fingers through her hair, it's already up in a ponytail, which makes it more messy.

"You okay? Who was that?" I ask, tossing my bag in the laundry room.

"I'm not okay," she mutters.

Grinning, I enter the kitchen and hold up the bakery bag. "Would a scone help?" She doesn't smile back, and it's then I notice how disheveled she is. Not in her usual cute way either, in a stressed-the-fuck-out way.

I drop the bag. "Hey, what's going on?"

"I need to show you something." She hurries to the dining room table and returns with her laptop, spinning the screen to face me.

Biting her thumbnail, her gaze is fixed on the floor as she paces. *What the hell?*

I squint to read the document she has pulled up. It's paperwork showing the funding being secured to move ahead with ownership of the Lakes. From B. Davenport Jr. *There's no way.*

"Is this real?"

She scoffs. "If it isn't, it's a really good forgery."

"And he's got a meeting set up with the board? How the fuck did he get approved?! The NHL spends around twenty grand just to evaluate prospective owners."

Her smile doesn't reach her eyes. "Yeah, you know who also uses that law firm?"

My face falls. This can't be real. "You're kidding."

"H&H."

This is because of my thing on the ice with Jordan. I'm sure knocking a few of his teeth out didn't help either.

"I called him—"

"What?" I never want her to have to listen to him again.

She slides her phone from her back pocket and holds her hands up. "I recorded the call. Just listen."

She hits play, and listening to him even speak to her makes my blood boil. He's a fucking snake. *"Have you told Camden yet? I'd love to tell him myself."*

My hands ball into fists as I listen. The second he says he wants Jordan, I scrub both hands down my face. Fuck, I want at him. She pauses it in the middle.

"I want to hear the rest."

She yanks it away. "No."

I rip the phone from her fingers and hit play.

"Cam, you don't need to hear it, I promise, I'm not leaving you!"

I hear her voice over the recording. Blood drains from my face, and my world stops.

He hit her? Choked her?

My body is vibrating. I see red. Rage seeps into every pore. The rest of the call plays through. I can't believe the balls on this motherfucker.

I stand, grabbing my keys. *I'll kill him.* "Stay here." This whole funding thing is moot because he'll be dead before the ink dries.

"No!" She jumps up, pressing both palms to my chest. "Stop! He'll be expecting you to resort to anger. He's prob-ably on his porch waiting. I won't let him take you away from me. Please, I need you to trust that I'm handling this. Things are already in motion."

Who was she on the phone with when I walked in?

"No way in hell are you dealing with him on your own." I go back to the PDFs he sent and scroll through them again. I can't believe what I'm seeing.

"It's been in the works for a while, I didn't want to involve you because I don't want you to get wrapped up in it. I'm going to stop him at the source.

"So am I."

She levels me with a stare. “It’s not worth the risk. Bryan’s a stain on society, and he’s mine to wash out.”

“What are you going to do?”

“I’m going to ruin his life,” she says. “But, sweetheart, I need you stay out of my way.”

I pull her close. “Jordan, how come you never told me he hit you?” It breaks my heart she went through that. And I hope someday she’s willing to tell me about it. “I would have been more careful with you and the things we did.”

“Exactly. I didn’t want special treatment. I knew I was going to take care of him eventually, so it didn’t seem necessary.”

I can’t believe I didn’t know the whole thing. “How often was it happening?”

She wraps her arms around herself. “He would grab my wrists here and there, but it didn’t seem that bad. When I met with him to end it, he became violent. That was the worst. It was the night of the fundraiser, the one I saw you at before I left.”

I swallow. *Fuck, I remember that night. I was right there. She needed help, and I let her leave with him.*

“I was ashamed. Embarrassed that I let it get that far. When I was getting ready that night, I overheard a conversation with Bryan and his father. He said spouses can’t be forced to testify against each other. I knew he was up to some shady shit, but I didn’t know what. I realized that night I needed to take my life back. And I wanted to hit him where it hurt.”

Jordan’s a fearless little bulldog most days, but I recognize the bloodlust that flickers in her gaze . . . even I wouldn’t fuck with her.

“On one condition, I don’t want you putting yourself in danger.”

She nods. "Agreed."

"And you tell me your plan." I want to clear it beforehand.

She hesitates. She can pout all she wants, but she's not doing anything without first letting me know what her strategy is.

"Remember when I was talking to your dad at Thanksgiving about Bluetower?"

"Yeah . . ."

Jordan takes a deep breath. "My job at H&H was to review contracts on the new companies they were purchasing and send it up the ladder for the head execs to gain investors. Bluetower was one of those companies, it was just some small startup acquisition." She bites her lip. "It doesn't exist. It's a dummy shell corporation."

"How do you know?"

"I had a guy look into it, he got me the documents—signed by Bryan Davenport Jr., by the way—to back it up."

"So are they being audited?"

"An audit would take too long, and it would give him time to cover it up. It needs to be a scandal. I want him publicly humiliated . . . I knew the circumstances around me being assigned the Bluetower account were suspicious, it was an IT company, whereas I dealt with the healthcare sector. Something didn't sit well with me. It was confirmed when I spoke with your dad at Thanksgiving."

That's why Jordan told my father not to invest. She said the returns were too high . . . It's coming together now. "He's running a Ponzi scheme."

She covers her mouth and nods. "Mm-hm."

"Holy shit."

"I know. And I'd be willing to bet that he's using it as collateral to bankroll his purchase of the Lakes."

"Why do you say that?"

"According to the falsified R&D documentation that Bryan signed off on, Bluetower works with wireless technology, the speed test results would be a technology leap equivalent to Apple releasing the iPhone. It would create a huge disruption in the industry—meaning massive payouts. As long as he's borrowing from one investment to pay the other. Investors don't care, so long as they're getting the returns they were promised. He probably offered it to your dad as some kind of poetic justice to get revenge on you as well. Use your father's money to help destroy your career."

My nose wrinkles. "But that's so risky. Why wouldn't he just use H&H Holdings to finance the Lakes buyout?"

"Because H&H is Daddy Davenport's. He'd never let Bryan get his hands on that. It's also probably why Bryan did it, he wanted to impress his father with some big new company he brought in. They have office buildings and everything. I looked up the employees on LinkedIn—their photos are AI generated. None of those people exist."

"But why wouldn't he just submit the offer on the Lakes? Why tell you to break up with me first?"

"Because this way he can take both of us down. You heard what he said, he doesn't give a fuck about the team. It's personal. He'd rather punish us. He likes to make people hurt. He made a grave miscalculation this time. He assumes I won't sink that low, but I've been at the bottom waiting for him."

She's a legion of one, taking no prisoners. "So, what are the next steps?"

"An audit would take months, but there needs to be a whistle blown from the outside, it has to be an ambush. We have to leak that the funds are coming from a fraudulent shell corporation to the financial agency. Fucking up his collateral will delay securing the loan, and he won’t be able to move forward.

“If I hand over the documents myself, they’ll ask me where I got them, and I refuse to implicate my source. I need them to come directly from Bryan himself. That part is already in the works.”

She’s going to plant the evidence. This woman’s blowing my mind. I scrub a hand down my face. Here she let me believe I was corrupting her, but she’s been her own villain all along.

“After, we take it to the NHL Board of Governors, packaged in a neat little bow with this recording.” She wiggles her phone. “He could show up with cash in hand, and they’d spit in his face.” *Clever girl.* “Then we’ll give the media a head start before the Davenports or H&H can begin damage control.”

“We should call—”

“Alexis,” she says, following my train of thought with a smile. She and my sister chatted about work a lot over Thanksgiving. Jordan knows she’s a journalist in Boston. Alexis is cutthroat. She’ll eat him alive.

“And she can use it as a jump start to expose the law firm that’s taking bribes on the side. I’m sure the NHL won’t be too happy to hear about it.” After a moment, her eyes soften, and she looks up at me. “I’m sorry, Cam. I never meant for you to get wrapped up in this.”

After hearing he laid his hands on her, it doesn’t seem like enough justice, but I’ll do whatever I have to to protect Jordan as she takes him down.
“Whatever you need, say the word.”

“I need you to trust me.”

Jordan is savage. On the outside, she’s sweet and feminine, but she’s got a fierce streak that’s almost frightening.

She's a bad bitch with zero fear. *And she's mine.* Just when I think I can't love her more . . .

As much as I want to beat Bryan into the great beyond, I recognize her need to enact vengeance and love her enough to restrain myself to give her the satisfaction.

She's thought this through, and Jordan's right—this needs to be strategic. Bryan only has the balls to do and say the shit he does because of his money, business, and reputation. I grew up with the guy, I know the way his brain works. He's nothing without cash and clout. He hides behind his prestige to give him the appearance of power.

And she's about to rip it all away.

FIFTY-ONE

Jordan

My car is warming up outside. I check the clock one last time as I pace—1:00 a.m.

It's time.

I flip up my black hood and tuck the burner phone in my pocket. The house is silent. Tiptoeing into the garage, I'm careful to face the mud room door as I make my escape. Walking backward toward my car—while praying Cam doesn't wake up—my fingers feel for the driver door handle, I pull it and spin around, ready to make a mad dash.

"You're up late." I jump out of my skin with a shriek when I see him already in the driver's seat.

"What the fuck?! You're supposed to be sleeping!"

"I could say the same to you." He waits for me to explain myself.

"I need you to get out of the car. I have an errand to run."

He chuckles. "Get in, Jordan. I'm not going to stop you from whatever this *errand* is, but you're not going alone."

My weight shifts. I don't have time to argue with him. It's now or never. I hurry around the car and climb into the passenger seat.

"Where are we going?"

I glare at him in the darkness. "Veronica's."

"Oh, is it a slumber party?"

"It is for *Bryan*."

"We're not about to commit murder, are we? Because if that's the case, I need to change my outfit."

"Cam, please don't joke. I need you to trust what I'm doing and not try to stop me. I didn't tell you about it because I didn't want to put you at risk. You cannot get in my way tonight."

He nods, and we drive in silence. When we arrive on the street, I tell him to turn off the lights, and we pass Veronica's house, parking behind Bryan's car—*my old car.*

"Turn off the engine." So far, he's been doing what I ask without question, and I appreciate it.

Bryan liked to keep tabs on my location. How convenient that I can still track the Lexus he once gifted me. He's been at Veronica's all evening, based on the car's tracker not moving, he's staying the night. I've been waiting for this. I know exactly where her security cameras are and am careful to stay out of sight. Her house will easily allow me to get in and out undetected. She has no neighbors across the street, which is helpful.

I didn't have confirmation they were still seeing each other, but when Veronica agreed she would end it, she told me everything I needed to know. I knew if I told her to invite him over to end it, he'd likely fuck her "one last time." Now that I'm free of his gaslighting, his narcissistic habits are easy to anticipate. He's so predictable.

I wait, needing to make sure the conditions are right to make my move. It's not quite time yet. Cam looks at me. "Now what?"

"I'm waiting for a phone call."

At 1:37 a.m., my burner phone vibrates with a call from an unmarked number. It's Seven.

"I'm here," I answer."

"His notifications will be disabled for the next twenty minutes. Is that enough time?"

"Perfect. Send me a bill."

"Pleasure doing business with you. I look forward to watching the news tomorrow."

I smile. "Me too."

I end the call and grab my personal cell to turn it on. Bryan enjoyed control over people and *things*. Which is why almost every device he owns is connected to our phones. I have no idea if he has proximity alerts set up for me on his phone, but he likely has them if his car is being tampered with, so I need to cover my tracks. Seven helped with that. I reach behind me for the duffel bag and unzip it.

Cam sucks in a breath. "Jesus fuck. How much money is that?"

The day I withdrew 20,000 cash, I requested a variety of bills. It took me hours to roll them into little bundles, giving the appearance of contraband. I've never touched the money with my bare hands, and I never will.

"It's a small price to pay to get even."

I crack the window of my car and listen. A police siren sounds in the distance, and I wait for it to fade before getting out of the car. Once it's quiet, I open my door and stalk to the trunk of his car, open the Lexus app on my phone, and pop the trunk. My breath is visible in the trunk's interior light. It's cold as fuck out here.

Next, I disconnect the taillight—*thank you, YouTube*—I attempt to push the light out, but it won't budge. I practiced on my car three times with no problems, but my hands are cold and stiff and shaking. Behind me, the passenger door quietly opens.

"What do you need?" Cam asks.

"To knock the taillight loose. Don't break it, just pop it out partially so I can thread some of the wires through." He gets his hands in there and does it in two seconds.

I delicately place the bag of money in the trunk. *Looks impeccably suspicious.* Last, I tuck the stack of papers regarding the financial statements for Bluetower, all with his signature, in the bag.

"'Kay. Let's go." I click the trunk closed and return to our car. We put our seatbelts on and pull away from the curb. *Please let this work.*

Cam gives an exaggerated exhale. "My dick is so fucking hard."

I chuckle and look over at him. Glad he's excited about it. I'll feel better once everything goes according to plan. Though, I am quite pleased with myself.

When we get home and climb into bed, we lie there staring at the ceiling.

"We never left."

"Nope."

In the morning, I'll track Bryan's location again. As soon as he's on the road, I'll report erratic driving from a Lexus with a busted taillight.

FIFTY-TWO

Camden

The adrenaline from last night kept us up, so we played Battleship. Not a euphemism. I made her strip every time I sank one of her ships, but in the end, she was fully-clothed and I was fully-naked. As competitive as I am, it was fun watching her kick my ass and get cocky about it.

Then we cuddled. And kissed. And cuddled again. I've never experienced anything so sensual without actually having sex. My heart was pounding, and she had me hard as fuck, but we connected with each other in a way that was equally powerful. We stayed in each other's arms until sunrise.

A few minutes ago, her phone beeped with a GPS notification that his car was in motion, and she's been wearing a hole in my rug since.

"Thank you," she says, to the 911 dispatcher, ending the call. She runs her fingers through her hair. "They're sending an officer."

Now that the erratic driving has been called in, it's out of our hands. "Come here."

She walks over to me, and I pull her back into bed. She groans and picks at her fingernails.

"Did Four send the information to the financial agency?"

She smiles and rolls her eyes. "His name is *Seven*, and yes."

"Dude sounds like a fucking psycho."

"Well, that *psycho* is the one who's getting our info to the right people." Jordan flips her hair. "He said I was a natural and even asked if I was interested in getting into his line of work."

I laugh. "Shit, I'd say the same after watching you go all *Mission Impossible* last night."

She giggles. "Did you call Alexis?"

"Yeah, she's already on her way to NYC to start digging."

She nods and takes a deep breath. "Now we wait."

"Now we wait . . . It's going to work."

She opens up her phone, and we watch the Lexus's GPS dot creep down the highway. A few minutes pass. Then it stops.

She jolts up. "It's stopped. Cam he's stopped. On the highway."

I appear calm on the outside, but my anxious thoughts are racing. I'm just as keyed-up as she is.

We wait . . . and wait . . . and wait . . .

The car never moves.

FIFTY-THREE

Jordan

The morning is quiet, but Cam finally convinces me to take a nap after making some of his famous macaroni and cheese for lunch. He crawled into bed behind me, and I was out within minutes.

My phone wakes me from a deep slumber. Cam stirs next to me. The lofty bed in the center of the room swallows us up in the warm covers. I'm not ready to wake up.

"Is that your phone or mine?" he asks groggily.

I lift my head and pick up my illuminated phone, bringing it under the covers with me. My mom's photo lights up the screen, and I slump back into the mattress.

I groan and silence the ringer. "It's my mom." I'll call her later, right now, I need more sleep. Sliding the phone under my pillow, I snuggle up and return to my nap. It rings again.

Cam grumbles.

I pull it from my pillow and answer it without looking at the screen.

"Hi, Mom."

"Turn on the news. Now."

My eyes fly open. *Is this it?* I clamber in the sheets, trying to throw the heavy duvet off me. My hand slaps the night-stand, and when my fingers land on the corner of the remote, I snatch it up and feel for the power button. It flickers on to a headshot of Bryan. *I remember when he took that photo*. He looks approachable in the picture, but he was an asshole to the photographer.

"Oh my God." My heart pounds.

Camden rolls over and rubs his eyes. "What's going on?"

"Are you seeing it?" my mom asks. "Jordan, you dodged a bullet. Thank God you got away from him!" Her words echo in my head as I focus on the headline.

"Call you back, Mom." I drop the phone and turn up the volume on the television. The reporter says H&H Holdings is under fire for their subsidy Bluetower.

"Holy shit," I mumble, with my fingers pressed to my lips. My eyes are glued to the television.

"We expected this, remember?"

Of course, but that doesn't make it any less monumental. I stare as the breaking news scrolls across the screen.

"Sucks to suck," he tuts.

"Do you think he knows it was me?"

He laughs. "I'm sure he does, but you were great at covering your tracks. Worst-case scenario, you get Eight to jump in there and delete any evidence."

"Seven," I correct. "I also made a semi-anonymous donation of sixteen million to the police department. I think they'll side with me on this one." I breathe a sigh of relief and lean against the headboard as I survey the fruits of my labor. *I won, you fucking monster.*

"You bribed law enforcement?"

"*Donation*."

He throws his head back and laughs. "Goddamn, I love you."

I lean into him, and my lips curl into a lopsided grin.

"How do you feel about it?" he asks.

"Vindicated."

We channel surf every major news network as we watch Bryan Davenport's life implode minute by minute. The news anchor reports that more than one fake subsidiary has been confirmed. *I fucking knew it.* This will shake out to be a Ponzi by dinner time. He built his own house of cards, all I did was breathe on it.

"Sources tell us that the board of directors have asked Bryan Davenport to step down from his role at H&H Holdings, no word as to what his response has been. A full investigation is being launched into the business conglomerate empire. A spokesperson for the company says there was no collusion with the founder, Bryan Davenport Sr., and that he's already set up a foundation to repay any investors that were swindled by his son."

I shake my head. Bryan Davenport Sr. is a snake, but in this case, I appreciate that Bryan Jr. is being publicly humiliated and renounced by his own father—the man he worshipped. I wouldn't be surprised if some of those fake subsidies were his dad's and now he's throwing his son under the bus to cover his ass.

They flip to bodycam footage of the arrest. Everything in the trunk is blurred, but Bryan is a broken record saying, "It's not mine!" which only makes him look more guilty. Another police officer is shown at the traffic stop, and I smile when I see the same one who pulled me over after Bryan said I stole my own car. No doubt he remembers that car and my *gift* to the department.

Through the large picture windows, a few intermittent snowflakes fall from the dense, low-hanging clouds stretched across the sky. It's blustery and cold. Even the trees appear to shiver as the wind passes through the bare branches.

"He must be so scared. I wonder if he's thinking about me?" I stare out the window with a grin. "He won't sleep tonight. Every person he fucked over is coming after him now. And he's alone, his own father won't help him. He'll look over his shoulder with every step . . . Poetic, isn't it?"

"Come here, Sunshine," he says, tugging me into his side. I sigh and sketch circles with my fingertip on Cam's chest. We snuggle in our warm bed while Bryan probably sits on a metal chair in a cold room, wondering how he let his life spiral out of control. Camden kisses my forehead and whispers, "Anyone ever told you how dark you can be sometimes?"

I smile bigger. "Who's the one who got off on corrupting me?"

"You were unhinged long before I got to you, I just taught you to embrace it." He climbs on top of me and peels my top off. "Clever Jordana, plotting away and ruining the lives of those who've wronged her . . . *so fucking sexy*."

He's always empowering me. One of the many differences between Cam and Bryan. One celebrates my brilliance, the other tried to extinguish it, steal it before I knew my own strength. We undress each other to the soundtrack of his reputation being ground to dust on national news.

He turns me to face the television and kneels behind me, my back to his front. With one hand, he holds my jaw straight to watch the TV while his other hand dives between my legs. I gasp and clutch his arms as he rolls my clit between his fingers.

He tucks his chin, skims his lips up the column of my neck, and whispers, "You did that."

I smirk. "I did . . . I made a difference in someone's life, Camden."

He chuckles and slips a finger inside me. "That's right, Sunshine."

He pumps faster and faster until I'm shaking and panting, still he holds my face steady.

"Does it make you wet to watch him suffer?"

I moan. *Cam makes me wet*, but this doesn't hurt either.

"Mm."

"Spread these pretty thighs wider."

His crown notches against my entrance, and he pushes me forward slightly as he thrusts inside. "Fuck." I bite my lip, and he pulls me to my knees as he palms my throat.

"Goddamn, you are gorgeous like this," he says, removing his hand from my clit and pointing to the mirror in the corner, where only a sliver of us can be seen on the edge.

"I wish he could see you now, bent over in the position he always made you get into . . . while you get off to his downfall."

I chuckle. "Wish he could see you behind me when I do."

Dropping onto all fours, I look back at him and smirk. He shakes his head at me.

"Ruthless." He draws out and plunges deep, my nails sink into the blankets as he takes me on all fours with long strokes. It's heaven. I love his touch, the way he grips and manipulates my body. Reality is fuzzy, everything feels so good. Slick arousal coats my thighs, and my stomach clenches, as the orgasm builds.

"You're dripping," he says, his hand wrapping around my hair. He wrenches my head back, forcing me to look straight ahead. "Look at him, Jordan. I want you to look at his pathetic fucking face as you come around my cock."

I love this man so much. I grind into him, and waves of

wild heat roll through me as my body is racked with tremors. His hand raises before he strikes my ass with a firm, sharp sting.

"Who owns you?" he grunts.

"You," I cry.

He pulls me up, my ass tight against his pelvis. "No, baby. No one owns you. You're too fucking vicious to have a keeper. But I'll worship and love you for as long as I live to make you stay."

My mouth nearly drops open. Turning my face to the side, I smile. "Which is why I give myself to you freely."

He loses all control. Pounding me from behind without mercy, his piercings thrumming as he punishes me with all of him, shaking me to my core.

"Say it again," he growls. "Tell me you're mine."

"I'm yours," I whimper. "And you're mine."

He grips my sides, and I fall to my hands again, dropping my shoulders and letting him fuck me into submission. A coil winds inside me, tighter and tighter.

His hand comes down on my ass again. "That's right, Sunshine. I'm yours."

His rough hand slides up my spine and wraps around the back of my neck. He holds me in place while doling out punishing pleasure and total possession. My mouth drops open as my climax overtakes me. Every part of me feels charged with electricity. *This is true love.*

He groans and snaps his hips. Hot ropes spurt inside me until I'm filled to the brim. Our chests heave, sweat dripping down our bodies. He curls himself over me while softly kissing up my spine—it's ecstasy. This man and I were meant to be He rolls us to the side. Our chests pound in sync, like two halves of the same thunderstorm.

"I will always love you," he whispers.

Ever so softly, he tilts my chin to the side and captures my lips. It's an emotional culmination of everything we've been through, everything that brought us to this moment. With his arms around me and his mouth on mine, I never want to come up for air.

Pushing my hair to the side, he kisses the back of my neck. "Me and you, Jordan."

"Me and you."

There are moments in life you desperately want to hold on to, wish you could freeze time and space, bottle it up and take it with you. Open and breathe it in whenever you need to remember what it felt like to be alive. You wonder why it can't be like this forever. It could disappear in seconds or hours, so you don't dare move for fear of losing grip on euphoria. That's what it's like with Camden every time his arms are around me. I want to feel this content, this safe, this *alive* forever.

FIFTY-FOUR

Camden

Valentine's Day is next week, and I want to do something special for Jordan. Unfortunately, everything I come up with feels so . . . *cliche.* She's not into gifting "things." It's not like I can whisk her off to a romantic getaway. With playoffs in a couple months, I'm about to be more involved than ever to ensure we make it. Which means I'll have less time with her, so whatever I do has to be good. Lucky for me, I know someone who's an expert at this stuff.

In the locker room, the guys are busy talking about their plans for Superbowl Sunday.

"How come my damn tape is always missing?" I grouse.

"Here." Barrett tosses me one of his rolls.

I sit next to him and begin wrapping my stick. *Now's as good a time as any.*

"Hey . . . how's the family?"

"Great. Raleigh's morning sickness is finally easing up. Arthur's loving kindergarten."

"Good, good . . . Say, wondering if you can help me with something."

He stops lacing his skates and cocks an eyebrow at me. "Depends on what it is . . ."

"I, uh, I need help coming up with a gift for Jordan . . . for Valentine's Day."

In my peripheral, he leans back and crosses his arms. I don't have to look over to know he's got a smug smile on his face.

"Look, you're always doing romantic shit for Raleigh. I want to do something for Jordan. Don't be a dick about this."

Silence. I look over, sure enough, smug as hell.

The corner of my mouth tips up. "Okay, asshole. Forget it."

"Oh, come on, you gotta let me enjoy this . . ."

I give him three full seconds to revel in the moment. "There. You done?"

He goes back to his skates. "Raleigh said Jordan's never had a normal Christmas before."

"Okay." I'm aware, but not sure where he's going with this.

"The girls were talking about it after Jordan got back from Monaco. Ral cried for a good half hour that night because Jordan never got to pick and cut down a Christmas tree." He chuckles.

Why? "The fuck was she crying for?"

"She's pregnant, man." He shrugs. "She's all up in her feelings. An ASPCA commercial came on the other day—shit, I thought I was going to have to take her to the hospital. You wouldn't believe how many fucking dogs we're sponsoring now."

My lip curls and I shake my head. "Jesus . . . okay, but focus, I need help with a gift."

"Give her a normal Christmas. Let her pick out a tree, make cookies, et cetera."

"It's February."

"That's why it's romantic, dumbass."

I suppose that could work. I scrape a puck over the fresh tape on my stick, thinking of all the things my family does for Christmas.

"Trust me," he adds.

"Alright . . . but if it doesn't go over well, I'm sending your wife a PETA brochure. Sure would be a shame to miss out on all that good Kalua pork next time you're in Hawaii."

He snatches the puck out of my hands and jabs a finger at me. "Don't even joke about that shit."

I chuckle and flip my stick to tape the handle. "Wait, where the hell am I supposed to cut down a Christmas tree? Are tree farms even open?"

A slow smile spreads across his face. "Who said you had to go to a tree farm?" He winks.

We stare at each other for a while until I know what he's getting at.

Grinning, I ponder aloud. "Didn't Sully say something about his new lake lot having nice trees?"

FIFTY-FIVE

Camden

Barrett was right. The Christmas idea was perfect. I've never seen her so excited. This morning, she woke up to find her name on a stocking, filled with her favorite candy. Chicken Salad got one full of treats. I ordered Christmas lights and a variety of ornaments so she could decorate the tree we're on our way to chop down.

We pull up to the private property midmorning, the fresh snow is sparkling. There's a construction crew on-site, so we park behind one of the trucks. *Shit, I wasn't prepared for anyone to be here*. Jordan looks around.

"What are we doing?" she asks.

"Wait herc a sec."

I hop out of my truck and find the foreman. One awkward conversation, a few hundreds, and eight autographs later, I return to Jordan, who's now standing outside of the truck, her eyebrows knitted together. She holds up her arms in a what-the-fuck gesture.

My hand feels around the truck bed until it lands on a handsaw. "You always wanted to cut down your own tree. So that's what we're doing." I point the saw toward Sully's future front yard, with those perfectly shaped trees he loves so much, and wave it around. "Any tree you want, Sunshine."

"Do I even want to know whose house—oh God, please don't tell me this is Sully's new lake lot. We're not stealing a tree, are we?"

I glance around the property and mutter under my breath, "Not the whole tree, just the part that sticks out of the ground—"

"Cam! That's his landscaping!"

"Jordan! That's why it's funny!" I say, imitating her.

She tries to keep a straight face but loses her battle with laughter.

I cup her rosy cheeks and kiss her. "You have your heists and I have mine."

She stares at me for a few long seconds, but eventually, her mouth tips up and she shakes her head. I step away so she can survey the property. "*Any* tree?"

"Yup. Might I be so bold to recommend ones with curb-side appeal?"

She purses her lips and tears her eyes away from me as she walks around, and I grin, pleased that she's going along with my scheme. She circles the nice trees in front, carefully inspecting each one. Something catches her eye across the road, and she hurries across the dead-end street.

I follow her. "The good ones are that way, babe." I point back to the yard.

"What do you think about this one?" she asks, dusting off snow from some of the pine branches.

"*That's* the one you want?" It's an ugly fucker. Real ugly. But if this is the tree that makes her happy . . . Damn, I paid off a bunch of dudes to say the tree from the front was already gone when they showed up. But this tree? We'd be doing him a favor by taking it down.

Her boots crunch in the snow as she walks around the hideous spruce. The "tree" looks more like an overgrown shrub with all the bare spots, it's round where it should be triangle-shaped. I wonder if she's secretly trying to interfere with my prank, but this is Jordan. She'd probably pick an ugly tree just so its feelings aren't hurt. I love that she's as compassionate as she is ruthless.

"Yup. This is the one," she says, clapping her chopper mittens together. "What should we name it?" I was right, she's already treating it like it's a pet.

I raise an eyebrow. "It's a tree, Jordan."

"It's gotta have a name."

Grinning, I tilt my head to the side. "Chris Smith."

She chuckles, and I drop down to my shoulder, shuffling under the lowest sappy-as-fuck branch with the handsaw, no doubt ruining my wool coat. "Next year, we're going to buy a precut tree."

"Never gonna happen," she says with confidence.

Squinting, I saw away at the trunk, trying to keep from getting any falling pine needles in my eyes. Can't believe this is the one we're walking away with. It doesn't take long before I slice through, the thing is barely three inches thick. I shove out from under it as the tree topples away from me. When I stand, she brushes off the needles and bits of bark from my coat.

"Thank you," she says with a big smile.

"Whatever the queen wants, the queen gets." I sigh.

I lift the trunk with one hand and drag the tree behind us back to the truck, a few workers stop hammering to look up at us, and laugh.

"How are we going to decorate it?"

"Everything's at home already. Although, the branches might be too weak for some of them."

"We can do the balls, those are light."

"If you play your cards right, you might do more than the balls tonight." I waggle my eyebrows, and she nudges me with her shoulder.

"You keep those puns up and I'll roast your nuts over an open fire."

"Oh!" I laugh, amused that she's joining in. "That'll put you on the naughty list." We stop at the truck, I drop the tree, and pick her up. She wraps her legs around me. That's what I'm talking about. I'm two seconds from fucking her in the snow, with my truck being the only thing blocking us from an audience.

"Is that a candy cane in your pocket, or are you happy to see me?" she whispers.

I grind into her. "Candy cane? More like the North Pole. You want to climb on Santa's lap and tell him what you want?"

She laughs and kisses me. "Maybe later. Put me down." I nip at her lower lip and let her slide down until her feet hit the ground. I wrap a mittened hand around her neck and bring her mouth to mine for a final kiss. If it weren't for her cold nose reminding me to get her home, she'd still have her legs around me.

I toss her the keys and heave the tree into the truck bed. She races around to her side and starts the engine while I strap down the pine abomination. Once it's finished, I wave to the guys before I climb in the driver's side. She holds her hands out in front of the heater and looks behind us, checking the tree and smiling.

When we get back to the house, she holds the door open wide so I can haul it inside. I don't mind the way it fills the space with the scent of evergreens. It actually smells a little like Christmas in here. It's nice.

I turn on the fireplace. "Why don't you go pour us a couple glasses of wine, and I'll do this part."

Surprisingly, I'm enjoying making it festive and cozy. It's something I never bothered to do before, other than paying for a company to come out and string up some exterior lights so I didn't look like the neighborhood Grinch.

"You're going to put it up *yourself*?"

I jerk my head, feigning disgust. "No! I'm putting it in the living room, *you sicko.*"

She gawks and gives me a small shove. Hopefully, we can get this tree stuff over with so I can put something else in that open mouth. With her eyes shooting playful daggers at me, she trudges off to pour the wine, and I get the tree locked into the stand. However, I quickly learn the trunk needs to tilt to the left so the off-balanced limbs don't cause it to tip over.

On her way back with the wine, she stops in her tracks. "Oh my God, Cam! It's incredible!"

Incredibly hideous. I stand and admire my work. Reaching inside the tree, I grasp one of the weird, oversized limbs and rotate the tree a couple degrees—obviously joking, it's not like this tree has a good side. I back up and she steps beside me, handing me a glass, and I hold it with the hand less covered in sap.

"Thank you." We observe the disfigured conifer, and our heads lean to the side at the same time. From this angle, the trunk seems slightly straighter.

"Oh, Chris Smith Tree, Oh Chris Smith Tree, how homely are your branches . . ." I mumble.

She turns and clinks her glass to mine. "Cheers."

"To our first Christmas . . . on Valentine's Day."

She takes a sip and smiles at me. "The first of many . . ."

"How come you wanted such an ugly tree? Don't deny it, a tree this mangled is only chosen on purpose."

A slow smile forms on her lips as she turns to marvel at the monstrosity like it's the most beautiful thing she's ever seen. "Since I've met you, you've encouraged me to question conformity and do what makes me happy. I've never had a tree that wasn't professionally cut, trimmed, decorated, and themed to perfection. I wanted something with . . . character."

She leans her head against my shoulder. It means so much to know that I've helped her get to this point. "Ready for lights?"

"Hell yeah," she says, her smile growing.

I love this Jordan, she's imperfectly perfect.

By the end of the night, I'm fucking exhausted. We've crammed about three weeks of Christmas into one day. We did the whole tree thing, baked cookies while listening to holiday music, ice skated on the lake—after I shoveled the recent snowfall, the ice underneath was shit, so that didn't last too long, and we opted for sledding instead.

We opened presents, well *she* opened presents, which consisted of more cliché Christmas gifts: an ugly sweater, socks, and the classic three-flavor tin of popcorn. All the candy canes are Sour Patch Kid flavored, because it's her favorite.

For our big dinner, we had takeout—her request—and now we're winding down, curled up watching *National Lampoon's Christmas Vacation* in what else but our coordinating Christmas PJs. I can't stop stealing glances as she watches the movie. I could stare at this woman for days. She kicks her feet up and laughs, falling into me, and I wrap my arms around her tighter. My fingers slide through her hair like silk. I make a vow to give her this Christmas every year for the rest of our lives.

FIFTY-SIX

Camden

Now that the Landrys are back from Monaco, we've decided to host a family dinner tomorrow to get everyone together. Our families run in some of the same circles, but as far as we know, they haven't ever had dinner together, outside of some charity shit. Jordan's family is in a higher bracket, whereas my family knows senators, her family knows the president. I'm really hoping this dinner party goes well.

Lonan's wife, Birdie, is one of the best chefs in Minneapolis. She came over and helped us put together the meal, which took some of the stress away. Especially for me, I've got enough on my plate already with what I plan to ask her dad. I'll marry Jordan whether or not I have his blessing, but getting it would make my life a lot easier. I'd like our families to get along.

The Landrys arrive first. They're early.

As I walk to the door, I give the house a once-over. Jordan has been watering "Chris Smith" tree for almost four weeks now, by some miracle it's still alive, and she refuses to take it down until it dies. I don't even mind, it reminds me of how much fun we had, it was a good day—and an even better night. I open the right side of the large half-rounded double doors and usher them in.

"Good to meet you face-to-face, sir," I say, holding out my hand to her father. He takes it with a firm handshake.

"Likewise." Jordan hurries into the foyer with a smile. Chicken Salad isn't far behind.

"Hi! How was your flight home?" Jordan asks.

"Uneventful," Frank Landry says, satisfied, hugging his daughter. He passes me a box of twenty-five-year-old Scotch from the Macallan Red Collection. *Fucking baller.*

We nod to each other. Patricia Landry hugs Jordan, and, surprisingly, gives me one too. "Thanks for coming over on such short notice."

"Of course."

Jordan leads them farther into the house. She uncorks a bottle of wine and starts pouring.

We chat in the kitchen, making small talk until Frank claps his hand on my back and says, "Camden, let's open up that bottle, shall we?"

"Yes sir." He doesn't mean here. Shit, he might not even be thirsty. He wants to get me alone to give me some speech about respecting his daughter, which is ironic because I know firsthand how much Jordan enjoys being disrespected. "I keep the glasses downstairs."

I lead the way, heading toward the open staircase.

"Let's keep it casual, nix the sir stuff," he says under his breath. Mr. Landry gets down to business.

"You got it."

Her mother gasps in the living room as we descend the stairs. "What on earth is that?"

"Our Christmas tree!" Jordan answers proudly.

"It's March!" she shrieks.

That's the last I hear of their conversation after passing through the double glass doors to the bar area. I open the plush box of Scotch, pull out the bottle and a couple of snifter glasses from the shelf. After giving each of us a pour, we nod and take a sip.

Frank Landry is from old money, so while he can afford a much more expensive bottle, this is probably his favorite, and that means a lot. *Also, it's really fucking good Scotch.*

"She talked you into getting that god-awful tree, didn't she?"

I bark out a laugh. "There's not much that'll stop her when she sets her sights on something."

His brows furrow. "Is that so?"

That response has me curious. "Does that come as a surprise to you?"

He sort of shrugs and stares into his glass. "Jordana always kept her fire inside. She never wanted to rock the boat. She was the perfect child—no, not *perfect*—she was an *easy* child. She obeyed and did what she was supposed to. Though, I always felt like we did something wrong. She had confidence, but zero passion to channel it through. Until lately, it seems . . ." He looks up at me with a smirk.

It's hard to be humble. "I wish I could take all the credit, but I think Bryan was the straw that broke the camel's back. She had enough, and she let him know it." I eye him carefully.

His eyebrows raise. "By herself?"

I nod. She single-handedly designed his downfall.

"Impressive."

Puffing out a breath, I nod. "I wouldn't fuck with her."

He laughs. "That's good to know . . ." His features turn solemn. "I tried to talk to her over Christmas, but Jordan never gave us the details of their . . . fallout. I can't help but assume there was more to it than the cheating."

I clear my throat and avert my eyes. That's something for Jordan to share how and when she's ready.

"We should have done more. Been there for her . . ." He reaches across the bar and sets his palm on my shoulder. "I want to thank you for stepping in."

I nod. I won't placate him with empty reassurances, because he's right, they should have done more for their daughter, but being a haven for her allowed me to get to know Jordan better than anyone. And though I wish it happened under different circumstances . . .

"Best thing I ever did. She's a remarkable woman." My hands are sweating around the glass. ". . . And you should know I plan on asking her to marry me. It would mean a lot to her if we had your blessing."

He smirks. "I wondered if that was coming. After seeing your *grand gesture* on the ice, your intentions were pretty loud. Jordan said it wasn't a proposal, but it looked official all the same."

I nod.

"You were there for her when we weren't. You protected her, and she's very happy with you. That's all we've ever wanted for her."

"I appreciate that."

He takes another sip and slaps his thigh. "Well, we should probably get up there before they come looking for us."

I close the decanter and follow him out.

"I hear you collect bikes," I say as we climb the stairs. I'd love to see what he's got.

The corner of his mouth tips up. "I hear you ride them."

I chuckle. "Are you looking for lessons?"

"Possibly. Jordan told me beautiful bikes should be ridden." He quirks an eyebrow at me.

Fuck. Cue nervous laughter. "I was talking about the bike."

"Uh-huh. In the future, let's leave my bikes out of your pickup lines, huh?"

"Understood." Normally, I wouldn't give a fuck, but knowing my future-fiancée's dad heard my double entendre, has the room temperature going up a few degrees.

"Camden, this tree is an atrocity." Patricia laughs.

"I tried telling her," I say.

"No, he didn't," Jordan says. "He was entirely supportive!"

Her dad laughs, rocking on his heels and taking in the giant shrub thing that takes up a good portion of the living room.

My parents show up minutes later, letting themselves in. The introductions go well, and apparently, our mothers are both involved in supporting the arts and have more in common than we knew. They are becoming fast friends, and I can tell it gives me Patricia Landry's full approval. That's a relief. Once they realized that Jordan no longer backs down and is comfortable enough with me to make waves—*not a double entendre*—I won them over.

We were made for each other. I needed Jordan to open my heart, and she needed me to heal hers. She changed my life, and I'm a better man because of her. This woman taught me how to love with my whole chest. Together, we're unstoppable.

At dinner, I make a small toast, then we dig in. Everyone is impressed by the dinner, including myself; *Birdie can fucking cook.* Within minutes, the moms are interrogating us with questions regarding our relationship. I look at Jordan and smile, we're in love and going at our own pace.

"Your sisters are thrilled you are settling down with someone," Mom says. "They really like you, Jordan. Have you two figured out what you're going to tell people when they ask how you two met?"

"I'll say we met at her wedding."

She tsks me. "This isn't a joke."

"People are going to ask," her mom adds.

"I don't know . . ." I rub the back of my neck. "I'll say . . . we met through a friend." I throw up my hands.

Jordan laughs, and her dad coughs, trying to suppress a grin. At least someone thinks I'm funny.

"Camden, the Lakes are doing quite well this season, do you think you'll be making the playoffs?" Frank Landry asks. *Thank Christ, a change of topic.*

"We're at the top of the standings, if we can keep it up, we'll certainly get there."

"Camden is an incredible captain. He's already made improvements to the lineup, and it's made a real difference. I'm very proud of him."

I thread my fingers in hers under the table. Her praise fills me with pride. Being the Lakes captain has been one of my greatest accomplishments, and I take the role seriously. That C on my chest has been the catalyst for a lot of my growth over the year.

"I'm going to do my damnedest to get us there. The boys deserve it."

"We're also proud of you, son," my dad adds.

By the end of the dinner, everybody is tight and we have plans to grab dinner at Demi. At the *Landry table*, unreal. We stand in the foyer, and thankfully, neither of our families are big on the Midwest goodbye. Jordan waves them off and leans against the door with an exaggerated sigh and a relaxed smile. "We did it."

"And nobody threw a punch." I reach under her thighs and pick her up, pinning her to the door. "God, I love you. How did I get so lucky?"

"I have low standards," she whispers. I slap the side of her ass, and she giggles.

"You think you're real cute, huh?"

"I'm adorable."

I slide the tip of my tongue up her neck and nip at her ear. "You are pretty fucking adorable. What do you wanna do now?"

"Honestly?"

"Yeah." I trail a line of kisses down to her shoulder.

"Watch a movie, get high, and maybe plow through a box of Little Debbie Zebra Cakes."

I laugh. "Vanilla or chocolate?"

Her lips tip up in the corners. "A respectable hockey girlfriend always buys both."

"A respectable stoner buys both." I chuckle.

"Okay, you get your stash, I'll get a movie queued up."

FIFTY-SEVEN

Camden

JUNE

Stanley Cup Finals

"Go, go, go!!" I scream from the home bench. My nerves are exploding, and I'm operating on a whole 'nother level today. We all are. Because we're playing for the one and only Stonkley Clonk, as we're calling it. The whole team is too superstitious to actually say the name until we've earned it.

It's the oldest trophy in professional sports, going back all the way to 1893, where it's been passed from team to team since. There are no reproductions, there is only one Stanley Cup. The one we all want our names on so we can live eternally in the Hall of Fame as champions.

We've had the most challenging season of all our careers, making it this far. Playoffs have always separated the men from the boys, and we've walked through hell to get here. We've been playing every other day for two months. Traveling and being away from our families. We've been wrestling with crippling fatigue, shot nerves, and injuries. All for a chance at greatness. We've worked our asses off. We are burned out and starving for it.

First period and we're down by two. 0-2.

I shout to the team, trying to boost morale after the opponent's second goal. "We're here to win a trophy boys, but this is our ice and our fans, so have some fucking fun out there! We play our best when we're happy, so I better see every one of you motherfuckers smiling!"

"Energy, boys! Energy!" the defense coach adds, clapping.

We are not underdogs, and we will not play like it. There's a ton of hockey left. We've got more than a chance at winning. Every single one of us can put a puck in a net, we've been proving it all season.

I clap Lonan and Rhys on the back as we swap out the defense line. "Let's get it, fellas!"

When it's my shift, my skates hammer the ice as I get into position. A puck battle breaks out along the boards near Florida's net. I'm able to flip it out to Rhys, who passes to Lonan. He takes the shot, and it sails through, right behind the goalie's left glove. We clamor onto him, screaming. "Fuck yah, Burke!!" From the bench, I hear the coach yelling, "It starts with one, boys! It starts with one! Let's go!"

1-2 at the first intermission.

In the locker room, we refocus. I sidle up next to Barrett and lean back, matching his posture. "How are you feeling?"

"Top of the world."

"Yeah?"

"How could I not? My last professional game and we're at the finals? I mean, how many players get a shot at winning their last game before retirement? It doesn't get better than that. I've been waiting for this moment my whole career. We made it."

"Wish we could have done it with Sully."

"Yeah, it would be nice to have him with us tonight. You had big shoes to fill, and you succeeded, right out of the gate."

"Well, you know what they say about big shoes . . ."

He chuckles and shakes his head.

I lean forward and knock my elbow into his knee. "Thanks for being my mentor this season."

"Thanks for being my captain. Proud of what you've done for this team and for yourself."

Shit, I'm gonna miss Conway. He holds his fist to me, and I tap it with mine. "If you make me bawl like a bitch, we're gonna have problems."

We get another short speech from Coach before we head back out. "Talk to the refs. Keep that line of communication open. Protect your brothers, protect the net. Dig deep, boys."

About ten minutes in, the tension is high. We're near our net, fighting like hell to get it away from there when their forward, Gilles, takes a shot on goal. I hold my breath. It bounces off the net post, and we all exhale. Dude's done it twice this period, and I can't help but give him shit about it.

"Damn, Gilles, you smoke pole like a champ. You get that talent from your mom's side or your dad's?"

"At least I know what end of the ice to stay on. Want me to draw you a map to our net, asshole?"

Matty recovers the biscuit, and we chase it to their end.

He sends the puck to me, I pass behind me to Paek, who sends it to Burmeister, who dekes and returns it to me. *Those two are stealthy as fuck.* I get the shot and take it. And it clears the net.

2-2.

The foghorn sounds, and the arena erupts into madness. We're tied. The guys crash into me. "Atta boy, Banksy!"

"Beautiful!"

It was a pretty stellar fucking pass between the guys, and Burmeister's deke was glorious.

I skate by Gilles and grin. "Thanks for that map, bud."

He gets in my face, skating toe to toe, and I smile big, waiting for him to do something.

The ref gets between us.

"Come on, Teller. Don't start shit," he warns.

"I'm not starting shit. All I said was thank you!" This official and I are on a first name basis. He's a nice guy, a solid skater, and makes fair calls. I respect him, even if he's had to escort me off the ice more than a handful of times.

"Well, don't *try* to start shit."

Gilles skates off, and I lift my shoulders and show my palms.

"I'm not trying to, Bob! You know me better than all these refs. Have I ever made trouble on the ice? I'm simply making friends, that's all . . . Gilles is just pissed because he woke up and realized his face looks like that."

Ref looks down, smiling. "Teller, I love you, but if you chirp the other players and create issues for me, I'm gonna run ya."

"Aww, I love you too, Bob!" I smile and skate off. He really does love me.

Spirits are up. Lonan and Rhys are working defense, dekeing and checking like their lives depend on it, to keep it away from Strassburg in the net.

"Get it the fuck outta there!!" Teddy yells next to me on the bench.

"Heads up! Heads up!" I shout when they start losing control. Rhys is already ahead of me, gets it away, and sends it around the back of the net to Jonesy. Neither team can keep it on one end long enough, which means everybody is covering ground like a goddamn bag skate, accomplishing nothing. We made two shots on goal, each ending with a disappointed "Oh!" from the fans. Florida's goalie is on his A game tonight.

The next intermission, I check my phone, and Jordan has sent me a couple text messages. The first few came in after my goal. The last one says, *I love you, I'm proud of you, and I'll see you on the ice.*

I'm too nervous to make any assumptions about seeing her on the ice later, but Jordan prefers to say those things out loud to manifest them into real life. I'll take all the help we can get. I text her I love her, and tuck my phone in my bag.

Making yourself drink water when your nerves are stretched thin and you feel as if you could vomit at any moment is no easy task, but we all force it down before we go back out there.

Third period. Tied game. Anything could happen. We all take our time to visualize, focus, and rub our lucky charms. Coach doesn't say a word or interrupt us until it's time to leave the tunnel. His speech is short and sweet: "Let's give our fans a game they'll never forget."

Back on the bench, a few guys pick up the smelling salts to get their adrenaline kicks. We're exhausted and running on fumes in our final period.

After the puck drop, it remains neck and neck for most of the period. We're on pins and needles, if it weren't for the fatigue, I don't think any of us would sit on the bench right now. We're all waiting to see what happens. I look up at the WAGs box, and Jordan blows me a kiss. I send one back. *Barrett's right, it's hard not to look up at your woman.*

During each of my shifts this period, Florida's bench has been chirping like a goddamn choir loft, desperate to throw us off our game. A few guys, myself included, have joined in.

We're itching to throw a punch, but neither team is willing to risk a power play against the other. It's too late in the game.

Jonesy's knee bounces next to me as he fidgets. "Fuck, dude. Somebody hold my hand. I can't take this pressure." He groans, grabbing my glove. I let him. I'm barely holding it together myself. Unfortunately, it's looking like we're gonna end up in overtime.

Florida swaps out their players, and two of their best defensemen take the ice. Coach responds by swapping our offense line with Barrett, Jonesy, and me. We do a quick line swap and prepare for the worst. 02:13 left in the game.

"Let's pull a fuckin' Sully," Jones says, jumping the boards.

A few seasons ago, Sully made the filthiest of filthy goals, and it's forever gone down in team history as one of the greatest plays to come out of the Lakes. After that game, we made Sully recreate it so we could all get a chance at it. It was difficult to master, but we'd bust it out to fuck with our goaltenders during practice every once in a while. I grin and nod. What the hell, we're probably hitting overtime anyway. If the opportunity presents itself, I'm down.

Their defense is all over us when we cross the blue line. They've got a big guy, and he checks me into the wall. Not the cleanest of hits, but I'll let it by.

Jonesy gains possession and slips it to me behind him. In my peripheral, Barrett closes in on the net. I rush the goalie in the opposite direction and transition on a dime, skating in the opposite direction and flip the puck up in the air, pulling away from the net at the last second. Barrett plucks it out of midair with his stick and deflects it, throwing the puck into a different trajectory, and right into the net before it even hits the ice.

3-2.

Pure chaos.

The horn blows, and we pile onto Barrett, slapping his helmet and screaming. Adrenaline courses through us. A couple rubber ducks are tossed onto the ice, a tradition created by fans, as they prepare for the win. Our bench is going nuts. The arena is exploding with energy.

I flag my buddy the referee and point to the puck while Jonesy's got his arms around me. Bob nods, snagging it up and dropping it off with Coach. Glancing up, Jordan is in the box jumping up and down with my parents, my sisters, and the other wives—her friends—by her side.

"Let's finish this!"

Rhys, Lonan, Barrett, and I stay on the ice. Jonesy is swapped with Burmeister, who plays defense but we're putting him in a forward position so we can better protect Kapucik, our goalie. All we need to do is defend our net for the next ninety seconds, and it's ours.

They drop the puck, and Florida gives their all. We fight harder than ever to keep it away from our end as the clock runs out.

We know we're almost there when another yellow rubber duck is chucked from the crowd onto the ice.

Then another.

And another.

Fans chant the countdown when there's ten seconds left. More ducks. Our smiles grow. It's hard to focus when we're so close to a win, we can taste it—more than taste—we can lick, suck, and swallow it. This is happening.

The horn sounds, and I turn into a fucking bitch with tears streaming my face. We toss our sticks, gloves, helmets, *everything* into the air. The rest of the bench floods the ice, and we form a huge pile. Fans are screaming, crying, and pounding on the plexiglass. Rubber ducks soar through the floating confetti. Sully stands next to Coach, and I wave him out. We form a giant mob against the boards, screaming and yelling.

It's absolutely surreal.

"The Stonkley—motherfucking—Clonk!" Jonesy hollers next to me.

"Stanley Cup!" O'Callahan corrects, now that we are in the clear to utter its name out loud.

"I'm still calling it the Stonkley!" he screams back. Half of us are crying. I'm sure half the Florida bench is crying too. I don't fault them.

Our coaches, managers, and owner get on the ice with us —along with media reporters looking for sound bites. We give a replay of the winning goal and answer "How are you feeling?" about fifteen times while panting and dripping with sweat.

It's a full-on celebration on the ice. Before long, they roll out the red carpet, and two men with white gloves bring out The Cup. They give a short speech and call my name up to take it for a victory lap. I nod for Barrett to join me. He takes one end as we both hoist it above our heads and make a lap around the arena. It's surreal. It's all led to this, and we saw it through.

"Hey, promise me something," Barrett says.

"What's that?"

"Don't do anything sexual with it when it's your day with the cup. I promised Arthur he could use it as a cereal bowl."

I bark out a laugh. "I promise I won't fuck Sir Stanley before I give it to you."

As soon as I see Jordan at the player bench, I split from the group. She's wiping away her happy tears next to Micky, Birdie, and Raleigh, and I scoop her up. She cups my face and kisses me between laughs.

"Camden! You won the Stanley Cup!"

That reminds me, Barrett's shot was the winning goal. I drop her to her feet and kiss her cheek, then grab the winning puck off the bench. "Be right back."

I skate to Barrett and thrust it into his chest. "This one is yours." It practically sends him into tears, which gets me choked up. Damn, he sure is going out with a bang. "Your last puck, and it won the Stanley Cup."

He throws his arms around me, and we hug it out before skating back to the bench to see everyone together. Rhys and Lonan are already there. Lonan kisses Ethan on top of his head and wraps an arm around Birdie, kissing her. Rhys cups his hands around Micky's neck as they make out. Barrett picks up his son, Arthur, and kisses his wife, Raleigh, who's holding their newborn daughter, Darby.

I smile at Jordan and sink my hands into her hair, crushing my lips to hers. She's the love of my life. I can't imagine celebrating this win without her.

FIFTY-EIGHT

Jordan

"Do you have to be touching it the whole time?" I laugh.

Cam's hand is firmly planted on the base of the trophy while I grind on his cock. "Yes. Yes, I do."

The Stanley Cup stares back at me from the nightstand, close enough to see my reflection in the silver.

"You're lucky it's this far away. It'd be in bed with us, except I promised Barrett I wouldn't do anything sexual with it since his kid's gonna be eating cereal out of it next week."

"Ew! Stop touching it, then!"

"No. You know how you had your nipples pierced because it was on your bucket list?"

I nod.

"Well, I've imagined fucking a pretty girl while holding the Stanley Cup since I was twelve. Let me have my moment." I smile and lean back to give a better show of my piercings as I slide up and down his length. "*Fuuuuck.* Just like that . . ."

He runs his free hand over them and plucks them with enough pressure to make a chill run up my spine. His hand skates from my breasts up to my throat, and I lean into his palm as I grind harder. *God, you can take me whenever. I've served my purpose for you, Lord.*

He pinches and growls the dirtiest things while I work my way to my orgasm. Kneeling above him, he pulls out, sliding his ladder up and down my clit, bringing me right to the edge.

"Come with me," I rasp.

He thrusts again, and I detonate, pulsing around him as he spills inside me. He smirks as we finish together—still, with his hand on the Stanley Cup. I roll my eyes and laugh as we collapse into a heap under the covers.

"Congratulations on not letting go the whole time." I heave breaths as he dots kisses across the top of my back.

"It was really hard at the end there, I wanted to tear into that tight pussy."

He brings both arms around me in a bear hug before slipping out of bed. The sound of our oversized soaking tub filling up makes me grin. I doze in and out of consciousness, blissfully relaxed.

Minutes later, he gathers me up and carries me to the en suite bathroom. The scent of sandalwood and eucalyptus surrounds me, giving our already luxurious bathroom a spa-like ambiance. He's set out sea sponges and bath oils and has even lit a few candles. It's romantic. I'm surprised he didn't bring *Sir Stanley*.

He perches me on the edge of the tub, with my feet submerged as I acclimate to the temperature. Cam sinks into the water first and brackets my waist with his large hands, dragging me into the bath. Tattooed arms cross over my front as he hugs my body close to his chest. My eyelids become heavy as I'm cradled in the warm water, and I sigh, totally at peace.

One of the candles crackles with a wooden wick. He dips a sponge in the water and wrings it out over my bare shoulders while his lips trail up and down my neck. His touch traces the tattoo on my thigh that matches the one on his chest, and I thread my fingers with his.

"I want to give you something."

My relaxed smile tips up. "Another orgasm?"

"No."

He reaches behind a stack of towels and produces a box. *A ring box.* With an arm on each side of me, he holds the small lush case in front of me, turning it in his hands. My breath catches in my throat. I'm too stunned to speak.

"I never thought I'd ask a woman to marry me. I never imagined I'd find someone who could make me feel something beyond physical attraction. I thought that being in love would feel like infatuation. Those heart-pumping, brain-scrambling, intense feelings of need. All the time. But it's the opposite. Love is calm—it's tranquil. It's a feeling of mutual connectedness whether I'm thousands of miles away or in the same room. It's companionship and friendship and understanding."

It's as if he pulled the thoughts from my own head. Camden's love is comfort and warmth and joy. And steadfast, despite our proximity or the situation we're in. He opens the box, and my jaw drops, instantly my palm finds my chest. I'm in awe. The diamond fire sparkles in the candlelight. It's the most beautiful ring I've ever seen. Absolutely breathtaking. It's simple, elegant, and *exactly* my style.

"Marry me, Jordan. Let me love you more every day."

The memory of Cam and I meeting in the coffee shop plays in my head when he took off the old one. Little did I know that our meeting that day would lead to him sliding on his own. The previous ring felt like a collar, but this feels like a promise. And that's the best thing about Cam. He encourages me to live my life however I want. I want to live it with him.

I bite my lip and spin in his arms.

"Yes."

His eyes sparkle almost as much as the ring that he places on my finger, which fits perfectly. He cups my chin and leans forward, parting my lips and sweeping his tongue over mine with a smile. I grip his shoulders, and he drags me into his lap, letting me straddle his thighs.

"I can't wait to make you my wife."

I will love this man forever.

EPILOGUE

Jordan

DECEMBER

The fresh snowfall last night makes everything look like a winter wonderland. Pockets of blue sky cut through the overcast clouds. It's chilly, but I've always welcomed the cold.

I peek out our bedroom window and see the cleared area on the ice. The lake isn't completely frozen over yet, but it's rock solid along the shore. Snow has been shoveled and packed down to form a walkway, which creates a semicircle at the end, there's only enough room for our immediate families—plus the Lakes team and their wives. I smile as my mom attaches my veil.

"Your father and I are so impressed by you and who you've become. We're glad you found Camden."

"That means a lot, Mom. Thank you." Over the last month, I have dedicated most of my time at Safehouse. I even spearheaded a new off-the-record project on the side—which involves walking some *very* fine lines with Seven—to assist the most severe domestic abuse cases. I've disclosed the story of Bryan to my family—minus the Bluetower details. Though, after seeing the pride in my dad's eyes, I suspect he already knew I was involved in his demise. Bryan is in prison, and he's probably safest there, considering the hundreds of investors who want his head on a platter. I stole his freedom, and I'm not giving it back.

My parents apologized for not being here while everything went down. Truthfully, I was thankful they weren't. It was something I needed to take care of on my own, but I'm glad to have them involved in our life going forward. Who knows what the future will bring for Camden and I. Good things, I'm sure.

"Oh, Jordan. We need your ring." I haven't taken it off since he put it on. I wiggle it off and notice an engraving on the inside that I didn't see before, one word: *Priceless.* A juxtaposition to *I love you this much.* I clutch my heart and smile to myself. These are the little surprises that make me fall more in love with him every day.

"Are you ready?"

I nod, barely able to contain my smile. Micky crouches down and grabs one of my snow boots, which I'll be wearing until I switch to the white stilettos after the ceremony. She helped me pick out the ivory, plunging V-neck crepe wedding dress. It's appropriate for winter, long sleeves with pearl buttons that go from my wrists to my elbows and match the ones on the back. My mom holds open my floor-length white wool coat, and I slip my arms inside.

Micky glances out the window and clutches my hand. "They're ready for you."

CAMDEN

I adjust my cufflinks one final time on the right side of the "altar," which is technically a patch of snow. My heart flips when I catch sight of her beaming at me as she makes her way to the edge of our lakeshore. That's my wife. *My fucking wife.* Since Jordan, I'm the happiest I've ever been. She seems pretty pleased with me too.

Beside me, Chicken Salad wags her tail, and the ice sings as soon as she steps onto the frozen lake. It gives me goose bumps.

Barrett, our officiant, chuckles behind me. "Singing ice is supposed to be lucky on your wedding day."

I hum in agreement, but truth is, there could be an earthquake and I'd still feel like the luckiest man alive. With every step closer, I fall harder. The belonging she makes me feel. The safety and stability my life has now that she's in it. She's made my world better—she's made *me* better. I hug her parents, and they hand her off. She gave herself to me long before today.

They step back to stand with my parents, and Micky takes Jordan's coat off her shoulders. *Goddamn.* She looks up at me through her lashes. Jordan is painfully gorgeous every day, but in that wedding dress? She looks every bit the queen she is. Without thinking, I lean in and kiss her. Barrett clears his throat behind us. He can't fault me for that. She's my ultimate weakness. Especially in this wedding dress.

I mumble, "When I get you upstairs later, I'm going—"

"Let's begin," Barrett barks. I roll my eyes and Jordan blushes.

"Behave."

Barrett's speech is touching, and I appreciate him being a part of our day. As we recite our vows, high and low pitches strum, like plunking echoes under the ice. Every kid who grew up playing on frozen lakes can attest to the mystifying, ethereal sounds of newly frozen water. It makes this day all the more special. We exchange rings, and when Barrett finally says I can kiss my bride, our lips lock and the distant ice cracks, shooting thunder across the lake from under our feet. It's beautiful. Our friends cheer, and we all hustle inside to warm up our rosy cheeks.

The caterers have set out some of the food—along with the pumpkin muffins and apple scones we requested—it was the obvious answer when we were asked about dessert options. Our reception is low-key and relaxed, exactly how we wanted it. Being with our favorite people, the ones who know us best. The ones we want in our lives because they enrich it. I'm thrilled that Jordan has found a family with the team as much as I have. The wives of the other players have welcomed her with open arms, she fits in effortlessly, and I love watching her laugh and tell stories with the other women as they clink champagne glasses.

The sun begins to set, and I stroll up to the girls. "I'm going to steal her away for a minute."

Jordan smiles at me, and I slip away to the foyer. When she follows me, I'm waiting with her coat, and she allows me to slide it over her shoulders. We wander to the shore again. The sky drapes in fiery pinks and oranges, making the sparkling snow around us appear in technicolor.

Hand in hand, we step onto the frozen ice. "I wanted one more moment out here with you."

She turns into me and wraps her hands behind my neck. "Will you dance with me?"

"Always, Sunshine." I pull her close, and she rests her head on my shoulder. I breathe her in and feel—*this is so fucking cliche*—I feel complete. We sway on the ice in each other's arms. "You know we can't ever move, right?"

"After getting married over singing ice? Yeah, no. We're never leaving. They'll bury us in this backyard."

I tuck my chin down to press a kiss to her hair. "Have you thought more about where you'd like to honeymoon?" We've already agreed to go during the offseason. It gives us something to look forward to, but we still haven't chosen a location.

"Raleigh and Barrett said we could use their place in Hawaii?"

"Hell no. I'm not having sex in their weird cum-covered, baby-making beds."

She laughs. "Yeah, I'm not quite ready for kids yet. Someday, though."

"The world could use more of me." I nod.

Jordan squeezes me tighter. "Definitely. There's a shortage of humble people."

I smile down at her and listen to the snow crunching under our feet and the pew-pew-pew of the ice. It's such a rare, magical experience, and to have it on our wedding day makes it even more special.

Glancing at the house, filled with all of our friends, the windows glowing with warmth against the landscape turning more blue as the sun sets, I imagine filling it with family someday. The world may not need more of me, but I wouldn't mind creating a few more Jordans.

She shivers against me, and I run my palms up and down her arms. "How much longer before I can take you to bed?"

"Only a couple more hours."

I groan and spend a few more minutes with her, watching the sun melt into the icy horizon. When we're ready to rejoin the party, she picks up the hem of her gown and we take our time trekking off the lake.

When we finally say goodbye to everyone, I'm practically shoving people out the door. As soon as the lock turns, I throw her over my shoulder and haul ass to our bedroom. She bounces when I toss her onto the bed and spreads her thighs. Gazing down at her, I remove my tie, unbutton my shirt, and push the suspenders off my shoulders, letting them fall at my thighs. She simpers.

I'm going to undo that column of buttons up her back and work her over in every way imaginable. With my thumb, I caress her tattoo. I love this woman.

"Thank you for not covering your freckles today . . . Now why don't you push up that white dress, Mrs. Teller, and show me how wet you are." I help her shove the billowy fabric out of the way, and my eyes nearly bulge at the hot-as-fuck bridal lingerie. *Goddamn.*

She props up on her elbows and pushes her stiletto against my chest. "Show me you're worthy, *Mr. Teller*. Put your face between my thighs and find out yourself."

My dick is so hard it hurts. It fills my chest with warmth to see her holding her ground with me. I'll happily get on my knees and do anything she asks. She's mine and I'm hers. Falling in love changed us.

I smirk, and my hand finds her throat so fast she jumps, her heel digs deeper into my chest. "I'm going to eat this fucking cunt because *I* want to. Don't forget, *wife,* in the bedroom, you kneel for *me*."

Standing, I stride to the plush navy high-back chair near the dressing mirrors and sit. I lean back and beckon her with two fingers. Her chest heaves with excitement even though she glares at me from across the room. With a tight jaw, she pushes off our bed, prowls over, and plants her feet in front of me with hands sweetly laced behind her back. I twirl my finger in a circle, and she turns, facing away. Palming the sides of her breasts, I slide down her sides and over her ass, admiring the shape of her curves. She's trembling, and her flesh pebbles as I unhook the pearl buttons, starting at the base of her spine.

I work quickly, after the last pearl, the gown tumbles to the floor in a pile around her sexy satin heels. I hold out a hand, and she grasps it while stepping out of the dress. My hands graze up and down her legs. I loop my thumbs into the lace garter belt and thong and drag them down her toned thighs; then spread her cheeks and loll my head to the side, admiring her plump glistening pussy and swiping a finger over her arousal. Her shudder puts a smug grin on my face.

"Grab your ankles."

She bends and clasps her calves. Her spine arches when I dive in and devour her from the back, dipping my tongue inside to lap her up. I'll never tire of this. For the rest of my life, Jordan will be the first thing I touch when I wake up and the last thing I taste before I fall asleep. It's cute how fast she submits when I'm sucking her clit. *Not so bold now, are we?*

Her moans drive me wild. With one arm safely braced around her, my fingers plunge inside, she's drenched. I sink my teeth into her ass, and she screams out. I've been looking at her all day, my patience is running thin. Curling my fingers, I peek around to glimpse her face. Her mouth drops open and thighs quake, shaking the stiletto heels as she takes her first orgasm of the night.

I smack her ass and spin her to face me. "Get on your knees and open your mouth."

When she does, I grip her neck and spit her cum into her own mouth. "Taste that?"

"*That's* my worthiness. The taste of my bride greedy for her husband's cock." Heat flashes in her eyes, and I drop a loving slap to her cheek. "My wife's such an eager little cumslut, even for her own pussy . . . God, you're perfect." I kiss her lips, and she mewls against mine.

"Everything but the heels and your wedding ring."

Thank Christ I'm sitting, because the way she grins at me when unhooking her shelf bra, makes me weak in the knees. Those nipple piercings are begging me to play with them.

"Now take out my fat cock and suck the way I taught you."

She unzips my fly, releasing pressure from the zipper against my ladder. My erection bobs out, she spits on it, and rolls her tight fist over me. I groan and cup her cheek. "That's right. Be my dirty fucking wife."

As soon as her lips seal over me, my eyes roll back. This woman could suck the chrome off a tailpipe. "*Fuck*, Jordan."

She moans around my length, and I pluck her nipple piercings, making her breasts jiggle. My palm rests on her throat, the diamond necklace tattooed on the back of my hand is centered perfectly with her neck, and I smile. My fingers tangle in her hair as I move with her, and she gradually hands over control. I increase the tempo, and we regard each other with endless trust and love. Her big brown eyes are fixed on mine, and my heart explodes for her. Her eyelashes flutter as I stroke her temples and praise her loud enough to hear over the glucking sound that soon fills the space.

"You have the sweetest fucking tongue . . . So precious, giving me control . . . That's it. Every inch . . . Yeah, whimper those sounds I love so much . . ."

The filthier I speak, the more she moans and shivers. I love how my praise affects her. Tears roll down her cheeks, and she drools a little. This woman is remarkable. I tug her hair back, pulling her off me so she can catch her breath. She gasps and pants, with trembling fingers on my knees. Her mouth opens again, and she nods when she's ready for more. I cup her chin and push between her full lips. Pretty manicured nails dig into my thighs, and I roar as I fuck her mouth, relishing the pain of her scratches.

"I know it's hard, but you're doing so well . . . Being such a good wife for me . . . You like that, don't you? Of course you do . . . You're so goddamn beautiful . . ."

When my balls draw up, I swipe my thumb across her chin and haul her into my lap, our lips crash together as she whines for more. My hand travels between her legs, and I smile when her arousal is practically dribbing down her legs. Gripping her ass, I stand and carry her to our bed where she leans against the pillows like a goddess. She looks like an angel—a sinful angel about to be well-fucked—but an angel, nonetheless.

One at a time, I unclasp the straps of her heels and press a kiss to each ankle.

"I want to be loved and fucked by you, every day, for the rest of my life," she whispers.

"Try and stop me."

She smiles.

I crawl over her and rub my piercings against her most sensitive spot. "Promise to love you more every day," I say, slipping inside.

Her fingers fan out against the sheets, and those raspy moans slay me. Each barbell drags in and out of her tight entrance. I've fucked her enough times to know when she's about to break, and she's on the precipice.

I need to see my bride fall apart while I'm buried deep. Her soft body clenches, and she kisses me with everything she has. I groan as my thrusts turn unpredictable. Her eyes flicker with emotion, and it sends me flying off the cliff I've been teetering on. She falls with me, and I tuck her into my chest.

My nose brushes up her neck as she writhes beneath me, her body constricting mine. She sighs and wraps her arms around my back, holding on with everything she has as the climax subsides.

I never thought I'd fall in love, and if I hadn't crossed paths with Jordan, I never would have—no matter how long I lived. It had to be her. They say if two people are meant to be, they'll find each other. That's what we did—that's how I know she's my soulmate. It wasn't luck that placed us on this earth at the same time, it was destiny.

She's my twin flame. My one and only. My forever.

She's corrupted me—in the best way imaginable.

THE END

ACKNOWLEDGMENTS

What a ride! This book rounds out my first ever series and I couldn't be more emotional over it. This last December, I was able to quit my full-time job to write, I owe it all to my readers who have spread the word and impacted my life in ways that have forever changed who I am. With so much love, *thank you.*

I couldn't write this without thanking Banksy and Jordan for their story. These two characters never left my brain throughout the entire writing process and it will be a while before I'll stop thinking about them. Thank you for closing out the series with a bang. (several of them)

Thank you to my husband who helped me design Jordan's revenge. I cannot put into words how much I appreciate the sacrifices you make to let me get in extra writing time, especially during the end when I'm holed up in my room editing for hours on end. You are my favorite love story. You've been supportive since day one and I'm so happy to have you by my side during this wild journey. Thank you to my kids for your patience. I still haven't figured out how to explain these books as you get older. I love you all so much.

This story wouldn't be what it is without the unbelievable sisterhood that is my beta team. Catie, Emma, Jess, Kailey, Leia, Lorelei, Megan, Nicole, Rachel, Sarah, Shannon, Tricia, Jenna, and Mackenzie. You are always there for me to celebrate my wins, mourn my losses, and tell me to add butt stuff when I feel like the story is missing something.

Shannon, my PA, my lovely ball of chaos. Thank you for somehow keeping me in line, showing me the ropes, and pushing me to be the best author I can be. You've taught me so much over this last year. You and Emma have been with me since before Before We Came and I don't want to know where I'd be if I hadn't found you.

My incredible ARC readers—I'm so grateful for the time and energy you put into reading my work and writing reviews. The responses I've received for Stand and Defend have blown me away. Your words keep me going and make every release better than the last. Thank you for being a part of release day and I hope you're celebrating as much as I am!

My line editor, Dee Houpt (Dee's Notes), can you believe the series is over? Thank you for taking care of Banksy and giving him the love he deserves. You called dibs on him early on but the connection you shared with this story has truly touched my heart. I love you so much I even gave up my "chews thoughtfully". You won. I hope you're happy.

Thank you to my developmental editor, Rachel Jeter. Rachel, you've done so much for me with the last couple books and taking on the Street Team, I knew that you would knock this dev edit out of the park and you absolutely did. I am so honored to have been your first dev edit and can't wait to have you work on every future book here on out.

My formatter, Mallory at The Nutty Formatter for converting all my text messages and notes into those gorgeous little text bubbles. Your formatting is a work of art!

This is the first time I've been able to thank a street team! Y'all. What would I do without you? You've been hyping this book for months and I cannot thank you enough! Most of you were readers for a long time before the team was formed and I love that my favorite people are all together in one group. I appreciate the work you do and helping me shine on your platforms.

I've got to give a shoutout to a few special readers. I'm sure I'm missing some people, I apologize! But thank you for consistently sharing my books and interacting with my posts. Amy, Tahnika, Leia, Christina, Chelsey, Mackenzie, Sarina, Katrina, Kenadhe, Leesha, Ashley, Katie, J.R., Kristen, Courtney, Brittany, (and so many more!) along with all of my alpha and beta readers.

To my friends Megan, Kate, Katie, Jenn, and all of my loves in Ohana—Mandi, Matt, Casey, Maddie, Tristan, Erik, Kelly, and Nicole. Thank you for your support even when I go dark for weeks at a time. You fill my cup and have a special place in my heart.

If you know someone being abused, or if you're experiencing abuse yourself, please seek assistance and know there is nothing you have done or are doing to cause it. It is always the choice of the abuser to continue.

Help exists, even in impossible circumstances.

For anonymous, confidential help, 24/7, please call the National Domestic Violence Hotline at 1-800-799-7233 (SAFE or 1-800-787-3224 (TTY.

I couldn't say thank you without mentioning these awesome content creators! I have found so many amazing readers through you and I'm so incredibly grateful for your awesome posts! Readers, grab your phone and follow each of these Booktokers and/or Bookstagrammers to find your next great read!

Mackenzie @readingwithkenzz

Ashley @ashleybooksandbarbells

Jamie @nerdthatreads

Chanelle @chanellehelle

Haily @hailyreads

Nina @author.nina.wolf.reads

Courtney @romancereadswithcourt

Chelsey @chelseyjeannee

Kassi @kassinicole.reads

Christina @christinareadsbooks

Sarina @booktrovert_rina

Brittany @happy.ending.always

Catie @catiesshelfofsmut

Bri @_books_with_bri_

Shannon @thebooksofshae

Jess & Ash @bestiebookshelf_

Kailey @kaileyd_reads

Nicole @nicoleleannemreads

Emma @thebooksofemma

The Wet Spot Pod @wetspotpod

Amanda @messterpieces1621

Trish @trishh_reads

MORE BOOKS BY SLOANE ST. JAMES

Lakes Hockey Series

Book 1: Before We Came

Lonan & Birdie

Book 2: Strong and Wild

Rhys & Micky

Book 3: In The Game

Barrett & Raleigh

Book 4: Stand and Defend

Camden & Jordan

HAVE A BEGGING KINK?

Well do I have good news for you!

If you enjoyed reading this book, please help spread the word by leaving a review on Amazon, Goodreads, Bookbub, Facebook Reader Groups, Booktok, Bookstagram, or wherever you talk books.

Please, tell your friends and followers. Recommend this book and share the hell out of it. If you already have, you have my endless gratitude. I hope you sleep well knowing that you are making some woman's mid-life crisis dreams come true!

I love to connect with my readers!
SloaneStJamesWrites@gmail.com
Instagram and Tiktok @SloaneStJames

Facebook Reader Group:
Sloane's Good Girl Book Club

Interested in being an ARC reader?
www.SloaneStJames.com

Looking for signed paperbacks and other merch?
www.SloaneStJames.com

Made in the USA
Middletown, DE
01 June 2024

55156694R00283